Her Royal Payne

The Survivors: Book X

Shana Galen

HER ROYAL PAYNE
Copyright © 2021 by Shana Galen

Cover Design by The Killion Group, Inc.

Also by Shana Galen

Dedication and Acknowledgments

Thank you to all my fabulous readers who suggested titles for this book. And thank you to Amy Dudley who hit on the perfect one.

This book is dedicated to my daughter who always asks me to tell her about the book I'm writing, then after two minutes says it sounds boring and I should write books like Tera Lynn Childs.

One

The German was enormous, and his right hook was deadly, but he'd been hit in the head one too many times. He was as dim as the stars shining in the London fog. That didn't mean Rowden wasn't dancing in the ring. He didn't want a ham-sized fist plowing into his face. But the German had no strategy. Rowden had lasted four rounds with the brute, and he could see the man was tiring. If Rowden could survive one round more, the German would be tired enough that Rowden could get in a few jabs and take him down.

Rowden danced back, twisted, felt the swipe of the German's fist a fraction from his ear. The crowd yelled and cheered, and Rowden flashed them a grin. Some of them had bet against him of course, but most of them were smart enough to bet against the German. Rowden wasn't known as The Royal Payne for nothing. He glanced at his manager, standing with arms crossed on one side of the ring. Chibale narrowed his eyes, reminding Rowden to focus. They'd be called to their corners soon.

7

Then he'd get a drink, take a breath, and start his attack. In another quarter hour, the prize money would be his. Fifty pounds wasn't a fortune, but it was nothing to scoff at. Once Rowden would have considered fifty pounds nominal. But that was before his father had disavowed him.

Younger sons of dukes didn't have many useful, practical skills. Rowden had tried the army, but he hadn't liked taking orders. Now he made his way in the fashion he preferred—with his fists.

He ducked as the German swung at him, then skipped behind the man and jabbed him in the lower back. The German grunted and swung around. That punch was easy to evade as the German hadn't even aimed it. Sweat poured from the giant's forehead, and his blue eyes were red-rimmed. Rowden could feel the fifty quid in his pocket already. Well, thirty-five quid. He'd have to pay Chibale fifteen pounds.

Rowden glanced at Chibale who nodded and raised a hand level to the ground. Hold steady.

Suddenly a loud bell rang out and a voice shouted above the men lining the ring. "Woe to ye, sinners! Repent and God will forgive thy sins!"

It was a woman's voice, and Rowden tried to ignore it, but the bell had been loud and unexpected and thrown him off balance.

"Flee this den of iniquity!"

Den of iniquity? It was a tavern with an area roped off for boxing in the back. A bit of drink and sport was hardly wicked.

"Flee now afore the fires of hell descend!" The bell rang again, and a burst of fire seemed to leap into the crowd. The men on the side of the ring closest to the fire moved aside, and Rowden couldn't stop himself from looking. Even as his mind screamed, *No!*, his head turned to glance at the spectacle.

It only took an instant for him to see the woman's companion held a torch. No one was in any real danger. Except for Rowden, in the ring with the German. That was the instant he should have turned back to his opponent. He should have ducked. He should have done anything other than lock eyes with the woman dressed in black. Her gown was severe with its high neck and coarse cloth. Her hair was covered by a white cap.

But her eyes.

Her eyes were the most beautiful shade of hazel he'd ever seen. Truly, they were remarkable. He stared at her, and she stared at him, and then she winced.

Like an idiot he turned to look at what had caught her attention, and pain struck the side of his head like a boulder smashing down on it.

And then he was down, and for a moment the world was gray and all but silent. Rowden felt as though he had fallen into a lake and was struggling to swim to the top of the water. Everything was murky and muted, but finally he broke through to the surface and a dark brown face was right above him.

"You lost," Chibale said.

Rowden shook his head. "No. I can still fight. Give me a minute." He tried to sit, but his head felt too heavy.

Chibale shook his head. "You've been lying on the ground for two minutes. It's over."

Rowden growled. He was suddenly hungry and thirsty, and his pockets were not fifty pounds fuller. "Goddamn it."

"I think that is exactly what happened, my friend." He offered a hand, and Rowden took it, allowing Chibale to pull him to his feet. "Those zealots came in and ruined everything."

"I shouldn't have let myself become distracted."

Chibale put an arm around Rowden, led him to a table, and signaled to a server to bring him a drink. "It's not like you to lose focus."

Rowden closed his eyes. He opened them again when he heard a cheer from the other room, then scowled when he saw the German and his friends raising their pints in celebration.

"Get me another match with him," Rowden said.

"And how am I supposed to do that? He knocked you on your unfocused, white arse. No one is interested in a rematch."

"Make them interested. That's what I pay you for."

Chibale sat back, crossed his arms, and looked up at the ceiling. "Neither of us made any blunt tonight. And we could have used it after your holiday a few months ago."

Rowden blew out a breath. "I was helping a friend, not on holiday." He'd spent most of October in the countryside at the home of his friend Nash Pope. Pope's father, the Earl of Beaufort, had offered to pay Rowden for his time, but Rowden hadn't felt right about taking the money. Now that Nash was planning a wedding and threatening to invite Rowden, he wondered if he should have accepted the money.

"I was hoping to buy a new waistcoat," Chibale complained.

Rowden rolled his eyes and then winced. His head was still ringing. "You're already the best-dressed man east of Mayfair. The last thing you need is another waistcoat."

Chibale nodded at the server who brought his ale and drank. "You could use a new waistcoat." He handed Rowden his shirt so he could pull it over his head and bare chest. "And a few new shirts, come to think of it."

Rowden drank his ale down. "Only get blood on them," he said. Rowden stared at his empty glass. "Besides I have no one to impress." He glanced at Chibale. "How is your sister's gown coming along?"

"It's finished," Chibale said, looking annoyed.

"And the modiste still hasn't succumbed to your charms?"

A few months ago, Chibale had drunk a bit too much wine when they'd been celebrating one of Rowden's wins, and he'd confessed he was half in love with a French modiste named Madame Renauld. But the dressmaker refused all of Chibale's efforts to court her, so he'd finally brought his sister to her to have a dress made. Apparently, that effort had not gone as planned.

"How's your head?"

Rowden turned to see where the voice had come from and immediately regretted the quick movement. Aiden

Sterling grabbed a chair and sat, laughing. "That bad?" He signaled to the server to bring another tray of drinks. "That German knocked you flat. I haven't seen you lose that badly since you fought that Spaniard in Portugal."

"Spaniard in Portugal?" Chibale asked.

"When we were in the army," Aiden said. "Before you started calling Rowden The Royal Payne and charging to watch him fight."

"Ah." Chibale nodded. "When you fought for free." His tone held a trace of contempt.

"It was those goddamn Methodists or Puritans or whatever the hell they were this time," Rowden said. "They threw my concentration." That wasn't exactly true. It was the woman who had distracted him. Those eyes. He'd never seen eyes like that before. Nothing else about her was remarkable. He couldn't even remember her face. She had seemed a black, shapeless thing yelling about sin and hell. Usually, the religious zealots stood on the street corners by the whores and harangued the men soliciting the prostitutes. Lately, they'd become bolder, entering taverns to preach about the evils of drink and sport. This was the second time they'd interrupted one of his mills, though he'd heard of other fights that had been disrupted by them. Last time he'd considered it a nuisance. This time he was angry. And bruised.

"A sect of Methodists, I think," Chibale said.

"You cost me five pounds," Aidan said.

"Only five pounds?" Rowden asked. "That's all you wagered on me?"

"No, I wagered ten."

"Then how did you lose only five?" Chibale asked, passing out drinks from the server.

Rowden glared at his friend. "Because he wagered five on the German."

Aidan smiled and lifted his ale. "You know me too well."

Rowden brought the ale to his lips then set it down again. His belly roiled and his head hurt like the dickens. "I'm done for tonight." He stood, wobbling a bit.

Chibale stood too. "I'll go with you."

Rowden waved him off. "Your rooms are nearby. It would be out of your way." Rowden caught the look Chibale and Aidan exchanged.

"I'll go," Aiden said. "I haven't eaten yet. I'll stop in at the Draven Club and see what Porter is serving tonight."

"I don't need a chaperone," Rowden said. But he didn't argue very forcefully. He'd rather Aidan go with him, hail the hackney, and haul him up to his flat. Rowden's head hurt too much to think about anything practical.

"Tomorrow at Mostyn's," Chibale said as the two men started away. "I made notes for improvement."

Rowden blew out a breath and leaned on Aidan as they stepped out into the frigid February night. Aiden raised a hand, and a jarvey just down the street called to his horse and started their way.

"I thought you didn't like taking orders," Aidan said.

"He works for me."

Aidan raised his brows but didn't speak. Rowden didn't like taking orders, but he also wasn't an idiot. That's why he'd hired Chibale. The man knew boxing, and he knew what Rowden needed to do to win. It was Chibale who had come up with the name The Royal Payne, and it was largely due to Chibale that the name was becoming known not only within London but throughout England.

So Rowden might not like having to go to the boxing studio tomorrow, but he'd do it.

And next time, no goddamn zealot would throw off his concentration.

***

Modesty Brown stood on the corner and watched as the fighter—they called themselves *milling coves*—climbed into a hackney with his friend. She heaved a sigh of relief. He had been hit so hard, and when he'd fallen it seemed the entire floor shook. She'd known it was her fault. He'd been looking at her when the other man hit him. She'd wanted to warn him, but she was supposed to be there to disrupt the sinful activities, not take part in them.

Beside her, her father called out Bible verses to men and women passing by. No one seemed to pay him any attention. She held her wooden sign higher. It read, REPENT! THE END IS NEAR!

The torch one of the other congregants held lit the words on the sign. The older woman with the torch would take over preaching when her father's voice tired. It was only half past ten, and they would probably be here until midnight at least. She did not like staying out that late. The later it became, the more intoxicated the people. The Fancy—what the men who liked to watch fights called themselves—were especially rude. Men and women alike yelled foul things and made vulgar gestures. Modesty always tried to look away. When she'd been younger, her father had covered her eyes. But now that she was almost four and twenty, she had seen just about everything the underground of London had to offer. A boxing match between two grown men seemed relatively tame to her, but she had not argued when her father instructed the small group of parishioners to follow him and disrupt the match.

Modesty never argued. Her mother had not argued. She had been an example of perfect womanhood—obedient, submissive, soft-spoken, and pious. Modesty wanted to be everything her mother had been. She wanted her father to love her the way he'd loved her mother.

And her mother would not have countenanced her staring at the pugilist as she was. Modesty averted her eyes from the hackney and tried not to think about the man. She'd seen bare-chested men before on other occasions when she had been in the party that disrupted a boxing match. She saw bare buttocks even more frequently. All she had to do was look down the alley to her right to see prostitutes pushed up against a wall and men with their breeches about their knees. She did not concern herself with matters of the flesh. It was the spirit inside the flesh that mattered.

But she had been sorely tempted tonight because the flesh encasing the pugilist's spirit was rather enticing. She'd have to ask for forgiveness later because she had looked far too long at his bare chest. And then she'd looked even longer at his almost-handsome face and his green eyes.

"Beware the serpent!" her father called out, and Modesty nodded in agreement. She did need to be wary.

"Beware the fires of—" Her father broke off and the other parishioners looked at him with alarm. He cleared his throat and continued. "The fires of hell!'

Modesty frowned. Something was not right. Her father did not sound like himself. "Excuse me. Brother John, please take my place for a moment."

"Father!" Modesty grabbed his arm. "Are you well?"

"The Lord is my shepherd," Brother John began.

Her father gave her a tight smile and wiped a bead of sweat from his cheek. Like the rest of the party, he was dressed in all black. His black hat obscured his face in the dim light, and she could not see his eyes.

"Yes, child. All is well. I see someone I must speak with. I will return in a moment."

He walked away, and Modesty rose on tiptoes to watch where he went. He passed several buildings then stopped in front of a younger man dressed in plain brown trousers and the sort of coat farmers wore. He removed his hat, and the two men stepped around the corner and out of sight.

Modesty felt her belly tighten with unease. Her father had never done such a thing before. He never left his preaching like this. The only time he left off was when someone passing by asked for a blessing or to pray with him. But if that man had wanted a blessing, then why had he not asked in front of all of them? Why had her father gone off with him in private? London was dangerous, and it made her nervous to think of her father alone and undefended.

But presently, he returned. She waited for him to explain himself, but he said nothing, just took over for Brother John. Modesty glanced down the street where her father had gone to meet the man and noted he was still standing on the corner. He still held his hat and he seemed to be watching her. Modesty looked away, feeling self-conscious. And when she looked back, he was gone.

Two

"Father, who was that man last night?" Modesty asked as she placed the last bowl of porridge on the table and poured her father tea.

"What man, my child?" her father asked, absently. He was studying a book of sermons by John Wesley, as was his habit in the morning. No matter how late they had been out the previous evening—and last night had been an early night as they had been in bed by quarter to twelve—he woke at six to read the Bible for two hours. She rose at seven to prepare breakfast and they ate at half past eight as he read one of his books of sermons. They were not wealthy, and the few books they owned were cherished and carefully tended. Even now, as he seemed to spoon porridge distractedly, her father pushed the book to the side, safely out of the path of any dripping food or tea.

"The man who summoned you last night. He looked like a farmer. You spoke with him for a quarter of an hour at least," Modesty said.

Her father did not speak for several moments, seemingly engaged with his book. "That is a matter that does not pertain to you," he said finally. His tone was not severe, but it did not invite further discussion. He looked up, his reading spectacles making his brown eyes look large. "Mind your place, child. Do not concern yourself with worldly affairs."

Modesty had to keep her brows from rising. Since when had her father been concerned with worldly affairs? But she kept her thoughts to herself and dutifully drank her tea and ate her porridge. After the meal, she washed and dried the plates while her father continued to read and sip his tea. Finally, she sat beside him, opened the Bible, and pretended to read. Her mind was too busy to concentrate on the words.

"I have a task for you today," her father said.

Modesty looked up, surprised. Her father believed idle hands were sinful hands, and everyday had its set tasks. Yesterday, she and several of the women of the church had cleaned the room they used to gather for worship on Sundays. They had polished the benches and mopped the floors and dusted everything to a dull gleam. Today was the day she would mend socks and shirts and the few other items in her mending basket. She usually began the mending closer to noon, when the most light shone through the small window in this room.

"I have the mending," she said, feebly.

"This should not take long. I would like you to deliver a basket of bread and cheese to Mrs. Kydd on Pall Mall."

"You want me to go to Pall Mall?" Modesty asked in surprise. "Alone?"

"I would go with you," her father said, "but I must work on my sermon for Sunday."

Today *was* one of the days he devoted to sermon-writing. But he had never before asked her to go alone to deliver a gift of charity, and he had never sent her so far as Pall Mall. It was a thirty-minute walk, at least, across London. She was rarely allowed to go anywhere by herself, and she felt a thrill of excitement at the possibility of an adventure. Normally, when she was out with her father or one of the church elders, she had to keep her eyes downcast. But if she were alone, she could study the ladies in their fine dresses or pause at the windows of shops and study the goods for purchase.

"When should I leave?" Modesty asked, now eager to be on her way.

"Within the hour," her father said. "Use the provisions in the storage room at the church to make up the basket."

"Of course. Is Mrs. Kydd ill? Should I make her soup?"

Reverend Brown waved his hand. "Nothing like that. She made a donation to our cause, and this is a small gesture of our thanks. I have her information written on this paper." He slid a slip of paper she had not noticed on the table toward her. It had the woman's name and the number of her residence on Pall Mall. "Bring her the gift. If she will see you, speak with her a little to express our thanks and tell her of our mission. Then come straight home." He looked at Modesty, his brown eyes meeting hers as he peered at her above his spectacles. "No dawdling."

"I understand, sir."

Her mother would not have dawdled. Her mother would have gone straight to Mrs. Kydd and come straight back again. And that's what Modesty would do. It took no additional time to catch glimpses of the world about her. She would walk quickly and still peer at shop windows. "Shall I go now, sir?"

"Yes, go now. Do not forget your coat and scarf, child."

"No, sir." She put on her threadbare coat and the scarf she had knitted the year before and tucked her hands in her pockets. She wished she had gloves or mittens, but she had only the one pair of gloves that she wore for church and those must be kept clean and tidy for Sundays.

She put her black bonnet over the cap she wore and tied the ribbons under her chin. A quarter hour later she set out from the church, a basket tucked into the crook of her arm. The sun was shining dully in the sky. Outside of London, the day was probably crisp, cool, and bright. Inside the city, with its endless coal fires darkening the sky, it was cold and less gray than usual. Modesty decided to walk briskly to keep warm and return quickly as her father had bade her. She kept her eyes down until she was out of sight of her home and the church and then she lifted her head and took everything in.

She passed a group of boys kicking a ball in the street and cheering wildly when one boy crossed a line invisible to her. She passed a fishmonger and a costermonger and a young girl on a stoop, a dirty dog beside her with his head in her lap. She lowered her eyes again when she passed a group of men outside a gin shop. In her shapeless black dress and bonnet, she was unlikely to draw their interest, but she did not want to chance it.

As she drew closer to the Kydd residence on Pall Mall, there were fewer gin shops and groups of boys playing in the street and more carts and horses, clerks in black carrying heavy ledgers, and ladies in fur-lined pelisses. She gave two men unloading a cart a wide berth. They looked to be carrying a table into a building while a well-dressed man stood with his arms crossed and watched. Modesty continued walking, slowing slightly when she reached a row of shops. Her arm ached from the weight of the basket, and she took the opportunity to switch arms. She might have paused slightly longer than she intended to study an array of bright bonnets in one window. They were bedecked with plumes in colors she had never seen on a bird in the wild. A few also had sprigs of what appeared to be grapes embellishing them. She did not fancy fruit on her bonnet, but she would not have minded flowers. One hat in pink was decorated with a cluster of white silk flowers, and Modesty thought it was lovely.

Of course, she would never be allowed to wear a bonnet that color, even if it didn't clash with her awful red hair. She had never worn anything but dark, sober colors. She had never owned a hat that was not either dark blue or black. Her undergarments were plain white as was the cap she wore over her hair to keep it in place. The bonnet had a wide brim to hide much of her face and all of her hair. She had once heard her father tell her mother that witches were known to have red hair, and her mother had remarked, very softly, that her own mother had red hair and was not a witch.

That was the beauty of her mother, Modesty thought. She was peaceful and never argued, but she had quiet authority. She'd never heard her father mention her hair again, although she knew he did not like it. Modesty kept it covered all the time, even at home in his presence. The only time she uncovered it was when she took it down before bed or to wash it. She made sure to keep her chamber dark so even she did not see her hair. She rarely looked in a mirror. Vanity was a sin. But when Modesty moved to the next window—she was dawdling now, but she could not seem to help it—and peered at the boots displayed, she also caught her own reflection in the wavy window glass. She was a pale face draped in black. She knew the glass distorted her image, but she looked so small and scared in the reflection that she turned away.

Time to be on her way. She hurried along the street, only slowing when she reached the bustling corner of Haymarket and Pall Mall. Then she took a deep breath and waded into the swarms of people. The streets were filled with private carriages and hackneys as well as coaches and heavily laden carts. The sidewalks were just as busy with men hurrying this way and that, ladies using their parasols to move anyone in their path aside, and mothers pulling recalcitrant children in their wake. It was a mass of people moving in every direction, and it was the epitome of London. Modesty would have paused to smile and take it in if she had not feared being jostled to the ground by those in a hurry behind her. She was not certain if people hurried to stay warm or because they were late.

She removed the slip of paper with the number she wanted on it and began to scan the numbers of the buildings she passed. The first section of the street was full of shops and offices, but there were residences interspersed. Finally, as the numbers neared the one she wanted, she slowed and, after being pushed aside by people hurrying past, paused in front of Mrs. Kydd's residence.

Modesty shifted the basket to the other arm again. It had felt so light when she'd left and now it seemed full of bricks. She climbed the steps to the residence and clutched the brass knocker, rapping repeatedly. A moment later a maid opened the door and smiled.

Mrs. Kydd had not wanted to see Modesty, so she left the basket and stepped back into the commotion of Pall Mall. On the return trip, she avoided looking in the shop windows and gazed at the street and at the people on the other side of Pall Mall. In front of her, a young child began to cry and threw himself on the ground. Modesty paused while his mother tried to coax him up and out of the way. She gave Modesty an apologetic look, and Modesty smiled at her reassuringly. While she waited for the mother to either calm the child or pick him up kicking and screaming, her gaze strayed across the street again. She narrowed her eyes as a man she recognized exited a gray building almost directly across from her.

He was a dark-skinned man of medium height, dressed very well in fawn breeches and a dark blue coat. His waistcoat was a deep burgundy color, and as she watched he adjusted his beaver hat on his head. She did not know his name and did not think he was among the parishioners of her father's congregation. Why should he look so familiar to her?

Her gaze strayed to the sign above the building he'd exited. It read *Mostyn's*. That told her nothing. Mostyn was most likely the surname of the owner of the establishment. But she had no idea what sort of establishment it was. The dark-skinned man began to walk along Pall Mall. It was just as crowded on the other side, and he had to jog to the side at one point to avoid plowing into another man. The way he moved released the trap on her memory. He was from the tavern the night before. She had seen him on the side of the boxing ring, yelling encouragement to the man the German had hit.

The pamphlets she had seen to promote the boxing match called the man The Royal Payne. She wondered if The Royal Payne was inside Mostyn's. Before she could think about what she was doing, she was taking her life into her hands and crossing Pall Mall. She let out a little scream as she was almost trampled by a horse and gave the coachman of a carriage traveling far too quickly a few choice—but still Christian—words. And then she was on the other side of the street and breathing heavily with relief. She looked up and saw the sign for Mostyn's. A large wooden door faced the street and there were no windows. She went to the door, pulled on the heavy latch and peered inside.

The interior was cool and dark with paneled wood walls and marble floors. The smell of oranges permeated the air, and she stepped inside and looked up at the high ceiling and the heavy but sturdy chandelier hanging from it.

"Help you?" came a low masculine voice.

Modesty turned and took a step back. The voice had been low and pleasant, but the man who greeted her was large and bald and had several bruises on his face. His nose had obviously been broken at one time as it was unnaturally crooked.

"I am sorry. I shouldn't have come inside," Modesty said. Really, what had possessed her to enter this place? Sometimes she was far too curious for her own good. Her mother would have gone straight home. She would never have crossed the street, much less opened the door to an unfamiliar establishment.

"No harm done," the man said with a smile that revealed several missing teeth. Modesty turned to go then heard a shout and a grunt and what sounded like several thumps. Then a loud cheer went up and Modesty couldn't help but look past the man who'd greeted her at the cracked door behind him.

"What is this place?" she asked.

"Mostyn's," he replied, seemingly happy to converse. "It's a pugilism studio for gentlemen wanting to learn to box. Most of the men who come here just want the activity. Boxing is quite energetic. Good for the lungs."

"I see," she said. "Is..." She should leave now. She should not say anything further. "Is The Royal Payne here?"

The man's brows shot up. "What does a woman like you know about The Royal Payne?" he asked. His eyes swept down her dour black dress.

"I should take my leave." She really should be on her way now. Determined now to do as she ought, she turned and walked to the door.

"Wait," the bruised man said. Modesty halted. "I'll fetch him for you."

She spun around. "He's here?"

"You're a strange one. I thought your sort didn't approve of blood sports, but I can see you're no different than every other chit in London."

"What do you mean?" Modesty asked.

"You're all in love with Rowden Payne. Stay right there. Don't move." He went through the door where the noise had emanated. Modesty didn't dare move, though she was half-afraid the man would return with Rowden Payne.

That was his name. Rowden. It was an odd name, probably a family name or a name he'd given himself. What would she say if Mr. Payne came through that door? What would she do?

She didn't have to wonder long because Mr. Payne himself stepped into the doorway a moment later. He was dressed only in shirt sleeves, and Modesty was grateful he wasn't bare-chested as he'd been the night before. He wiped his face with a cloth, and when he lowered it his green eyes fastened on her.

"*You*," he said. "You owe me fifty quid."

***

Rowden was immediately sorry he had said it. The woman paled visibly, and she was already quite pale beneath that large black hat. She was on the shorter side of medium height, and she seemed to shrink when he spoke, and he stepped forward to reassure her.

Which was exactly the wrong thing to do because she took a step back, clearly not reassured. "I'm teasing you," he said, though in truth, he wasn't quite ready to forgive her the fifty quid she'd cost him. But he'd also caught another flash of those amazing hazel eyes, and he didn't want her to run away quite yet.

"Teasing me?" she asked. "Like *na-na boo boo*?" Her voice was not weak or quiet, as he'd imagined it would be. It was strong and unwavering.

Rowden bit his cheek to keep from smiling. "I meant that I spoke in jest."

"But I did cost you a win last night. The German fighter knocked you down."

"Thanks for that reminder." He put his hands on his hips. "Did you come to offer to compensate me?" He hadn't meant it in a suggestive way. God knew she was primmer than a nun. Still, his tone had a suggestive hint to it he hadn't meant to put there.

"I don't have anything to offer," she said, seeming not to notice his tone. "I do not really know why I came. I suppose I wanted to apologize."

Rowden cocked his head to the side. "You wanted to apologize."

She nodded. "Yes. I didn't intend for you to be hurt."

He touched his temple gingerly as the bruise there was still tender. The blow had been glancing, but he still had a blooming black rose of a mark for it. "But you wanted to stop the fight."

"Of course." She nodded, and her eyes darted about the entryway as though it were a museum of curiosities. Rowden couldn't think why it should capture her attention. There was nothing of interest. Ewan Mostyn was not one for many words or embellishments. The walls were bare and the only items in the entry were a brass receptacle for umbrellas and walking sticks and a coat tree laden with several greatcoats.

"Why?" he asked.

Her gaze focused on him again, puzzled. He liked having her gaze on him and decided to ask more questions when it strayed. Of course, Rowden had an idea of why she objected, but he wanted to hear it from her.

"We don't believe in violence. We believe in peace and compassion." Her gaze strayed again, and she spoke almost as if by rote. "Jesus said, 'Love ye your enemies, and do good.'"

"The German wasn't my enemy. Our managers arranged the fight, and I did plan to do good with my winnings. I'd promised to donate them to an orphanage."

Her gaze locked on his face, eyes wide. "Really?"

"No." He smiled. "I would have done nothing so noble, only paid my landlord and bought food so I don't starve."

Her eyes lowered and then she seemed to realize she should not be looking at his body, and her gaze shot up again. "Is there not some honest way you can make a living?"

"I can't think what would be more honest than a fair fist fight. Do you want to have a look around the studio?" he asked, gesturing behind him to the door leading into the practice room.

"*Inside*? No!"

Rowden jammed a shoulder against one wall and made himself comfortable. "You don't want to risk your soul in a den of iniquity? I promise you it's not nearly as seedy as the tavern last night. I'll introduce you to the owner, Ewan Mostyn. He and I fought in the war together."

"You were a soldier?" she asked, clearly interested despite herself.

He laughed wryly. "I was a lot of things once upon a time. Come on." He waved for her to follow him and then, not checking to see if she did, opened the door to the studio and held it for her.

For a long moment she stood rooted in the entryway. Rowden could almost see her mind working, and he did see the play of emotions on her face. She was clearly torn between curiosity and morality. In the end, curiosity won, as it always did. She moved forward and stepped through the door and into the studio.

Rowden tried to see it through her eyes. It was a large, cavernous room, painted white. The ceilings were high and a row of rectangular windows along the top of the outer wall shed quite a bit of light into the room. Several crystal chandeliers hung from the ceiling as well, a nod to fifty or so years ago when this had been a ballroom. Two large rectangular areas had been raised and roped off in the center of the room. On the sides were sacks of flour and other weighted items designed for building strength.

Mostyn's was not crowded at this time of the day. It catered to gentlemen—not necessarily peers, who preferred Gentleman Jackson's, but gentlemen nonetheless. And those gentlemen tended to sleep until noon, just like their brethren with the title of *Lord* before their name.

Today there were just five of them in the room, not counting...

Rowden couldn't believe his bad manners. He hadn't asked her name.

Well, there were five men in the room. Ewan Mostyn was in the center rectangle. Ewan was a giant of a man with cropped white-blond hair and pale eyes. With his strong features and fierce expression, he resembled a Norse warrior. In the ring with Ewan was a young man of perhaps twenty. The man also had blond hair, but it was dark with sweat and pushed off his brow. He was proceeding through a series of quick steps and jabs, punctuated by Ewan's grunts of approval or censure. The lad was bare-chested, showing a scrawny chest with no hair yet to boast of. Ewan wore buff breeches, boots, and a shirt open at the throat. His coat had been discarded almost as soon as he'd arrived, and he rarely wore a neckcloth of any sort.

Outside the ring was the lad's father. He had removed his hat and greatcoat, but he still wore his coat and a cravat expertly tied. He had his hands on the ropes, clutching them tightly as though he could somehow infuse his strength and spirit into his son.

The other man Rowden knew only as Burr. He wasn't certain if it was the man's Christian name or surname, and he didn't ask. Burr was large, not quite as tall as Ewan but equally as brawny, and Burr was bald. He had bruises all along his face, and Rowden also hadn't asked if those were from practice sparring or a fight outside the studio. Burr had been a professional fighter, like Rowden, but he was mostly retired now. Rowden liked to think he could best Burr, but the two men hadn't tested that yet.

"Forgive my bad manners," Rowden said to the woman looking about the studio as though it were the first ring of hell. "I should have introduced myself. Rowden Payne." He gave her a stiff bow, and she blinked at him before finally nodding.

"My name is Modesty Brown."

Rowden almost laughed. It was the perfect name for her, so perfect it was almost a caricature. But he held his laughter and ushered her closer to the ring. "When they pause, I'll introduce you to Mostyn."

She dragged her feet, but finally they stood on the side of the rectangle adjacent to the lad's father. He watched as the lad stepped forward and back, jabbing with his hands, weaving and bobbing as he moved.

"It looks like a dance," Miss Brown said.

"Yes." Rowden had considered that comparison before. In the ring, it often felt like a dance, except there would be no champagne or stolen kisses at the end of it. You danced well or you were flat on your back.

The lad paused, grasped a towel from the corner and wiped at his sweat-streaked face. He looked at Ewan, and Ewan made a circular motion with his hand, indicating the lad should do it again. The lad looked as though he might argue, then he thought better of it and began the exercise again. Rowden glanced at Miss Brown. She seemed intrigued despite herself. Her face was a study of contrast. Her eyes, those exotic eyes, were fixed on the lad with interest. But her mouth, almost too ordinary to share a face with those eyes, was pursed disapprovingly. Rowden thought he could like that mouth—not as much as the eyes, but he could definitely like that mouth if she softened it. It was a very kissable mouth.

Almost as soon as the thought materialized, Rowden pushed it away. Rowden liked women, and they liked him. But this was not the sort of woman a man dabbled with. He doubted she had ever held a man's hand, much less been kissed.

"Why must he repeat the steps over and again?" Miss Brown asked. She spoke in a hushed tone, and he had to lean closer to hear her.

Rowden glanced back at the lad. "There's not much time to think when you're in the ring and another man is throwing punches at you." He glanced at Miss Brown, and she was looking at him with interest. His belly tightened unexpectedly, and his face warmed. "Your body acts instinctively. Training will overcome instinct only if that training has become second-nature. So the lad learns to weave and dodge and punch rather than flinch or duck or run."

"God gave man those instincts to protect us from harm. It seems foolish, if not sinful, to work against them." She didn't say working against them was like working against God, but Rowden took her meaning.

"God also gave us the capability to train and to learn. Maybe it's His will we defeat our instincts."

She didn't answer, merely looked back at the roped-off area. No doubt she had an answer ready, though Rowden thought his rejoinder had been strong. After all, man's every instinct was toward what the Miss Browns of the world would call sin. But she either did not like to argue or, more likely, had been told it was unbecoming and unwomanly.

Too bad. Rowden would have liked to argue with her, to see those hazel eyes flash at him with temper.

The lad finished, lifted his towel again, and said, "I'm ready for something new."

Ewan didn't speak, merely lifted one eyebrow slightly in challenge.

"I am!" the lad protested. "I've mastered this."

"Mostyn will say when you've mastered it," the lad's father said.

The lad scoffed and shook his blond hair. "He doesn't say anything. *I'm* telling you both, I'm ready for the next lesson."

"Uh oh," Rowden said under his breath.

"What is it?" Miss Brown asked.

"He's rolling up his sleeves." Rowden watched Ewan finish with one cuff and begin on the other.

"What does that mean?"

"It means, Miss Brown, you are about to receive a demonstration. Stand back a step or two, would you?"

She didn't argue, just took two steps back from the ring.

Ewan moved to the center of the ring and crouched slightly. He rarely spoke, and he rarely needed to. It was clear what he intended. The student gave his father a look, then tossed the towel aside, and assumed a defensive posture. Ewan advanced, and the student retreated.

"You see," Rowden said quietly, speaking close to Miss Brown's ear. "That's instinct." Then more loudly, he called, "Use what you just learned, lad!"

The student glanced at him, nodded, and began to repeat the steps he'd been practicing. He jabbed at Ewan who easily deflected, and then Ewan threw a light punch, and the student was able to evade it.

"It seems he has learned the lesson," Miss Brown observed. Her hands were folded together, giving her a very prim appearance in her black garb, but her voice held a note of excitement.

"Keep watching," Rowden said, doubtfully. And indeed, in the next moment, Ewan threw another punch and another. The lad, who had looked so confident a moment before, stumbled and faltered. One of Ewan's punches glanced off his shoulder, and the dash of pain was the beginning of the chaos. The carefully choreographed dance was gone, and the lad scurried and lurched about the ring. He was an easy target, and Rowden counted the student fortunate when Ewan punched him lightly in the breadbasket. It was hard enough that the student doubled over and went down. A punch from Ewan, even a light one, flattened a man.

Ewan looked at the lad's father, and the man nodded his head. "We'll be back tomorrow," he said. Then Ewan climbed over the ropes and stood to the side, rolling his cuffs back down.

"Come," Rowden said, reaching to touch her back and lead her toward Ewan, but he stopped just short of touching her. "I'll introduce you."

She did not move. "I did not come to see him. I came to apologize to you. I have done that."

"Don't remind me," he said, thinking again of the fifty pounds. "But you can't come to Mostyn's and not meet the man himself." He moved forward and beckoned her, and finally she followed, a mutinous look on her face. The look was brief and then slid into a compliant smile, but Rowden had seen it.

And he wanted to see it again.

"Miss Modesty Brown," he said as he approached Ewan. "Might I present Mr. Ewan Mostyn, the owner of this fine establishment."

Ewan looked down at the little figure in black as a hawk might study a field mouse. He nodded then looked at Rowden, a question in his eyes.

"Miss Brown came to apologize to me. She and her fellow Crusaders interrupted my match with the German last night, and the distraction cost me fifty pounds."

Ewan's gaze shifted to the bruise on Rowden's temple, and Rowden clenched his fist to stop himself from touching it. He sighed. "Yes, I know what you say about distraction."

Rowden looked at Miss Brown. "Mr. Mostyn has absolved you of blame."

Miss Brown wrinkled her brow. "He did not speak."

"He doesn't have to. I know what he's thinking, and it's that boxing is all about focus. Lose your focus and lose the fight. I lost my focus." Rowden looked at Ewan. "But can you blame me? Look at her eyes."

Ewan scowled. "I'm not allowed to look at another woman's eyes."

"How is Lady Lorraine?" Rowden asked. He leaned closer to Miss Brown. "Mostyn's wife is…how do I say it the polite way?" He gave Ewan a questioning look and Ewan shrugged. "In the family way?"

"Oh!" Despite his attempts to use the most unobjectionable term he could find, her cheeks still turned quite pink. Rowden stared and almost forgot what they were discussing. The transformation from the pale, drab creature into a blushing woman was remarkable. She looked almost beautiful. She stared hard at the floor then recovered herself. "What a blessing," she whispered.

Ewan blew out a breath as though he did not consider his wife's current state a blessing. Rowden did not know Ewan's wife well, but she was the daughter of a duke, and as he was once the son of a duke, their paths had crossed many times. He knew her brothers better than he knew her, but he'd been at a dinner party or two with Lady Lorraine and she was—for lack of a better word—effervescent. He couldn't imagine she would have turned cross or sour because of pregnancy, but she might be even more excitable than usual. After all, Rowden had once had sisters, and he'd watched the amount of planning and hysterics that went into every aspect of their weddings. He could only imagine readying the nursery was much the same.

"Mostyn," Burr called. "Mr. Johnson is here for his lesson."

Ewan clapped loudly and started for the ring, and Miss Brown jumped about a foot. Rowden put a hand on her back to steady her. She jumped again, as though his touch had burned her.

"You're rather skittish, aren't you?" he said.

"I should depart."

"No need to run off. You could watch Johnson's training. He's a good deal better than that puppy in here earlier. Or you could watch me. When you arrived, I had just begun my own daily regimen."

Her gaze strayed to the rectangle on the far side of the studio, and Rowden almost thought she would stay. But then she shook her head vehemently enough that her ugly black bonnet nearly fell back. "I must go home."

"I will see you out," Rowden said. When they reached the entryway, he grasped the door handle and pulled it open. She stepped through, and he looked about for her escort. Seeing no one waiting for her, he frowned. "Did you come alone?"

"I did. I came to pay a call to Mrs. Kydd, who lives just there." She pointed to a row of terraced houses down the street. "She is a benefactress for the church. But I have tarried too long. Good day, sir. I do hope you recover quickly." She raised an ungloved hand, almost as though she might touch him. Rowden wanted to lean forward so that she might brush her fingers against his skin, but she lowered her hand quickly and looked away. "Good day."

"If you wait a moment, I will fetch my coat and hat and see you home." She was relatively safe walking through this part of the city in the middle of the day, but he would feel better seeing her safely home. "Step back inside, out of the cold. I will be just a moment."

She stepped back into the entryway, but her step was hesitant and her gaze on the street. Rowden hurried back into the studio, gathered his coat, and all but sprinted to the entryway where his greatcoat and hat hung. He was not surprised to find her gone when he returned.

He grabbed his hat and ran out of the studio, hoping to catch her. But he looked this way and that and couldn't spot her anywhere. It didn't help that all of London was out and about on Pall Mall. Rowden swore and went back inside. It was for the best, he told himself, hanging his greatcoat back on the rack. He did not want responsibility for the woman. And he needed to train. Chibale would organize another match soon, and this time Rowden must win.

But when he stepped through the ropes a short time later, her hazel eyes still haunted him.

Three

Across town, Chibale lingered across the street from Madame Renauld's. He'd stood there for about a quarter of an hour, trying to work up the nerve to go inside. The feelings he had when he thought of Madame Renauld were not like anything he'd ever experienced before. His chest felt tight and his heart beat fast. He felt slightly lightheaded, and he'd spent part of the last quarter hour taking deep breaths and talking himself into walking inside the modiste's shop. He was Chibale Okoro, son of Gamba Okoro, who was son of Thimba, the great warrior and lion hunter. If his grandfather could hunt down a lion, Chibale could face a woman with nothing more deadly than a needle and thread.

A woman passed in front of the shop, stopped, peered at him, and crossed the street. Chibale recognized her belatedly and straightened. "Why are you standing out here?" Bethanie asked. She was his younger sister and the favorite of his siblings. Although she was almost seventeen, she looked much younger. Like their mother, she was short and slim. She wore her hair in a pinned-up twist, and she wore a day dress of light blue which suited her copper complexion. Chibale himself was dark, like his father. As such, he preferred bolder colors, but the pale blue suited Bethanie.

"I was waiting for you," Chibale said.

Bethanie gave him an odd look. "It's freezing out here. You should have waited inside."

Chibale offered his arm, giving himself one more silent lecture to be brave. Though he was not religious, he called upon the spirit of his grandfather anyway. He could use the lion hunter's bravery. He led Bethanie across the street and opened the door of Madame Renauld's. A large man stood nearby. He gave the two a look then went back to scowling at the shop in general. Chibale had seen Madame Renauld's bully boys before. They were employed to keep thieves and ruffians away. Chibale had read in the papers of groups of boys who swarmed shops and, while the dressmakers tried to shoo them out, grabbed handfuls of the fine fabrics on display. But just as the bully boy—er, bully man—moved away, Chibale was startled by a fluttering of feathers. A large, brightly colored bird looked down at him from a perch. The bird cocked its red head and said, "Would you like to see the fine lace? Fine lace!"

Bethanie smiled and clapped. "Oh, I forgot about the beautiful parrot!"

Chibale could have sworn the bird preened. "Hello!" it said.

"What is your name?" Bethanie asked.

"What is your name?" the bird repeated.

"Bethanie," she replied.

"Fine lace!" the bird said.

Bethanie looked at Chibale. "Do you think his name is Fine Lace?"

"Her name is Bleuette," a pretty woman with light brown skin said, coming forward. "And she will talk to you all day, Miss Okoro."

"How extraordinary!" Bethanie said.

Chibale found talking birds more disconcerting than extraordinary.

"She is," Miss Phaedra agreed. "You are right on time. And hello to you, Mr. Okoro."

Chibale nodded. "Miss Phaedra, good to see you again. My sister is here to see her dress. Is it ready?"

"Of course! Madame Renauld is upstairs making the final alterations as we speak. I will take you to the dressing room. And you, Mr. Okoro, we have a private parlor where you may wait." The bell above the door tinkled as a well-dressed woman entered, and Miss Phaedra turned and signaled to another woman, who came out and greeted the lady. But not before Bleuette asked if the woman would like to see the fine lace.

"This way, please."

Chibale and Bethanie followed Miss Phaedra up an enclosed winding flight of stairs to the first floor of the shop. The ground floor was clean but a bit cluttered with goods to tempt the shop's customers. But the parlor he was led into was quiet and dim with no sign of clutter. Or talking birds. The room was cool and dark, the heavy draperies pulled almost all the way closed. A couch had been positioned behind a raised platform and was flanked by a grouping of chairs. In the back was a table and a door to a dressing area.

Chibale's breath caught in his throat as he finally spotted Madame Renauld. She stood by the table with a small smile on her face. "Mees Okoro," she said, coming forward. She had the loveliest French accent Chibale had ever heard. When he spoke, the sounds of London punctuated every word. When she spoke, he could almost see the Seine and the stained-glass windows of Notre Dame. "We have anxiously awaited your arrival. Thees dress ees a masterpiece, if I do say so myself. I know you will be pleased."

Bethanie clasped her hands and beamed. Chibale felt almost guilty. He hadn't thought how much pleasure such a fine dress would bring his sister. He had only been looking for an excuse to see the modiste. He made to follow his sister toward the room behind the table, but Madame Renauld raised a hand.

"Monsieur will wait in here." And with that, she followed Bethanie into the dressing room and closed the door.

"Would you like coffee or tea?" a blond woman asked. Chibale had not even noticed her.

"No, thank you," he said.

"Something stronger then?" She gestured to several crystal decanters Chibale assumed held brandy and sherry and such. He could have used liquid courage right now, but he declined the offer. Then the blond too went through the door, and he was left alone. He did not know how long he paced the room. It was probably ten minutes, no more, but when the door opened again, he turned eagerly, expecting to see his sister. Instead, Madame Renauld emerged.

She wore a gown in deep burgundy. The waist was high, as was the current style, and though she wore a fichu at her bosom, it was sheer and did little to hide the plumpness of her breasts above the neckline of the dress. The gown had long, tight sleeves and threads of gold running through it, making the wearer seem to shimmer when she walked, especially in the candlelight of the parlor. Without saying a word, Madame Renauld went to one of the decanters, poured amber liquid into it, and crossed to him.

Her hair was swept into an elegant chignon, and the upsweep highlighted the strong cheekbones in her face and her dark eyes, framed by long, thick eyelashes. She had a generous mouth with lips a bit too red to be natural, and Chibale liked to imagine kissing that mouth until the paint had been rubbed away so he could watch as she reapplied it.

She held the glass to him, and he took it and drank. He was suddenly very thirsty.

"Mees Okoro ees *très belle*," she said.

"What does that mean?" he asked, stupidly. At least he felt stupid. All of that time spent gathering his courage, and this was the first thing he said? He knew a bit of French, but now she would think him ignorant.

"You will see for yourself, monsieur." She moved away from him, trailing a long, elegant finger along the back of the couch. "The dress ees a little long. Phaedra is making the adjustments to the hem, and then *voilà*. The reveal." She gestured to the raised platform.

"Will we have to return?" Chibale said, hopefully. Perhaps he would have another chance to make a better impression.

"No." Madame Renaud waved her hand. "The hem ees a small thing. We always leave it unfinished for adjustments. My girl Betsy can finish it like that." She snapped to illustrate.

Chibale set his empty glass on a table and removed his hat, crushing it in his hands as he drew on the courage of all his ancestors. "Madame, have you given any thought to the proposal I made when we last spoke?"

She smiled at him. "Ah. I was wondering if you would mention thees matter again."

"So you have considered it." Chibale felt lightheaded. He did not know if he should hope or prepare for despair.

She inclined her head. "As a businesswoman, I carefully consider every proposal. I have not been in London for very long. Not even two years."

Though Chibale knew this, he was still surprised. She had made a name for herself in Paris, and when she arrived in London, her reputation had preceded her. Even so, London had its own modistes and women were notoriously loyal to their dressmakers. Just as many men were devoted to their tailors, himself included. But Madame Renauld had done very well for herself in such a short time. She dressed the wives and mistresses of some of the most important people in the country, if not the world.

"And yet I have heard of the Negro Merchant's Guild. I would like to know more."

"It would be my honor to escort you to the ball," Chibale said.

Madame Renauld gestured to the dressing room door, where the murmur of women's voices could still be heard. "And what of your sister? Will you leave her without an escort?"

"My parents will be in attendance. Miss Okoro will not be without a chaperone."

Madame Renauld perched daintily on the arm of the couch. She was a small woman, but she seemed to possess enough authority for two women. And yet, every movement she made was the height of grace and elegance.

"Then it ees your parents who are members of thees guild, *oui*?"

"Yes."

"You are not a member?"

Chibale relaxed his grip on his hat. "No. I am not a merchant, Madame."

"No, you are not. You are a…" She made a punching motion.

"I am not a pugilist, Madame. I am a businessman. I arrange the boxing matches for my client, Mr. Payne."

"He ees the one who lost to the German last night?"

Chibale dropped his hat then fumbled to scoop it up. "Y-you heard of that?"

Madame Renauld looked at the dressing room door. "My seamstress Phaedra talks of thees pugilists when she thinks I do not overhear. She has an affection for the one called The Plague—no, that is not right. The Black Death?"

Chibale made a face.

"I see you know thees man."

"I was his manager—very briefly—several years ago. Miss Phaedra would do better to find another man more deserving of her affections."

Madame's eyes opened wider. "You will have to tell me more."

The dressing room door opened and Phaedra herself peeked out. "Madame, we are ready."

"And so are we!" Madame Renauld said. "Bring her out, *mes filles*."

She moved to the side to stand near Chibale. He caught her scent, a mixture of oranges and cloves. Bethanie came through the door, her smile wide but her eyes on Chibale, as though she was still not quite certain about her appearance. Chibale was conscious of Madame Renauld's gaze on him as well, and he smiled broadly at his sister. When she climbed on the platform and turned around for him, he clapped.

She wore a cream-colored gown with a wide neck that dipped low but not so low that Chibale felt he had to avert his eyes. The sleeves were sheer and white and fluttered prettily on Bethanie's arms. Pearls adorned the bodice of the gown and were placed in a lattice pattern on the skirt, giving the dress a sort of ethereal feeling.

"She will put pearls in her hair," Madame Renauld said quietly, "and the effect will be stunning."

Yes, Chibale could imagine it. Bethanie's dark hair would contrast with the gleaming pearls, and she would shine in the candlelight.

"You look more beautiful than I have ever seen you," Chibale said to his sister, who seemed to relax a bit at his compliment.

"Do you like it?" Bethanie asked, turning to look at herself in the mirror, though she must have looked at herself for the last ten minutes.

"It is your opinion that matters," Chibale said. "Do *you* like it?"

"I do," Bethanie said. "I adore it."

"Then it is yours," Chibale said, smiling. He was genuinely pleased with the dress and more so with his sister's pleasure. He glanced at Madame Renauld and found her watching him with a curious expression on her face. She looked away and glided to the platform. Madame inspected the gown, fluffing the skirts and ensuring each pearl was securely attached. Finally, she declared it *très magnifique,* and Bethanie was whisked back to the dressing room.

Madame Renauld gestured to the exit and led Chibale back down the stairs to the showroom. "We will bring her down when she ees dressed again." She approached the counter and gestured for the clerk to give her a quill and an ivory card. "Write the address here, and we will send one of our boys to deliver the dress thees evening." She lowered her voice. "And you may send him back with a note telling me the day and time you will collect me for the merchant's winter ball. I trust you have a carriage?"

"Of course," Chibale lied.

Madame Renauld gave a slight curtsy. "Good day, Mr. Okoro."

"Good day, Madame Renauld." He watched her glide through the room and back to the stairs and then turned his attention to the card, having no memory whatsoever of what he was supposed to do with it.

***

Modesty tried to think of excuses all the way home. She knew as soon as she walked into the house her father would want to know why she had been away for so long. She imagined how distraught he must be. He was probably pacing, unable to concentrate on writing his sermon. What reason could she give for causing him such anguish? As she hurried back home, she shivered with the cold. Her hands were numb and her ill-fitting shoes made her feet hurt. Tears sprang to her eyes not only because she was cold and hungry, but because she felt wretched for making her father worry.

She did not often disappoint him, but when she did, she felt miserable for days. Once, when she was eight or nine and had transgressed in some way, her father said he needn't punish her because she punished herself more than he ever could. Modesty was already punishing herself with mental flagellation. The next week she would do extra chores and pray an extra hour a day. This was in addition to whatever punishment her father would give her.

Modesty opened the door to their home, head down, apologies on her lips, and was greeted with silence. Not only was the house silent, it was dark. The ground floor consisted of a sitting and dining area with a small kitchen in the back and a small room her father used as a study. Modesty could cross the entire room in ten steps. She knew almost immediately upon entering the house was empty. The curtains had been drawn and the lamps extinguished.

"Father?" she called, thinking her might be closed off in his study.

He did not answer.

"Father, I'm home." She moved cautiously toward the table where she kept the tinder box, lit a candle, and started toward the study. But she did not take a step before she inhaled sharply and stared. The room was in shambles. No one who did not know the usual state of the room would think it in shambles. But to her eye, the room looked as though it had been ransacked. A chair was pushed away from the table where she and her father had broken their fast instead of pushed in. A teacup stood half full on the table rather than in the sink. The candlesticks had been allowed to burn down to the nubs, and she could still smell the scent of tallow in the air. When Modesty finally dragged her eyes from the destruction, she saw the door to her father's study was open. "Father!" she called, now more worried for him than for any punishment she might receive. She started across the room, stepping over a table that was a good two inches out of place, and peering into the study. It too was empty. Her father had about a dozen precious books and two of them had not been replaced on the shelf and lay willy-nilly on the desk. One lay open.

Modesty gasped with horror as her father was always very careful and protective of his books. They were the only thing of value he owned. She hurried to pick up the two books on the desk and restore them to the shelf where they belonged. It was only when she'd righted the book that she had the terrible thought: if her father's books had been so badly mistreated, what had happened to her father?

She searched the rest of the house, including her small bed chamber and his on the first floor. They were empty as well. Modesty shook with fear and bewilderment now, but she forced herself to sit on her bed and set the candle on her nightstand so as not to drop it. Her hands were shaking so violently that the light jerked wildly and made eerie shapes on the wall.

Her room had not been disturbed. The normally closed door had been open, but her few possessions had been undisturbed. This did not surprise her. After all, who would want her other black dress and black bonnet hanging on pegs on the wall or the white underthings she kept in a small trunk? She had opened the trunk to be certain and saw her mother's hairbrush, all Modesty had left of her mother, still rested on top of her chemise as she'd left it there after brushing her hair this morning.

Modesty hadn't searched her father's room. She never entered it unless she was to sweep and polish and even then she kept her eyes down, but from the doorway, it also looked undisturbed. His narrow bed was tidy, and his other black coat hung on a peg.

Modesty couldn't say how long she sat on her bed, willing her hands to stop shaking. It seemed hours before she could take a breath and think clearly enough to know what she should do. She would go to Mr. Pliney's house. He was one of the church elders, and he would know what to do.

Modesty went back downstairs and stepped outside, surprised to see it was still light outdoors. It had seemed like hours and hours had passed, and it must be night by now. She walked the ten minutes it took to reach Mr. Pliney's home and was greeted by his wife, who took one look at her, dropped the hem of the apron she'd been wiping her hands on, and took Modesty in her arms. Modesty promptly burst into tears and attempted to tell her story between sobs and hiccups.

***

Mr. Pliney enlisted the aid of some of the other elders of the church, and they investigated and discussed but had no more answers than Modesty herself.

Modesty stayed with the Plineys until Sunday. In her mind, Sunday was the day her father would return. He *had* to return as he never missed giving his sermon on Sundays. But when she and the Plineys arrived at the church Sunday morning, her father was not there. Nor did he make an appearance as the small congregation prayed and sang hymns. And when the service was over, Modesty knew one thing for certain: something very bad had happened to her father. He would never have missed church if the decision had been his own.

When she returned home with the Plineys, Mr. and Mrs. Pliney pulled her aside.

"The elders have made inquiries and searched for your father," Mr. Pliney said, "but there seems to be no trace of him. No one saw him leave that day, and no one has seen him since."

"You know we have enjoyed having you here. We love you like one of our own," Mrs. Pliney said, still patting Modesty's hand. "But the house is too small and, well, it's been a struggle to find enough money to feed even one more mouth. Not that you eat much!" Mrs. Pliney waved her hands as though refusing an offer. "You're a bird, but, well, Mr. Pliney and I thought it might be better for you to stay with family. Is there someone we can write to or send for?"

"Do you have an aunt or uncle? Cousins? Perhaps your mother's people?" Mr. Pliney suggested.

Modesty knew very little about her mother's people, as Mr. Pliney called them. Her father had a brother, but he had emigrated to Canada when Modesty had been just a little girl. Her father's parents were dead, as were her mother's, but...

"My mother has a sister," Modesty said. "I only ever saw her once. She came to the door when I was very young, and I only caught a glimpse of her." Modesty did not add that she had been hiding behind her mother's skirts. Her aunt had seemed very tall and very grand. She'd had a large bird plume on her hat, and Modesty had stared up at it. She'd also had a loud, sharp voice, and though Modesty did not remember what she'd said, whatever it had been had upset her mother. Catherine Brown had rarely spoken in anything other than mild tones, but she had raised her voice that day. She'd said, "Are you quite finished, Augusta? Yes? Then go home." She'd slammed the door, which had made Modesty jump.

Her Aunt Augusta had not returned and when Modesty's father arrived that afternoon, her mother did not speak of it.

"Is she in London?" Mrs. Pliney asked.

Modesty wasn't certain, but said, "Yes. I've seen her in London," which was true, even if it had been fifteen or more years ago. She now understood what this was—the Plineys wanted her gone—and Modesty was mortified that she had stayed as long as she had. This wasn't her family, and she was a burden to them. They would continue to allow her to stay out of Christian charity, but they did not want her. And Modesty could not imagine staying another moment under a roof where she was not wanted. Her mother had always said to make yourself useful or get out of the way.

Modesty had tried to make herself useful, but the truth was the Plineys had plenty of daughters to cook, clean, and sew. Modesty was just an extra mouth to feed. If she had been a man, she might have found a job and earned money. She could still find a job in a factory or a shop, and then she could pay the Plineys for her meals. But the fact was they were not her family, and she was not a child who had nowhere else to go. She had a house and an aunt. She even had a father... somewhere.

Modesty sat straight and tried to look hopeful. "I am so pleased you have mentioned her. I was thinking of seeking her out myself."

Mrs. Pliney squeezed her hand. "Were you?"

She had just now thought of it. "Yes. In fact, I would go first thing tomorrow. Would you mind if I stayed one more night?" Her bed was infinitely preferable to the hard floor of the Plineys' girls' room, but she just couldn't go back home. Not yet. It would be too empty without her father, too upsetting to wonder what could have happened to him.

"Of course." Mrs. Pliney patted her hand again, and Modesty tried to smile rather than cry.

***

The next morning she washed her face and hands and set out. She declined to break her fast, saying she was certain her aunt would have plenty. In truth, she did not want to take anymore from the Plineys, who had been so generous toward her.

She made her way toward Mayfair and when she reached St. James's Park, she sat on a bench and rested. The park was empty and the grounds stretched out before her, lightly frosted and sparkling in the morning light. She had no idea where her aunt might live. She did not even know how to inquire after her. Modesty's mother's maiden name had been Ryan, but if her aunt had married, would it do Modesty any good to inquire after an Augusta Ryan?

Plus, it was the middle of winter, a fact made abundantly clear as she shivered on the frozen park bench. Modesty's mother's family had been wealthy. Modesty had pieced this together after hearing her father make comments about how Catherine Ryan's parents hadn't approved of her marrying a penniless minister. Didn't wealthy people go to the country during the winter months to...do whatever people in the country did?

Modesty had only ever traveled outside of London once. Inside of London, she tended to stay close to home. She had rarely been to Mayfair as the wealthy did not look kindly upon people who called out their vices on the street, and her father had been hauled away by bully boys or footmen and tossed on his ear one time too many to bring Modesty there.

Modesty supposed there was nothing to do but go home. She did not know how to find her aunt. She did not know how to find her father. She did not know how she would afford to pay for the house or meals or any of the other things she needed. She could go to the church for charity, but how could she stand the shame of it? At the services yesterday morning, she had known people were looking at her and whispering about her. She knew what she would have thought if she'd been in their shoes. She would have assumed her father had done something awful and run away before he could be discovered. That or he owed money to someone and the collector had carried him off for punishment.

But Modesty knew her father. He didn't owe anyone money. He couldn't have done anything awful. He didn't have secrets from her.

Except...why had he sent her to Mrs. Kydd's the morning of his disappearance? Who was the man he'd met with the night before?

Modesty stood and paced to keep warm. Her head ached from the cold and from hunger. She couldn't go back to the Plineys. She couldn't go home. She didn't know where her aunt lived, and she didn't know anyone of her aunt's station she could ask.

Or did she?

Modesty stopped pacing and thought of the day she had visited Mrs. Kydd. Afterward she had stopped into the boxing club. She hadn't belonged there, not just because she was a woman but because the men who paid to attend the club were gentlemen. Of course, she had been taught to believe all men were equal in the eyes of the Lord, but she was well aware the upper classes did not share that sentiment.

The Royal Payne was from the upper classes. Perhaps he would help her or would ask some of the gentlemen from the club about her aunt.

She had not thought of Mr. Payne in days. She'd been too preoccupied with worry about her father, but now that she did think of him, her face felt warm and her heart sped up. She wanted to see him again. Her father would not have liked it. He would not have liked her going to the boxing club. But perhaps she had found Mostyn's because God knew she would need to go back again later. God always had a plan, and even a man like Mr. Payne could be part of it.

Modesty really had no other options at this point, so she straightened her hat and started for Pall Mall. It was still too early for Mostyn's to be open, but she could stand outside and wait. Surely it wouldn't be long. Ignoring the gnawing in her belly and the throbbing of her head, Modesty began to walk.

Four

Rowden woke to the sound of pounding. He pulled the pillow over his head and pressed it tight over his ears. He closed his eyes and tried to go back to sleep, but the pounding continued.

After a moment he heard the door of his bed chamber open and the plodding steps of his manservant Trogdon. "Someone is at the door, sir."

Rowden scowled under the pillow. "Make whoever it is go away. That's what I pay you for."

"Yes, sir," Trogdon said. He shuffled away. Rowden closed his eyes and was almost asleep again when Trogdon shook him. "He won't go away, sir."

Rowden threw the pillow. "If I have to—" Rowden squinted. "Burr?" He glared at Trogdon. "What is *he* doing in my rooms?"

"I let him in, sir."

"Of course, you did," Rowden muttered.

"We have a bit of a situation, Payne," Burr said.

Rowden snapped his fingers at Trogdon, who gave him a confused tilt of his head. "My dressing gown, Trogdon."

Trogdon looked about, clearly unsure where the garment might be. With a sigh, Rowden lifted it from the foot of the bed himself and donned it. "What sort of situation?" he asked as the last vestiges of sleep fled and his head cleared.

"I found that girl curled up in front of Mostyn's door. She was shivering and didn't wake when I shook her," Burr said, rubbing his bald head.

"What girl?" Rowden asked. There were any number of orphaned children living on the streets of London, though Rowden couldn't remember any sleeping in the doorway of Mostyn's. They tended to seek out places with food for obvious reasons.

"The girl who came last week. The one in black," Burr said.

Rowden stilled. "Miss Brown?"

"No, she was wearing black."

Rowden shook his head. "Where is she now? Still in the doorway?"

"I brought her here," Burr said. "I laid her on your couch."

Rowden gave Trogdon a sharp look. "Is there a woman lying on my couch, Trogdon?"

"Yes, sir.

"And why did you not mention this before?" Rowden asked, pushing past his manservant and Burr to pass through the bed chamber door.

"You didn't ask, sir."

Rowden would have throttled Trogdon, but he spotted the small black form on his couch. She wasn't moving.

Rowden cursed under his breath. He was a man who went to great lengths to avoid any sort of serious responsibility toward others. He'd had enough of that in the war and...before. The last thing he wanted was responsibility for a woman lying unconscious on his couch. And yet, what was he supposed to do? Put her out in the cold? He cursed again.

Rowden crossed the room and knelt beside the couch. "Open the drapes and light a lamp, Trogdon."

She was turned away from him, and Rowden touched her shoulder. It felt ice cold.

"Bring me a blanket and a pot of tea," he ordered. "Miss Brown?" Rowden said, patting her shoulder. She did not move. Where was the blanket? Rowden looked up to see Trogdon standing in the middle of the room, unmoving. His feet were bare as were his calves. He wore his nightshirt and a long cap over his golden curls. He scratched at those curls now, clearly confused.

"Trogdon!" Rowden bellowed and the servant jumped. "What are you doing?"

"Trying to remember, sir. You gave me so many orders, I forgot the first one."

Rowden blew out a breath. "Go make a pot of tea, Trogdon. That's all you need to do. Make tea."

"Make tea, sir." He repeated it under his breath as he moved away.

"What are you planning to do with her?" Burr asked.

Rowden bent and scooped her into his arms. "Right now I need to warm her up. Watch out." He carried her past Burr and into his bedchamber. She weighed practically nothing, though he could feel she wasn't skin and bones. That at least was a relief. She was undoubtedly cold but hopefully hadn't been out on the streets and starving. He set her on his bed, pulled the blankets up and around her, then strode to the hearth and stoked the fire. When it began to crackle, he returned to the bed and looked down at her. Her face looked very small under the large brim of the black hat. It couldn't be comfortable to lie with that hat on, so he reached under her chin and tugged the ribbons loose. Gently lifting her head, he removed the hat and stepped back in surprise.

She wore a plain white cap under the hat, but it couldn't disguise the deep auburn hair at the crown of her head. No wonder her skin was so pale. She was a redhead. He wouldn't have thought it.

"You'd better not be thinking of taking anything else off," Burr said, his voice closer. Rowden looked over his shoulder at Burr, who was right behind him now.

"Are you concerned I plan to take advantage of her?"

"You put her in your bed and started undressing her."

"I put her in my bed to warm her and removed a hat. You will be relieved to know that's as far as my intentions go." Rowden moved away from her and checked on the fire again. It was blazing now, far too warm for Rowden's comfort, but he added more coal nonetheless. "Why did you bring her here?" His voice held a note of accusation, and he didn't try to disguise it.

"Don't know," Burr said, moving to stand at the head of Rowden's bed, almost as though he were Miss Brown's protector. "I didn't know what else to do with her."

Anything else but bring her here.

"Here we are," Trogdon said, entering with a blanket over his arm. He'd dressed and combed his hair. His cravat was perfectly tied, his golden curls expertly tousled. He offered the blanket and when Rowden didn't take it, he nodded at it. "You said to fetch a blanket, sir."

"Trogdon, do you see Miss Brown?" Rowden said, his voice low and deceptively calm.

Trogdon looked at the bed. "Is that woman Miss Brown?"

Rowden nodded.

"Then yes, sir, I see her."

"Do you notice anything about her, Trogdon? For example, do you notice what is on top of her?"

"Blankets, sir?"

"Right. Which is why I asked you to fetch tea. I have blankets. I do not have tea."

"I distinctly remember you asking for a blanket."

Rowden made a low sound in the back of his throat, and Trogdon backed away. "If you want tea, I will make it now."

"Thank you, Trogdon," Rowden said between clenched teeth. With exaggerated care, Trogdon set the blanket on a chair in the corner and turned to leave the bed chamber. Rowden could have sworn he heard him muttering about how some people were never happy.

"Seems he has apartments to let," Burr said, tapping his head.

"Yes, he's not the brightest lamp in the larder. I would let him go, but who else would hire him?"

And that was precisely the problem with responsibility. Rowden did not need anyone else relying on him.

Rowden went to the window and parted the curtains slightly to look out. It wasn't that he cared so much for the view. His rooms overlooked St. James's Street, and there was not much to see this morning. It was more that he needed something to look at rather than the woman lying in his bed. The weather outside was cold and gray. The sun had risen, but the light was weak, and the clouds promised rain that day. It wasn't cold enough for snow—it rarely was in London— but that didn't mean the temperatures weren't frigid, especially for a woman in a thin coat and no gloves. Rowden looked back at the small form under his bedclothes. How long had she been out in the cold? Hours? Days? Surely not days. But judging by how cold and pale she'd been, however long she'd been out in the elements was too long.

Trogdon appeared in the door again this time with a tea tray. "Shall I set the tea on the dresser, sir?" he asked, his voice tight. His gaze did not meet Rowden's, and it was obvious the man's feelings had been hurt. Rowden would make amends later.

"Yes, the dresser."

Trogdon set the tray on the dresser and poured a cup, adding lemon as Rowden liked it.

"It's not for me, Trogdon," Rowden said. "See if she will take some."

Trogdon straightened. "You want *me* to play nursemaid?"

Rowden frowned. "You've tended me when I was sick."

"Yes, but you are a man." Trogdon pointed accusingly at the bed. "That is a woman."

"Women drink tea the same as men."

"But I am a *man*servant, sir. I serve men, not women."

Rowden opened his mouth to explain that was not what *manservant* meant but decided it was not worth the effort. "You may go, Trogdon."

Trogdon did not waste a moment, moving to exit more quickly than Rowden had ever seen him. Burr made to follow. "Where are you going?"

Burr stopped, looking like a small child caught in mischief. "Mostyn will wonder where I am," Burr said.

"Mostyn is still in bed with his wife."

Burr shifted but started toward the door again. "He has a lesson in two hours. I'd better ready the studio."

"Ready the studio? How long does it take to open a door?" Rowden followed Burr into the drawing room, but Burr was already closing the outer door behind him.

Rowden looked about. He had a woman who came a few days a week and cooked and cleaned, but he had no idea if she came today or what time. Miss Brown needed attention now, and he supposed there was no one else to do it. He returned to his bedchamber and noted she hadn't moved. Lifting the tea tray, he brought it to his bed and placed it on the other side of her. He used a spoon to fish the lemon out of the cup of tea Trogdon had prepared and then held the cup in one hand as he awkwardly slid an arm behind her head with the other.

The tea had cooled enough that he could have brought it to her lips. Instead, he wafted it beneath her nose as though it were smelling salts. He had no idea why he was doing this. It seemed rather stupid until she fluttered her eyelashes. Rowden's heart beat faster. Fearing she might wake with a start, he set the tea back on the tray. "Miss Brown," he said quietly. "Miss Brown, wake up."

Her eyes fluttered again, opened, then closed. Then opened wide and stared at him. The look of abject terror on her features made Rowden want to pull her close and assure her she was in no danger, but he rather thought that would not be helpful—for either of them. "You're safe," he said. "I won't harm you."

Her gaze stayed on his face for a long moment then slid down to his neck and lower. Rowden looked down and realized he was still wearing his dressing gown. The open neck revealed a V of the bare skin of his chest. He released her and stood, pulling the dressing gown closed. She looked around and then, seeming to realize where she was, tried to jump up. She stumbled and almost fell, and Rowden forgot his clothing and pushed her back into bed.

"Not yet, Miss Brown. You need to eat something first, I think."

"Why am I here? What do you intend?" she demanded. Because of course her puritanical mind jumped to the conclusion that he had put her in his bed to take advantage of her.

"You are here because you were found unconscious on the doorstep of Mostyn's, and Burr didn't know what else to do with you. I had intended to make you drink tea and give you something to eat so you could regain your strength. But now that I realize you are in my bed, I will have to ravish you."

Her eyes widened and she pulled the covers to her chin.

Rowden blew out a breath. "I was not serious." As though he would have any woman who did not want him, especially some little church mouse dressed head to toe in the dourest black.

Although, she did not wear all black now. In her struggles the moment before, the white cap over her hair had come loose, as had some of her hair. The auburn waves fell around her face and shoulders, and Rowden couldn't deny that she looked rather tempting with her hair down. He'd been careful not to look into her eyes, but he knew the combination of that hair and those eyes would turn any man's head. He turned his back to her, walked to the door, and called for Trogdon to bring toast.

Then he leaned on the door frame, crossed his arms over his chest, and nodded at the tea tray. "Drink some tea. It will warm you."

"How do I know you haven't put spirits in it?" she asked, narrowing her eyes.

"Why would I put spirits in tea first thing in the morning? The only thing that's been in the tea is lemon. It's on the saucer there. You can add it, if you like, or there's cream."

She glanced at the tray but made no move to lift the teacup.

"Go ahead and sniff it if you don't believe me. You'd be able to smell the spirits."

She seemed to accept that idea and lifted the cup gingerly, sniffing it. Then she took a small sip and swallowed.

"You see? No spirits."

She closed her eyes, and Rowden moved forward. "What's wrong? You're not feeling lightheaded again, are you?"

"No." She took another sip. "I just haven't had tea this lovely since..."

To Rowden's horror, her eyes seemed to well with tears. Oh, hell. He was not at all good with tears. "Don't start crying."

She sniffed and, panicked, Rowden went to the door again. "Trogdon! Toast! Now!"

"I'm fine," she said, wiping her eyes.

Rowden gave her a suspicious look, but she seemed to be telling the truth. She sipped more tea, and he thought perhaps some color had returned to her cheeks. It seemed an eternity before Trogdon finally appeared with the toast. Rather than enter, he handed the tray to Rowden and fled again. Rowden brought the tray to the bed, set it beside the tea then stood at the foot, one arm on a bed post.

"Do you want to tell me why you were sleeping on Mostyn's doorstep?"

She took a piece of toast and nibbled at it. "I didn't know where to go," she said, glancing at him quickly from under her eyelashes.

"Why not sleep at home?"

"I didn't mean to fall asleep. I was hungry and cold, and I just closed my eyes for a moment."

"Which still does not explain why you were not at home."

"Something has happened," she said.

"I gathered that."

She didn't speak, just nibbled her toast.

"I don't want to be presumptuous, but am I correct in assuming the reason you were at Mostyn's was to see me?"

"Yes. I was hoping to see you," she admitted. She set down the toast and straightened her shoulders. "I thought you might be able to help me. You don't have any reason to, of course. I don't expect—"

"I'll help you," he said. Anything to get her out of his bed and his flat. He had found, in the past, that short-term responsibility usually meant avoiding it in the long-term.

"Thank you," she said. "I am looking for my aunt, Miss Augusta Ryan."

Rowden waited for her to say more, but that was apparently it. "How would I know your aunt?"

"She might be married now. Her surname might not be Ryan. I thought you might know her because I think she is— or at least, she seemed to me to be—of the upper classes."

"And you think on the nights I'm not having my head bashed in at a tavern, I'm attending balls at Almack's?"

"No, but the men who frequent the boxing studio are gentlemen. I thought you might have heard of her or know something." She shook her head. "I see now that I was not thinking clearly. I just have no idea where to begin if I'm to find her."

"You could hire someone."

She looked down, and Rowden knew he'd said the wrong thing. Of course, she didn't have any blunt to hire someone.

"Never mind. I can ask around. I'm sure someone knows of her, and I do have connections."

She looked up at him, and tears were in her eyes again. "Thank you."

"No crying." He pointed at her. "No tears."

She nodded and wiped at her cheeks with the back of her hand. Rowden went to a drawer, pulled out a clean handkerchief, and handed it to her. She took it with a watery smile and dabbed at her eyes. "I'm feeling a bit better now," she said.

"Good. Eat another piece of toast, and I'll take you home."

Her expression froze. Rowden swore in his mind. "What's that look about? Why can't you go home?"

She picked up the toast and nibbled again. "I can go home."

"Why the hesitation? And good God, just eat the toast already. Don't nibble at it like a bird."

Her eyes flashed at him, and he forgot he was not supposed to be looking at them. Was this how they looked when she was angry? Almost green and brilliant with light. Her cheeks were red as well. What the hell had he done to anger her? Tell her to eat?

"Sir, I must ask you not to take the Lord's name in vain."

He squinted at her. "Take the…when I said *good God*?"

She pointed a finger at him, and he almost took a step back. "That is twice now."

"Point taken. No blasphemy. Now do me a favor and stop dissembling. Something must be very wrong if you were unconscious on the doorstep of Mostyn's. What's happened? Where is your father?" That seemed to unlock the vault because as soon as he mentioned her father, she slumped as though she'd been shot.

Rowden moved around the bed and sat on the edge. "It's your father then. What's happened?" Now he was making progress. Get her back to the father and be done with her.

"I don't know," she said, her voice sounding perilously close to tears. Rowden clenched his fist and remained where he was. "That day I met you at Mostyn's was the last time I saw him."

Rowden tried to think back to when he'd seen her last. It had been the day after the fight with the German. That was almost a week ago. "Go on," he said, resisting the urge to ask questions. It was better to let her tell it in her own way.

"He sent me to visit Mrs. Kydd. She lives on Pall Mall, and she had made a donation to the church. I brought her a basket with our thanks, and on my way back, I stopped into speak with you at Mostyn's. How I wish I'd never done that! If I had come home sooner. If I had not dawdled…"

"What did you find when you returned home?" Rowden had to ask because she was tearing up again.

"The house was empty. Not just empty," she said. "It was in shambles."

"And you've had no word from him since?"

She shook her head, using his handkerchief to catch several rogue tears.

"No messages have come to the house? He has not stopped in to change his clothing or gather funds?"

She dropped the handkerchief. "I didn't think of that. Perhaps he has been at home. I never thought to check." She tossed back the covers now and Rowden prepared to catch her if she should stumble, but she seemed steady enough on her feet.

"Where have you been?" he asked, watching her warily.

"I couldn't stay in the house alone. I have been with the Plineys. Mr. Pliney is a church elder."

She brushed the wrinkles out of her ugly black dress. Rowden watched her, thinking that even in the awful gown, she was still very pretty, especially without that hat. "You haven't been home then?" he asked, an idea forming. "You haven't tidied the house?"

"I put the books away," she said. "I couldn't leave those lying about." She frowned as she noticed her hat on the floor. Slowly her hand went to her bare head and then she gasped. "Turn around!"

Rowden spun around, expecting nothing short of an assassin behind him. When he saw nothing but the door to his dressing room, he turned back. "What the devil—"

"Don't use that phrase!" she said. "Turn back around."

He turned back around. "May I ask why I am turned around?"

"You didn't tell me I had lost my cap and hat."

"I removed your hat so you could lie back comfortably, and your cap fell off of its own accord."

"You should have told me!"

"Forgive me," he said, staring at the paper on his walls. His gaze traveled to a table with a wash basin and pitcher. A mirror had been hung above the basin, and he could see her frantically pinning her cap back in place. "I was more concerned with the fact that you were cold and unconscious. I wasn't looking at your hair." Not much, anyway.

"Good. I don't—I don't like to be without my hat," she said. She'd paused her movements when she spoke, obviously not certain how to explain her distress.

When she raised her hands to twist her hair up, the bodice of her shapeless dress stretched over her breasts. He hadn't really thought she had breasts or any sort of body under that sack. He rather wished he didn't know she had a body under that sack as now he would be thinking about it.

He looked back at the walls. "I have an idea," he said, changing the subject. "Why don't we return to your house and look for information about your aunt there? Surely your mother—I presume she has passed—had a miniature or letters or something with your aunt's information on it."

"I hadn't thought of that," she said. "Perhaps in my father's room. But I never go in there. You may turn back around."

He did, disappointed to see her back in the oversized hat that obscured most of her face. "I think he would understand you trespassing in this case. It seems to be an emergency."

Her gaze had drifted from his face down to his robe, and he realized the neck had opened to reveal a swath of chest again. "My eyes are here," he said, teasing. But she turned as red as a cherry and began to stammer apologies. He waved a hand. "It seems to me the place for us to begin to find your aunt and discern what might have happened to your father is your home. I'll dress and we can be on our way."

"You don't intend to dress with me present?" she said, sounding horrified. Rowden knew he still had the vestiges of a bruise on his temple, but he didn't think he was that hideous to behold.

"No. I thought you might have another cup of tea and more toast in the drawing room. Trogdon!"

For once the manservant was nearby. He entered immediately and gave a small start when he saw Miss Brown. Rowden could hardly blame him. She did look rather frightful in that costume. "Trogdon, will you move the tea tray and toast to the drawing room for Miss Brown then return and help me dress?"

"Of course, sir." Trogdon gathered the tray and led Miss Brown away. Rowden moved to his desk and snatched a piece of parchment. He'd need to pen a quick note to Chibale explaining why he would be late to Mostyn's. His manager had secured him another match the following evening, and Rowden really needed to practice. But it would have to wait. He felt annoyingly protective of Miss Modesty Brown. She had chosen her words carefully, but he understood the implications of her situation well enough.

She was alone in the world. No mother. Father missing. Relying on the charity of friends. He'd seen what happened to women in that position, and he didn't like to think of Miss Brown begging on the corner or raising her skirts in a back alley—not that he could imagine that. She'd probably insist on keeping her hat on.

He smiled briefly at the image then shook it off and dipped his quill in ink.

***

Modesty sat primly on the couch in Mr. Payne's drawing room. As soon as his manservant had returned to the bedchamber and closed the door, she finished the toast she'd been nibbling in two bites and reached for another piece. There were four triangles of toast in all, and she planned to devour each one. She drank tea in between, her gaze darting to the bedchamber door lest she be caught eating like a starving dog. But she was starving, and once the toast was in her belly, she sat back and closed her eyes, feeling the worst of her headache fade slightly.

She was used to meager provisions, but she'd never gone hungry under her father's roof. Under the Plineys, she'd been slowly starving. It wasn't that they'd intended to starve her, there just wasn't enough for everyone, and Modesty could see the children were hungry, so she often gave half of her small provision to one of them.

Now she did not even have the Plineys. She would probably have to go to the church and ask them to feed her. She'd fed the hungry many, many times, but she never imagined she would be one of those waiting in the line.

Modesty opened her eyes and looked about the drawing room. This one room was almost as large as her entire ground floor. Obviously, The Royal Payne wasn't always being knocked out by opponents. It appeared he did quite well for himself. She ran her hand over the upholstery on the chair where she sat. It was a dark purple, soft and velvety. His bed had been soft and the bedclothes thick. She hadn't realized beds could be so large. Hers was short and narrow, the mattress lumpy and uneven. Her sheets were always clean, but the material was rough and scratchy. She shouldn't be concerned about these material things. They were not what mattered. Life on earth was fleeting, but some nights certainly felt very long...

Modesty turned her head to look at more of the room and her gaze landed on a bookshelf on the wall behind her. She turned more fully and stared at what appeared to be two full floor-to-ceiling tiers of shelves full of books. With a gasp, she rose and went to the wall of books and peered at the shelf at eye level. She read the titles of the books, mostly poetry volumes, and mostly authors she had never heard of. Though she did recognize the name of Lord Byron. Oh, but she had heard her father preach against him in church. He was said to be quite evil.

Modesty looked behind her and, seeing no one there, pulled the volume off the shelf. Her heart beat fast and she told herself she should not be looking at the book. But she wanted to see what was so scandalous about Lord Byron. She opened a page and had to steady her hands so the page would stop shaking.

Hers is the loveliness in death,

That parts not quite with parting breath;

But beauty with that fearful bloom,

That hue which haunts it to the tomb,

Expression's last receding ray,

A gilded Halo hovering round decay,

The farewell beam of Feeling past away!

Modesty stared at the verse, then took a breath and read it again. These lovely words couldn't be evil. They seemed to pierce her heart, right into her soul. They seemed to be speaking directly to her, reminding her of those awful days when her mother had died and been laid out and tended on the table in the dining room.

The night before the funeral, when her mother would be laid to rest, Modesty had sneaked down from her bedchamber. She'd been all of five, and she'd stayed awake until the house had gone quiet. She knew she would not be allowed to attend the funeral, and this was her last chance to say good-bye to her mother in private.

She'd carried a candle down with her and set it on the table beside her mother's body, which had been dressed in a clean black gown and her best pair of shoes. Modesty had taken her mother's cold hand and looked at her face for the last time. Her thoughts, though not as poetic as Byron's, had been similar. Her mother had looked so beautiful in death that it was hard for Modesty to believe she really was gone. She half expected her to open her eyes and smile at Modesty. The doctor who had come a few times while her mother had been in bed said her mother's heart was weak. It did not beat like everyone else's and it had finally given out. But Modesty didn't believe the doctor. Her mother's heart had been fuller and stronger than anyone else she knew.

And though she had looked pale and haggard in her last days, struggling to breathe or even sit, on the table she had looked so much like Modesty always thought of her—serene, beautiful, and, in the light of the candle, haloed.

She hadn't wanted that beauty covered by dirt and put in the ground. She'd wanted her mother to stay with her always. She'd been very naughty the next morning, refusing to come down when the undertaker had come to collect the body and the men had left for the funeral. Modesty preferred to remember her mother as she had been that night.

Modesty replaced the volume and stepped back. Why would her father call such lovely words sinful? The words had been secular, yes, but they weren't evil. Of course, her father called much of what he saw in the world evil. Modesty always verbally agreed with him, but sometimes she privately disagreed. Was a prostitute who gave herself to a man in a dark alley wicked or was she doing what she must in order to feed her children? Was a fighter like Mr. Payne immoral? It was difficult to see a man who possessed a book of poetry like the one she'd just glanced at as evil. She might not want to hit another person for money, but hadn't Jacob spent a night wrestling with God? If God was against pugilism, why had He engaged in it?

Her father would have had an answer. He would have explained the meaning behind the story—how Jacob was not simply physically wrestling with God but wrestling mentally as well. He was learning that one must give up control and give everything to God. So was it merely a story then? If it was true, how could she fault a man who did what God himself had done?

The door opened and Mr. Payne stepped out. He looked about until he spotted her and then he raised a brow. "You look like you've been doing something you shouldn't."

"I was simply admiring your library."

He glanced up at it. "Some of those came with the flat, but I have added to it." He strode into the room. "You finished the toast, I see."

Modesty barely heard him. She couldn't help but stare at his attire. The few times she'd seen him before he had been dressed informally—*too* informally, some would say. But this morning his dress could only be described as the height of fashion. He wore fawn-colored knee breeches, with highly polished black boots, a berry-colored waistcoat with dark green vines embroidered on it, a white neckcloth, and a navy coat that fit tightly and emphasized his broad shoulders. His short black hair was artfully styled, brushed rakishly to one side.

Payne looked down. "What's wrong?"

Modesty shook her head and smiled, not trusting herself to speak.

He offered an arm. "Shall we?"

Modesty hesitated a moment then took his arm, feeling rather silly. After all, she was not one of those debutantes she occasionally glimpsed traipsing in and out of shops and carriages with their wild curls and their plumed hats. She must look ridiculous on his arm, but she didn't release it.

Once on the street, Payne hailed a hackney, and once they were inside, he raised his brows at her expectantly. She gave him the address, and he relayed it to the driver. Then he sat back and peered out the window. Modesty had expected to be peppered with questions, but he was quiet until finally he sat forward. "Is there still a pie cart on the corner near that old fountain? The one that never has any water?"

She knew the fountain. It had been dry ever since she could remember. "I know the fountain, and I do think there is a man with a cart who often sells his pies there."

"We'll stop and buy one." He looked at her. "Two."

"I'm perfectly fine," she protested, though her belly gurgled at the idea of pie rich with sauce and potatoes, carrots, and a flaky crust.

"I can't very well eat if you do not, and I haven't had one of those pies in years."

"You know Bowling Square?"

"When I started as a fighter, I used to have matches in the Rose and Thorn."

She knew the place. It was a tavern she'd never seen the inside of, though she'd passed it practically every day of her life.

"The early matches are the newer fighters, those who haven't made a name for themselves yet, so when I began I would often finish a match before the pie seller—what is his name? Isaac?"

"I believe it is Elias." She'd always called him Mr. Elias when she passed. She'd asked for his surname, but he told her it was just Elias. She'd never bought one of his pies. She didn't ever have any coin to spare, but they always smelled divine.

"That's right." He snapped his fingers. "Elias. I would often buy his last three or four pies before he left for the day. Then I became better known and my matches moved later and to better taverns—not that there's anything wrong with the Rose and Thorn—and I didn't see him anymore." He sat back, a wistful look on his face. "I miss those days sometimes. I certainly miss those pies."

Modesty always felt slightly ill in a carriage but listening to Mr. Payne speak seemed to help with the queasiness. "What do you miss about those days?"

"It was simpler," he said, looking out the window again. He appeared to be watching the people on the streets, but Modesty imagined he was seeing the inside of a tavern from years ago. "Two of us would decide to fight and we'd strip down, push some tables aside, and men would place bets. I didn't earn much, but it was real."

"And it isn't real now?"

He shrugged. "It's all show. The pamphlets plastered to every wall, the parading around the tavern, the managers hurling insults. When I lost before, my friends would buy me a drink and we'd laugh it off. Now the newspaper writers publish columns speculating as to whether my career is over."

Modesty hadn't considered that his profession, if one could call it that, would be a source of any stress for the man. She had just assumed the men pummeled each other. She hadn't thought of it as a business. "I don't read the papers, but I can't believe anyone would think your career over. You're still young and...virile."

He looked away from the window. "Virile, am I? I didn't expect compliments from you."

Now she looked out the window. It made her stomach clench to see the buildings pass so quickly, but she wanted to look at anything but his eyes. "It's not a compliment. It's just an observation."

"What else have you observed about me?"

She did look into his green eyes now. "You are rather arrogant." To her surprise, he laughed at the insult.

"I won't argue with you there, but I will say I'm knocked on my arse just often enough to keep my arrogance bearable. At least that's what Chibale says." He pulled out a pocket watch and winced at the time. "Speaking of Chibale, he'll have my head if I'm too late to the studio." He replaced the watch. "Can't be helped, I suppose." He knocked on the roof of the hackney. "Just over there," he called, pointing out of the window.

The conveyance stopped near the fountain and Mr. Payne climbed out then handed Modesty down. He paid the driver then took her arm and led her to Elias and the pie cart.

"Well, well, well," Mr. Elias said, beaming at Payne. "I never thought I'd see ye again."

"I've been dreaming of your pies," Payne said. "I had to come buy one. Actually, two. One for the lady."

Elias nodded at her. "Good morning, Miss Brown."

"Good morning, Mr. Elias."

The pie seller didn't ask why she was with a fighter, but he gave her an inquisitive look. "I heard about yer loss to the German," Elias said, opening a cupboard and removing two pies. "Ye planning a rematch?"

"I leave that to my manager these days," Payne said, "but I believe plans are being made."

Elias wrapped the pies in paper and handed them over. "I haven't seen ye fight in years, but I'd pay to watch that one."

"No charge for you," Mr. Payne said and handed Elias a coin. Elias looked down at it.

"This is too much, sir."

Mr. Payne raised a hand, refusing to take the pound back. "Come see me fight, and I'll consider myself repaid. Good day, Elias." He tipped his hat and led Modesty to the edge of the fountain. She sat and he handed her a pie then sat himself and unwrapped his. He took a bite and smiled. Modesty unwrapped her own, her mouth watering at the scent. She took her own bite, and it was so good she forgot how cold the stone of the fountain was underneath her or how brisk the winter breeze or even how worried she was for her father. She just enjoyed the wonderful flavor of the pie. She couldn't remember when she'd ever tasted something so wonderful.

"Shall I buy you another?" Mr. Payne asked.

She looked down and realized she'd eaten the entire pie in only a few minutes. She felt her cheeks heat. "No, I couldn't eat another bite."

"We'll see," he said. "For now, show me where you live."

She rose and took a deep breath. "It's this way."

Five

Rowden didn't realize they'd arrived until she went to a narrow door and produced a key. He wouldn't have thought this a house at all. There were no windows facing the street, no knocker, nothing to indicate someone lived here. But she opened the door and stepped inside, and he turned sideways to fit through and follow. He had to stoop to pass under the door and once inside the ceiling wasn't much higher. Mostyn would have had to duck, but Rowden just kept an eye out for low beams. They'd entered a room with rectangular windows in the back. The sun was creeping higher in the sky, allowing some light to filter through, but Miss Brown lit a lamp and lifted it, shedding more light on the room.

The chamber was cold and had the musty smell of disuse, but it was in perfect order. A table sat on one side of the room and a couch and chairs were closer to the window. "I thought you said the house had been ransacked. This looks neat as a pin."

"Neat as a—look!" She went to the table and lifted a teacup. "This tea has been sitting here for days. My father was drinking it when I left that morning, and he left it right here. And see this chair? It isn't pushed in. "

"So he didn't push his chair in or put the cup away before he departed. That's unusual, I take it?"

"Yes. And see here. This table is out of place and his study!" She started for a door at the other end of the room. Well, it was about five steps away. She opened the door to reveal what Rowden would have deemed a closet. It held a desk, a chair, and a shelf of eight to ten books. She took two off the shelf. "These were lying open on the desk. Just left open to the pages he had been reading."

"That's unusual?"

"Yes!" Her color was high, and he could see he was exasperating her. He didn't mean to. Obviously, something had happened to make her father leave without explanation, but he was beginning to doubt foul play.

"He never leaves his books open. He says that damages the spine. They are always returned to their proper place."

"Is anything else amiss?" he asked. "Is any money missing?"

"We had no money to steal. The rooms upstairs appear undisturbed."

"May I see?"

She ducked her head, and he could have sworn her cheeks went even redder. "Of course."

She led him up a narrow, steep staircase. He had to turn sideways to fit his shoulders and duck to avoid giving himself a concussion. At the top of the stairs were two doors, both closed. She opened the first, and he knew immediately it was hers. It was tiny, barely big enough for the narrow bed. On the wall hung a dress and hat exactly like the one she wore now. Under that was a trunk which he imagined held her underthings. The room had nothing else. No window. No paintings. Not even a rug. It was the most spartan chamber he had ever seen.

One look at the crisp white bedclothes, and he knew it had been undisturbed. "Did you right anything in this room?" he asked.

"No. It hadn't been touched."

"The other door is your father's?"

She led him out, closing her door behind him then opening her father's door. It was only a little larger than hers, and it was equally as spartan. There was a bed, a peg with a black coat hanging on it, and a trunk underneath. The one difference was that on Mr. Brown's trunk was a framed picture. Rowden stepped inside to look at the picture. When

Miss Brown didn't follow with the lamp, he looked over his shoulder at her.

"I don't usually come in here," she said. "I'm not allowed."

"I think we can dispense with the usual rules in this situation. Bring the lamp closer."

She did, and Rowden lifted the drawing and studied it. It had been done in charcoal and was the likeness of a young woman wearing a dark dress with a white collar. She wore a cap over her hair, which was, of course, black, as the drawing was in charcoal. Her eyes were black too, but Rowden knew those eyes. They had the same shape as Miss Brown's. "Your mother?" he asked.

She nodded. "Her name was Catherine."

"Catherine Ryan and then Catherine Brown, yes?" He set the portrait on the floor beside the trunk. "Could your mother read?"

"I think so." She seemed to consider, her unusual eyes lowering and then meeting his. "Yes. She read me the Bible and taught me my letters."

"Then your aunt might have corresponded with her."

"I hadn't thought of that."

"Is there any place your father might have kept something like that? Letters or other mementos?"

"Perhaps in his desk," she suggested.

"Perhaps." He reached for the trunk.

"What are you about, sir?"

He gestured to the trunk. "The portrait is here. Other items of your mother's might be here too. Perhaps one will give us an idea of the whereabouts of her family and your aunt." He didn't say it, but he thought the contents might also give them a clue as to where her father had gone. Perhaps they'd find he owed a large sum of money and had fled to the Continent to avoid paying. Rowden opened the trunk and indicated Miss Brown should move closer with the lamp.

She did so reluctantly, and Rowden looked down at a pile of neatly folded white linen. He carefully lifted the shirts and neckcloths out of the way, revealing a wooden base. "False bottom," he said.

"Don't be ridiculous. This top shelf lifts out. My trunk is the same." She reached down and lifted the wooden insert. She brushed against him as she leaned over, and he caught the scent of starch and soap. Underneath there was another fragrance, something light and feminine he had caught in her chamber. He knew that fragrance—not perfume but the scent of soft curves, silky hair, and satin skin. It was the fragrance of a woman.

"I keep my brush and hair pins on this top shelf," she was saying, oblivious to the fact that he was half-drunk on her scent. "Underneath are my…are clothing items."

Rowden looked up at her, their faces closer than she realized because she immediately stepped back. For just a moment, he'd been imagining those clothing items—chemises and stockings and stays. The sorts of women he knew generally wore frilly underthings with ribbons and silk. But he imagined Modesty Brown lived up to her name, preferring sensible, plain items made of starched, scratchy fabric. Rowden could imagine her in it, imagine her lifting her arms to unpin her hair, as he had watched her pin it this morning. The curve of her breast would be revealed, sweet and round and tempting in the prim chemise.

"There, you see?" she said, gesturing to the trunk. Rowden forced himself to look back at it. "It's just a hat."

"No one keeps a hat in a trunk," he said, lifting it out. "Hats are hung. Ah. Here we are." He lifted a packet of letters wrapped with twine. "Correspondence." He held the packet out to Miss Brown, but she didn't take the letters, merely looked at them. "Do you want me to read them?" he asked.

"No," she said. "I…it's just, I…"

Rowden waited, but she didn't seem inclined to say more. And she didn't take the letters. He had the urge to check his pocket watch. He knew he would be late for his appointment at Mostyn's, but the question was how late.

"Why don't we go downstairs, make tea, and look through these? You don't have to open them. But we can sit down and see what we have."

She stood very still and then gave the briefest of nods. Rowden rose and started for the door, letters in hand, but she made a tsking sound and crouched to replace the items in the trunk as they had been. Finally, she followed him out, closing the door behind her. Once downstairs, she went into the kitchen and seemed to stand there as though she had never seen it before.

"Do you need me to light the stove?" he asked. "You can fetch water while the stove heats."

She nodded and took a bucket off a peg on the wall. Then she paused, went to a shelf, and took down a tea tin. She looked inside and shook her head. "Never mind. We have no tea." She held the tin out, and he saw there were but one or two leaves stuck to the bottom. "We use the leaves over again," she said. "My father likes a cup of tea while he works, and so I did not lay them out to dry when I left. He must never have had that second cup of tea." She gestured to the tea pot on the small table near the stove. If the leaves were still inside, they would be moldy and unusable now.

Rowden wasn't sure what he should do. She was safe in her own home, but she was all alone. She wasn't a lady, who required a chaperone or servants, but was she safe here on her own? What if something nefarious had happened to her father? Perhaps the evildoers would come back for her.

He rather doubted that, considering the house had been untouched, but Rowden didn't feel right simply taking his leave. He looked about the kitchen and noted the bare shelves. She had what looked to be a bit of flour and perhaps some potatoes, but how would she buy more provisions? Surely her church would help her, but hadn't she said the church elder had turned her out and instructed her to look for her aunt? Others might be willing to help, but Rowden knew what it was to rely on the charity of others. He supposed family was different. Of course, when his father had disowned him, no one in Rowden's family had dared oppose the duke.

He simply needed to help her find her aunt. Then he would know she was safe and cared for and he could be through with his obligation to her. "Gather what you need," he said. "You're coming with me."

She lifted her head and stared at him. "I am not."

"I can't leave you here with nothing to eat and no blunt, and I can't have you sleeping on Mostyn's doorstep again.

We'll bring the letters, and you can read them at Mostyn's. He has a comfortable room away from the boxing rings where you can read and have a cup of tea."

"I don't think I should frequent a place full of half-dressed men," she said. "My father wouldn't like it."

Rowden wanted to say that her father had left her in this predicament, but he knew when to keep his mouth shut. "I'll send for Lady Lorraine," he said. "She is Mostyn's wife and the daughter of the Duke of Ridlington. You can't object to her."

"The daughter of a duke?" She looked down at herself, and for the first time Rowden detected a note of self-consciousness about her ugly attire. "I think she has better things to do than take an interest in me."

"You think that because you don't know her. She's not so high in the instep, and she loves—" He had been about to say *interfering* but he stopped himself just in time. "She loves helping others."

"I don't know." She smoothed her skirts.

"Well, consider it in the hackney." He withdrew his pocket watch and winced at the time. "I am late, so we must go now. Fetch what you need. Hurry up," he said, giving an imperious flick of his hand. He might be a bare-knuckle fighter, but he still knew how to behave like the son of a duke.

She hesitated slightly then went to do as he asked. Less than ten minutes later, she returned with a small, worn valise. He took it from her, lifted the letters and slipped them in his pocket, then led her out of the house. She locked the door and tucked the key in a pocket, and then he bought her another of Elias's pies while they searched for a hackney. Of course, she protested she was not hungry, but she ate it, and Rowden was pleased to see her face regaining some color and her movements filled with more energy. If he could do nothing else, he could make certain this woman did not starve.

***

Mr. Payne's manager was pacing outside Mostyn's when they arrived. Modesty had thought Payne well-dressed this morning, but his manager was a sight to behold. He wore a tall beaver hat cocked to one side, a coat the color of a deep red wine, a cream-colored waistcoat with embroidered designs that were the same color as the coat, and tight fawn-colored breeches. His boots were even glossier than Mr. Payne's. She thought he might be cold as he was on the street without a greatcoat, but he seemed to have been pacing for some time and perhaps that had kept him warm.

As soon as Mr. Payne helped her out of the hackney, his manager called to him. "You're late."

"Couldn't be helped," Mr. Payne said, giving her a reassuring smile. He was always doing that—trying to reassure her. She appreciated the attempt, even though she was beginning to realize that life as she'd known it was over.

"It could be helped if you arrived on time." He stopped pacing and stared at her. "Why is she here? First, she cost you fifty guineas, and now she makes you late? What good is another match with the German if you won't train?"

Mr. Payne stiffened. "You arranged another fight with the German."

"Not yet."

Payne waved him away and started for the door to Mostyn's. Modesty couldn't do anything but follow.

"But I know how to make it happen."

"Go on," Payne said, opening the door and allowing her to pass inside. She remembered the small entryway from the week before. The door to the studio was open, and Mr. Burr swept a spot near one of the roped off areas.

"He'll fight you again," the manager said as he stepped inside.

"When?"

"When you win against Abraham Strong."

"Strong?" Mr. Payne yelled the word so loudly Modesty jumped.

"Stop bellowing. You're frightening your companion."

"I'm quite alright, Mr. Chibale," she said.

He looked at her directly for the first time. "It's Mr. Okoro, but everyone calls me Chibale. This lout here hasn't given me the pleasure of your name."

"Miss Brown," the lout in question said.

Mr. Okoro gave her a slight bow. "I wish I could say it was a pleasure, Miss Brown, but as you seem to be a distraction, once again, for my client here, I'm afraid I'm left wondering why you are here."

"I'll explain later," Payne said, moving into the studio. "Why do I have to fight Abraham Strong? I beat him last year."

Mr. Okoro followed him. "Then beat him again."

Payne stopped and narrowed his eyes. "The German doesn't want to waste his time with me, is that it? He wants me to prove I can win before he'll fight again."

Burr glanced at them and swept a bit more eagerly.

"His manager didn't put it that way."

"No, I'm sure he was far blunter. Tell him no. Wait. Tell him *hell no*. I'll fight the German or no one."

"I am the manager here," Okoro said. "You fight who I say or get another manager."

Payne stared at him, and Modesty half expected him to dismiss the manager. Mr. Mostyn had emerged from a room a few feet away, and Modesty wondered if that was the room Mr. Payne thought she might use.

"Arrange the match," Mr. Payne said.

Mostyn, leaning on the door to the antechamber, nodded his head in approval. "Oh, shut up," Mr. Payne said, though the other man had said nothing.

"The match is already arranged," Mr. Okoro said. "Tomorrow night at the Cock and Bull. You're the last fight of the night."

"How much?"

"If you win, twenty pounds." He paused. "And we split it."

Mr. Payne gaped. "You're taking fifty percent now? That's highway robbery."

"I earned it with all I had to do to arrange this match. Besides," Okoro said, walking toward the center ring. "I need a new coat. I'm taking Madame Renaud to the Negro Merchant's Guild winter ball."

Payne's face broke into a grin. Modesty had seen him smile before, but this smile was almost boyish in its enthusiasm and exuberance. "She said yes?"

"Of course, she said yes."

"You weren't so certain of yourself a few days ago." He turned and Mr. Okoro helped him out of his coat.

"I knew my charm would win in the end."

Mr. Payne slapped him on the shoulder and tugged his neckcloth loose. In that moment his gaze landed on Modesty, and she realized he'd all but forgotten her. He stiffened. "Miss Brown. Let me show you to the antechamber." He looked for her valise, scooped it back up, and started for the room where Mr. Mostyn stood leaning against the door.

Payne's footsteps faltered. "Mostyn, Miss Brown—you remember her?"

The tall blond man nodded slightly.

"She's hit a bit of a snag, and I offered her use of the antechamber this morning. She has some reading to do. I hope I haven't been presumptuous."

Mr. Mostyn lifted one eyebrow, which Modesty took to indicate Mr. Payne had been presumptuous. But then the blond man stepped aside and held out a hand, indicating the antechamber.

"I may have use of it?" she asked, wanting to be certain before she entered.

"Yes." He had a deep voice but not an unkind one, and she smiled at him and stepped into the chamber. It was small but quite a contrast to the utilitarian boxing studio. The chamber held a large desk with two chairs behind it. One was more feminine in style and the other large and functional. A low fire burned in the hearth across from the desk and a velvet couch-type furnishing faced the hearth on a rug of deep blues and golds. Several other chairs were pushed against the walls, obviously ready for use should they be necessary, and Modesty was quite at a loss for where she should sit. The couch looked inviting, but if she were to read, perhaps the desk would be better. She'd never had so many choices in seating.

She glanced at the door to see if Mr. Mostyn would give her any guidance and saw Mr. Payne had one arm around Mr. Mostyn's shoulder. Mostyn was leaning his head down to listen to Payne who was speaking earnestly. Mostyn glanced in her direction, and Modesty realized they must be speaking of her. Then Payne looked at her and gave her a reassuring smile. She tried to smile back, but it was all she could do this morning not to burst into tears yet again.

"You write, and I will sign," Mr. Mostyn said. It was the most words Modesty had ever heard him utter.

Mr. Payne looked a little taken aback, but he didn't argue. He entered the chamber, went to the desk, and opened and closed drawers until he found a blank sheet of parchment. Then he dipped a quill in ink, scrawled something quickly, and held the pen out to Mostyn. When Mostyn entered, the room seemed to grow very small and quite warm. The tall man bent, and with his tongue lodged at the corner of his lips, he made his mark. Then he replaced the quill and returned to the studio. Modesty could see why he used this room. The angle of the door allowed her to see almost the entire studio. She saw Mostyn hand the paper to Mr. Burr and then Burr nodded and left.

"Lady Lorraine will be here soon," Mr. Payne said. "In the meantime, make yourself comfortable. Do you need anything?"

She tried not to look at him. When she looked at him, she couldn't help but notice he did not wear a coat, and she could see the slimness of his waist where the waistcoat met his breeches. He had broad shoulders and unlike some men she knew, he did not need the coat to emphasize them. They were quite impressive even in shirt sleeves.

"Miss Brown?" he asked.

She quickly looked away. "Where should I sit?" she asked.

"Anywhere you like. I believe Lady Lorraine favors this chair, so you might find it comfortable." He indicated the feminine chair behind the desk. "Or you could sit on the chaise longue." He indicated the couch before the fire. "Then you're sure to be warm. I'll be in the ring if you need anything." He started for the door then paused. "Try not to make a sudden appearance when I'm in the middle of sparring," he said. "My head has just stopped ringing from the last time."

"I apologize again," she said. "I didn't mean—"

"I was teasing you. You haven't been teased much, have you?"

She shook her head. She couldn't remember ever having been teased until she met him. She had always thought of teasing as an unwanted thing. A boy pulling a girl's hair or calling each other rude names. But the sort of teasing Mr. Payne employed was not unpleasant at all. It was sort of a friendly banter.

"Right. I'll be in the studio," he said. She watched him leave and wondered if she should close the door behind him. While she wondered, he stripped off his neckcloth and his waistcoat and handed them to Mr. Okoro, who laid them on a chair at the side of the ring. Then Mr. Payne sat on the chair and removed his boots and stockings. Modesty knew she should close the door now. At the very least, she should look away. There was nothing sinful about the human body. God had made it, and it was good—as was everything in His creation—but the direction of her thoughts was anything but pure. And Paul had instructed the church at Philippi to think on "whatsoever things are just, whatsoever things are pure, whatsoever things are lovely."

Mr. Payne's calves were certainly lovely. They were round and muscled and covered with a light dusting of dark hair. And then he tugged his shirt over his head, and though she had seen his chest before—just this morning, in fact— her mouth still went slightly dry at the sight of his bare chest. Not only were his shoulders broad, they were muscled. She had seen statues carved out of marble, and she had thought the sculptors quite inventive in the way they portrayed the chiseled form of man.

But now she knew men like those rendered in marble existed. Men who had flat bellies with ridges of muscle, thick biceps, and—Payne rose and gave her a view of his bare back—and Lord, help her, backs that all but rippled with muscles. Mr. Payne bent to duck under the ropes marking the boxing area, and Modesty quickly turned her back. She should not ogle him. She would not like to be ogled were she in his place. She would read the letters.

She withdrew the packet from her coat pocket then decided it was too warm with the fire and removed the coat. There was a coat rack by the door, and she hung the coat there and then, a bit reluctantly, hung her hat there as well. She tucked stray pieces of hair into her cap and hoped not too much of her awful red hair was visible. Of course, standing so near the door she could not help but peek out. Payne was in the arena, going through a complicated set of jumps and lunges and dropping to the floor, all at what appeared to be Mr. Okoro's direction. She realized he must be warming up his muscles, and since her thoughts were drifting to those muscles again, she looked away and took her packet of letters to the longue.

The twine on the packet had been tied tightly as though to keep the letters undisturbed. Her efforts to loosen the knot only tightened it. Modesty wondered if her difficulty was a sort of sign. Perhaps she was not meant to read the contents of the letters. They were private. But how could she justify not reading them if they might give some indication as to the whereabouts of her father? What if he needed her, and the clues to finding him were in this packet of letters?

She struggled with the knot further, and then gave up, went to the desk and searched for a letter opener. She found a quill knife and used it to sever the twine. The pieces unraveled and pooled on the desk. She swept them away and dumped them in the rubbish bin. Looking up, she noted she had an even better view of the studio from the desk, so she made a point of returning to the longue before she watched Mr. Payne too long.

She was staring at the letter on the top of pile and wondering at the unfamiliar writing on it when she heard the first thud. She couldn't stop herself from looking up and immediately witnessed another thud. Mr. Payne had hit Mr. Mostyn's upraised palm. Mostyn had joined Payne in the ring. Mr. Mostyn had removed some of his clothing as well but retained his shirt. He was not moving around as Mr. Payne was. He was holding his hand up and moving it about as Mr. Payne danced around, jabbing high and low at Mr. Okoro's orders. Mr. Okoro stood outside the ring, seeming to direct the activities inside.

Modesty completely forgot the letters she was supposed to be reading—or perhaps *not* supposed to be reading—and stared at the action in the ring. The way Mr. Payne moved was mesmerizing. He was so fluid and quick. His muscles bunched and rippled as he moved, and it was almost beautiful. And then Mr. Okoro called out something and both men went to different corners. Mr. Mostyn leaned against the ropes on his side as though quite bored while Mr. Payne wiped his face with the towel Mr. Okoro offered and listened as Okoro gave him a litany of directions. Finally, he nodded and tossed the towel on the ropes. He went back to the center of the ring, and Mostyn joined him.

Their stances were different now, tighter and purposeful. She realized the sparing was about to begin in earnest. The men circled each other, both crouched, Payne's fists raised, Mostyn's hanging loosely at his sides. Payne jabbed and Mostyn ducked. This went on for some time, with Mostyn seeming to easily avoid every punch Payne threw at him and not offering any of his own.

And then suddenly that changed.

Suddenly, as if some undetectable cue had been given, Mostyn threw a punch. Mr. Payne seemed ready for it. He ducked, turned, and punched back. Modesty winced at the thud of Mr. Payne's fist connecting with Mr. Mostyn's chest. She put her hands on her cheeks, ready to cover her eyes if necessary. She really did not want to see anyone hurt.

The two continued their dance—advancing, retreating, one jabbing and then the other. Mr. Payne hit Mr. Mostyn again, and Modesty covered her eyes. Her fingers were spread, though, and she saw the smile Mr. Mostyn flashed. It was not a smile filled with any sort of humor.

Faster than she could close her fingers, Mostyn feigned moving to the left. Mr. Payne shifted away, and Mostyn, who had only looked as though he would go left, had an opening and punched him hard in the belly.

Mr. Payne doubled over, and Modesty ran toward the ring. She didn't even realize she was running until she was at the ropes and pausing to figure out the best way to get through them. Finally, she decided there was no ladylike way to get through them and just crawled under one. Vaguely, she heard Mr. Okoro calling her name, but she ignored him, climbed to her feet and stood between Mostyn and Payne who was now looking up at her in confusion.

"Step back!" she ordered Mr. Mostyn who looked down at her impassively. "Don't you dare hit him again."

He didn't move, which was not a promise not to hit Mr. Payne again, but at least wasn't aggressive. She turned to Payne. "Are you hurt?"

He gestured and moved his lips, but she couldn't hear and had to step closer. Closer to that bare chest, which was now glistening with perspiration. "I'm fine," he wheezed. "Just had the breath knocked out of me."

She turned back to Mostyn. "Why would you hit him so hard? This is supposed to be practice."

Mostyn looked at her then Payne then finally to Mr. Okoro as though he expected one of them to do something with her. Mr. Okoro entered the ring. "It is practice, Miss Brown."

"But Mr. Mostyn hit him very hard." She gestured to Mr. Payne who was now covering his eyes as though humiliated.

"Let me help you out," Mr. Okoro said. Modesty allowed it and then allowed Mr. Okoro to escort her back to the antechamber. He went to a cabinet, lifted a pitcher, and poured a liquid into a glass. She took it and sniffed.

"It is only water. You seemed overwrought."

"I am not overwrought." She was overwrought. She must be if she was climbing into boxing rectangles. "I do not understand why that big brute would hit Mr. Payne."

Okoro smiled. "Rowden hit Mostyn first, and harder than he should have for a practice fight. Mr. Mostyn was repaying him in kind. It's a sort of game with them. They have been friends for a long time, and they like to see who can land a punch."

"Hitting each other is a game?"

"You do not have brothers, do you, Miss Brown?"

"No. What has that to do with anything?"

"Never mind. I assure you Mr. Payne is fine. He is also a big brute. If Mr. Mostyn wanted to flatten him, he could have. He pulled that punch at the last moment."

She sipped the water and sank onto the longue, considering. "It did not appear that he pulled it, as you say."

"I assure you he did. Moreover, you needn't concern yourself with the practice. I am there to make certain Rowden is ready for his fight tomorrow. He won't be ready if Mr. Mostyn knocks him flat. But you should let me watch out for him. Men do not like to be rescued by women." He lowered his voice. "Hurts the pride."

She thought of Mr. Payne with his hand over her eyes. "I didn't think of that."

"I daresay this situation is all new. Mostyn's lady will come soon, and she will explain everything."

"Fine." Modesty nodded, rather embarrassed now that she had obviously overreacted. When Mr. Okoro returned to the studio, she rose and closed the door after him. She had come here to read the letters and read the letters she would.

No matter how much they scared her.

Six

Lady Lorraine swept in with a lot of noise and commotion as she always did. She wore a velvet dress in deep green with a matching cape. Burr hurried in her wake and she had two maidservants with her as well. As soon as Rowden heard her laugh, Mostyn cocked his head and climbed under the ropes. In the middle of the round. What man walked away from a fight before the bell was rung?

Rowden put his hands on his hips in annoyance as he watched Mostyn greet his wife. She smiled up at him, her cheeks pink from the cold. The cape concealed her figure, so Rowden couldn't see if there was any sort of bump indicating she was with child, but she certainly didn't act like she had slowed down at all. She was speaking rapidly, as usual, directing everyone in her wake hither and yon.

She came to a stop before the ring and looked up at Rowden. He gave her a slight bow. "A pleasure to see you again, my lady."

Mostyn threw his shirt at him, hitting him square in the face.

Lady Lorraine laughed, and Rowden tugged the shirt over his head. "It is a pleasure to see you as well, my lord."

He raised a hand. "I'm not a lord any longer."

"You should be," she said definitively. "And I will simply never get used to calling you *Mr.* Payne. You are Lord Rowden Payne to me. I deem it so."

"How can I argue then?"

"You can't. Now, where is my charge?"

Rowden shook his head. "She isn't a charge, exactly." It was best if Lady Lorraine didn't begin to think of Miss Brown as a little injured bird to take under her wing. Rowden was trying to keep himself from thinking that way. Yes, Miss Brown needed help, and yes, he wanted to help her insofar as he could. But there was only so much he could do. She needed someone to assume care for her, and he was not a relation or a husband, and therefore couldn't do more than he'd already done.

In fact, a young unmarried woman like her should not be associating with him too frequently. Even if she did have captivating eyes...

But he had to put her out of his head, as he had been doing, because she wasn't the sort of woman he could have anything to do with or would want to have anything to do with him. Better to give her to Lady Lorraine and have her assist. She was always looking for something to do.

"She needs help finding her aunt, one Augusta Ryan."

"Never heard of her, but I can make inquiries."

"I thought you might. She's in a bit of a fragile state. Her father has gone missing and she has nowhere to go. Burr found her sleeping on the stoop outside this morning and brought her to me."

"Why you?" Lady Lorraine asked.

"That's a long story. Mostyn can tell you."

She glanced at her husband. "You know he will never tell me."

Rowden pointed to the closed door of the antechamber. "She's in there." He climbed under the ropes. "I'll introduce you."

"So your fall from grace did not strip you of all your manners, I see."

He winced. "I suppose that pun was intentional."

"Anyone with the sobriquet *The Royal Payne* must appreciate a good pun."

Mostyn moved ahead of them and opened the door to the antechamber. He stopped, stared, and looked back at his wife. "She's asleep."

Lady Lorraine peered around him. "Why is she dressed like that?"

"She's a Methodist or some such thing," said Rowden.

"The Methodists I know don't dress like that."

Rowden didn't know any Methodists. Or if he did, they hadn't confessed to it. Come to think of it, she'd never said she was a Methodist. He'd just assumed. "Maybe she's not a Methodist. She's part of one of those churches who stand outside taverns and yell at the soiled doves to repent. Her mother is dead, and her father is missing, and all she has is some memories of an aunt. She was supposed to be reading these letters we found to see if they contained any information on the aunt."

Lady Lorraine moved into the room and looked down at Miss Brown, who was curled into a ball, her face pressed into the cushions of the longue. The letters were clutched in her hand.

"Poor thing. And why were you involved again?"

She did not surrender easily.

"Mostyn will tell you. I have to get back to the studio." But he didn't move. Instead, he watched as Ewan's wife bent and put a hand on Miss Brown's shoulder. "What is her name?" she asked quietly.

"Modesty Brown."

"Miss Brown." Lady Lorraine shook her slightly. "Miss Brown, time to wake up."

Miss Brown's striking eyes opened, and she sat quickly. "I fell asleep."

"That's quite alright. You must be very tired after your ordeal."

"Lady Lorraine," Rowden said, "may I present Miss Modesty Brown."

Miss Brown got to her feet. "Should I curtsy?"

Lady Lorraine held out a white-gloved hand. "Why don't we shake hands?"

Miss Brown shifted her letters to the other hand and took Lady Lorraine's.

"Did you read the letters?" Rowden asked.

Miss Brown looked sheepish. "Not yet. I was about to, but I must have fallen asleep."

Rowden believed her, but he didn't think that was the whole of the reason. He would have thought she would start reading the letters immediately, almost as soon as he removed them from the trunk. But she had hesitated to even take them. Was she afraid of what she might find out?

"You must be tired and hungry," Lady Lorraine said, taking her arm. "You will come home with me, and after you have rested and eaten, we can talk about the aunt you're searching for. I know almost everyone and surely someone knows someone who knows who and where Augusta Ryan might be. I have the carriage, and we can be home shortly."

"Lorrie," Ewan said, his voice a warning. He was a man of few words, but he didn't need them. Clearly, he was not happy with the plan for Miss Brown to travel to his home.

"I will see you this evening," Lady Lorraine told him. "I'll tell Cook to prepare your favorite for dinner tonight." She led Miss Brown out of the antechamber then directed one of her maids to return and gather any correspondence. "I'll read it, and we can discuss any necessary replies after dinner," she told her husband. He scowled at her, but she merely waved and was gone.

Everyone who had served closely with Mostyn in the war knew he couldn't read very well. Although Colonel Draven also had a stake in the studio, Rowden suspected Lady Lorraine was far more involved in its operations than anyone but Mostyn himself. It was her connections that brought the initial clientele in for lessons, and it was obviously her participation in the actual business affairs of the studio that were making Mostyn's such a success.

"Well," Chibale said, coming to stand beside Rowden. "That's done."

Yes, it was. Rowden was relieved.

"How about another round?" Chibale suggested.

Mostyn shook his head. "Lesson in a quarter of an hour."

Chibale nodded toward a set of leather sacks filled with grain. "Let's see how you do against those. Your left hook could be stronger."

Rowden wanted to object that he was done for the day, but he had to win the fight with Abraham Strong and win it soundly. Then the German couldn't possibly refuse to fight him again.

***

Lady Lorraine chatted all the way to her home. Modesty hardly heard what she said. She was too busy gaping at the ornate interior of the carriage. The door handles appeared to be gold and the curtains framing the windows were velvet. As a child, the chance to sit in the back of a wagon or take a brief ride in a hackney was an enormous treat. And of course, she had seen the conveyances of the upper classes pass by on the street. Lady Lorraine's was by no means the grandest she had seen. Once she had glimpsed the Duke of Devonshire's and had stopped to stare.

But even in her wildest imaginings about the interior of the Devonshire carriage, she had not imagined comfort like this—plush seats, a soft blanket and hot bricks to keep her feet warm, and Lady Lorraine had even produced a tea service.

"Ah, here we are," Lady Lorraine said, and it took a moment for Modesty to tear her gaze from a panel under Lady Lorraine's seat, which she had been informed held a small library.

Modesty looked out the window and spotted a small white house with trees out front and greenery across the door. It was not one of the terraced houses but freestanding. She imagined in the spring the trees were lovely with green leaves and buds. The empty flower boxes in the window were probably filled with color. "It's lovely," she murmured.

"I should have had the greenery removed after Epiphany," Lady Lorraine said, "but I rather like it. The front of the house looks so bare without it."

The carriage halted and a footman came forward to lower the stairs and open the door. Lady Lorraine alighted with ease and Modesty followed more clumsily.

The interior of the house was just as spectacular as the carriage. The foyer was wide and airy with a grand marble Y-shaped staircase. While Modesty looked up and up at the high ceiling, Lady Lorraine spoke with a housekeeper who gave Modesty dubious glances before taking her coat. Then Lady Lorraine led Modesty to a small pale blue parlor where she immediately sat on a couch and put her feet on a footstool. A small white and brown dog trotted in, sniffed at Modesty, and then climbed on the couch and put its head in Lady Lorraine's lap.

"This is Welly," she said, stroking the dog's soft ears. She sighed. "The problem with pregnancy," Lady Lorraine said, "is that I am tired all of the time."

Modesty glanced at Lady Lorraine's midsection. There was just the slightest protrusion where her waist would be. As even the mention of pregnancy embarrassed Modesty, she quickly turned the subject. "I am sorry to trouble you. I assure you, you needn't have gone to this much effort on my account."

Lady Lorraine waved a hand. "When I have my breath back, I will write a few letters and we will discover what there is to know about your aunt Augusta Ryan. Until then you are welcome to stay here. It is just Mr. Mostyn and me, so obviously we have plenty of room to spare."

"His boxing studio must do very well," Modesty said before she could think better of such a comment.

But Lady Lorraine laughed and did not seem offended. "Mr. Mostyn is absolutely making a name for himself in addition to the notoriety he had acquired from being a war hero and a younger son of the Earl of Pembroke. But this house was a wedding gift from my father, the Duke of Ridlington."

Modesty had been to a wedding breakfast once or twice. She had given the newlyweds a basket with bread and jam. Clearly, she had stepped into a different world.

Uncertain what to say in response to Lady Lorraine, Modesty pulled the packet of letters from her pocket and looked at them. She had not been able to read them earlier that day. She had wanted to. She had even stared at them for a long, long time, willing herself to open the first one.

"Do you require privacy?" Lady Lorraine asked. "I can certainly give you privacy. I can retire to another room or have one readied for you or…what is the matter?" She rose and went to sit beside Modesty. A moment later the dog trotted over as well.

"I am a great coward," Modesty said, wiping her eyes. She must stop crying and acting as though her father was dead. She must have hope and faith. She must be strong. Modesty couldn't ever recall her mother crying, and Modesty must show the same resolve in difficult times. God was still with her and though it might feel as though the whole world was against her, she knew that was just her fear speaking.

"You cannot be a coward," Lady Lorraine said, patting her shoulder. "You spent the morning with my husband and

Lord Rowden. That takes a great deal of courage." She smiled.

"Lord Rowden? Do you mean Mr. Payne?"

"Yes. I forget that he is Mr. Payne now. His father is an idiot."

Modesty knew she should not gossip, but she still hoped Lady Lorraine would continue. Instead, the lady tugged at a bell pull and when the door opened to admit the housekeeper, she said, "Is Miss Brown's chamber ready? Show her to it, will you? She requires some time to refresh herself."

Modesty rose and Lady Lorraine took her arm. "Are the other items in your valise as…black as these?" she asked, indicating Modesty's dress and hat.

"Yes. We believe sober dress shows humility."

"It certainly does. If you would like a change of clothing, I might be able to find something suitable. You and I are not of a similar size." This was true as Lady Lorraine was several inches taller than Modesty and had more womanly curves, though that might have been due, in part, to her condition. Even so, Modesty could never wear the sort of clothing Lady Lorraine wore. It was not even afternoon, and she wore a gown that revealed her collarbone and showed the swells of her breasts. A gauzy fichu did nothing to hide the flesh on display. "Nell might be able to find something. She is my lady's maid. Send for her, will you?" she directed one of the footmen standing outside.

"Come down when you are ready," Lady Lorraine said. "I will fortify myself with tea and then begin my correspondence. I have to think who is still in Town," she said almost to herself as she turned away.

Modesty followed the housekeeper, a Mrs. Keefer, to a chamber on the second floor. It was a small chamber but still grander than any Modesty had ever seen. It was papered in mint green and contained a large bed with an inverted V-shaped draping of silky fabric at the head. There was also another of those chaise longues, this one in cream, and a table with a pitcher of water and a basin.

"The fire hasn't had time to warm the room much," Mrs. Keefer said. "But you should be cozy enough in a quarter of an hour."

"I am perfectly cozy now. Thank you."

The housekeeper turned to leave then hesitated and turned back again. "I hope you don't think to take advantage of my lady. She is trusting and kind, and sometimes those qualities cloud her judgment of people."

Modesty understood the warning clear enough. "I assure you, I have no ill intentions. I am grateful for her generosity."

"Good. Mr. Mostyn is a gentleman, but he is protective of Lady Lorraine and her unborn babe. I wouldn't want to anger him."

Modesty wouldn't want to anger him either. She nodded and when the door closed, she removed her hat and went to the wash basin. She washed her face and hands then took a seat on the longue and stared at the letters. She had put it off long enough. Nothing in these letters could change her life more than it had already been changed.

She didn't mind that some of it had changed. If she never had to stand outside a tavern and yell about sin again, she would be perfectly happy. But she did miss her father, and she missed the routine of their days and listening to his sermons on Sunday. She missed the comfort of being in her own home and knowing what the next day would bring. Now everything was uncertain, and she feared life would never return to what it had once been. More importantly, she worried she might never see her father again.

Modesty opened the first letter and began to read.

And then she understood how very naïve she had been because, after only a few words, she realized her whole life had been a lie.

Seven

Across town, Thérèse Renauld had started that day with a problem of her own. And that problem was called Madame LeMonde.

Thérèse was actually French, unlike many of her contemporaries, including Madame LeMonde. It was fashionable in London to patronize a French modiste, and so every one of her competitors, saving a few who had been established for decades and served the older members of the upper classes, had suddenly sprouted French accents and lineages. Thérèse's fashions would not appeal to a dowager of four score, but they were becoming rapidly sought after by the younger, most fashionable of the *ton*. Lady Daphne FitzRoy wore Renaud gowns exclusively, and now that she was willing to wear colors other than pink and not drape herself in bows, other ladies of her set had taken notice.

Even the Duchess of Mayne had bought two gowns and a pelisse from Thérèse and had promised to return. The patronage of a duchess was nothing to scoff at. Indeed, it was a sign that Madame Renauld was making a name for herself. And that brought out the worst in her competitors, namely her nemesis, Madame LeMonde. Madame LeMonde, according to Phaedra, had "done it again."

"I have not had enough coffee," Thérèse said, opening Bleuette's cage and placing her inside. The parrot immediately began preening and fluffing her feathers. "Betsy!" she called, then looked at Phaedra. "Betsy ees still with us?"

Betsy appeared, her blond hair pinned neatly in a bun. "Yes, madame?"

"Will you see to Bleuette thees morning and bring me *un café au lait*." She gestured to Phaedra to follow her to her office in the back. It was a small office, but the door opened into the room where her seamstresses worked, allowing Thérèse to oversee their progress when necessary. The girls had not yet arrived, but their stations were all neat as a pin. Thérèse produced a key from her reticule and unlocked her office. She had taken to keeping it locked after several design sketches had gone missing a few months ago. She motioned to the couch and took the padded chair behind her worktable. A quick perusal of her space showed her everything was as she had left it. Phaedra had been with her from the start. She had been a seamstress for the shop's last owner, and when

Thérèse had bought the store, Phaedra had stayed on. Thérèse had quickly seen the young woman's value. She was smart and hard-working and had an eye for which colors and materials would best suit a client. Thérèse had soon made the woman the manager of Madame Renauld's and had never felt a moment's regret.

Betsy entered with a tray holding the coffee and set it on the worktable, a safe distance from the papers filled with sketches of gowns. "Lady Royce will be here at eleven," she said. Thérèse glanced into the seamstress's workroom and spotted Lady Royce's gown, displayed on a dress form.

"What progress on Mrs. Bartlett's pelisse?"

"I will ask Mrs. Farmer when she arrives, but I believe it is almost finished," Phaedra said. Mrs. Farmer oversaw the sewing and was an accomplished seamstress herself. She often attended to the more delicate final touches on a piece.

"*C'est bon*," Thérèse said. Mrs. Bartlett was not titled, but she was very wealthy. Thérèse, like any good businesswoman, cared as much for wealth as prestige. She gestured for Betsy to depart and after a sip of her coffee raised her brows at Phaedra. "Well?"

"Mary Marker did not come to work yesterday. Her friends Anne and Meg said she was sick, but I sent a spy to Madame LeMonde's."

"Go on." But Thérèse already knew what she would say.

"She is there. That makes the third seamstress Madame LeMonde has stolen from us in a year."

"Thees cannot be tolerated. I pay our girls a good wage."

"Madame LeMonde offers them more and then a few months later reduces their wages. She does not care if they leave after that. By that time, she has all the information on your designs she desires."

"And *mes filles* have not realized thees yet?"

Phaedra adjusted her black hair, which was swept over one shoulder instead of in an elegant chignon as usual. "They have, but Mary Marker apparently needed the blunt now. Her son is sick and needs a doctor."

"Then why did she not come to me? I have told them to come to me. You will speak to *mes filles* today, *oui*?"

"I was thinking of calling a morning meeting." Phaedra smoothed her hair over her temple. She did not normally fuss with her hair. "I will remind the girls that you're here to help, and that if they leave for LeMonde, or anyone else, you won't hire them back."

"And no other modiste will either. No one wants a traitor. Phaedra, what ees wrong with your face? Why do you hide it?"

Phaedra stilled. "Nothing, madame. I thought I'd try a new style with my hair today."

Thérèse narrowed her eyes. "I prefer it out of the way." She waved a hand. "Go and rearrange it before we open."

"Yes, madame." She rose and then sat back down again. Thérèse said nothing. Waiting. Phaedra swallowed. "I can't put it up today, madame."

"Let me see," Thérèse said.

Phaedra lifted her hand and pushed the hair back. A mottled red bruise marked the light brown skin at her temple and the upper part of her cheek.

"Where else did he hit you?"

"It were an accident, madame." Phaedra had pulled herself out of poverty in the rookeries and taught herself to sew. She'd worked hard to speak in a way pleasing to the ladies of the upper class. But her accent grew heavy when she was tired or upset.

"He hit you on accident? A prizefighter does not hit by accident."

"I made him angry."

Thérèse rose, too irritated to sit still. "That ees no excuse. I am often angry when a sleeve ees sewed wrong or a hem poorly tacked. I do not beat *mes filles*." She gestured to the work room.

"He's a man. He can't control his temper."

Thérèse gaped at her. "Thees ees a lie, an even bigger lie than Madame LeMonde, that snake, tells. You do not deserve thees treatment, Phaedra. You will leave him and find another man."

Phaedra bit her lip, and Thérèse saw tears in her eyes. She had never seen Phaedra close to tears, not even when the Marchioness of Ware threw a vase at her because her pregnancy had made her waist too thick to fit in the dress she'd ordered. Phaedra had caught the vase and then patted the marchioness's shoulder while she sobbed.

Thérèse knelt before Phaedra. "Tell me."

"I have thought of leaving," Phaedra said, wiping at her eyes.

Thérèse sat back on her heels. "But he will not let you. Ees that why he hit you?" When Phaedra did not answer, Thérèse gently took her arms. Phaedra winced. Thérèse released her immediately. "So the bruises we do not see are worse than those we do. Go home. You should not be here today."

Phaedra shook her head. "I would rather be here, madame. I want to work. I need to keep busy."

"Very well." Thérèse had often used work to distract her from her own problems. Sewing or sketching were wonderfully calming for an anxious mind. She had known men like Phaedra's prizefighter. She had fled her home and family in Toulouse to lose herself in Paris because of a man like that. She had been fortunate enough to find work in Paris and to make herself into the businesswoman she was today, but the back alleys of Paris and London were littered with the women who had not been so fortunate.

"I should have believed you," Phaedra said.

Thérèse raised her brows.

"You told me never to trust them. Men, that is. You told me I was better off without them. Now I don't know what to do." She closed her eyes and whispered. "I'm afraid he'll kill me."

"I won't let him," Thérèse said, though how she would stop a prizefighter she did not know. "You leave thees to me." The door to the workroom opened, and several seamstresses filed in, chatting quietly and shaking the rain off their coats.

"But madame—"

"No questions. Time to work." She shooed Phaedra away.

"Yes, madame." Phaedra rose and gave the girls a smile, chatting with each as though nothing was amiss.

Thérèse closed her door and sipped her coffee, which had gone cold. No, she could not stop a prizefighter. But perhaps she knew someone who could.

***

By late afternoon Modesty had read all of the letters twice, her face burning, her heart aching, her head throbbing. She wanted the letters to be wrong. After the first time she read them, she made herself read them all again, because she was certain she'd misunderstood something.

But, of course, she hadn't. She might be sheltered and naïve to the ways of the world, but she wasn't dull-witted.

The letters were from another woman. A woman who was not her mother, although some of the letters were dated from the time when her mother had been alive. The early letters had made Modesty's cheeks heat. She had read Song of Solomon in the Bible, and these letters were just as eye-opening. This woman, who signed her name as Fanny, wrote of her longing for Samuel Brown. It was a physical longing. She'd described it in great detail. She'd also described what she wanted Modesty's father to do with her and what she'd enjoyed the last time he'd visited her.

The letters spanned years, and the later letters were less passionate and more of a practical nature. Fanny talked of her children—*their* children. Modesty had not known her father had another family and other children. She had not known there was another woman in his life, a woman who was like a wife to him. He sent this woman money and he visited her on occasion. Modesty had never known. She had never even suspected that every Sunday, while her father preached truth and light and against the evils of fornication, all along he was lying to everyone he knew and fornicating for years.

But perhaps he was not lying to everyone he knew. Perhaps he was only lying to her? Perhaps everyone but her knew.

Her mother had known.

That was the most shocking letter of all. One of the letters mentioned Catherine Brown. Fanny wrote that she was relieved Samuel's wife had forgiven him. Did that mean Modesty's mother knew the relationship continued? Had she condoned her husband's infidelity? Had she too pretended to be good and pure and, in reality, led a life of lies and duplicity?

A tap sounded on the door, and Lady Lorraine entered. "I have sent the first batch of letters," she said entering the room. "Did the letters give you any clues as to the whereabouts of your aunt? It would help to know if she lives in London or…" She wrinkled her brow and looked down at

Modesty, sitting on the floor with the letters strewn about her. "Are you well?"

Modesty wanted to say, *Yes, I am quite well. Thank you for asking.* But she couldn't pretend. She *would not* pretend. She would not *lie.*

"No," she said. "No, I'm not well at all."

The lady moved forward, her eyes wide. "What's happened? Has something in the letters upset you?"

"You could say that." Modesty jumped up and kicked at the letters. "He is a liar, my lady. My father. He lied to me for years." She began to pace, feeling the need to move. She was so angry, angry like she'd never been before in her life, and she could not contain her feelings. She had to do something with that emotion. And she would not cry. No. No more tears for her lying father. Where was he now? With his mistress? With his other family? And did he care that Modesty was scared and alone? Had he even sent so much as a note to assure her he was alive?

She wasn't sure how much of her thoughts she said aloud, but it must have been enough that Lady Lorraine began to understand the nature of things. "I am certain he cares. Something must have happened to prevent him from sending word. I still think we should seek out your aunt—"

"Do you know what I think, my lady? I think I am tired of wearing this black, itchy dress. I am tired of standing on street corners half the night and telling loose women they are bound for hell. I am tired of having beer and curses thrown on me—and much worse, I assure you. I have tried to follow my mother's example for years. I have tried to be good." Up and down the carpet, back and forth she walked.

"Of course, you have."

"But my mother looked the other way while my father sired children with another woman. We lived in poverty so he could send any spare money he had to this other woman. I thought my mother was so good and pure. But she was weak and pathetic. I hate her. I hate them both."

"My dear, you don't mean that." Lady Lorraine sat on a chair. "You're angry right now. You've realized that parents are human, like the rest of us. They make mistakes."

"They never allowed me to make mistakes," Modesty said. "They expected me to be perfect. I don't want to be perfect any longer. I want..." She looked around the chamber, not certain what she wanted. And then her gaze landed on Lady Lorraine. The lady looked so lovely in a green dress with sheer sleeves and that gauze at her throat. She even had a green ribbon woven through her light brown hair.

"I want ribbons," Modesty had said. "I want a pink dress."

Lady Lorraine's eyes widened. "Not pink with your coloring. What about yellow?"

"Yes. Yellow. I want a yellow dress with ribbons. I want to let my hair down." She ripped off the black hat and unpinned the cap she wore, then shook out her hair so it fell down around her in long, auburn waves.

Lady Lorraine nodded with excitement. "I'll send word to a modiste, and my lady's maid is a wonder with hair."

"I need somewhere to go. An assembly?" She'd dance all night, even though she knew no dances. Mr. Payne would teach her. She didn't know why she should think of him. He'd pawned her off on Mostyn's wife. But she wanted to see him again. She wanted him to look at her as he had that morning in his bedchamber. She wanted to steal a kiss and see what it felt like.

Lady Lorraine was shaking her head. "There aren't any assemblies this time of year."

"The fight then. What are they called? Mills? I want to attend the mill tomorrow night."

Lady Lorraine clapped her hands. "That would be most exciting. Leave everything to me. Why don't I have a bath sent up? You bathe and refresh yourself while I see to the modiste and the prizefight."

"And the ribbons. Don't forget the ribbons."

"Lorrie!" came a male voice that made Modesty jump.

"It's just Mostyn," Lady Lorraine said. "I'll send up the water." She left and Modesty heard her call. "Ewan, I need ribbons!"

As soon as Lady Lorraine departed, Modesty had second thoughts. She had spent years doing everything she had been told. She had dressed and behaved soberly and humbly. She had been frugal, buying only the necessities and eating very simply. She dared not even allow herself to look at a display of pretty hats or imagine what it would be like to eat one of the sugary confections she sometimes saw when passing by tea rooms. She never drank anything stronger than tea, never swore, never went anywhere but church and to rail against sin. She'd never danced, never read anything beyond the Bible and books of sermons, and never even played a card game.

And what had been the point of all the deprivation? To be as perfect as her mother? Well, her mother's life had been a lie. To please God above? Modesty rather doubted God cared if she wore a pretty dress or danced. After all, even the Bible said there was a time to dance. She wanted to dance.

A tap sounded on the door, and Modesty turned, wondering if Lady Lorraine had found some ribbons already. But it was two footmen with a large hip bath, followed by a maid with a towel and a wooden box. The footmen set the tub down, and the maid opened the box. "Would you like me to scent the bath water, Miss?" the maid asked. "I have scents of rose, lavender, or lemon."

Modesty looked down at the box and saw vials of scents as well as soap for the body and the hair. "I don't know which to choose," she said. "You choose."

"Yes, miss." She went to the tub and soon the scent of lavender filled the room. "Would you like me to help with your bath?"

Modesty shook her head. "I can manage."

"Then I'll stoke the fire and return with a robe for you to wear after you bathe. Shall I have your garments cleaned for you, miss?"

Modesty wanted to tell her to burn them, but she had learned never to be hasty or impulsive. "Yes, please."

The maid bobbed and hurried away. Modesty undressed and sank into the fragrant water. She felt as though she was washing her old self away and revealing the new.

Eight

That night Aidan tossed a paper on the table in front of Rowden and sat in the chair on the other side. Rowden was at the Draven Club where the men who had served in the war with Colonel Draven often gathered. There had been thirty in the troop at the start, and a dozen had returned. Only a few were in attendance at the club that afternoon.

Rowden drank coffee, rather than his preferred brandy and soda, in preparation for the fight the next night. His muscles were sore from the practice session today, but a good session in the morning—lighter and not too strenuous— would warm him up and leave him in good shape.

"Looks like we're traveling to Hungerford," Aidan said.

Rowden lifted the paper and smiled. A mill had been arranged at a racecourse in Hungerford for the week following. Details were scant and would not be made known to the public until a day or so before the actual match. This way the magistrates were not alerted to the bout too early, although many of them would probably attend as spectators

155

anyway. The pamphlet did say the German would be there as well as Tom Cribb, serving as an umpire.

"I'll have to tell Chibale."

"I'm sure he already knows. You beat Abraham Strong tomorrow and the German will have to fight you. Do it at this venue and the winnings will be…" He whistled.

"I could make enough to retire."

"You could retire anyway. You have enough from selling your commission. But fighting has never been about the blunt for you."

Rowden drank his coffee and wished it were brandy. Aidan wasn't wrong. At first, he'd fought for the money. He needed it after his father cut him off. But when he'd heard how angry his success made the duke, Rowden had wanted to fight all the more. He wanted to stick a thumb in his father's eye and dig it around.

"Not everything is about blunt to me, no," Rowden agreed. "Difficult as that is for you to imagine."

Aidan smiled. He was rumored to be the bastard son of the Marquess of Cranbourne by a chambermaid. The marquess had provided for Aidan and his mother, but he hadn't codified the arrangement. Aidan had been twelve when his father had suddenly died, and he and his mother had become destitute. He'd had to resort to stealing to survive.

Colonel Draven liked to say the army had reformed Aidan, but Aidan had just learned more socially acceptable ways to steal. He'd used the money from the sale of his commission to buy shares in various companies and schemes and made a hundred times what he'd invested.

Aidan was now one of the richest men in England, and certainly the wealthiest of the Survivors. Even the Duke of Mayne's wealth couldn't hold a candle to Aidan's.

"Don't you have a house in Hungerford?" Rowden asked. The inns would be full, and even this far in advance, all the rooms would be taken. He didn't relish sleeping in a stable or out in the cold.

"No. How many houses do you think I have?"

Rowden considered. "Eight."

"Only six."

"My mistake."

"Nicholas's breeding farm is near Hungerford," Aidan offered after a moment.

"Do you think he'll have us?"

"He won't shoot at us like Nash, though he's probably equally as surly. I'll write to him." Aidan rose and left the reading room just as Ewan stalked in. Rowden shrank back involuntarily. The look in Ewan's eyes was deadly.

"What's wrong?" Rowden asked as Ewan towered over him.

"Miss Brown," Ewan said.

Miss Brown? How could she be any trouble? In fact, since Rowden had handed her over to Lady Lorraine this noon, he'd hardly given her another thought. Hardly, of course, being the operative word because every once in a while, when he wasn't making an effort to control his thoughts, they wandered back to the sight of her auburn hair falling over her shoulders as she lay in his bed.

Ridiculous. Rowden would have about as much chance to bed a nun as Miss Brown. And that was fine. Women were a distraction. He'd been in love once, and it had all but destroyed him. Sleeping alone was a choice and a lonely one at that. But that was his choice, and he preferred it that way.

Ewan sat and gestured to one of the footmen to bring him a drink. "What's that?" he gestured to the pamphlet Rowden held.

"There's an exhibition in Hungerford sometime next week. The German is fighting."

"Then so are you."

"Yes."

The footman delivered the brandy—straight, no soda—and after Ewan had consumed about half of it, Rowden broached the subject of Miss Brown again. "What is the matter with Miss Brown? Can't find her aunt?"

Ewan lifted a shoulder and finished the brandy. Rowden raised his brows and waited. Ewan lowered his glass. "Don't know anything about an aunt, but she has my wife running around with ribbons."

This made absolutely no sense. Miss Brown had only been with Lady Lorraine for a half day. Rowden gave Ewan a moment to say more, but the man was taciturn as usual. "Well," he finally said, "I am sure Miss Brown will be on her way to her aunt's soon enough."

Ewan signaled for another drink. This was serious then. "She wants to come tomorrow."

"To the mill?"

Ewan inclined his head. "I said no."

"That's reasonable. It's not safe for a lady in her condition."

Ewan grunted. Rowden hated to ask. He could see Ewan was in a state and might haul off and punch him if the mood struck, but Rowden was curious now. He so rarely witnessed Ewan this riled up.

Rowden pushed his chair back an inch. "Who wants to come to the mill, exactly? Lady Lorraine?"

"Both."

Rowden shook his head. "That doesn't make any sense. Miss Brown is against prizefighting."

Ewan muttered something else about ribbons.

"Are you certain Miss Brown wants to come to the mill?"

Ewan growled, and Rowden shut up. A half hour later he was on his way back to his flat in St. James's. Ewan's foul mood had emptied most of the club, and Rowden thought it prudent to remove himself as he was responsible for Ewan's trouble, at least in part. He still couldn't figure out how Miss Brown could be any trouble at all. He'd imagined she would read the letters and then seek out her aunt. If the letters didn't hold a clue to her aunt's whereabouts, Lady Lorraine would find out. She knew everyone in Town and had a way of making people talk to her.

She'd found a way to make Mostyn talk to her, and he never talked to anyone more than was necessary.

Rowden reached his door, opened it, and was greeted immediately by Trogdon. Rowden was impressed as his manservant usually had to be summoned to take Rowden's coat and hat. He was about to praise the man when Trogdon stepped close. "You have a guest, sir," he said quietly.

"How can I have a guest?" He turned so Trogdon could remove his coat. "I just arrived."

"He is waiting for you in the drawing room, sir."

Rowden was tired and wanted to eat and rest his tired muscles. He did not want to make inane small talk with someone who hoped to profit off his prizefighting and had a grand moneymaking scheme. "Why is he waiting for me? Why didn't you tell him I was not at home?"

Trogdon's brow creased. "But you are at home, sir."

The door to the drawing room opened, and Chibale poked his head out. "It's just me."

Rowden was not reassured. "If you want me to go back to Mostyn's tonight, you can forget it."

"I didn't come about that," Chibale said, moving backward as Rowden entered the drawing room and closed the door. "I came about her."

"Miss Brown?" Had she done something to anger Chibale too?

Chibale cocked his head. "Who? That little Methodist?" He waved a hand. "No. Madame Renauld."

Rowden sat. "Really? What about her?"

"She sent for me."

"Then why aren't you in *her* drawing room?" He settled in a chair, putting one leg over the arm. He signaled for Trogdon to bring him a drink.

"Just water, Trogdon," Chibale said. He reached in his coat and produced two oranges. "For before the fight," he said. "They'll give you energy."

Trogdon took the oranges and left. Rowden hoped it was to fetch him something stronger than water.

"She said to come when her shop closes and her seamstresses have gone," Chibale said. "I thought I'd wait another hour." He sat then stood then sat again. Rowden watched him, feeling a mixture of amusement and bewilderment. Chibale was always so confident, so sure of himself. When he'd first approached Rowden about becoming his manager, Rowden had brushed him off. He'd brushed off every other man who approached him, offering to take fifty percent of his winnings for acting as a glorified bottle man. But Chibale had been so self-assured. He'd had a plan to make Rowden's name famous throughout the country. Rowden had been using Rowdy Rowden, but Chibale said The Royal Payne had more class and would highlight his lineage. People would pay to see the son of a duke fight or be knocked out. And Chibale offered to only take thirty percent of his winnings. He said Rowden would make so much, thirty percent would end up more than the fifty percent any of the other men who'd offered to manage him would make.

Rowden couldn't refuse. Even though he'd still been skeptical, he wanted to give Chibale a chance. Chibale had not disappointed. He was a tireless promoter, an ardent supporter, and a relentless trainer. He had negotiated fights and prizemoney with some of the most notorious criminals in London in some of the seediest venues in Town. He moved equally well among the upper classes at puffed-up exhibitions held at garden parties. Never had Rowden seen Chibale ill-at-ease—not when speaking with a countess, not when arguing with an arch rogue and his fellow coves, not when things went wrong and they were running for their lives.

But clearly this modiste was different.

"She probably has a question about the ball."

Chibale paced. "I sent her the information. The time I would collect her, a copy of the invitation with the date, and so on. She must want to cry off."

"It's not a wedding."

"And it never will be at this rate."

Rowden sat. "Are you thinking of marrying her?"

"Who wouldn't want to marry her? She's a brilliant businesswoman and beautiful besides. And that accent. Can you imagine her whispering in French in bed?" He looked at Rowden. "Don't imagine that."

Rowden scowled. "I have no desire to imagine you in bed with Madame Renauld or any other woman. But if that's what you want, why not be bold?"

"I was bold. I invited her to the ball."

"She's a modiste, not a debutante. I doubt she cares how well you waltz. Tell her what you want. Seduce her with kisses and sweet words or tell her you intend to make her your wife. If she says no, then you needn't waste more of your time."

"If she says no, I'll never recover."

Rowden stared at him. "Who the devil are you? I've never seen you act like this. She's a woman, Chibale." Rowden stood. "There are a hundred more just like her."

"You would say that," Chibale shot back. "You kick a woman out of your bed almost as fast as you get her in it. What would you know of love?"

Rowden clenched his fists. "Get out."

Chibale held his hands up. "I'm sorry. I didn't mean that. I forgot."

"Go to your modiste."

"Rowden—"

"Here is the orange juice you requested, sir," Trogdon said, carrying a tray with a glass of orange liquid.

Rowden gritted his teeth, his gaze still on Chibale. "I asked for a drink, Trogdon. The oranges are for the morning."

"But, sir, you always have toast in the morning," Trogdon said. This was true, and Rowden was too tired to argue. He took the glass of juice from the tray. "Thank you, Trogdon. I'll dine in a few minutes. Mr. Okoro was just leaving."

"Very well, sir. Mr. Okoro, I will show you out."

"I can see myself out, Trogdon." He made a shooing gesture with his hand, and with a huff, Trogdon departed. Rowden hoped he would put the dinner Cook had made on the table, but there was no guarantee.

"I spoke without thinking," Chibale said. "I'm overwrought."

"It's fine," Rowden said, sinking back into his chair. The anger had left him. He'd been angry for years, and he'd burned with it for so long that he had very little left. Chibale often said this was what made him a good fighter. Other men became angry at their opponents. Rowden was cool and focused.

Chibale sat as well, dangling his arms between his legs. "You really think I should tell her how I feel?"

"Life is short," Rowden said. "Too short for games. Too short to be without the person you care for. If you care for her, tell her."

"I will. Rowden, I—"

Rowden raised a hand. "I'm fine. I'll see you at Mostyn's in the morning, yes?"

"Yes." He eyed the orange juice. "I'll bring more oranges."

Rowden nodded and when Chibale had gone, drank the juice. He didn't even like oranges.

***

Half an hour later, Chibale knocked on the back entrance of Madame Renaud's. In her note, she had asked that he not use the front door, lest he be seen. The back door opened almost immediately, and Madame Renauld stood in the doorway, holding a lamp. She peered out, looking into the alley behind the shop. Apparently satisfied with what she saw, she moved aside to allow him entrance.

"Thank you for coming."

Chibale looked around the room he'd entered. It was a workroom, with tables placed against the walls and chairs set at each. Shelves of thread and fabric rose to the ceiling and several dress forms were swathed in women's fine fashions.

"I need your help," Madame Renauld said. "Come, Mr. Okoro. We can speak in here." She led him to a small room with a view of the workroom and indicated a couch. He sat and wondered if she would sit beside him or behind the desk. This room was not so neat as the workroom. Several papers were scattered over the desk, and some drawings as well as pieces of charcoal had fallen on the floor around the rubbish bin. The parrot he had seen in the showroom when he'd come with Bethanie also perched on the desk, her head under her feathers, tugging and fluffing them.

"Call me Chibale," he said, focusing on her again. She wore a dark purple dress with black trim and looked effortlessly elegant.

"Chibale?" she said, head cocked. He liked the way her French accent sounded on his name.

"My given name," he said. "If you need help, and we're to meet in private like this, it seems we might as well use given names."

She considered for a moment. "Very well. I am Thérèse." She indicated a marquetry cabinet behind her desk and opened it. "Would you like tea or something stronger?"

"Nothing for me."

"Do you mind if I partake? It has been a long day."

"Not at all." He rose. "Sit and I will pour for you."

She waved a hand. "Thees ees not necessary."

"I insist," he said. She inclined her head and sat on the couch, placing herself on the far edge from where he had been sitting.

"Sherry, *si'l vous plait*," she said.

"Pour the sherry," the parrot said, startling Chibale, who had almost forgotten her.

"Oh, hush," Thérèse told the bird, and she went back to her fluffing.

Chibale lifted a clean, heavy crystal glass, found the sherry, and poured her a generous portion. He brought it to her and sat on the couch again. His heart was still pounding and his insides shaking with nerves, but he'd managed to calm them enough to act more himself. Rowden was right. He should be bold and confident. Meek and hesitant were unlikely traits to attract a woman like Thérèse Renauld.

"I assume this is not about the ball," he said.

"The—no."

Chibale tried not to let his face show his disappointment. She had forgotten about the ball. That was a good sign, was it not? That meant she still planned to accompany him. Didn't it? "You received my note with the details?" he asked.

"*Oui.* I am quite looking forward to it, but I need your help with a different matter, monsieur. It ees the matter of my assistant, Phaedra."

"Ah." Chibale understood immediately. "The one who is…shall we say *involved* with the Black Plague."

"*Oui.* She came to work thees morning bruised and battered. I do not know the full extent of her injuries, but any man who hits a woman ees a monster."

"I quite agree. She should stay away from him."

"It ees not that simple."

No, of course it wasn't. "He needs a bit of incentive to leave her alone."

"*Oui.* Thees word I like. Incentive ees what he needs." She sipped her sherry and eyed him from under her lashes. "And do you know anyone who can provide thees incentive?"

"I believe I do." Chibale stroked his chin. "He's fighting at the Cock and Bull tomorrow night."

"Fine lace," the parrot interjected.

Chibale smiled. "Not much lace at the Cock and Bull. We'll have a word with the Plague after his mill."

"Just a word?" Thérèse asked, raising her brows.

"In a manner of speaking," Chibale said. "Words don't always have to be given verbally. Actions sometimes speak louder. Isn't that what they say?"

"I have heard that saying." She reached forward and set her glass on the desk. "I appreciate your help, monsieur—Chibale."

"I only wish you had asked sooner, Thérèse." She rose, and he rose too. "Before I go, I was hoping to say something more to you."

"Fine lace!"

Chibale ignored the bird.

"About the ball?" Thérèse asked.

"No. About why I asked you to the ball, Thérèse."

Her dark eyes met his. "And why ees that, monsieur?"

"I asked you," he said, moving closer to her, "because I admire you. Because I find you quite the most remarkable woman I have ever known."

"You hardly know me."

"I hope to rectify that," Chibale said. "But I believe the better I know you, the more my regard will grow."

"We will see," she said. "Shall I show you out?"

"If you'll permit me," Chibale said. "I thought I would illustrate my feelings with an action. I think it might be clearer than my words." His words had seemed to stick in his throat, and it was a good thing else he might have gushed about how beautiful she was and how much he adored her.

"Go ahead," she said. "You have made me curious, monsieur."

"Chibale," he murmured. He lifted a hand and gingerly placed it on her shoulder, drawing her closer to him. The scent of her enveloped him, musky and sophisticated, like the finest perfume. She looked at him, the height difference between them only four or five inches, and he brought his hand to her cheek. Her skin was soft and burnished to a deep golden brown in the lamp light. Giving her plenty of time to change her mind, he lowered his head. Rather than move back, she stood where she was and even leaned forward and into the kiss. His lips slid over hers, his heart beating so hard that he feared she would hear it.

Her lips were full and so lush as he explored them, kissing her gently but with undisguised passion. Her mouth parted slightly, and he tasted the sherry she'd been drinking. He wanted more of her, wanted to slide between those lips and cup the back of her head, kissing her deeply.

She wanted more as well. She grasped his coat and her fist tightened on the material, bringing him closer. His body told him to lower her to the couch. His mind told him to leave her wanting more.

Slowly, he withdrew and looked down at her. Her eyes opened, her dark gaze unfocused and her lashes lowered seductively.

"I hope that makes my feelings for you clear," he said, voice low.

"I am beginning to understand," she said. "But perhaps another demonstration would illustrate your point even better." She pressed into him, and Chibale was sorely tempted. He was more tempted than he'd ever been. But he wanted more from this woman than a tumble on the couch. He wanted her heart and her hand.

"Fine lace! Pour the sherry!" the bird said, and Chibale was glad the bird had broken the mood.

"Tomorrow," he said. "After the fight. I'll come to you," he said and stepped back.

She gave him a long look then nodded. "The Cock and Bull, you say?"

Alarm bells rang in his head. "You shouldn't come. Bad area of town. Questionable crowd."

"You will be there?"

"I have to be. My client is fighting. If he wins, we go to Hungerford for a mill with the German."

"The German who beat him before? Why would he fight him again?"

Chibale spread his arms. "For honor, of course."

"I am sure the winning purse ees also quite large."

Chibale grinned. "That too." He gave Thérèse a bow. "I'll come to you tomorrow and let you know how our discussions proceed."

"I look forward to it, monsieur." She led him out of her chamber and to the back door, unlocking it and opening it for him. "*Bonsoir.*"

"*Au revoir.*"

"*Au revoir,* monsieur." And she closed the door. Chibale leaned against the building and put his hand to his heart.

Nine

The Cock and Bull was teeming with people—the Fancy, they were called—though the name did not fit this motley group. Modesty did not know if she had ever seen so many people. The sound and smell of them, after the quiet and clean scents of a night and day at Lady Lorraine's house, was almost shocking. She was thankful Mr. Mostyn had accompanied them—not that they'd had any choice about it. He entered the tavern and people made a path for him. A few people seemed to know him and moved forward as though to greet him, but with one look, those men thought better of it and moved away.

Modesty followed Mr. Mostyn and Lady Lorraine to a table near where the boxing area had been set up. It was a square of about eight feet that had been roped off with stakes in each corner. Two men were already inside the ropes, swinging at each other, but Modesty did not recognize them. The table Mostyn had chosen was occupied, but when

Mostyn stood over them, the men who'd been sitting there lifted their drinks and moved.

Lady Lorraine removed her cloak and laid it over her chair and motioned for Modesty to do the same with the cloak she had borrowed. She leaned close to be heard. "If you drape the cloak over the chair before you sit on it, your dress will stay clean."

Modesty nodded. She reached for the ties at the cloak's throat and then had to take a deep breath. When she'd put on the dark blue dress in her chamber at Lady Lorraine's home, she had felt rather daring in it. Lady Lorraine had assured her the bodice was modest, but Modesty had never worn anything where her neck showed, not to mention her collarbone. Instead of being shapeless, the dress had a "waist" just beneath her breasts and the fabric there was fitted to show her figure. The hem had to be altered slightly so as not to drag on the ground and the sleeves were a bit long as well, but they'd been easily tucked and pinned under. Her arms were covered as were her legs. But she still felt exposed when she opened the cloak and laid it on the chair.

Modesty started to put a hand over the pale flesh at her neck then resisted and sat, placing her hands in her lap.

"When does Lord Rowden box?" Lady Lorraine asked.

"Last," Mostyn said.

"Of course." One of the men in the ring hit the other quite hard in the face and both Lady Lorraine and Modesty shrank back. Lady Lorraine turned to Modesty. "You look very pretty. I can't believe you were hiding that glorious hair under a cap. You should have allowed Nell to have her way with you."

Modesty put a hand to her hair, which had been arranged in a sophisticated upsweep. Lady Lorraine's maid had wanted to leave some of it down and falling over her shoulder in curls, but Modesty had refused.

"Isn't this exciting?" Lady Lorraine asked, looking about them. "I confess I do not like boxing much, but look at all of these people. Some of them appear quite dangerous."

"I have no doubt," Modesty said, having been in her share of taverns over the years. "We are fortunate to have Mr. Mostyn with us. May I ask you a question?"

"Of course."

"Why do you refer to Mr. Payne as Lord Rowden? You said earlier his father was an idiot."

"I'm not sure I should tell you if he hasn't divulged it, but I suppose it's no secret," Lady Lorraine said. "He is a younger son of the Duke of Comerford. I know him as Lord Rowden because my father is a duke, and we were often thrown together in Society when we were younger. But Lord Rowden's father disowned him when he married."

Modesty's heart clenched tightly, and it seemed the room began to swim. "Why?" she asked, careful not to betray her feelings.

"The woman he married was Catholic. I believe his father refused to consent to the match, and he married her anyway." Mr. Mostyn put a glass of water in front of her and she smiled at him and sipped it. A server put a glass in front of Modesty as well.

"But that was a long time ago. It was before he went into the army and became a war hero. We all thought his father would forgive him after that, but apparently even his son distinguishing himself in battle was not enough for Comerford."

The crowd roared as one of the men in the arena went down and did not rise. One of the men in his corner rushed to the side of the ropes and yelled at him to get up, but he could only climb to his knees and then went back down again. The umpire then took the standing boxer's hand, raised it, and declared him the victor.

The noise level in the tavern became too loud for speaking, and Modesty sat back and tried to digest what she'd just been told. Not only was Mr. Payne the son of a duke, he was a war hero. But more important than either of those matters, Mr. Payne was married. Modesty hadn't quite admitted to herself that she was attracted to Mr. Payne. It wasn't the sole reason she had come to the match this evening, but it had certainly been a factor. She wanted to see him again. She wanted to see the look he'd give her—that one that made her cheeks feel warm and her belly flutter.

But he was married. He shouldn't be looking at her like that, and she should not want him to. She would have asked Lady Lorraine to take her home right then, but a glance at the lady showed Modesty she was smiling at her husband and quite obviously enjoying herself. Modesty wouldn't cut her enjoyment short. The lady had spent hours writing letters to inquire after Augusta Ryan, and then she'd spent even more time helping Modesty dress for this evening.

Two more men were entering the boxing area, both of them dark-skinned and shirtless. The tavern owner introduced one as John "The Mighty" Jones and the other as "The Black Plague." Modesty frowned. What sort of sobriquet was that?

"What the devil are you doing here?" a voice asked from behind her. Modesty looked up and into the green eyes of Rowden Payne. His gaze shifted from her to Mr. Mostyn. "You brought her?"

Lady Lorraine rose and extended her hand. "Oh, how lovely to see you, Lord Rowden. Yes, the weather is quite cold this evening. We are fine, thank you for asking."

"You shouldn't be here," he told her.

Mostyn crossed his arms over his large chest and nodded in agreement.

Lady Lorraine scowled. "And why is it, exactly, you think you have the right to tell me where I can and cannot go?"

"Fine," Mr. Payne said and turned his gaze back on Modesty. "Why are you here? And what are you doing dressed like that?"

Modesty looked down at her dress and wished she could pull the cloak over herself again. It had been a mistake to come. She hadn't known about the wife, and now it was obvious that Mr. Payne did not want her here.

"She looks very pretty," Lady Lorraine said.

"That's the problem," Mr. Payne said. "Half the men in this place are staring at her."

Modesty looked around, but no one seemed to be looking at her. Most everyone was staring at the fight, although a few people close by were watching the scene at their table.

"If you are determined to be disagreeable, then go back to your corner," Lady Lorraine ordered.

"I can't," Mr. Payne said. "Chibale wants a word with him." He cocked his head toward the one they called the Black Plague. "I'm supposed to make sure he doesn't leave this way."

"What's the problem?" Mr. Mostyn asked.

"He has a rough hand with women," Mr. Payne answered, and his gaze flicked toward a corner of the room. Modesty recognized Mr. Okoro there, sitting in a chair and speaking to a beautifully dressed woman, who was crying. The woman looked up briefly, and Modesty gasped when she saw the woman's eye was swollen and red. She had obviously been hit.

Modesty felt the heat of indignation rise in her. The blood seemed to rush to her face.

"That man hit her?" she asked, indicating the large boxer in the ring.

"Yes," Mr. Payne answered, his gaze flicking to her then away again. He obviously did not like what he saw, but then she should be glad of that as he was married and should not be looking at her.

"But he is so much bigger than she," Modesty said.

Mr. Payne nodded, still not looking at her. "I believe the plan is to make him aware of that issue, among others." He grabbed a nearby chair and sat beside her. "I won't trouble you with my presence long, Miss Brown. I just want to make sure he doesn't slip away before Chibale and I can have a…word." He turned his attention to the boxing match for a few moments, and that gave Modesty a chance to admire his profile. He had a strong chin and forehead. His nose was not quite perfectly straight. She assumed it had been broken at some point, but it was still a better nose than many men she had known. He glanced at her, and she quickly pretended to be immersed in the fight.

"Did you read the letters?" he asked, when the men had gone to their corners for thirty seconds.

"I did," she said. "They were…not what I expected."

"I see."

She could feel his gaze on her face, obviously trying to read her emotions. "The letters were not from my aunt." They had not been from her mother either, but she did not want to mention that.

"Lady Lorraine is making inquiries into your aunt's whereabouts?" Mr. Payne asked.

"Yes. She's been very kind."

"Would've been kinder not to bring you here," he muttered. The mill began again, and the noise level rose with the men. Mr. Payne had to lean closer. Modesty could not help but catch the scent of him—something dark and musky mixed with the smells of beer and ale from the tavern. "Did the letters give any indication of where your father might be?" he asked.

She had thought of that. Modesty had considered that perhaps her father had gone to be with his other family. But certainly, he would have written to assure her he was well. He would not abandon her. Still, what if this other woman knew something she did not? It might be helpful to seek her out.

Modesty would have had to read the letters again and pick out places they'd referenced. She hadn't had the stomach to do so yet. Truthfully, she wasn't certain she wanted to see her father again. It might be better to find her aunt first. Her aunt had loved her mother and might take Modesty in.

"They might," she answered finally. And then because she was thinking of her mother—thinking of scorned women—she made a show of looking about. "Is your wife here tonight, Mr. Payne?" she asked.

184 | *Shana Galen*

He stilled. To Modesty, it felt as though the entire tavern stilled, though of course, no one but he could even hear her. Quite obviously, he hadn't liked what he heard. It was as though a door opened and the cold night air rushed inside.

"My wife?" he asked. "Did she tell you about her?" He nodded toward Lady Lorraine who was watching the fight with her eyes covered but her fingers spread.

"Yes. I asked why she called you Lord Rowden, and she told me the story."

"It appears she forgot a key part."

"What's that?"

"My wife is dead." He rose and walked away.

***

The fight in the arena went on, but for once, Rowden didn't see it. He didn't know who was winning, and he didn't care. He hadn't cared since he saw Ewan Mostyn walk in with his wife on one arm and a beautiful woman trailing behind. But she wasn't just a beautiful woman. It was Modesty Brown.

Rowden had caught glimpses of her beauty before. When he'd been mesmerized by her eyes for long enough to allow the German to plant a facer, he'd gotten a peek. Yesterday morning in his bedchamber when pieces of her hair had come loose, he'd caught another glimpse. But looking at her tonight, her beauty hit him like a punch in the chest. He hadn't seemed able to breathe.

And perhaps it was his imagination, but it seemed the rest of the tavern had held its breath as the beauty with the ravishing red hair made her way through the swath of people Ewan willed out of his way.

And then they'd reached the table and Miss Brown had removed the cloak she wore, revealing a half moon of skin below her throat, and Rowden had made his way to the table to ward off every other man who had the same idea. It wasn't even that the amount of skin she showed was scandalous. It was far too modest for a venue like this one, where more of the ladies' chests spilled out of their bodices than was contained inside. It was just that combination of pale skin and dark blue fabric pulled taut over perfectly shaped breasts. Sometimes what was only hinted at was far more tantalizing than what was on display.

But Rowden had quickly remembered himself. The mention of Mary had dampened his lust. Mary, who had been dead for ten years now, and who he sometimes believed was only a figment of his imagination. He was a different person than the impetuous boy who'd married her. He was a man now, and a man who knew Miss Brown was no lightskirt to be trifled with. And Rowden didn't want any more from a woman now. Perhaps ever.

Chibale rose and stopped Rowden before he could sit back at the table where they'd been watching the fighting. Madame Renauld's assistant sat there now, her head down to hide the bruised skin near her eye. It would be puffy and swollen in the morning. "I finally got her to admit it," Chibale said, jerking his head toward the table. As soon as the Black Plague had entered the tavern, Chibale had spotted Phaedra and pointed her out to Rowden. She had cowered behind the big prizefighter, keeping her head down and herself out of the way. She reminded Rowden of street dogs he had seen who slinked along back alleys, hoping not to call attention to themselves lest they be kicked.

"Admit what? We all know he did that to her." He cut his eyes to the square, where the men were resting for thirty seconds, and the Black Plague cast a dark look at Chibale and then the assistant at their table.

"Do you know why?"

"He's an arsehole?"

"That and because she tried to call it off. She told him she didn't want to see him any longer and locked herself in her flat. He broke the door down, beat her, raped her—she says *took liberties*—and made her dress and come tonight."

Rowden clenched his fists. He knew a thousand other women in London lived that same story this evening, but it still angered him. It always angered him when the strong picked on the weak. His first fistfight had been in the yard at Eton. His opponent had been a bully who kicked a younger boy, causing the lad to trip and bloody his nose. So Rowden, who had been big for his age, gave the bully a bloody nose.

But it would take more than a bloody nose to stop the Black Plague. "Want me to kill him?" Rowden asked, angry enough that he was only half-joking.

Chibale frowned. "I want you to start preparing for your mill." He tapped Rowden's forehead. "Up here. I'll take care of him."

"On your own? His friends will have his back, and even if you do manage to give them all what for, he'll only break her door down again tomorrow."

"I know someone who will take her in and keep her out of view for a few days. I thought Trogdon could take her out of here while I take the arsehole out back for a word."

Rowden shook his head. Trogdon was currently sitting beside the Black Plague's woman, inspecting a glass of amber liquid with a frown. Rowden had brought the manservant to act as his knee man. Chibale would act as a water man and give him advice during the match.

188 | *Shana Galen*

"That's too much responsibility for Trogdon. He'll muck it up, and this situation is delicate."

"Then what do you suggest? I want her out of here before I take him on."

Rowden looked about the room, his gaze going inadvertently to Miss Brown before he forced it to move away. "Why don't I take her out the back? I'll put her in a hackney to—"

"Madame Renauld's shop."

"Very well. I'll walk right by the ropes, so he sees me with her. When his fight is over, he'll head out that way to look for us. That's when you have your…discussion. I'll wait for you in case you need my help."

Chibale nodded. "I won't need your help, but it's a sound plan. There's still another mill before yours. It should be enough time for you to get back and warmed up."

"A good skirmish always warms me up," Rowden said with a smile, and he felt that old burst of energy flow through him. Lately a mill hadn't given him that excitement, but a fight to protect a woman—that was always a pleasure.

He and Chibale returned to the table and Trogdon set his glass down. "Is it time, sir?" he asked.

"No. Stay where you are and hold the table."

Trogdon gripped the edges of the table with both hands. Rowden sighed. "I mean, don't allow anyone else to sit here." Rowden looked at the woman with one hand covering her swelling eye. "Miss—"

"You can call me Phaedra," she said peering at him with her good eye. "And I know who you are—The Royal Payne." She gave a small smile, and Rowden winced when he saw the cut on her lip split.

"You can call me Rowden," he said. "Our mutual friend"—he gestured to Chibale—"indicated you might be more comfortable elsewhere. Would you allow me to put you in a hackney and pay the fare?"

"He'll only find me if I go home." Her gaze strayed to the fight in the roped area, and there was fear in the way her eyes widened.

Chibale leaned over and whispered something to her. She looked at Rowden again then nodded her head. "Are you ready now, sir?" she asked.

"More than ready, Miss Phaedra." He went to her, pulled out her chair, and offered his arm. She took it and turned toward the nearest exit. Rowden steered her toward the roped off area instead. She gave him a terrified look, and he gave her a steady one back. "This way," he said.

She let out a shaky breath and allowed herself to be led in front of the ropes. She kept her gaze on the floor, but Rowden turned his head to watch the mill. The Black Plague was staring at the two of them, hate in his eyes. A moment later, he issued a dart to his opponent, who swayed but stayed on his feet. And then Rowden was through the crowds and in the kitchens. The cook gave him a look, opened his mouth to scold, and then thought better of it. Rowden tossed the man a coin and led Miss Phaedra out the back door.

The night air bit into his overly warm skin like a tiger. Miss Phaedra held an outer garment, and she dropped Rowden's arm and tried to pull it on. Clearly, she was bruised all over as she struggled. He helped her don the garment, and when tears streamed down her cheeks, he handed her a handkerchief. "None of that now," he said, patting her shoulder awkwardly. "You're stronger than you think."

"I don't feel very strong today."

"You've made it this far," he said. "Now we put you in a hackney and send you to this Madame Renauld. Chibale will come check on you later."

The back door burst open, and Ewan came spilling from it, his wife and Miss Brown right behind him. "Idiot," Ewan said. Miss Phaedra gasped, but Rowden put a hand on her arm.

"They're friends," he said. "Usually."

"Do you want to die?" Ewan asked.

Rowden made a show of looking at his shoes. "If the devil wants to dance, I'm more than ready."

Ewan gestured back toward the Cock and Bull. "He's in a rage, beating that man bloody."

Miss Phaedra gasped and tensed. Rowden shrugged. "Then the plan is working. Ewan, stop a hackney for me, will you? This lady has another appointment tonight."

Ewan looked at Phaedra, assessed the situation, then stalked toward the front of the tavern. Lady Lorraine seemed winded, her wide gaze going from her husband's retreating form to Miss Phaedra and back again. But Miss Brown's brows were pulled together in a look of concern.

"Are you well enough to travel on your own?" she asked. "Should I go with her?"

Rowden almost rejected the idea, but Miss Phaedra was in more pain than she allowed them to see. He had gone from touching her arm to comfort her to holding her up. "Do you mind, Miss Brown?" he asked. "I will come fetch you later and return you to Lady Lorraine's."

"I don't mind at all. Where are we going?"

"My employer's shop," Miss Phaedra said. "Madame Renauld."

"I thought you looked familiar," Lady Lorraine said, coming forward. "Who did this to you? The fighter?"

"Let's talk about it later," Rowden said as Ewan came back and gestured to them to come with him. "He'll be out here as soon as his fight is over, and I'd rather we weren't all standing around."

"Lorrie!" Ewan called, and she lifted her skirts and followed him. He'd stopped two hackneys, and he opened the door of one and gestured to Rowden. Then he led his wife to the other, had a brief discussion with her, and put her in the second. He was sending his wife away, and Rowden was glad of it. If things did not go as Chibale hoped, there could be a riot. Who knew what might happen when men were drunk and excited by shows of violence?

Rowden handed Miss Phaedra into the first hackney then Miss Brown. He held her hand a little longer than was necessary, and when she looked back at him, he pressed some coins into her hand. She looked down. "This is more than the fare."

"I know, but just in case you need it."

She squeezed his hand, and the simple gesture made his heart tighten. He pushed the feeling away. He did not want these emotions. He'd allowed his emotions to rule him once before, and he'd lost everything. Never again.

He released her hand, stepped back, and closed the door. Then he told the driver to take the ladies directly to Madame Renauld's.

The jarvey peered down at him. "She'll be closed this late, guv."

"That's not your concern. See them there safely or I'll come looking for you tomorrow."

"No need for threats, guv. I'll get them there." He made a sound and the horse started away. Ewan came to stand behind him.

"Chibale wants a private discussion with the arsehole," Rowden said.

Ewan shrugged.

"The way I see it, he can have his discussion, but we can also put in a word."

Ewan flexed a fist the size of a boulder. "I find myself with plenty to say."

Rowden put an arm around his shoulders, and the two men made their way back behind the Cock and Bull, where the sounds of raised voices could already be heard.

Ten

Modesty hardly heard where the hackney was headed. She'd been shocked by the condition of the crying woman in the seat beside her. She'd started off across from the woman, whose name she found out was Phaedra, and then when it became clear the woman was sobbing silently, she'd moved to sit beside her.

"You're safe here," Modesty said, patting her back as she might a small child's.

The woman shook her head. "I'll never be safe. He'll never let me go. He said he'd kill me first."

What was Modesty supposed to say to that? It was probably true. "Mr. Payne and Mr. Mostyn will make sure he knows you are protected. He'll leave you alone."

"Mr. Payne is a good man," Phaedra said, raising her tear-streaked face. Modesty handed her a handkerchief. "So many of the milling coves have a mean streak in them. Not him. I thought Jahleel was the same. He was so good to me at first."

Jahleel must be the Christian name of the Black Plague, though it was hard to see anything Christian about a man who made a woman's face look as swollen and bruised as Phaedra's. "You're safe now. You made the right decision to leave him."

"Now." Phaedra gave a bitter laugh. "What about a year from now? Two years? What's to stop him from waiting until I've no one around to protect me and come for me next winter? I'll never be safe."

Modesty had gone on patting Phaedra's back, but the lump in her throat grew so that it became hard to breathe. How many times had she stood with her father and preached to fallen women to leave their evil ways? And how many times had the women scoffed at her? A few had even said things like, "And who'll help me? You?"

Her father had always answered that God would help them, but the women had shaken their heads and walked away.

They'd needed more than platitudes to save them from a life of poverty and whoring. Most had pimps who expected to be paid else the women would be beaten within an inch of their lives. They couldn't just walk away and hope God would protect them. Where would they go? How would they survive and feed their children? How ridiculous Modesty had been and how presumptuous. To stand on a box and think she knew more about those women's lives than they did.

And her father...her father had been lying the entire time. He'd been preaching against fornication, all the while practicing it himself for years. She'd always liked Bible stories where God humbled the mighty, but it didn't feel so good when she was being humbled.

"We'll think of something," Modesty said, but she had no idea if she could ever think of anything. And if she couldn't find her aunt or her aunt wouldn't take her in, what was to stop Modesty from becoming just like the women she'd railed against all those years? She had no way to earn a wage. She could sew, but would that make enough to pay for a house and food? And who would protect her if her landlord decided he wanted to take payment in another form?

The hackney stopped, and Modesty peered out the window at the dark windows of a shop with a sign above it reading *Madame Renauld's*.

"Where are we?" she asked.

"The modiste. I work here." Phaedra opened the door and climbed out and Modesty followed.

"Cove said I was to make sure ye got in safely," the jarvey said. "So I'll wait until yer in."

Phaedra steered Modesty to the shop door. "I'll go in around the back. You wait here, and I'll come through the shop and let you in."

Modesty nodded and stood in the doorway, shivering with cold. It seemed hours passed as she stood in the dark with the gaze of the jarvey upon her, and then finally the door opened, and a woman who was not Phaedra, but who was dressed just as elegantly, opened the door. "Come in, *chérie*." She waved to the jarvey then closed and locked the door behind Modesty.

"Come to the back with me. I want no light seen in the windows."

Modesty followed the woman through a shop like those she had passed many times. She'd always stared at the windows and the expensive hats and lace and fabrics. She'd never been inside. The place smelled of lavender and floor polish. Several tables were spaced about the shop floor, each with a dizzying assortment of beautiful things—ribbons and velvets and dress forms adorned with lovely gowns. Modesty couldn't see very well in the dim light, and she had to force herself to keep walking instead of stopping to touch the silks and satins and hold them to her nose.

Finally, she was led through a corridor and into a back room, which was much more austere with white walls and no embellishment. Tables lined the walls, and each was a neat workstation. Modesty understood at once this was where the seamstresses worked. She sewed her own clothing and recognized the tools arranged neatly about the room.

A boy of about twelve had made a bed in the corner of the room and was sitting, rubbing his eyes. Modesty smiled at him, but he looked annoyed to have been roused from his sleep. Phaedra had taken a seat in one of the chairs at a worktable. The elegantly dressed woman turned and studied Modesty as she entered. "You are Payne's woman, *oui*?"

"We?"

"It's French for *yes*," Phaedra told her. "This is Madame Renauld. She's a modiste."

Modesty nodded politely at the modiste. She had dark hair piled elegantly on top of her head with a section trailing over her shoulder in glossy black curls. This was similar to the style Lady Lorraine's maid had wanted to create for Modesty. She almost wished she'd consented because it was an attractive style. But even if her hair had been sleep-tangled, this woman would have been beautiful. She had luminous skin burnished the color of copper in the lamplight and large brown eyes with arched brows that seemed to hint at amusement.

"I'm not Mr. Payne's woman," Modesty said. "He is…" She didn't know how to finish. What was he to her, exactly?

"That ees a pity," the modiste said. "He ees a handsome man." She looked at Phaedra. "But sometimes looks can be deceiving, *oui*?" She knelt before Phaedra. "You look worse than you did yesterday, *ma fille.*"

"I tried to leave him," Phaedra said. "I tried, but…" Her voice broke, and she began to sob again.

Madame Renauld did not embrace the other woman or pat her back as Modesty had. Instead, she stood and straightened her shoulders. "He will not touch you again. If Payne and Okoro do not stop him, then I have my own methods."

Modesty could only wonder what those might be as the woman said nothing more. She went into another room and returned a moment later with a folded paper. "Boy," she said, and the child on the pallet rose and walked sleepily to her.

"Name is Twig," he muttered.

"Twig ees not a name. I told you to give me a real name or I will call you boy. Do you have a real name?" She looked down at the child, hands on her hips.

"Name is Twig," the child said.

Madame Renauld sighed. "A man or two will come late tonight. They may be together or come separately. Show them thees paper when they knock."

The boy took the paper. "How am I supposed to know it's the man you want and not a ruffian?"

"Ruffians do not knock," Madame Renauld said. "You can do thees, *oui*?"

"Alright."

"Come with me then," Madame Renauld said, gesturing to Modesty and Phaedra. "You are safe here, but we will be safer in my apartments. They are not far."

Before Modesty could consider whether she should stay here or go with the modiste, the woman was already shooing her out the door and leading the other two through a wide alley lined by doors to other shops. Once on the street, she led them over one block and then into a building and up a flight of stairs. Producing a key from her reticule, she opened the door to a small entryway where she hung her coat and Modesty's cloak. The entryway opened into another room, a parlor of sorts that Modesty saw more clearly when Madame Renauld lit a lamp. Modesty's eyes must have widened because the modiste laughed. "Have you never seen a sitting room, *chérie*?"

"Not like this."

The room was painted a sapphire blue with couches and one of those chaise longues placed in a cozy arrangement on a gold rug. The furnishings were in jewel tones of ruby and amethyst and the fabrics were sumptuous velvets and satins. It looked a room that belonged in the palace of King David.

"But what are you wearing?" the modiste asked, coming closer to inspect Modesty's dress. "Thees is not a gown for the evening. I do not think it was made for you either. The fit ees not quite right."

"A friend allowed me to borrow it," Modesty said. "My own dress is more…" Funereal? "Subdued."

"More subdued than thees?" Madame Renauld asked. "If I were to dress you, I would put you in greens or purples. You have the coloring for it. I think you could even do red. Yes, a bold, deep red. Not scarlet but the red of currants or wine."

Modesty shook her head. "I could never wear red."

The modiste lifted a shoulder. "We shall see. Now, you must make yourself comfortable. I will put Phaedra to bed."

"Madame, no. That's not necessary," Phaedra said, though she was practically asleep on her feet.

"No arguments," the modiste said. "To bed with you. And you will stay there until I tell you to rise. Do not even think of coming to the shop tomorrow. I have half a mind to close for the day."

"But Madame, the Countess of Blinn has an appointment."

"Ah, of course. We cannot disappoint the countess."

Their voices tapered off as they moved into another room and then behind a closed door. Modesty looked about and tried to decide where to sit. She finally decided on a plush chair upholstered in emerald velvet. It was close to the fire, and she took the poker and stirred it until it came back to life. She would have added coal as there was a full bin nearby, but she did not know if the modiste rationed her coal and had used her supply for the day.

She closed her eyes and thought back over the events of the past few days. Lady Lorraine had been so kind. Her husband was terrifying as usual. And Mr. Payne. It was hard not to see Mr. Payne every time she closed her eyes. His eyes were the green of the chair she occupied. She hadn't seen him fight, but he'd been in only a coat and linen shirt at the Cock and Bull, and she had seen the strong lines of his neck and width of his shoulders. She'd watched his mouth as he spoke and wondered what it would be like to kiss that mouth.

She would never know. She had hurt him with the mention of his wife. She'd done so inadvertently. She hadn't known the woman was dead. And she certainly shouldn't feel about it as she did—relieved? Almost…happy?

But there was no point in fantasizing. If she was fortunate, she would find her aunt. If she were not, she had years of a workhouse to look forward to.

Or worse.

***

Ewan patted Rowden on the back and smiled. Since one of Ewan's pats was akin to a blow from a racing stallion, Rowden had to struggle not to fall flat on his face. "Just like old times, eh?" Rowden said, smiling back at his friend.

Rowden surveyed the three men crawling away on the dirty ground. The Black Plague had started the fight strong, but he'd been tired from his mill in the tavern and hadn't lasted long against Rowden. His two friends had been easily knocked down by Ewan, and they'd wisely decided to stay down.

Rowden went to the Plague and crouched beside him. "As I told you earlier, I think you need a holiday. Do you prefer Scotland or the Continent?"

The man turned his bruised face—most of the bruising due to his earlier fight—to glare at Rowden. "The Continent."

"My friend here will put you on a ship tonight." He leaned closer so no one else would hear. "And if you ever come back and so much as pass within a mile of Miss Phaedra, I'll kill you myself."

He stood and wiped his hands on his trousers. "He'd like a sea voyage," he told Ewan. "Can you escort him to the docks and put him on a ship?"

"Can I hit him again?"

"Not unless he provokes you."

Ewan slammed a fist into his palm. "Too easy."

"Not as much challenge without the snipers shooting at us."

Ewan laughed, and Rowden shook his head. He would have never thought one day they would be laughing over the times they'd almost been killed in the war. At the time, he hadn't minded being labeled *expendable*. He was the disinherited younger son of a duke with three older brothers and little chance of ever inheriting the title. Most men still wouldn't have wanted to die, but Rowden had just lost his wife—the woman for whom he'd relinquished his name, his family, and his position. He'd loved her more than life itself, and death seemed easier than living in those days.

Now he was thankful for the times Ewan had protected his back while Nash covered them with his rifle. He was thankful for all the times Stratford had devised a strategy that saved their lives or Phineas negotiated for more provisions or Rafe collected information that helped them avoid ambush. It was a cold, dark night in February, and he stood in a filthy alley with stinging knuckles, but he was glad to be alive.

The tavern door opened and Chibale stepped out. "Warmed up?" he asked, surveying the men on the ground.

Rowden nodded. He'd almost forgotten he still had a mill. "Mostyn will take our friend to the docks. He's opted for a trip abroad."

"I'll take him," Chibale said.

"But he might provoke me," Ewan protested, sounding disappointed.

"If he provokes me, I'll hit him for you," Chibale promised. "Can you coach Rowden in the mill against Strong?"

"I'll be fine," Rowden said.

"I'm not leaving you with only Trogdon for support."

"I'll stay," Ewan told Chibale. He gave the man on the ground a last look before opening the door. Ewan followed Rowden back through the kitchens and into the tavern, now so full of people they must be spilling out into the streets. The roped off area wasn't raised, and Rowden couldn't see the progress of the mill, but he could hear the groans, which usually signified the beginning of the end.

Ewan started through the crowd, and Rowden followed, but he'd gone no more than three or four steps when a man stepped in front of him. "Mr. Notley. I think you'll find your man outside, lying in the gutter where he belongs."

Notley's perpetually red face turned redder still. He was a short man with a bulbous nose, unruly black hair, and bushy side whiskers. When Rowden had begun to catch the notice of the Fancy in the boxing world, Notley had approached him with an offer to manage his career. It had been more of an order, really—*I'll be managing you from now on.*

Rowden had declined the offer in less than polite terms. A few months later, he had asked Chibale to manage him, and Notley had taken it personally. They'd been on rocky footing ever since. Now Notley had lost all his prizefighters to injury, cheating scandals, or drink, and he had only the Black Plague left. Or at least he had before now.

"If you and that blockhead damaged his right hand—" Notley began.

"His hand should be fine, but he won't be fighting for you anytime soon. He's taking an unexpected trip abroad."

Notley stared at Rowden, his mouth dropping open and his face turning such a dark shade of crimson it verged on purple. "Why, you—"

"Stop right there," Rowden said. "No need to say anything you'll regret. Your man had a heavy hand with the ladies. Since you did nothing to curb those bad tendencies, someone else had to step in."

"Is this about that whore he's been seeing?"

"I'll have to ask you to watch your language. The lady is employed by Madame Renauld, and Mr. Okoro will not take kindly to any disparagement of her name or that of her employees."

Rowden was still feeling exhilarated from the fight, and he'd known he was preening just a bit too much. But right then he realized he'd said too much. Notley's eyes narrowed, and Rowden wished he'd kept his mouth shut. He shouldn't have brought the modiste into this.

"Payne," Ewan said from behind him. He'd obviously realized Rowden wasn't right behind him and had come back. "Let's go."

"Right." Rowden gave Notley one last look and followed Ewan back to the table where Trogdon was looking about. Trogdon stood, looked at his chair then under the table then lifted a glass and checked under it. "What are you about

Trogdon?" Rowden asked, pulling his coat off and sitting to remove his boots. He would fight bare-knuckled and barefoot, wearing only breeches and a growl.

"I can't find the oranges, sir," Trogdon answered, his face long and his expression regretful. "I suppose you will have to let me go."

Rowden could have let him go a dozen times over for more cause than losing oranges at a mill. But he eyed the bulging pockets of Trogdon's coat. "Have you checked your coat, Trogdon?"

"Yes, sir. I put them in the pockets, but somehow they made their way out again."

Rowden pulled off his stockings. "Check again, Trogdon."

Trogdon patted his pockets, discovered the oranges and produced one from the left and one from the right. "I say, sir! You've found them."

"So I have."

The tavern owner came by then and leaned down. "Ready, sir?"

"I'm ready." Rowden stood and pulled his shirt over his head. Abraham Strong was already at the ropes and Rowden looked at Ewan. "Are you coming?"

Ewan was staring at Trogdon as though he couldn't quite believe the man was serious about the oranges, but he nodded and followed Ewan to the ropes. Trogdon plodded after him, holding an orange tightly in each hand. The tavern owner was introducing the final milling coves of the evening, though Rowden and Strong needed no introduction. Still it gave the patrons a last chance to place their wagers, and since the winner would receive not only the prizemoney but a portion of the stakes, Rowden was in no hurry to begin. He held out a hand to Trogdon, who placed an orange in it. After peeling it, Rowden ate it in three bites then took water from the cup Ewan offered.

He spotted Aidan in the crowd and nodded to the man. Aidan was a shrewd investor who rarely lost in speculation or wagering, so Rowden hoped his friend had bet on him. Being that Aidan was a man who put money above just about everything else, Rowden didn't expect loyalty.

Ewan leaned close. "Hit him hard and end this quickly. I'm ready to go home."

Rowden was ready too. He would have to fetch Miss Brown and take her to Mostyn's before he could go home, but he found himself eager to see her again. She'd still be wearing the blue dress, and he wanted to see if she looked as good in it as he remembered. He was allowed to look, even if looking only made him wish he could touch.

Rowden climbed under the ropes and met Strong in the middle. The two men shook hands and went to their corners. Rowden had nothing against Strong. He was a fair fighter and a good one at that. They were evenly matched, but something told Rowden he would win the fight. Maybe it was the blood still thrumming through his veins after the sight of Miss Brown and the warmup tousle with the Black Plague. Maybe it was the confidence Ewan exuded behind him. Maybe it was the way Aidan sat back at a table beside the ropes and crossed his arms, looking at Rowden smugly, as though he knew Rowden would make him a pretty penny tonight.

When the umpire rang the bell, Rowden was ready. He stepped forward shuffling a bit to keep his muscles warm. Strong looked eager too. That was the problem with fighting last. One was impatient to finally have a crack at the other fellow.

Strong threw a test punch, missing Rowden. But that hadn't been the point. The point was to see how Rowden reacted. He leaned back just enough to avoid the blow but didn't overreact or shuffle backward. He didn't intend to give Strong a warning shot. He intended to do as Ewan said and hit hard and fast. The two went around the ring, Strong throwing increasingly more serious punches and Rowden easily evading. The crowd began to protest. They wanted to see blood. Rowden didn't intend to disappoint. He made to shuffle left then shifted right and threw a quick jab to Strong's midsection. When Strong reared back in surprise, Rowden caught him in the chin when his head arced forward.

Strong went down and the umpire separated the men and sent them to their corners. The crowd cheered, and Rowden took a seat on Trogdon's offered knee. Ewan handed him a cup of water, and he drank. He looked up. "Well?" he said.

Ewan looked at him.

"Don't you have any praise?"

"No."

"Censure?" Rowden asked.

"No."

"Advice?"

"Keep hitting him."

"Remind me to tell Chibale to never again allow you to take his place."

"Another orange, sir?" Trogdon asked, sounding pained at Rowden's weight on his knee.

"Not yet," Rowden said, rising as the bell sounded again. He was once again face-to-face with Strong, but this time the man had blood in his eyes. Good. Anger made it difficult to focus, and that worked to Rowden's benefit. He let Strong tire himself by throwing more punches, which Rowden avoided. Not all of them were easy to avoid, but he was quick on his feet.

The crowd booed again, but Rowden didn't fancy a split lip to give them a good show. Strong threw another punch. Rowden ducked and went under it then came up behind Strong, wrapped an arm about his neck, lifted him off the ground, and slammed him down. There were very few rules in a fight like this, but Rowden wouldn't stoop to kicking a man when he was down. He waited to punch Strong when he crawled to his feet, but the umpire shoved him into his corner.

Ewan held out another cup of water, looking increasingly bored. "Stop playing with him."

Rowden took the proffered orange from Trogdon and tried to catch his breath. "I'm not playing with him. He's good."

Ewan rolled his eyes to show what he thought of that assessment.

"Look," Rowden said between bites of orange, which he forced down so he didn't have to taste it, "I want to go home as well. I still have to fetch Miss Brown and deliver her back to you. The sooner I finish him, the closer I am to Hungerford and the German." And the closer he was to seeing Miss

Brown in that blue dress again. "So if you have any suggestions, I'm all ears." He ate the last of the orange and wiped his fingers on a towel.

Ewan leaned down, and Rowden almost stepped back, half afraid Mostyn would punch him for challenging him.

"He favors his right side," Ewan said quietly. "He always offers his left."

Rowden considered. He thought about the way Strong moved. He did angle his body to present the left side, which was unusual as Strong was not left-handed. "Was he hurt on the right?" Rowden asked.

Ewan shrugged. Chibale would have known, but Chibale wasn't here.

"Hit him on the right," Ewan said.

Aidan appeared next to the ropes. "So what's the plan? Should I double my wager?"

"How much have you wagered on me already?" Rowden asked.

Aidan gave a number that had even Ewan's brows shooting up.

"And how much on him?" Rowden shot a thumb toward Strong, who was still eating his orange.

Aidan smiled. "Not as much."

"Cagey bastard," Rowden said. "Yes. Double your bet and hurry up. Ewan has other plans for the evening."

The umpire called for the next round. Rowden started for the center of the square even as Ewan made a show of checking his pocket watch.

Strong looked to have recovered from the last round. He was moving quickly, and Rowden watched carefully. The other milling cove definitely angled his left side forward, which was inefficient since he then had to punch with his right arm. It made him slower and was probably part of the reason Rowden had easily dodged his strikes. Well, maybe not *easily*. Rowden saw the way to bring Strong down now. He could wait until the man tired and his protection of his right side flagged. Or he could trick Strong into exposing his right and end this fight right now.

He glanced at Ewan who stood with arms crossed, pocket watch swinging impatiently from one hand. If Rowden hadn't been anxious to go home as well, he would have made Ewan wait just to annoy the man.

Instead, he moved forward carelessly, giving Strong an opening to punch him. Strong took it, and Rowden didn't move back to lessen the blow. The punch glanced off his cheek and sent a bloom of pain through to the back of his head and then down to his very toes. But he took the punch and when Strong's hand glanced away, his right was fully exposed. Rowden punched and punched hard. He hit Strong on the right side of his jaw with the first punch and then in the ribs with the second. The ribs were the source of the problem for Strong. Rowden felt Strong crumple as soon as his fist made contact.

The man went down, and he didn't get up again.

The umpire raised Rowden's hand and declared him the victor. The room cheered, but Rowden looked down at Strong, still lying on the floor of the dirty tavern and saw himself in a few years. He felt no pleasure in his victory.

He collected his winnings and his share of the stakes coldly and then joined Ewan and Aidan outside. Trogdon would already be on his way home, tasked with readying the flat for Rowden's return.

"How's your face?" Aidan asked when Rowden emerged into the brisk night.

Rowden had forgot about it, but at Aidan's suggestion, the pain reemerged. "Hurts like hell."

"You'll have a blooming rose on that cheek tomorrow," Aidan said. "But now you're bound for Hungerford and another shot at the German."

"Will you be attending?" Rowden asked. "Or do you need to buy up the other half of London that week?"

Aidan smiled. "I can take a few days off. London will still be here when I return. I've already asked my secretary to write to Nicholas to ask if we can make use of his spare chambers for a few days."

Rowden nodded and looked at Ewan. "Are you coming?"

Ewan shook his head. "I'll make one of my carriages available," Aidan offered. "You could bring your wife."

Everyone in Town knew about Aidan's carriages. They were widely touted as the epitome of comfort and style. Some said they were the pinnacle of ostentation, since no one really needed a carriage so lavishly equipped. But Aidan had spent the first part of his life on the streets until his uncle, the new marquess, had taken his illegitimate nephew in. And a few years later, Aidan had joined the army and spent years with Draven's troop, sleeping on the ground in rain, sleet, and snow. Rowden could hardly blame Aidan for wanting his comforts now. And if Aidan was offering to share, Rowden wouldn't turn down his friend's generosity.

"I'll take that offer," Rowden said. "If Nicholas won't have us, we can always sleep in the carriage."

Aidan wrinkled his nose, though Rowden knew at least one of his carriages had a seat that pulled out wide enough to convert to a small bed.

"Leave the accommodations to me," Aidan said. "I know you have family obligations, Mostyn. Rowden, fancy a drink?"

"Not tonight," Rowden said. He didn't want to explain that he had obligations as well.

"You don't want to celebrate your victory? Very well. I'll celebrate for you."

A hackney pulled up then, and Aidan jumped forward and claimed it. Ewan growled, and Aidan waved, seeming to take pleasure in having beaten Ewan to it. But that was Aidan. He liked to win.

Ewan signaled to another hackney and, as it pulled up, he looked at Rowden. "A large purse offered in Hungerford."

Rowden nodded. Talking to Ewan was sometimes like talking to a wall, but Rowden asked anyway. "How do you know when you're finished?"

Ewan shrugged. "I was never a bare-knuckle fighter."

"But you walked away from Langley's."

Langley's was a gaming hell Ewan had owned a share in. Mostly he'd served as the strong man who threw out those who'd over imbibed or tried to start brawls. But he'd sold his share and bought the boxing studio with Colonel Draven. Now he was his own man and seemed happier than ever before. Of course, Ewan rarely showed any emotion, but Rowden assumed he was happier.

Ewan opened the door to the hackney, and Rowden thought he might not answer. But then he looked back, his focus somewhere far away. "When it loses its shine," he said and climbed into the hackney then sped away.

Eleven

Once Phaedra was put to bed, Madame Renauld returned to the sitting room. But she was far from easy. She paced and checked the window and paced more. She'd poured tea for Modesty and herself, but she hadn't touched her own cup. Modesty had drunk hers, mainly to keep warm until the room heated up after Madame Renauld built up the fire again.

Somewhere in the house a clock chimed one, and Modesty heard a squawk. "Was that a bird?" she asked, desperate to say something to end the tense silence.

"*Oui*. Bleuette, my parrot. Her cage ees covered, but she likes to echo the chimes."

"I didn't realize you had a parrot. I've never seen one."

Madame Renauld sat on the edge of a chair upholstered in amethyst and lifted her teacup. "You should come to my shop. You can meet her and be fitted for a dress that will leave men unable to look away from you."

Modesty raised her brows. "I'm not sure I want men unable to look away from me."

"Ah," Madame said. "You are like me. I must blend in lest I upstage my customers."

Modesty looked at this woman and wondered how she ever blended in. She was so beautiful.

"But surely there ees some man you want to look at you," Madame Renauld said, sipping what must by now be cold tea.

Modesty didn't speak, but she could feel her cheeks heating.

"Perhaps the fighter. Payne," Madame said, eyeing Modesty over the rim of her cup. "Phaedra said he would come to fetch you."

"He's been very kind," Modesty said. "I think he must feel sorry for me."

"Perhaps," Madame said, but she looked unconvinced.

"In any case, I won't trouble him again after tonight. He has done quite enough for me."

"I see."

Modesty heard the sound of a coach approaching, and she and Madame Renauld rose and went to the window overlooking the street. When Mr. Payne alighted from the conveyance, her heart beat a little faster, but she noticed the modiste slumped slightly. She wondered who the other woman was expecting but did not ask.

A moment later a knock sounded at the door, and Madame went to answer it then ushered Mr. Payne into the chamber. The sitting room, which had looked so spacious and cozy before, now seemed too small and cramped. Mr. Payne seemed to fill it, and when he came into the light, she spotted the dark bruise on his cheek.

"Did you win?" Madame Renauld asked, after introductions were made.

He grinned then winced and touched his cheek. Clearly the bruise pained him. "Of course." He jiggled his coat, which jingled from the weight of the purse holding the coins in his pocket. Then his expression grew more serious. "How is your assistant?"

"She ees sleeping. I gave her some tea laced with brandy."

"The best thing for the swelling is a cold compress. If she can stand it, apply ice wrapped in cloth for a quarter hour." He glanced at the window. "It should be cold enough to turn water to ice tonight if you put out a pan."

"I'll do that. *Merci.*" She glanced at the window. "Ees Mr. Okoro not with you?"

Mr. Payne's brow drew down. "No. He had…" He glanced at Modesty. "Some other business. I thought he would have finished by now, but his errand took him to the docks, and it might take some time to drive back. I can wait with you—"

"No, monsieur. This poor lady ees weary. You must take her home and see to your own injuries."

He nodded but pulled a card out of his waistcoat, which he wore unbuttoned under his coat. "Send for me if you need anything."

"*Merci.* You are very kind." She gave Modesty a pointed look. "And you, *chérie.* You must come to the shop. Bring her, monsieur. I will make her a dress you will not soon forget."

Mr. Payne bowed and looked at Modesty. "Miss Brown, are you ready?"

She nodded and took his arm. He led her out of the flat and into the street, where the hackney still waited. Once in the vehicle, she missed the warmth of his body pressed against hers as it had been in the narrow passageway. She burrowed deep into Lady Lorraine's cloak and tried not to think about how this was the last time she might ever see him. But if it were, she needed to apologize to him.

"I am sorry about this evening," she said. He'd been looking out the window, but he moved to face her.

"I won. There's nothing to be sorry for."

"No. I am sorry for what I said. About your wife. I didn't know, and it was careless to—"

He held up a hand. "She died a long time ago."

Modesty nodded. "I understand, but that is no excuse for my carelessness." She looked out the window. "And time does not always dull the pain."

She didn't know why she'd said that. She hadn't meant to say anything of the sort, but she was thinking of her own mother so much these last few days. Mr. Payne hadn't replied, and she thought he might allow the comment to pass unacknowledged.

"You speak as from experience," he said.

Apparently, the comment would not go unacknowledged.

"My mother died when I was five. I miss her still, though some would say I hardly knew her." After reading the letters and discovering her mother had known of her father's unfaithfulness, Modesty did feel she hadn't known her mother. "And perhaps I didn't."

"Was there something in the letters that troubled you?"

Modesty was sorely tempted to tell him that, yes, something in the letters had troubled her very much. But she was not ready to reveal her father's sins to Rowden Payne.

"They mentioned my mother only in passing. There was nothing about my aunt."

"What happened to your black clothing and that awful hat you usually wear?"

Modesty shrugged, a gesture she had never been allowed to make before. Her father considered it the height of rudeness. But what did she care what he thought now? She'd wanted to be a woman like her mother, a woman he would respect and love. But he hadn't respected her mother at all. "I don't see the point of dressing in black."

Payne's brows went up. "I thought your church dictated it?"

"They dictate modest dress, but it does not have to be black. My father and mother always dressed in black and dressed me thus as well. But I don't see the point in adhering to those strictures anymore."

He sat back. "Whatever was in those letters must have shocked you."

She looked out the window again. "I don't wish to discuss them." And that pledge lasted all of three heartbeats. "But have you ever believed one thing about someone and then it turned out that you were wrong? They were not the person you thought at all?"

She felt ridiculous for saying such a thing. How could anyone possibly understand what it was like to feel as though she had lived with a stranger her entire life? Her father was not who she thought. He had another family!

"Yes. I can understand that. My own father turned out to be very different from the man I always supposed him to be."

"I don't mean to pry," she said.

He waved a hand. "You have probably heard the duke disowned me. No doubt you think I did something to deserve it."

She shook her head. "On the contrary, I heard you were a war hero."

He gave her a faint smile. "That might be overstating it somewhat. But I fought in the war after I was cut off. And all the accolades heaped on me in the prevailing years did nothing to sway my father."

"I'm so sorry."

"Again, it is not your doing, and there is nothing to apologize for." The hackney stopped, and the jarvey called down that there was some sort of obstacle ahead.

"I'll see if I can find a way around, guv."

"If I may?" Payne said and moved across the conveyance to sit beside her and peer out the window. As he had occupied the rear-facing seat, he hadn't been able to see ahead of them. Now he lowered the window, peering out and frowning. The conveyance bounced, and she fell against him, righting herself quickly, but not so quickly that she didn't feel the warmth of his body or catch the scent of him.

She did not know what a warrior might smell like, but if she had to guess, she would have said it was the scent of Mr. Payne that evening. She detected a mixture of sweat, blood, wool, and—strangely—oranges. The scent wasn't unpleasant, as she might have expected. In fact, it drew her closer. The voice that always arose in her mind bubbled up again, telling her she should sit back and move away.

But Modesty pushed it away instead. Following all the rules had not kept her mother alive or made her father a faithful husband. Following the rules had not kept Modesty from being abandoned and becoming, essentially, homeless and penniless. What did it matter now if she moved away from him or allowed herself to soak up the heat and scent of him a moment longer?

He sat back and looked at her. "An overturned cart. They are already clearing it."

She nodded, unable to speak. She couldn't see the color of his eyes in the dim light, but she knew they were a lovely shade of green. She also knew he had a bruise forming on his cheek, but she couldn't see that either. Right now all she could see was his strong jaw and mostly straight nose. He was warm, his big body taking up more than half the seat, one of his thighs pressing against hers through layers of linen and wool.

He looked at her for a long moment then cleared his throat. "I should move back." But he didn't move, and she didn't speak. The hackney lurched to a start, and he caught her shoulders with both hands before she could tumble to the floor. Then the vehicle stopped again, and she was only cushioned by the fact that he held on to her. It took a moment before she realized she could feel his hands on her arms, and she looked down to see her cloak had come loose and fallen off her shoulders.

"Allow me," he said. He pulled the cloak up and over her shoulders then crossed the ribbons that had come loose at her neck. But instead of making a bow, his hands stayed where they were and one finger trailed along the bare skin just below her neck. Modesty gasped, but she did not pull away. Payne's gaze met hers. "I neglected to tell you how well you looked in this dress tonight."

230 | *Shana Galen*

She couldn't reply. She didn't know what to say, and even if she had, she didn't think she could have produced the sound. She wanted him to kiss her. She knew she shouldn't want that, and she had never wanted something like that before, but he was so close and so warm, and that one finger left a trail of fire over her bare skin. And then both his hands slid back, letting the cloak fall away again, and he leaned forward and placed a chaste kiss at the base of her throat. His soft lips pressed against her bare skin, causing her to tremble. She couldn't say why she should tremble. She was not cold—in fact, she was very, very warm—and she was not afraid. He would stop if she gave the slightest indication that she disapproved. So why should she tremble?

He looked up at her. "I shouldn't have done that. I'm not myself. After a fight, I always find it hard to be a gentleman."

"Your blood is stirred?" she said, her voice low and husky. She hardly recognized it as her own.

"Agitated," he murmured.

Had he gone home to his wife after boxing matches years ago and found a release for that excess passion in their bed? Was he looking for that same release now?

She reached up and touched his bruise, very lightly. He did not flinch, did not move as her hands slid down his cheek and over his jaw and then up to press two fingers over his lips, tugging the lower one down as she moved away again.

"You're trembling," he said, still holding her.

"I've never been kissed," she admitted.

He shook his head. "I shouldn't be the man to—"

She swallowed and dropped her hand. "I didn't mean to suggest—I would never ask you to do something you don't want—"

"Oh, I want," he said, and the tone of his voice left no question as to that fact.

"Then why do you hesitate?"

If she'd expected a spoken answer, it didn't come. He lowered his head to hers, his lips almost brushing hers. "Do you want, Miss Brown?"

"Yes," she whispered. And then she did something that would have shocked her but a week ago. She took his face between her hands and kissed him.

***

Rowden's belly tightened, and his cock hardened. These were familiar sensations—arousal and desire. But his heart clenched in his chest, and that was unfamiliar. That he had not felt in a very long time. He knew why he felt it now. The way she kissed him was so sweet, so innocent.

Her lips pressed against his as tenderly as a child might kiss the cheek of her parent.

And it moved him. It moved him that she would give him this part of herself, this sweet, untouched part of herself. Her first kiss. It felt like his first kiss, the way her lips almost baptized him of his previous sins.

The kiss might have stayed chaste if the arousal wasn't flowing through his veins along with the hot blood from the fights earlier that night. He needed more than this, and he was curious what her reaction would be if he opened the door, just a little, to the passion and pleasure beyond.

He pulled back, and her brow pulled in. Her hands dropped. "Was that not right?"

"It was…" He didn't have the words. "It was perfect," he said, allowing his hands to slide down her slim shoulders. She'd almost stopped trembling. "May I kiss you now?"

She nodded.

"The words, Miss Brown. Tell me *yes*."

"Yes." The word was a whisper, and her eyelids fluttered closed as she waited. He slid his hands up her back then bent to kiss her neck again. Her pulse beat so hard he could feel it against his lips. Her breath came quickly, so quickly that if he'd pulled her just a bit closer, her breasts would have heaved against him. He tried to remember he was a gentleman, despite his cock's best efforts to convince him otherwise. Rowden trailed his lips up the column of her neck, and she let out a little gasp of pleasure. Rowden paused just under her chin at that rapidly beating pulse point. And then his hand was in her hair and his mouth found hers, and it was as though he had been kissing her for years. Their mouths fit perfectly, and her lips parted to receive him without him even having to nudge for entrance. She didn't kiss him back at first, but he showed her what to do, and when he paused, she imitated the press of his lips and the pressure he'd used.

God how he *wanted*. He wanted to sweep his tongue inside her mouth and taste her. He wanted to pull her onto his lap and run his hands under her skirts. He wanted to touch her in that hot, wet place he knew must be aching right now.

She was so sweet, so delicate, so innocent—and he was not the man who should be taking any part of that innocence. He'd done enough. Even as kisses went, this was only one step away from chaste, but it was more than he should be allowed. He pulled away, pressing his lips to her temple and then her forehead because he couldn't stop touching her quite yet, and he didn't trust himself to move his lips lower. That straining bodice was all too tempting.

He looked down at her and wished, with everything he had, that he had a lamp. Her face was flushed and her hair slightly mussed, and he could sense how beautiful she would look in warm candlelight.

"That is kissing?" she asked, her voice sounding low and raw as though she'd just awakened. He wanted to kiss her again just hearing it.

"More or less," he answered.

At some point, perhaps when they were kissing, the carriage had begun to move again. Now he looked past her and out the window and saw they were close to Ewan's home. "We're almost there." He pulled her cloak up and tied the ribbons efficiently then reached to smooth her hair before thinking better of it. The less he touched her, the better. Instead, he drew the hood of the cloak over her head. Her hair would seem mussed from the fabric rubbing against it rather than his hands.

"Is this good-bye?" she asked, sitting up and starting to resemble the prim and proper young miss he'd seen that first night.

"I think that's for the best," he said because he didn't want it to be good-bye any more than she. "Lady Lorraine will help you find your aunt, and I have to prepare for the mill in Hungerford."

"Hungerford?" She sat up as though she'd just sat on a pin.

"Yes. I'm to fight the German there. There are other renowned pugilists slated to fight, and since it's likely to draw enough Fancy to attract the attention of the magistrates in London, it's being held in Hungerford."

The coach slowed and the jarvey banged on the top. "Here ye are, guv!"

Rowden opened the coach door and helped her out. At the Mostyn's door, he rapped quietly, and a manservant answered immediately. He had obviously been instructed to wait for Miss Brown to return. He stepped back to give them privacy.

She turned to go in then hesitated. "I can't thank you and your friends enough for what you've done for me. I…" She looked down. "I admit I misjudged you."

"You thought I was a criminal," he said, smiling.

She started to shake her head. "Well, yes. But you must admit, boxing is illegal, so technically, you *are* a criminal."

Rowden bowed. "And so we end as we began. Good night, Miss Brown."

"Good night."

Rowden went back to the hackney and ordered the jarvey to take him to his flat. Normally, he might go to his club or a tavern and celebrate his victory. He could never sleep right after a fight. The thrill often did not wear off for days.

But tonight Rowden didn't want crowds and drink and buxom women on his lap. He couldn't imagine kissing another woman after that kiss with Modesty Brown.

Rowden could only hope that thrill would wear off eventually as well.

Twelve

The lad who had answered the back door at Madame Renauld's shop had shown Chibale a letter with the address of this modest building just a few blocks away and instructions to knock on the door where he stood at the moment. Chibale certainly hoped this wasn't some sort of trick because if Madame Renauld—Thérèse—did not answer, Chibale imagined whoever did would be rather annoyed to be wakened after four in the morning.

He tapped lightly on the door, waited approximately three seconds, then turned to go. Behind him the door opened.

"Monsieur?"

He turned back to find Madame Renauld—he dared not think of her as Thérèse in that moment—standing in the doorway in an elegant gold silk robe, her hair in a braid curving over one shoulder.

"It's late. I shouldn't have disturbed you," he said.

She waved his apology away and opened the door wider. "I have been waiting for you. Come in."

Chibale did not need to be asked twice. She closed the door behind him, took his coat, then led him into a beautiful parlor with furnishings in colors he had never imagined before. "Please sit." She sat on a chair of ruby red and lifted a teapot. "Tea? I made a new pot not long ago, and it ees still warm."

"Yes, thank you." Chibale didn't want tea, but he needed something to do with his hands. Holding a teacup was better than nothing. He took a seat on an emerald green chair and tried not to stare at her. The material of her robe draped elegantly, but it was thin and left little doubt that she wore only the flimsiest nightgown underneath—if that. He didn't want to stare too closely, but he was a man, and she was a beautiful woman.

She poured the tea, asked how he preferred it, then rose to hand him the cup. She settled back in her ruby seat and raised her brows. "Well?" she asked. "Will you tell me of the events of the evening? Mr. Payne was less than forthcoming. I think he did not want to speak in front of Miss Brown."

"Of course." Chibale set the teacup on the saucer. "I forgot to ask. How is Miss Phaedra?"

Thérèse's mouth hardened into a thin line. "Worse than yesterday. You saw her at the Cock and Bull?"

"Yes."

She gave a curt nod. "I put her to bed after a cup of tea with brandy."

"She's here then?" Chibale asked, surprised that a modiste would allow an employee such a liberty as staying in her house.

"I could not send her home. He might come for her."

Chibale shook his head. "He won't be seeing her any time soon. He's on his way to the Continent. I paid his fare on a ship that won't dock until it reaches Italy."

"If we are fortunate, the ship will sink."

"If we are fortunate, he will find men to box in Rome or Venice and stay away for years to come."

"You have done me a great service, monsieur." She rose and went to a table then slid open the drawer. "You must tell me what I owe you for the fare."

Chibale had risen when she did. "I wouldn't dream of taking your money. I did it for Miss Phaedra. And for the other women he's hurt. And don't think I didn't get any satisfaction out of seeing him lying on the ground after Payne and Mr. Mostyn were through with him. They went easy on him, but he won't soon forget the feel of their fists."

Thérèse slid the drawer closed and moved away from the table. Chibale was disconcerted to realize that put her closer to him. And she moved closer still. "But I must pay you something," she said. "A reward of some kind."

Chibale swallowed. His throat had suddenly gone very dry. "You have already agreed to attend the ball with me—"

She shook her head and moved nearer, so near now that he could smell the scent of her perfume. He thought it might be jasmine. The silk of her robe brushed against his coat. "That benefits me as I am always looking for more customers and good deals from textile merchants." She put a hand on his coat. "I want to express my appreciation to you, monsieur." Her hand slid up and down his coat as though appraising the quality of the superfine wool.

"I couldn't—"

"I could," she said, wrapping her arms about her neck. She looked up at him with those beautiful brown eyes and all of that smooth, creamy skin. Her body, and he could feel it perfectly, pressed against his. "Do not make me beg, Chibale."

Chibale prided himself on self-control, but every man had his limits. At quarter to five in the morning with a beautiful woman wrapped around him, he was at his. Chibale lowered his mouth and kissed her.

The kiss was exquisite—almost as exquisite as she. She tasted of tea with cream and something richer. He realized she must have put brandy in her own tea, and he liked the flavor that gave her. His hands slid around her waist, the silk rippling under his fingertips. It would have slid so easily off her shoulders and down her arms, over her hips, and into a puddle on the floor. Then he would know what she wore—or didn't—under it.

Chibale pulled back and had to grip the material of her robe to keep from running his hands up and down her lush body. She leaned into him, burying her nose in the side of his neck and inhaling. "It has been a long time since I've stood in a man's arms," she said. "A long time since I have met a man I wanted to kiss."

"Why me?" Chibale asked, unable to stop himself.

"I can see you are different." She looked up at his face. "I admit I was unsure of you at first. A man in the world of boxing." She shook her head as though disapproving. "Such a man can be violent. But not you. You are a protector."

Chibale had never thought of himself in those terms, but he supposed it was true. He had younger siblings, and he had always looked after them and protected them. "Do you need protecting?" he asked.

She gave him a rueful smile. "No."

He'd known the answer before he even asked it. She was strong and independent. She didn't need anyone. That was clear enough. But there was something in her smile, something sad and slightly wistful that made him think perhaps, at one time, she had needed protection.

"I should go." He forced himself to step back.

"So soon? Ah, but you are protecting me again. I promise you, monsieur, I do not need it. Another kiss?" She reached out and caught his coat, tugging him closer.

"I don't think that's a wise idea. I'm tired, and I don't trust myself."

"I trust you. Besides, I'd like to see you misbehave. I'll start, shall I?" She reached for the tie of her robe and loosed it, so it opened several inches, showing the lacy white undergarment she wore. Swathes of her skin were visible between sections of lace, sections placed very strategically to tempt and tease and hide very little.

Chibale drew in a breath and forced his gaze to rise to Thérèse's. She crooked a finger at him, and this time he did not hesitate. He went to her, swept her up and pressed her hard against the sapphire-painted wall. Her arms went around him, and her hands went to his hair, her fingers closing on the close-cut curls. The kiss this time was not gentle or teasing. He kissed her deep and thorough, showing her what he wanted, what she did to him. Her legs parted, and he slid his knee between them, pressing up and against the heat of her core.

"Chibale," she whispered. He kissed her neck, slid the robe off her shoulders and kissed those as well. He might have moved lower and tasted her breasts, but a moan sounded from another room, and they both froze and listened.

"Phaedra," Thérèse said.

Chibale stepped away. "She might need you. I should go."

Thérèse gave him a disappointed nod. "*Oui.* She was in great pain earlier."

"I can see myself out."

Thérèse reached for his arm. "Will I see you again? Soon? The ball ees…" She made a gesture to indicate it was too far away.

"I'll call on you."

"*Oui.* Soon, monsieur."

He took her hand, kissed the back of it, and saw himself out. A moment later, he heard the lock click on the door and her footsteps as she walked away. Chibale leaned back against the wall and smiled. He wanted to shout for joy. He felt like the luckiest man in the world. At that moment, he believed he was the luckiest man in the world. Rowden had won his match and a nice purse, the Black Plague had been sent out of London, and Chibale Okoro had kissed Thérèse Renauld. Even though the weather was cold and unforgiving that night, Chibale didn't look for a hackney cab. Not that he would have found one that late anyway. He didn't feel the cold. He didn't feel the ground. He floated all the way home.

***

He soared through London the next morning and sailed up the stairs to his parents' rooms above the spice shop. Chibale always loved coming home. He loved walking through the door and smelling the scent of exotic spices from India, Africa, and China. He loved his mother's cooking, especially her currant buns.

This morning, he loved the roaring fire that melted the ice from his gloves.

"Is that you, Chibale?" his mother called from the kitchen.

"Yes, Mama. I hope you have enough for me."

She came to the doorway, hands on her hips and a smile lighting up her dark face. "I always have enough for you. You don't kiss your mother anymore?"

Chibale went to her, bent, and kissed her. She smelled of yeast and dough, as she always did. "You aren't by chance making currant buns this morning?" he asked with a smile.

"It just so happens I told Alice to put some in the oven." Alice was their maidservant. His mother had never hired a cook since she liked to cook herself. "I had a feeling you would come by today." She made a shooing motion. "But go into the dining room and see your father. He has been waiting for you."

Chibale obeyed, entering the dining room, where his father sat with a cup of tea and the paper. He lowered it to show a round face with large, intelligent dark eyes. "Your mother said you would visit. She is never wrong." He had a deep baritone voice that seemed to resonate through anyone he spoke to. Although he had been born in London, his father had come from Africa, and Gamba Okoro seemed to retain some of the lilt of his father's native tongue.

Chibale sat in the chair to his father's left. He kept the right open for his older brother, but his father motioned to it. "Your brother Thimba is at the warehouse today. He wanted to inspect a new shipment from Morocco."

"And Bethanie and Dakarai?"

"They'll be here as soon as Alice announces the meal. I hear you'll be traveling to Hungerford."

Chibale smiled. His father always seemed to know the news from the boxing world, though he was not a part of it. "Rowden will fight the German again. This time he will win."

"I want to go," said a voice from the doorway. Chibale glanced over his shoulder to see his brother of fourteen, Dakarai, standing in the entry listening.

"Every time I see you, you've grown," Chibale said.

Dakarai straightened his slim shoulders. The boy looked like some great hand reached down and stretched him out. He was skinny and all legs.

"Grown enough to go to Hungerford with you?"

Chibale shook his head. "Not yet."

Dakarai's shoulders slumped. Chibale rose and put an arm around his brother. "I will be too busy to make sure you are safe, and along with the Fancy all the rabble will come too. Maybe next year."

"But The Royal Payne might not still be fighting next year," Dakarai complained, taking a seat.

"Then Chibale will find another pugilist just as talented."

Chibale wished he felt as confident of that, but it warmed him that his father had such faith in him. But then his father had always supported each of his children in all their endeavors.

"Bethanie!" Alice called and entered with a tray of currant buns. His mother followed. The two women were such a contrast—Charlotte Okoro with her dark features and her small stature and Miss Alice with her white skin, enormous bosom, and red hair barely contained under her cap. She gave Chibale a huge smile. "Mr. Chibale! Heard ye had some luck last night, eh?"

"Hard work," he said. "Not luck."

"Ye think The Royal Payne will win at Hungerford?"

"Let's not speak of it," Chibale's mother said. "Bethanie will be here in a moment."

"She's already heard all about it," Bethanie said from the door. She wore a pretty pink day dress, and her hair was put up in a style that made her look closer to twenty than seventeen. Chibale wished he could stop time and keep his siblings from growing up so quickly.

She kissed Chibale then her father on the cheek and sat. "You will be back in time for the ball, won't you?" she asked.

"I would not miss it," Chibale said.

His mother took her seat and Alice served them, then returned to the kitchen to make fresh tea. There was a moment of silence as they all enjoyed their meal. Then Bethanie looked up. "Chibale is taking the modiste to the ball."

Chibale felt every eye land on him. He swallowed a now flavorless bite of currant roll. "Madame Renauld has agreed to accompany me, yes."

"Madame Renauld? Is she French?" his mother asked.

"She is, yes."

"Is she a Negro?" Dakarai wanted to know.

"Yes," Chibale said.

"You should invite her to dinner," his mother said. "Before you leave for Hungerford."

"I—" Chibale tried to think of a reason to demur, but there really wasn't one. His family was successful and honorable. He loved his parents and his siblings. He failed to see how Thérèse could not love them as well. "I will."

Bethanie clapped her hands. "What should I wear, Mama? She is so beautiful and stylish. I'm sure I have nothing suitable."

"I am certain we can find something," his mother said with a smile.

Chibale smiled too because now he had another reason to call on Thérèse.

***

"I didn't mean for you to take me to see her," Modesty said in Lady Lorraine's coach later that morning. "I was idly wondering how Madame Renauld's assistant was faring."

But Lady Lorraine waved a hand. She'd looked a bit green since they'd begun the drive to Madame Renauld's shop.

"Are you feeling well?"

Lady Lorraine nodded. "I'll be fine once we arrive. Too much jostling before afternoon makes me queasy." She frowned. "I hope that doesn't mean the baby won't like carriage rides. I was hoping to take him—or her—to my father's estate when he—or she—is old enough to travel. It's simply beautiful there. But we won't be able to go if he dislikes carriages *this* much." She made a clutching motion toward her slightly rounded midsection.

"I believe most women have some nausea in the morning when with child," Modesty said. She had not spent much time with Lady Lorraine, but already she was coming to understand that though she herself had lived a sheltered life, Lady Lorraine had probably been even more sheltered. She seemed not to know things Modesty took for granted— like women in the early stages of pregnancy often felt nauseous in the morning.

"Oh, good. In any case, the discomfort is well worth it. I have been wanting to pay a call on Madame Renauld for some time. My mother always patronized Madame LeMonde, but her styles seem a bit old-fashioned to me. I want something new, and I probably need something with a bigger waistline."

Modesty could see very little evidence of that, but she wasn't certain whether it was better to agree or to disagree, so she kept silent. Lady Lorraine wore a pretty day dress of light green with a darker green pelisse over it. Modesty wore the same dress she had worn the night before. It was that or dress in all black.

"And even if I didn't need a new dress, you certainly do," Lady Lorraine said.

Modesty shook her head. "I could not afford a Renauld."

"But I can," Lady Lorraine said.

"No." Modesty shook her head. "Please. You have been so kind to me already."

"Kind? I haven't even managed to locate your aunt yet. But"—she raised a gloved finger—"I anticipate news later today. The ladies will be at their morning correspondence even now. So, you see, we need a diversion, and it's much too cold for a walk and I must confess I dislike sewing. And I've never been a great reader."

Modesty imagined that was because she liked to talk too much. She'd probably read a line and then tell everyone all about it before reading the next. "We could go to the studio. There's always work to be done there, and we might see Lord Rowden—"

"No."

Lady Lorraine raised her brows at Modesty's quick response.

"I mean, I have seen enough fighting for now. But if you would like to go—"

"I can wait," Lady Lorraine said. Then, "Oh, how charming!" She peered out the window at the shop with a white sign reading *Madame Renauld's* in black script. Under that, in block letters, it said MODISTE.

The shop too was painted white with a shiny black door and a large window showing several hats in various colors and styles. A ribbon of blue seemed to descend from one of the hats and ripple as it flowed over the green material that made up the background. "And look there's a tea shop just there," Lady Lorraine said. "We can have tea after we shop."

Modesty nodded, not arguing with that idea because she'd noticed Lady Lorraine had eaten almost nothing at breakfast, though her husband had piled her plate quite high with an assortment of pastries and every other sort of food Modesty had never so much as tasted, much less imagined eating daily.

The coach stopped, and a footman opened the door and handed Lady Lorraine then Modesty down. She was still not comfortable with the servants. Lady Lorraine assured her she had very few compared to other houses, but as someone who had never had any, Modesty did not know how to behave around them. "Thank you," she said.

He didn't respond. They never did. Modesty followed Lady Lorraine into the shop. As soon as they entered, someone said, "Hello!"

Modesty jumped, but Lady Lorraine looked up. "Hello," she said to a brightly colored bird.

"Fine lace," the bird answered.

Modesty wanted to turn around and walk right back out of the store. She had never seen a bird talk, and she was afraid this might be the work of Satan. Lady Lorraine put a hand on her arm. "It's a parrot," she said. "They are able to imitate human voices.

"Bleuette ees pretty!" the bird said, in what sounded like a French-accented voice.

"Is that your name? Bleuette?"

The parrot tilted its head as though it understood. Most unnerving. "What's your name, pretty bird?" the bird asked.

"Lorrie," Lady Lorraine answered. "Nice to meet you, Bleuette."

"My lady, welcome." Madame Renauld herself was coming toward them, dressed in black and looking just as lovely as always, though she had been up as late, if not later, than Modesty. "Ah! And Mees Brown! I had hoped you would come. Where ees Monsieur?"

"He's not with us," Modesty said, feeling her cheeks heat.

"We came to inquire after your assistant," Lady Lorraine said. "I hope she is well."

"Fine lace!" the parrot interjected, making Modesty jump again.

"Come away," the modiste said. "Bleuette will talk to you all day. In fact, come upstairs with me. We can speak in private there and perhaps some tea will settle your stomach," she said to Lady Lorraine. Modesty couldn't have said how she'd known the lady's stomach was at all unsettled. Lady Lorraine looked much better now that she was on solid ground again. The color had even returned to her cheeks.

Modesty followed the modiste up the stairs and out of the shop, moving slowly so she could take her time and see all the shop had to offer. She had walked by many shops like this, but she had never been able to do more than peer in the windows and admire from a distance. Now she was among the bolts of beautiful fabric, spools of lovely ribbon, and swathes of gorgeous lace. She would have liked to run her hands over all of it, hold it to her nose and inhale deeply.

The Bible said vanity was a sin, as was coveting. But, oh, how she coveted the beautiful gowns on display, and how she longed to wear one herself. She should be pleased with the one she had. Never had she worn anything as fine as the dark blue dress. She hadn't realized how scratchy and stiff her black clothing was. The material was inexpensive and rough. She imagined some of these silks would make the wearer feel as though she wore nothing at all.

Modesty blushed at that thought. It was not the kind of thought she should be having. But she'd had many such thoughts lately, and especially last night and this morning after that kiss with Rowden Payne. She'd had a hard time sleeping last night after that kiss. She'd wondered if she would go to hell for her wantonness. And then she'd decided she didn't care.

She was fairly certain she would absolutely go to hell if she did not repent for the dream she'd had when she'd finally fallen asleep. She dreamed of Rowden Payne kissing her neck and her collarbone, then opening her bodice to kiss her bare breasts. She'd woken too warm, and with her breasts feeling heavy and sensitive, almost as though his hands had been on them.

"Sit down, Mees Brown," the modiste said. "You are not used to climbing thees stairs."

"I'm fine," she said, but she knew why Madame Renauld seemed concerned. Modesty could feel her cheeks burning.

One of the assistants brought tea, and Lady Lorraine inquired after Phaedra. After they'd had some refreshment and been assured Phaedra was resting and being looked after, Madame Renauld had rung for another assistant named Betsy who had brought a beautiful wool in a deep brown with red undertones—the modiste's words, not Modesty's—for Lady Lorraine. Lady Lorraine exclaimed over it and was taken to be measured for a new walking dress and matching spencer.

The modiste stayed where she was, and when Lady Lorraine was in the dressing chamber, Madame Renauld turned her dark gaze on Modesty.

"And what shall we make you, Mees Brown?"

"Oh, nothing, thank you. I have no money."

The modiste angled her head toward the sound of voices in the adjoining chamber. "She will pay. She has a generous nature. Or I can send the bill to Monsieur Payne. The way he looked at you last night led me to believe he would rather see you in *déshabillé*, but we must lead the man on a merry chase, no?"

Modesty shook her head. "I've never—"

The modiste put a hand on her knee. "I am teasing. But only about the men chasing. I never tease about fashion. You must have a day dress and a walking dress and a—"

"I cannot! I have imposed on Lady Lorraine's kindness too much as it is."

"Then I will make you a day dress as a gift."

"No!"

"It ees the least I can do to repay you."

Modesty shook her head. "I have done nothing."

"Bah. You have brought her here." She indicated the dressing chamber. "To have the daughter of the Duke of Ridlington and the wife of a war hero patronize my shop will bring me many customers."

Modesty was still shaking her head, but the modiste rose. "I insist. I will measure you now and we can have a dress for you in two days' time."

"So quickly?" Modesty asked, excited despite herself.

"For a day dress, *oui*. An evening dress would take longer, but you will want no embellishment, so *mes filles* can finish like thees." She snapped her fingers. She pulled Modesty up and brought her to the dais where she could see her reflection in a large mirror. The modiste began to unbutton the blue dress, and Modesty pushed her hands away.

"You can't measure me with the dress on?"

"Of course not. No need for shyness with me, Mees Brown. I have seen more women than I can count in their chemise and stockings." She finished with the buttons and started on the tapes and laces. "When I first began, my customers were often actresses and opera singers. Some were courtesans."

Modesty's eyes widened. She saw them do so in the mirror and immediately tried to hide her shock.

"They would often strip bare, wanting a dress that would not accommodate even a shift and might even plunge so low that stays were made unnecessary."

"Oh, dear." Modesty could not imagine wearing something so revealing. On the other hand, it seemed rather daring and exciting to do so.

"*Oui*! I made them gowns so risqué my name became too—what ees the word?" She linked her hands together.

"Associated?" Modesty offered.

"*Oui*. I was associated with thees style and that ees one reason I came to England. I wanted to start over." She finished removing the dress and petticoats, and Modesty stood in her old chemise and much-mended stockings. The modiste did not comment on the ragged underthings, just took the measuring strip from a pocket under her dress and began to measure. She did not write anything down, just muttered to herself in French. Fortunately, the sounds she made seemed positive.

She promised Modesty she was almost finished when Lady Lorraine and Betsy returned from the other chamber. Modesty felt quite exposed on the dais in only her chemise, and she felt more so when Lady Lorraine's mouth dropped into an O.

Modesty glanced in the mirror to see what the matter might be.

"I would hate her if she were not so good," Lady Lorraine said to the modiste. "You should see the black, shapeless dress she usually wears." She nodded to Modesty. "I had no idea, even in the blue dress, that you were hiding this."

Modesty looked down, confused.

"She ees quite unaware," the modiste said, with a flourish of her hand. "She has no idea. But I will make her a dress so exquisite that—" She broke off, remembering who she was speaking to. "But of course, yours will be even more exquisite."

Lady Lorraine laughed. "Make her that exquisite dress. She will show it off better than I." She touched her belly. "Were you thinking a day dress?"

"*Oui*. In green, I think, to bring out the green in her eyes."

"Very good." She leaned close and whispered something to Madame Renauld whose eyes sparkled before she nodded.

"May I step down and dress now?" Modesty asked.

"Of course." Lady Lorraine nodded to Betsy who began to help Modesty dress. "We shouldn't whisper. It's terribly impolite. It's just that you have a figure most women would envy."

The modiste nodded. "Your measurements are almost perfect, and the imperfection ees in your favor. Such a tiny waist and such generous bosoms. You will show my fashions perfectly."

"I will wear the one dress," Modesty said. "I can't accept more."

But the way Lady Lorraine looked at Madame Renauld gave Modesty cause to suspect those two had other plans.

Another quarter hour was spent in pleasant conversation, and then Modesty and Lady Lorraine stopped in at the tea shop and had more tea and small delicate sandwiches. Everything tasted so wonderful and so new to Modesty, who had spent all of her life eating nothing grander than hard bread and thin soup.

But she couldn't allow herself to get used to this sort of life. She had no idea if her aunt would be found, and if she were, if she would take Modesty in. With her father still missing, Modesty would have to rely on charity or find a position of her own. With the possibility of having to search for work looming, Modesty had not argued too much over the new day dress. A pretty dress might help secure her a position as a shop girl. Perhaps Madame Renauld needed someone to sweep or straighten the displays. She could sew, but not well enough to be hired as a seamstress. But perhaps she could learn on her days off and then she could hide away in the back of the shop and not have to pretend she was happy and cheerful when her life had been crushed into un-recognizable pieces.

After tea, the ladies returned home, and one of the manservants brought a silver tray with letters on it to Lady Lorraine. Though the lady looked tired, she took the mail and brought it to the parlor where a window provided decent light, even on a gray winter day like this. She opened one letter, read it, tossed it aside, and opened another. She did the same with all four letters, leaving one unopened and ignored.

"Well," she said finally, looking at Modesty. "I have received responses to my inquiries regarding your aunt."

"Tell me," Modesty said.

"I've had four responses. Your aunt is indeed unmarried and still called Augusta Ryan. One of my friends does not know her at all, and one has heard of her and passed that information along. Another of my friends does not know her but was able to discover that she lives in London."

Modesty felt her heart kick with happiness.

"Unfortunately, she could not say if she was in Town at the moment. Another friend said the same and could also not say whether she was in Town. That friend thinks your aunt has gone to the countryside for the winter. Apparently, your mother's family has some property in Shropshire?"

Modesty blinked. "Really?"

"Your grandfather was a gentleman, and his eldest son provides for your aunt." She lifted one of the letters and passed it to Modesty. "See here."

Modesty read the letter slowly, skipping over the greetings at the beginning and the polite inquiries about family. The part in the middle was about the Ryan family. They apparently had land in Shropshire and were known to manage it well. The son had married and lived on that land, and the older daughter had never married, but her brother provided for her. She had a house in Town. No one knew what had happened to the younger sister.

Modesty read that line again.

No one knows what became of the younger sister. Perhaps there were only two children.

Her mother's life summed up in fifteen words. Forgotten by her family and by Society after she had married Samuel Brown. Even her husband had seemed to forget her. But Modesty had not. And she wondered why her mother had been forgotten. Had her father disapproved of her marriage to Samuel Brown? It was possible. His religious views were strict and unpopular. He would have seen a landowner as a sinner. Men were to give up all of their worldly possessions to follow Christ and help the poor. None of the members of their church had anything but what they absolutely needed.

"Look on the second page," Lady Lorraine said, prompting Modesty to turn the letter over. "That is where Lady Lindsey thinks Miss Ryan lives in Town. She is my mother's dear friend—Lady Lindsey, that is—so I say this with affection. The woman is quite the gossip. She knows everyone and everything. Shall we go now and knock on the door?"

Modesty wanted to say yes. She wanted to run all the way to the address given and pound until someone answered and gave her information. But she could see Lady Lorraine was tired. And Modesty did not want to admit this, but she was scared. What if her aunt was in Shropshire? How would she find her? Could she show up on her doorstep, even though she was the child of the sister who had been disowned?

"If you do not mind, might we go tomorrow morning? I am a bit fatigued from our exploits today, and I would like to think how I should greet my aunt."

"Oh, of course!" Lady Lorraine said. "I will see to my correspondence while you rest."

"Very good."

Modesty went back up to her chamber and took the letters from the drawer where she had secreted them. She did not want to read them again, but she did so. This time she read them with an eye to the mention of places, roads, and inns. She noted that her father's mistress lived in Berkshire. She also mentioned the distance from London and...finally, Modesty found it. The mention of Hungerford. She had known the reference Mr. Payne made was familiar. The woman who had borne her father's illegitimate children lived just outside Hungerford. Modesty did not know if she would find her father there, but she knew she might find some answers about his whereabouts.

She folded the letters again and made a decision: if her aunt was not in London, Modesty would ask to go to Hungerford with Mr. Payne and meet her father's mistress.

Thirteen

Two days later, Rowden was at Mostyn's with Chibale when the missive arrived. He called it a missive because it seemed he had little choice but to respond. He'd been drinking water and wiping the sweat from his face when the boy had run up to him and held the paper out. Rowden had taken it then realized he didn't have a coin as he wore only his breeches. Chibale flipped the child a coin and motioned for Rowden to go ahead and read it.

Still heaving from his exertions with the punching sack, he opened the letter. He read it then marched to Ewan's office and went in without even knocking. "Do you know anything about this?"

Ewan looked up from a ledger. "No." He looked down again.

Rowden crossed to the desk. "You didn't even look at it. It's from your wife."

Ewan looked up again, closed his eyes briefly, then went back to his ledger.

"She wants me to come to your house. She doesn't even ask. She tells me to be there at four."

Ewan checked his watch. "You should hurry then."

"Why does she want to see me?"

Ewan shrugged.

"You're coming with me," Rowden said.

"I have work," Ewan said.

Rowden reached over and closed the ledger. Ewan made a sound like a growl. "It's your wife."

"I trust you." Ewan opened the ledger again.

"I mean, she's your problem, not mine." Rowden shut the ledger.

Ewan looked up and nodded at the letter. "Looks like she's your problem right now." He opened the ledger and caught Rowden's hand in a painful grip before he could close it again.

"Fine. But don't blame me if she talks me into some dangerous scheme." Rowden stormed out of the office and went to Chibale. He snatched up his shirt and pulled it over his head. "We're going to see Lady Lorraine."

Chibale frowned. "Why?"

"How the hell do I know, but I would not go alone. You're coming."

"I hardly know the woman."

Rowden made a half-hearted effort to tie his neckcloth then pulled on his stockings and boots. By the time he had his arms in his coat, Ewan was waiting beside them. Rowden looked at him and was about to make some pithy comment, but Ewan looked at him with murder in his eyes.

The three made their way to Ewan's home, Chibale trailing behind Ewan and Rowden as though he'd rather be anywhere else. However, when they neared the house and caught sight of the carriage in front of it, Chibale practically sprinted in front of Ewan and Rowden.

"And here I thought you didn't want to come," Rowden said, less annoyed at the short walk than he'd expected. The cold air felt good after hours in the hot studio.

Chibale looked back and pointed at the coach. "That is Madame Renauld's coach."

Rowden looked at Ewan. "Why is she there?"

Ewan shrugged. "Who is she?"

"The modiste," Chibale reminded him. "You beat the Black Plague outside the Cock and Bull for hitting her assistant."

He nodded. "Oh, that was why."

Rowden laughed. Ewan had never needed a reason for a fight.

"Hurry up," Chibale said, reaching Ewan's door a good minute before Rowden and Ewan. Ewan opened the door and they entered to a small vestibule filled with women. There were probably only five, but it sounded like far more than that. Rowden pressed himself against a wall and spotted Madame Renauld, Lady Lorraine, and Miss Phaedra, the assistant. He wondered where Modesty Brown had gone. Perhaps her father had returned or Lady Lorraine had summoned him to tell him they had reunited Miss Brown with her aunt.

Everyone was talking at once, but rather quickly, Chibale escorted Madame Renauld outside and her assistants followed. Ewan took his wife's arm and pulled her into an open door. And Rowden stood in the vestibule with another woman. He'd thought she was one of the assistants at first, but now he realized she was dressed too well in a pale green day dress. Her auburn hair was pulled off her face and secured by combs, but it rolled over her shoulders in waves.

Feeling as though he should introduce himself, he stepped forward and looked into her face. And then he could not speak.

Because he recognized the eyes. And suddenly his gaze was all over her again, taking her in even as he told himself it was wholly inappropriate.

But how could he stop himself? She was utterly beautiful. Of course, he'd seen beautiful women before. He was a man of two and thirty, not a boy. He had to stop gawking at her and behave like a man.

"Miss—" He cleared his throat as his voice came out ragged. "Miss Brown, you look…different."

Idiot. He was as bad as Chibale.

Her cheeks colored, and he realized she didn't know whether he was complimenting or censuring her. "I mean to say, you look lovely. Did Madame Renauld make the dress for you?"

"She did, and thank you." She walked toward a door and opened it to reveal a parlor decorated in soft shades of yellows and blues. It was most likely used by Lady Lorraine. "Might we speak in private?"

"Of course."

Why the devil had he said that? He was supposed to be distancing himself. He'd told her good-bye three nights ago. And he knew it was not wise to be alone with her, especially not now that he was remembering their kiss. He had thought that was a good-bye kiss. He'd wanted it to be a good-bye kiss because there couldn't be more between them. He didn't want more.

She entered the parlor and left the door slightly open when he followed. Rowden was glad of that and waited until she sat on a cream-colored chair before he followed on one that matched it.

"First," she said, swallowing as though speaking was hard for her. "I want to thank you for your kindness toward me. I certainly do not deserve it after I was part of the reason you lost your fight to the German."

Rowden waved a hand. "The fault is mine for allowing myself to become distracted." Thank God she hadn't looked that night as she did now. He would never have seen the blow coming and would have taken it full force.

"But you also took me in from the cold and introduced me to Lady Lorraine, who has been far more generous than I have a right to expect. And I fear I have imposed on her too long."

"I doubt that," Rowden said. "She likes to talk, and you seem to be a good listener."

Miss Brown smiled. "Yes, but if I stay further, I will be taking advantage. And I cannot help but think Mr. Mostyn might like to return to his evenings alone with his wife."

"Then I take it you have not been able to locate your aunt."

She shook her head. "She is not in London at the moment, and we are uncertain where she resides in Shropshire. It would be even more difficult for me to travel to Shropshire, especially as I don't know what sort of welcome, if any, I will receive."

Rowden was beginning to see her dilemma. She could not stay with Lady Lorraine, and she did not have anywhere else to go. "You don't want to go to your church for help," he said. If she had, she would not have relinquished the black sack she usually wore.

She shook her head. She seemed as though she wanted to say more, but instead she pressed her lips together and swallowed hard again. Rowden had the urge to go to her, to comfort her, but he couldn't touch her. This was already more than he wanted to know, more involved than he wanted to be. He waited, hands clenched and feeling impotent.

Finally, she smiled slightly. "From the letters you helped me find, I have come to understand that my father might be near Hungerford. If he is not there, a woman who lives there might be able to give me more information about him."

"Hungerford?" Rowden frowned. The back of his neck was prickling ominously. "That's a coincidence."

"Perhaps it's providence," she countered. "Divine providence."

"I don't believe in divine providence."

"I'm not sure I do either, but the fact remains that you are traveling to Hungerford soon, and I also wished to travel there. I hate to ask another favor of you—"

"Then don't." He wouldn't be able to refuse her. He didn't know why he seemed unable to refuse her whatever she asked—and even things she didn't ask—but it seemed outside his capabilities. He was perfectly able to refuse other women. Why should Modesty Brown be any different?

"I must. Will you escort me to Hungerford?"

"I will be traveling with Chibale. It's not proper for you to travel with two men."

She shrugged. "I'm not a lady with a reputation that must be kept pristine, and I can trust you and Mr. Okoro, can't I?"

"That's not the point." He'd evaded her question because he didn't want to lie. He did not think he should be trusted alone with her. "But I suppose Lady Lorraine will want to come. If she is there—"

Miss Brown shook her head. "I would ask you to try and dissuade her. She seems tired lately, and I don't think a journey over bumpy roads would be good for her right now."

"You try and dissuade her. No one but Mostyn can ever talk her out of anything she has her mind set on, and even then he's only moderately successful."

Rowden heard the click of nails on the marble outside the parlor and then the parlor door opened further. A small brown and white dog trotted in. "Who's this?" he asked as the dog nosed at his boots and his leg and then went to Miss Brown and put his paws on her knee, obviously asking to be picked up. She obliged him.

"This is Welly." He settled in her lap and she patted him. "He is very spoiled."

"He'll leave hair all over your new dress."

"I don't mind. Mr. Payne, you haven't answered me. Will you take me with you to Hungerford?"

The door swung open further and Lady Lorraine entered, smiling, while Ewan scowled fiercely just behind her. "Of course, he will," Lady Lorraine said. "We'll all go. I've already spoken to Ewan, and he thinks it will be great fun."

Rowden didn't think Ewan looked like a man who was about to have a great deal of fun. He looked like a man who wanted to hit someone.

Rowden decided rather than be that someone, he would take his leave.

***

Outside, Thérèse sent Phaedra and Betsy back in the carriage and took Mr. Okoro's arm. The day was cold but sunny, and she would not have another chance to go outside until after dark. "Are you sure you have time to walk?" Chibale had asked.

"*Oui*. The fitting with Mees Brown took less time than I had scheduled. The dress fit her perfectly, but I suspect even if it had not, she would not have complained."

"I am certain that is a welcome change."

She smiled at him, looking up into his handsome face. He had high cheekbones and light brown eyes. He wore his hat cocked to one side, and as a modiste she could not help but notice his clothing was always impeccable. He was a handsome man, and it was no hardship to take his arm. "When do you leave for Hungerford?" she asked.

"A few days. Mr. Payne's friend has offered the use of his carriages, so we will not have to rely on the public coach."

"I do hope you will call on me before you go."

He glanced at her, and she gave him a direct look. Sometimes these English were so obtuse.

"I would like that," he said. "In fact, I would extend a dinner invitation."

Thérèse could imagine a cozy dinner in her flat with dessert in the bedchamber. "I will have my cook order something for us."

"Actually," he said, "my mother and father would like you to dine with us."

Thérèse stopped walking. "You are inviting me to dine with your family?"

"Yes. My mother and father would like to meet you. And you already know my sister, Bethanie. I have two brothers as well."

She stared at him, uncomprehending. She was not the sort of woman men brought home to meet their mamas. Thérèse did not *want* to be the sort of woman men brought home to meet their mamas. "Why don't we discuss it over dinner tonight?" she asked. "Just the two of us."

He looked as if he might object, but then he smiled and inclined his head. "What time should I arrive?"

***

Thérèse opened the door to him at precisely nine o'clock that night. He was punctual, which was something she liked in a

276 | *Shana Galen*

man. He was also dressed in a blue coat of superfine, tight fawn breeches, and a scarlet and gold waistcoat that emphasized his trim waist. The look of him was definitely something she liked. "I've given my maid the night off, so I will have to take your greatcoat," she said, hanging it on the coat tree. "And your hat." She took it as well." She would have liked to take the rest of his clothing, but she didn't want to scare him away by moving too fast.

In her drawing room, she poured him a glass of wine and asked him about himself, while skillfully avoiding answering anything about herself. He clearly loved his parents and siblings. They seemed a close and happy family.

As she served dinner, he asked about her family, and she told him they were in France and little else. What should she tell him? That her mother had been a high-paid courtesan and she did not know who her father was? That she had learned to sew because her mother needed new dresses to attract protectors when she was between lovers? That her mother had sold Thérèse's virginity to the highest bidder when she'd been barely a woman and that man had been so possessive, he had almost killed her before she was finally able to escape him? Her childhood had not been full of laughter around the dinner table or her mother making currant buns in the kitchen.

But then the topic moved to pugilism, and she liked the way Chibale's eyes lit when he spoke of it. "My older brother will take over the family business," he said. "And I've never had much interest in importing or exporting, but my father used to take me to Gentleman Jackson's to watch the men train, and I never tired of that."

"What about it appealed?" she asked.

"The grace of movement," he answered, "and the danger. One wrong move, and it's over. But the combination of right moves is a thing of beauty."

"And did you ever box?"

He nodded. "I did a bit, but I soon realized I was much better at teaching than doing. Rowden Payne is my third milling cove, and the other two before him retired with fat purses."

"And what will you do when Mr. Payne retires?" she asked.

He shrugged. "Find another man with raw talent. Perhaps the next Tom Cribb or Mendoza."

They'd finished dinner, so she rose and offered her hand. He took it and stood. "I like your ambition," she said.

"I like yours."

"Shall we have dessert?" She led him to her bedchamber, where a fire was blazing, and the bed clothes had been turned down. Releasing his hand, she stepped back toward the bed. He looked about.

"Where is dessert?"

"Here." She opened her arms, inviting him to come to her. To her surprise, he hesitated.

"Are you sure?"

She nodded. "I am perfectly certain. You?"

He came to her. "I know exactly what I want." He kissed her then, and Thérèse, who had expected to dictate the events of the evening, found she was not quite so in control as she had planned. Her head spun as his lips slanted over hers, making it difficult for her to remember she was supposed to be seducing him. When he finally pulled back, she caught her breath and went to work undressing him. She pushed the coat over his broad shoulders and down his arms and loosed his neckcloth. Next came his shirt, which she unfastened at the neck then pulled over his head.

Looking at his muscled chest, it was difficult to believe he was not the one who was the prizefighter. He was powerfully built with a tight, flat stomach that she had the urge to kiss. In the firelight his skin glowed warm and burnished. She trailed her fingers over it then trailed kisses as well.

He swept her up in his arms and laid her on the bed, coming over her and kissing her until she was hot and wriggling for release. "I want to see you," he said, his voice ragged with need in her ear. "I want to touch you. Everywhere."

He helped her unfasten her dress. She'd worn one she could remove herself, but her hands were suddenly shaky, and she felt clumsy and inept. He stripped her of the dress then the underthings until she was in nothing but her chemise and he in nothing at all. Kneeling across from each other, he lowered the sleeve of her chemise and kissed her shoulder then her neck then her ear as he revealed her breasts. His mouth soon ventured to her nipples, taking them gently between his teeth and making her groan with need. He seemed in no hurry, though she could see he was aroused and ready, but he took his time exploring her body, revealing it little by little and then kissing each part and—she did not know how else to put it—worshipping her until he moved to the next.

When he reached her sex, she thought the torture would finally end. He would see she was wet and ready, and he would push her back and take her. She wanted him to take her, rough and hard. He did push her back, but he made no move to lever himself over her. Instead, he kissed her belly then the thatch of dark hair at the junction of her thighs, then parted those thighs and kissed her there. Thérèse had been with more men than she liked to count, and no man had ever shown her this much care and tenderness. No man had ever licked and sucked and settled between her thighs as though he had all the time in the world to make sure she climaxed.

"I want you inside me," she said, her voice sounding like someone else's, someone weak and needy and on the verge of ecstasy.

"There's time for that yet," he answered, his voice rumbling against her thighs and making her shiver. He spread her legs wider, and she gasped as he pressed a finger inside her, all the while his skilled mouth moving over her in the most intimate of strokes. She couldn't hold back any longer. Her body pulsed and she cried out, her muscles tightening and then releasing with the most delicious satisfaction.

Now he would plunge inside her. Now he would take her, but he did not. He continued his exploration of her body, kissing her legs and her knees and her ankles and even her toes.

"Chibale, *s'il vous plait*," she murmured. He was working his way up again, and though she should feel sated, she was beginning to feel the need for him again. "Must I beg?" she asked.

"Never," he said, and to her pleasure, he settled himself between her legs. The feel of him, large and powerful over her and against her, was at once frightening and erotic. And when he slid into her, she gasped with the pleasure of it. But though she had thought she wanted rough and hard, he did not give her that. He took her slowly, carefully, gently.

She'd never been taken this way, never been...she did not know how to describe it except to think she was being cherished. As he moved inside her, his eyes met hers. He showed her the rhythm he liked, and she matched it then varied it, and they found a rhythm they both enjoyed. She raised her hips, and he angled higher, giving her more pleasure each time he slid deep. The act became not something he was doing to her, but something they did together.

And when he brought her to climax again, she clung to him, holding him tightly as he came a moment later. He held her tightly afterward, their bodies both gasping for air, their hearts seeming to beat in unison.

Thérèse did not know what to do, how to feel. She'd wanted to take him to bed. She'd hoped for pleasure. She hadn't expected an experience like this. She hadn't known there was such an experience as this.

Finally, he rolled away, lying back with one arm behind his head. She looked over at him, and she couldn't help but feel she wanted to look over at him like that every night.

"Now, I really must introduce you to my family," he said.

Thérèse pulled the sheet up to cover herself. "There ees no hurry. I rather like our intimate dinners."

"I like them too," he said. He rolled to face her. "I especially like dessert."

She smiled and relaxed slightly.

"But I want more than this." He indicated the bed. "I want more than a few weeks or months in your bed."

Thérèse clenched the bed clothes.

"I want to marry you."

The words were like a knife in her heart, and she jerked as though stabbed.

"What's wrong?" he asked.

She rose and pulled on a robe. "I am not the kind of woman you marry," she said, cinching the robe at her waist and turning to face him."

"You seem exactly the kind of woman I want to marry." He sat up, still not bothering to cover himself. And why should he? He was so beautiful, and honest, and she was so…scared.

"I am not looking to marry," she said. "If that ees what you assumed, then I am sorry to have misled you."

"I didn't assume anything," he said. "I'm telling you what I want so there is no confusion between us."

"Then let me be equally forthright," she said. "I will never marry."

Fourteen

The next morning Modesty made her way down the stairs, valise in hand. She paused when Mr. Mostyn opened the door for a man in a black coat then closed it again behind him. Her steps, which had been rapid and full of excitement and trepidation, slowed. Something about the way Mr. Mostyn held himself concerned her. He was usually loose-limbed, moving like a prowling lion. This morning he was stiff and almost wooden.

"Is something amiss?" she asked. It was probably the first time she had spoken to him directly. He still made her nervous.

He looked up at her, and she saw his eyes were red-rimmed. Modesty's belly tightened and she imagined the feeling akin to a blow.

"No," he said, though she could see that plainly he had been crying. And then to her shock, he sat hard on the marble floor of the entryway. Modesty didn't think. She went to him and put her hand on his shoulder. She had done this thousands of times over the years with parishioners in her father's church. She had mourned with them as often as she had rejoiced with them, perhaps even more.

"What is it?" she asked, kneeling beside him. "Is it Lady Lorraine?" She swallowed hard, not wanting to say more but forcing herself. "Is it the baby?"

He nodded.

Modesty felt cold all over, and her skin prickled as though icicles trailed over it. "Shall we pray?" she asked.

Mostyn gave her a helpless look. "Yes."

And so she prayed. She said the prayer she had heard her father say so often in times of trouble, and she tried very hard to believe God heard her prayer. In this last week she had begun to feel there was no God, or if there was, he did not care about her. It scared her to think that for years she might have devoted herself to a God who either did not exist or was, at best, indifferent to her. But then she'd believed her father a different man than he was, and she'd believed her mother a different woman than she was. And maybe she'd been wrong about God too.

After the prayer, they sat in silence for a long time. Most people wanted to talk about their fears and sadness, but Mostyn seemed to be comfortable in the silence. Modesty didn't want to pry, but she also knew the carriage taking her to Hungerford would arrive soon, and she did not know if she should stay to be with Lady Lorraine.

"May I see Lady Lorraine?"

Mostyn nodded slightly. "She's in the bedchamber."

Modesty rose and went in the direction she had seen Lady Lorraine go when retiring. She found her lady's maid, Nell, outside the door, handkerchief patting her eyes. Modesty stopped and put a hand on Nell's arm. "You must be strong now," she said. "She needs you."

Nell nodded. "I know. I'm trying."

"I find having a task to do sometimes helps in hard times. Would you make tea for Lady Lorraine and bring a tray?"

Nell nodded. "Yes. Yes, I can do that." She left and Modesty opened the door.

The day was gray, but the curtains were open to allow what little light there was to penetrate the room. It was a warm room, the walls papered in blue and the large mahogany bed draped in white. Lady Lorraine looked small under the white bedsheets, but Modesty found her. She was sitting, one hand on the back of her dog who had snuggled in beside her.

"Oh, Miss Brown," Lady Lorraine said. "I am so sorry. I will not be able to go to Hungerford."

Modesty waved a hand. "Don't trouble yourself with that. Tell me what's happened. Is the baby…" She did not know how to finish. Obviously, the baby was not well or the doctor would not have been there.

"The doctor says he thinks the baby is fine. I've had some bleeding, and he says I must rest and be quiet and still for a few days. If I can do that, then the child might be saved."

Modesty went to her knees and grasped Lady Lorraine's hand. "Oh, my lady. I blame myself."

"Don't be ridiculous. It's no one's fault. And goodness, after the confidence I have just shared, would you call me Lorrie?"

Modesty nodded. "I should not have asked you to come to Hungerford with me. You have been doing too much."

Lorrie shook her head. "You did not ask me. I invited myself, and I always do too much. I don't like to be idle. Besides, the doctor said no one is to blame. Not you. Not Ewan, though he blames himself, of course."

Modesty frowned. "Why would Mr. Mostyn be to blame."

"He thinks because we…" She paused and she did not need to finish for Modesty's cheeks to heat. Lorrie smiled. "Yes, that. Because of that he caused the baby harm. You think it's because I was readying to travel to Hungerford.

Nell thinks it is because…well, I don't know why she blames herself, but she does. But the doctor says if I rest for a few days, I should be fine." She bit her lip. "But no traveling. He doesn't want me bounced about."

"Of course. I will tell Mr. Payne I cannot go. May I use your parlor to write him a letter?"

"No." Lorrie's hand tightened on hers. "You will go to Hungerford. You said yourself you do not need me as a chaperone. Besides, you will stay with Lord Nicholas and his sister, Lady Florentia. They live a few miles outside of Hungerford, and I have heard their estate is beautiful. It's all arranged."

"I don't want to leave you alone."

"And I won't be the reason you don't find your father. If he is in Hungerford, you need to find him. Besides, I won't be alone. Ewan will hover over me until he drives me mad, and if you wouldn't mind, I'd like you to write to my mother, the Duchess of Ridlington. Ask her to come for a few days."

Modesty took a breath. "You wish me to write to a duchess?"

"I promise you she reads left to right like anyone else. Funny how in times like these we want our mothers at our sides."

Modesty nodded. She understood that sentiment. She had wanted her mother this past week quite often.

"Then give me a kiss and start writing. Lord Rowden and Mr. Sterling will be here within the hour, and you don't want to make them wait."

Modesty kissed Lorrie's cheek and went out of the room. Mostyn was waiting on the other side of the door. "She's fine," Modesty said because she knew he wondered but wouldn't ask. "She wanted me to write to her mother and ask her to stay for a few days."

Mostyn gave her a pained look, and she patted his arm then went to the parlor to write the letter. She was still sitting there, looking over the letter and hoping she'd addressed it properly when Mr. Payne arrived. She heard his voice in the entryway and went to meet him, letter in hand. "Mr. Payne, Lorrie—Lady Lorraine—is not feeling well. She won't be traveling with us, and she asked me to write to her mother. I've never written to a duchess. Have I done it correctly?"

He seemed to absorb all of this information quickly and held his hand out to take the sheet of paper. He read it quickly then handed it back and nodded. "It's perfect."

"How do I address it?"

"The duke and duchess are at their country home?" he asked.

"Yes."

"I'll do it."

She followed him into the parlor, where he folded the paper into another and wrote on the outside, *Her Grace The Duchess of Ridlington* then scribbled the name of their country home and the other particulars. "Does she have a seal?" he asked.

"There." Modesty pointed to the heavy gold item.

Payne melted a bit of wax, swirled it on the back of the paper, and pressed the seal into it. Then he carried it to the entryway, flicked a finger at a footman, and handed the letter to the man. "Have this sent immediately." He handed the servant a few coins. "For the post," he said.

Modesty watched him, impressed. If she had harbored any doubts he was the son of a duke, she did not now. He had an authority that did not brook argument. He'd obviously grown up in a world of privilege and knew how to navigate it.

"How's Mostyn?" he asked.

"He's with her now," she said, deciding it would be best not to point out he'd been crying earlier. She was no gossip.

"I gather from the letter she hasn't lost the baby, but it's tenuous?"

Modesty did not know how to answer without saying something that would make her cheeks flame. "She says the doctor thinks all will be well with rest."

Mr. Payne let out a breath. "Rest isn't in her nature, but Ewan will strap her down if he has to. I suppose it's just the two of us then."

Modesty looked up sharply. "What do you mean?"

"Mr. Sterling, who has given us the use of his carriage, has business in Town and can't get away until tomorrow. He has another carriage and will meet us at Battle's Peak."

"Battle's Peak?"

"That's the name of Lord Nicholas's estate—well, his brother's estate, but his brother is...I don't know where the hell his brother is. In any case, we will be lodging there."

"And Mr. Okoro?"

Mr. Payne ran a hand through his hair, tousling it in a way she found very attractive and very tempting to smooth back into order. "He will come separately this evening or tomorrow. He sent a letter very early this morning to say he was unavoidably detained."

"I see." She straightened her shoulders. "Well, as I said, I do not need a chaperone."

"Lady Florentia is at Battle's Peak, and Sterling has equipped us with two outriders and a coachman. I think you'll be well protected."

But those men would be outside the carriage, and she would be alone inside. With him.

***

Rowden watched Miss Brown's eyes widen as she settled into Aidan's carriage. Rowden thought the interior looked more like a drawing room than a carriage. There was room for both of them to stretch their feet out or a footrest could be supplied with the pull of a lever. The interior was covered in the same plush fabric as the squabs, and the ceiling had been painted with a mural in the Greek style. A panel in the wall opened to supply wine and water on her side, and something a bit stronger on his. Aidan knew his drink of choice was brandy and soda and had made sure both were stocked. Another panel revealed wrapped sandwiches. On her side, that same panel held a pillow and slippers. A velvet blanket in cream had already been tucked about her and a warm brick was at her feet.

She looked a bit like a princess wrapped in velvet. But instead of a crown, she wore a simple bonnet, her hair gathered at the nape of her neck in a fiery coil.

He'd been annoyed at Chibale and Aidan for abandoning him, for leaving him solely responsible for Miss Brown. But he'd decided to make the best of it. He could keep their relationship shallow and platonic. He did not have to invite any intimacy.

"Mr. Sterling must be very wealthy," she said as they started away. Rowden smiled. Speaking of money was extremely gauche, but it didn't bother him. He liked that she was without pretense.

"Some say he's the richest man in England."

"What about the king?" she asked.

"Definitely richer than the king," he answered. And then because he wanted to see her cheeks pinken again, he said, "It's my understanding that your seat pulls out into a bed."

Her cheeks did turn rosy. "I suppose that is in case the traveler is forced to shelter in the carriage due to a storm."

He grinned at her. "I imagine that's a good reason for a bed too." Rowden opened the panel with the wrapped sandwiches. "Refreshment?" he asked.

She shook her head. "I've only broken my fast a couple of hours ago."

"Then you must be hungry again." He handed her a sandwich and opened his own. She laid hers down and peered out the window.

"Have you been out of London before?" he asked.

She nodded. "Once. When I was young, my father took us to Bath. It was lovely."

"Did you try the water at the Pump Room?" he asked. Speaking of drinks, he was thirsty. He opened the other panel and fixed a brandy with soda. He could definitely become used to this.

"I did, but the water was horrible," she said. "Are you drinking before noon?"

He raised his glass. "Want one?"

She shook her head. "I don't drink spirits. They—" Then she seemed to reconsider. "I would like one."

Rowden hadn't thought she would agree, but he poured her a drink anyway and passed it over. She tasted it and cocked her head. "This isn't bad."

Rowden sipped again. "You're drinking." He gestured to her dress. "Wearing colors. Attending mills. Whatever was in those letters must have been momentous."

She pursed her lips and drank again. Rowden mentally slapped his head. Why had he said that? It was the sort of comment that invited intimate revelations.

"I no longer see the point in standing on street corners yelling at people. To tell the truth, I never saw the point of that. Or the point of dressing as though I'm in mourning. I did it because I wanted to obey my parents."

"And you don't want to obey them anymore?"

"No, I don't," she said, finishing her drink and handing the glass back to him. He was about to replace it in the cabinet, when she said, "Another, please."

Rowden narrowed his eyes. "That's probably not a good idea."

"I'm tired of always being good. It's all a lie, you know. It's all pretense."

"I didn't know that, no," Rowden said, pouring her a splash of brandy and a great deal more of soda.

She took the glass back. "All of these years while he was pretending to be a man of God, he was lying and going against his own teachings."

Careful here, he told himself. *Step lightly*. "I suppose your father is human, just like everyone else. He made a mistake. Or mistakes."

"For twenty years? That's not a mistake." She set her glass down, and Rowden was relieved she seemed to be drinking this one slower. "And my mother." Tears were gathering in her eyes now and Rowden groaned silently.

"She knew, and she just looked the other way."

Rowden did not consider himself a particularly intelligent man, but neither was he a fool. Quite clearly, she'd discovered her father had a mistress and her mother had known about it. She swiped at a tear trailing down her cheek, and Rowden swore under his breath. If there was one thing he could not stomach, it was tears. They made him nervous and uncomfortable. Already he could feel the back of his neck growing warm and had the urge to get away.

But he couldn't get away unless he wanted to jump from a moving coach. That being an attractive but also unpalatable option, he crossed to sit beside her. She immediately threw herself into his arms, and the feel of her body pressed against his made him forget that he didn't relish tear stains on his coat.

He patted her back and shushed her and murmured soothing words. When she'd finally quieted, he found himself thinking back to his relationship with his own parents. His father had always been rather a remote figure. Rowden and his siblings had seen the duke in passing as he returned from Parliament and left for his club or when they chanced to pass by his study and his solicitor was leaving and they caught a glimpse of him from the crack in the door.

Their mother had been kind but always flitting here and there. She'd had balls and soirees and dinners to attend.

Rowden remembered her in a cloud of perfume and silk. As he'd gotten older and been home from school on holidays, he had come to see them a bit more. Those were formal evenings in the drawing room or at dinner. They took an interest in him, but they had several children, and all of them vied for their parents' attention. Rowden felt he hardly knew his parents or they him.

He did not argue when his father told him he should become a soldier. Rowden was just glad he would not have to become a clergyman or join the Navy. He was given a commission in the militia and quartered in the countryside, where he was able to attend balls and invited to dinners by the mamas of pretty girls. It was at one of those dinners that he'd met Mary.

He didn't want to think about Mary, and he didn't want to hold Modesty Brown. It seemed that every time he tried to escape Miss Brown, he ended up thrown together with her anyway. But that didn't mean he had to give in to temptation. He'd made that mistake when he'd met Mary at the tender age of eighteen. He was a man now, and he knew his own mind much better. And he did not intend to ever marry, to ever fall in love again.

"It's a hard lesson when we realize our parents are not the paragons of perfection we've made them to be in our heads," he said. She lifted her face and looked up at him. He was pleased to see she'd stopped crying.

"I hadn't thought of it that way. I suppose I did think of my father and mother as perfect, but of course, no one is without sin."

He pushed a strand of auburn hair off her cheek and tucked it behind her ear. "That's what I hear," he said. But he was having a hard time finding any fault with her. Those beautiful hazel eyes were looking into his, and he could lose himself in them.

"I think the brandy has gone to my head," she said. "I feel like I'm floating."

"I'll keep you tethered to earth."

"I like it when you hold me," she said.

Rowden raised his brows. "I think the drink has done more than create the sensation of floating."

"Everyone says spirits loosen the tongue and the morals. I suppose it's true because I can't stop thinking that I wish you would kiss me again."

Rowden carefully set her back and tried to move away. "That's not a good idea."

"I trust you," she said.

He laughed. "That's one of us."

She frowned at him. "I don't understand."

"Then let me make it clear." He moved closer again because he wanted to scare her a little, let her understand that he was not someone to play with. "I want you, Modesty. I've wanted you since I first saw you in that ugly dress and hat. I wanted to strip it off you and see what lay beneath."

Her eyes, so expressive already, widened.

"And every time I see you, I want you a little bit more."

She bit her lip, and he wanted to groan at the ache that caused. He wanted to take that mouth with his, feel her small white teeth nip at him.

"I want to kiss you again, but I don't want to stop at kissing you. And I have to stop there because I don't intend to marry you. That's not a slight. I don't intend to marry any woman, and you're not the kind of woman I can have without marrying. Do you understand?"

She nodded. He thought that would be the end of it. He even began to move back across the seat, but she grabbed his hand. "I don't intend to marry either."

Rowden shook his head, slowly. "You don't know what you're saying. You're young. You'll change your mind."

"I won't," she said, releasing him.

He moved back to his seat and lifted his brandy, suddenly thirsty. "Why is that?"

"Because it's a lie. I used to think it was a sacred covenant. Of course, I knew some men and women broke their vows, but not the men or women I knew. Not men like my father. I was a fool. My poor mother was made to look like a fool. I won't take that same path, accept that same fate."

He understood now that the contents of the letters had changed everything for her. Rowden wanted to tell her there was little her mother could have done, but he didn't think that was the point. She'd looked up to her mother and her father, emulated them, and then realized she'd been emulating a lie.

"What's in Hungerford?" he asked.

"My father's other wife. Well, he calls her wife. I don't know if he married her after my mother..." She made a gesture with her hand, and Rowden held his breath, hoping she did not begin to cry again.

She didn't.

"If you don't intend to marry, what do you intend? Most women marry out of necessity, not love."

She straightened—or at least tried to straighten. She was a bit disheveled in a way he found reminded him of a woman just rising from bed. "I have been thinking about that. I would make a good lady's companion, don't you think?"

He didn't want to mention that lady's companions were usually the impoverished daughters of gentry. "Lady

Lorraine would no doubt give you a reference," he said. And this was true and might be enough to secure her a position that, while it might not be in the upper classes, could mean a placement with a respectable lady of modest means.

"Do you think it would be presumptuous to ask her?"

"No," Rowden said. "You should ask when you return to Town."

She nodded then looked at him from under lowered lashes. "Did you mean what you said a few moments ago?"

Rowden knew exactly what she was referring to, but he would rather not bring it up again. "I don't remember what I said a few moments ago. And you should probably forget it as well."

***

Chibale should be on the way to Hungerford. He should be with his fighter. He should be enjoying the comforts of Mr. Aidan Sterling's coach. Instead, he was still in London, still at home, trying to decide how he could change Thérèse's mind.

His mother always said once a woman's mind was made up, there was no changing it. She liked to say she'd made up her mind to marry Gamba Okoro just hours after she'd met him, and once she'd set her cap for him, he didn't have a chance.

Chibale's father, for his part, had taken a bit longer to realize his future was inextricably linked to Charlotte's, but he'd given in at the end. Chibale had been pursuing Thérèse with this same precept in mind. She would realize they were meant for each other in the end. But since her declaration she would never marry, he had begun to doubt. She was not simply giving him a merry chase. She meant it. And as Chibale did want to marry, he wondered if he should simply let her go her way while he went his own.

He put his head in his hands and groaned. Rowden would tell him not to give up so easily. But Chibale's father would tell him that when a woman says no, she means it. Still, she hadn't exactly told him no. She still wanted him in her bed. She just didn't want him as her husband. Might he persuade her at some point that she *did* want him as her husband?

Not if he didn't know what her objection was. Did she hate marriage in general or was there something about Chibale in particular?

A rapid tapping came at the door, and someone called out. "Mr. Okoro? Mr. Okoro! Answer if yer home."

Chibale checked the clock on his mantel, noted the early hour, and called. "Who is it?"

"Twig, sir."

Chibale frowned. Did he know a Twig?

"From Madame Renauld's."

Chibale took the distance in two large strides and pulled the door open. "What's happened?" he demanded, staring down at the boy.

"It's 'er shop, sir. It's been turned topsy turvy. All ransacked, like."

"Ransacked?" Chibale grabbed his hat and overcoat and pulled them on, closing the door of his flat and following the boy. "Was anyone hurt? Weren't you there?"

"No, sir. Me ma was home last night. She works at a factory, and I don't see 'er much. She came by to fetch me before dinner. I stayed with me ma last night."

Chibale walked briskly through the cold drizzle falling over the city. "Does she come to fetch you often?"

"Nah. Only on Christmas and Easter, like."

"I see."

Twig ran to keep pace with Chibale's long strides. "Why'd you say it like that?"

"Because yesterday was neither Christmas nor Easter."

Twig stopped then ran to catch up again. "Ye think me ma turned the shop all topsy turvy?"

"No, but I think it convenient she was given a half day yesterday and the one night you're away, the shop is vandalized."

"I still don't…"

But Chibale saw the shop in the distance now. The sign was hanging askew and the front window was broken. He all but ran to the door and pushed it open. Several overturned tables impeded his progress. The parrot was not on her perch, but he spotted Thérèse standing in the center, directing her employees to this task or that.

"Thérèse," he said. She looked up, her face wearing the mask she wore when greeting customers, but as soon as she saw him, it dropped. Chibale jumped over the broken dress forms and bolts of silks to reach her and take her in his arms. She allowed him to embrace her but remained stiff. He realized she had to appear strong in front of her employees. "Let's go to the back for a few moments."

She looked as though she might object, but Chibale put a hand on her back and guided her. "Your women have things well in hand. You can step away for a few minutes."

The back room, where the seamstresses worked, looked just as bad as the front. Worktables were smashed, cloth had been strewn everywhere, and a dress on a female form had been slashed, the scissors still hanging from where they'd done the damage.

Thérèse opened the door to her office, and Chibale was relieved to see it had not been damaged. The parrot was there as well, preening at her feathers. She looked up at his entrance and said, "*Merde!*"

Chibale raised his brows at the French curse, and Thérèse let out a sigh. "*Silence*, Bleuette." She looked at Chibale. "Some days one does not want to hear the words repeated back, no?"

"What happened?" he asked.

"You see." She waved a hand expansively, making the lace sleeves of her dark blue dress flutter. She looked as elegant and beautiful as ever. "Someone broke down the door and did thees."

"Not this door." He indicated the door to her office, which he examined. The wood had been dented, as though kicked, but it was a thick, sturdy door with a good lock and had withstood the battering. Still, if the people who had done this wanted to break it down, they could have. But perhaps they were in too much of a hurry.

"I have a good lock on thees. I keep my designs in here." She reached for a bottle of wine on the marquetry cabinet behind her, but her hands shook, so Chibale rose and took it from her.

"Allow me."

"It ees early to drink, but I am shaking with rage."

With a bit of fear, too, he thought, though he didn't say it. "Have you sent for the magistrate?"

"*Oui*. He will come at his own pace. I have dealt with him before when I have caught thieves. He ees very helpful to the white shop owners. He does nothing for me."

Chibale could do little about magistrates who treated Black merchants differently than white. His own parents had faced similar problems, but they were at least citizens of England, whereas Thérèse did not have even that advantage.

"Do you have any idea who would do this?" He handed her the glass of wine he had poured.

"No," she said flatly. "I have thought about it. Madame LeMonde and I are rivals, but she would not do something like thees."

Chibale made a note to call on Madame LeMonde anyway. "Where were your bully boys last night? Your protection?"

She sipped the wine. "I pay them to be here when we are open. To…what ees the word? Deter?"

"Yes."

"To deter the thieves. They are not here at night. The boy who calls himself tree or branch—"

"Twig."

"*Oui*. He is usually here. But yesterday his *maman* came to fetch him. Perhaps it ees good he was not here."

Chibale sat on the couch. "Perhaps so. But I wonder."

"*Merde!*" the parrot screeched.

"*Silence!*" Thérèse said and put her head in her hands. "She will have to stay in the back or curse at the customers. If we ever have customers again."

"You will. You will clean this up in no time. But you will have to cancel your appointments for today."

She nodded. "I have already sent Phaedra to call on the ladies personally with our regrets. What ees it you wonder?" she asked.

"Ah, yes. How often does the boy Twig's mother come to fetch him?"

"Not often. She works in a factory and has lodgings there. She offered to pay me for his board and food here, but I told her no. To keep her money, and he can watch over the shop. She makes so little, how can I take it from her?"

"And yet she came yesterday. Unexpectedly."

Thérèse narrowed her eyes. "Thees ees true, but she would not do thees." Thérèse rose, went to the door and called, "Boy! Come here!"

"*Merde!*" Bleuette called. This time it was Chibale who told him to keep quiet. The bird looked at him. "Shall we have dessert?" the bird asked in a voice that sounded very much like Thérèse's.

Thérèse gasped and turned to glare at the bird. She sputtered something at the animal in French, which was too rapid for Chibale to understand. Apparently, the bird had been listening the other night at dinner—or, rather, after dinner.

Twig trudged into the workroom and then slouched through the door of Thérèse's office, where she had taken a seat behind her desk again. "Why did your mother come for you yesterday?" she asked. "It ees not usual."

Twig shook his head. "I've been thinking about that too," he said.

Chibale waited, but the boy said nothing more. "And," Chibale prompted. "What is your conclusion?"

He shrugged.

Chibale tried a different approach. "We don't blame your mother for this"—he gestured to the workroom—"but it is more than coincidence that she came to fetch you the night the shop was ransacked. Was she with you all night?"

"Course. We slept at me aunt's house. I got eleven cousins there, so we slept on the floor, but she were beside me all night."

"Did she say why she was given a half day?" Thérèse asked.

Twig shook his head. "She just said the forewoman came to her and told her she could take a half day."

Thérèse looked at Chibale, and he looked at Twig. "You may go help clean up now."

"Shall we have dessert?" Bleuette asked.

Twig paused. "There's dessert?" he asked, eyes widening.

"No," Chibale said, pushing the boy out the door. "Not that kind of dessert." He shut the door. Looking back at Thérèse he raised his brows. "Are you sure you have no enemies? I am not certain, but I think someone paid the factory manager or the forewoman to give that boy's mother the night off so the shop would be empty. A few coins would do the trick."

"I think you are right, but I can think of no one who would do thees to me."

"I'll help with putting things to rights," Chibale said. "And I'll stay with you tonight."

"Shall we have dessert?" Bleuette said.

Chibale glared at the bird. "To keep you safe. Not for...dessert."

"Perhaps we can do both." She glanced at him from under her lashes. "But I realized after I sent for you that I am imposing. You do not need to go to Hungerford?"

"I do, but I can go tomorrow. I sent Rowden early so he can rest before the fight."

"Then come to me tonight. But you must have other things to do besides sweep glass and right tables."

Chibale shook his head. "If you need me to sweep glass and right tables, then I'll be here all day."

Fifteen

The brandy and soda had not only gone straight to her head but also to her bladder. She'd been squirming in her seat and was glad to be able to use the necessary at the posting house where Mr. Sterling's horses were changed.

Mr. Payne had waited for her behind the posting house and taken her inside for tea. She took a few sips and then decided it might be best not to drink anything else. "I would like some air," she said. "Now that the rain has stopped."

"I think we outran it," Mr. Payne said.

"There's a yard in the back," the proprietor told her. "The grooms use it to walk the horses and brush them, but it should be empty right now if you want to take a turn."

"Thank you."

"I'll come fetch you in a moment," Payne told her.

She went out the back and found the yard. It was not as muddy as she had supposed it might be and though there were a few puddles, she could easily avoid them. She wished she hadn't given in to temptation and drank the brandy. She could

313

see why it was considered a vice as it had loosened her lips and she'd said things she now wished she hadn't. She'd told Mr. Payne she liked it when he held her, and then he'd said—

Her cheeks felt hot when she recalled his words.

He wanted her.

She wasn't exactly sure what that meant, but she rather wanted to find out. Even though she knew that was probably a greater sin than the spirits. And what did she care anymore? Was anything about sin or damnation what she had believed it to be? Her father had not worried about the fires of hell he so often preached about when he was with his mistress.

Mr. Payne did not want to marry. She was not a clever woman, but she could deduce his reasons. He'd loved his first wife. He'd given up everything for her. And she'd died. Of course he did not want to risk his heart again.

Modesty didn't want to risk her heart either, but she feared it was too late for that. Every time she thought of Mr. Payne or was in his presence, her breath came short and her head spun. He was a handsome man, but more than that, he was a good man. She hadn't said it to him in the coach because thankfully she hadn't had *that* much brandy, but she wanted him too. She did not know how to *un*want him. Though she feared her own heart would be broken if she did not find a way.

She neared the stables where she could hear the horses moving about and snorting softly. She was not at all comfortable with horses. She'd been born and raised in London and had never been very near to a horse unless it was racing toward her as she crossed a busy street. She usually tried to stay out of their way. But now she moved closer to peer into the stable, wondering just how many horses might be inside.

As soon as she moved under the eaves of the building, a hand closed about her mouth.

Modesty froze, forgetting for a moment what her father had taught her about how to defend herself. One didn't venture into the vice-ridden areas of Town without knowing how to protect oneself. Her father had been attacked many times and Modesty had to fend off a few amorous advances herself. But then she'd been ready for an attack. Now she was completely unprepared.

The man dragged her backward, into the stable, causing a few of the horses to snort in what sounded like fear. It was dark, and she couldn't see who he was, but her shock was beginning to fade. She struggled to elbow her captor in the ribs or kick him between the legs, but he managed to evade her limbs. Modesty began to panic now, her heart racing and her breathing coming quick and shallow. She knew panicking was the worst thing she could do, but she couldn't seem to free herself. She couldn't breathe well with his hand over her mouth.

"We'll see how he likes having something of his taken away," the man said, yanking her deeper into the dark. Modesty scrambled to remain on her feet, but she lost her balance and was dragged into a stall. Once inside, she was tossed against one of the walls, barely having time to lift her hands in an effort to keep her head from hitting the wood at full force. As it was, she was spared the worst of it, but when she bounced back, her leg scraped against a sharp corner of something in the stall—a feeding box, perhaps—and she heard the material of her new dress tear and felt the pain as her skin opened up.

Dimly, she heard voices in the yard, and she tried to call out to them. The man put his hand about her mouth again. "You deliver a message for me," the man said, his face close to hers. Modesty couldn't see him in the dark of the stable, and all she could smell was hay, leather, and horse. "Tell Payne this is just the beginning."

His hand hadn't fit as tightly about her mouth this time, and Modesty bit his palm as hard as she could. He swore and backhanded her then moved away. "Help!" Modesty called, her voice breathy. "Help!" she tried again, this time her voice carrying.

She heard footsteps running and a man burst into the stable, making the horses shift and snort again. "Miss Brown? Modesty!"

It was Payne's voice. "I'm here," she said, rising to her feet and stumbling out of the stall. He caught her, his strong arms wrapping protectively about her. "He went that way." She pointed toward the back of the stable.

"Who? Are you hurt? What happened?"

"He grabbed me and pulled me in here," she said.

Payne held her shoulders. "Who? One of the grooms?"

"I don't know." She stumbled, her injured leg buckling under her, and he bent and swept her into his arms, carrying her out into the yard, out of the darkness. Two men ran toward them.

"Sir, what's wrong? Is the lady injured?"

"Go fetch my outriders," he ordered.

One of the men ran off and the other stayed by their side. "What happened, sir?"

"She was dragged into the stable by a man."

"Who?"

Modesty shook her head. "I didn't see him."

The next quarter hour was a blur. Mr. Payne eventually set her down, and she was given tea laced with something that made her sleepy. A woman came in and tended her leg, and she was asked to look at all the men from the posting house, but she just shook her head. She hadn't seen the man who'd grabbed her, and these men looked too young and thin to be the man she'd struggled with. Finally, the men went to search the area, and one of the outriders helped her to the coach, where the seat had been pulled into the bed discussed earlier.

She laid down on it without protest and closed her eyes. Sometime later, she opened them again, and blinked up at the painting on the top of the coach. The conveyance was moving, and she was rocking gently. She didn't mind as she'd been wrapped under the velvet blanket and was warm. She glanced to her right and saw Mr. Payne on the seat just a foot or so away. With her seat extended, there was virtually no room between them.

"How are you feeling?" he asked.

She smiled. "Sleepy."

"That's the brandy they put in your tea. You had quite a shock. You were shaking so badly, we thought you needed it."

"I was shaking?"

"Yes. You seem better now."

She did a mental evaluation. She did feel better now. Her leg still ached, but her head did not hurt. She reached up to touch where she had hit it against the wall of the stall. It was still tender but not painful. She ran her hand down her hair, noting it was loose.

"It came down at some point, and I didn't know how to fix it," Payne said. "One of the men found your hat in the stable." He lifted it from the seat cushion beside him. It looked misshapen and dirty.

"Madame Renauld would be so disappointed," she said.

"I'll buy you another."

"It won't match the dress, though," she pointed out.

"About the dress."

"Oh, no!" She sat up, found her head spun, and had to wait a moment for the world to right itself. She pulled the blanket away from her skirts and stared down at the tear in her hem. "At least it is on a seam," she said. "I think it can be repaired.

"We'll find a seamstress in Hungerford," he said. "Or perhaps Lord Nicholas has a servant handy with a needle."

Though she knew it wildly inappropriate, she laid back on the bed. She should have asked Mr. Payne to remake the bed into a seat so she could sit, but she was warm and the rocking motion of the coach was soothing. She rather liked looking up at the painting on the top of the coach.

After a few minutes, he spoke again. "Can you tell me what happened? I caught bits and pieces earlier, but I'd like the details if you can remember them and they won't upset you."

Modesty smiled at him. He treated her like one of the ladies from the upper classes, ladies who were so delicate they could not bear to even think of unpleasantness, much less be presented with it. But she had grown up surrounded by poverty and suffering, and she was made of stronger stuff.

"I was taking a turn in the yard and as I passed the stables, I looked in. I suppose I was curious about the horses. That's when someone—a man—put his hand about my mouth and dragged me inside." She turned her head, her gaze level with Mr. Payne's seat and saw his hands were clenched tightly on the squabs. "For a moment," she said, watching his knuckles whiten, "I forgot to fight. My father taught me how to protect myself, but I was so surprised. He dragged me into a stall and threw me against one of the walls. I put out my arms and caught myself, but I hit my head and fell back."

"Go on," Mr. Payne said. "Did you see the man? Did he speak?"

She looked up at him, meeting his pretty green eyes. "He did. He said something like, 'Let's see how he likes having something taken away.'"

"What does that mean?"

"I don't know. But he was speaking of you."

"Me?" Mr. Payne leaned forward. "How do you know?"

"He said, 'Tell Payne this is just the beginning.'"

He sat back, his face a mixture of rage and confusion. "And you saw nothing of the man?" he finally asked.

"No. Do you think it was one of the men from the posting house?"

"That was my first thought, but they were all accounted for. No one was in the stable when you were there, and by the time we thought to search the stable and the area behind it, we didn't find anyone."

She remembered that she had hurt her leg in the stable and sat to take a look. But of course, as soon as she pulled the blanket back, she realized she couldn't lift her skirts to look at her leg with him right there.

"How is your leg?" he asked.

"The injury does not feel serious."

"Let's take a look." He knelt down beside the bed and reached for her torn hem. Modesty knew she should object to his lifting her skirts and peering at her legs, but she said nothing when he did just that. Her stocking was ruined and had been torn away so that it hung open to reveal a white cloth bound about her shin. "May I?" Mr. Payne asked.

Modesty nodded and he untied the cloth and looked down at her leg.

"Nasty scrape," he said.

"Yes." But she could see it might have been much worse. It hadn't even really bled. The top layer of skin had been removed, leaving a raw, red jagged swath. She began to shake and put her arms around herself to try and stop it. She didn't know why she was shaking. Seeing the mark on her leg made her remember the dark of the stable and the helplessness of being dragged inside.

Mr. Payne wrapped her leg again then sat on the bed beside her and pulled her into his arms.

"I'm fine," she said, burying her head in his chest.

"You're shaking and your skin is cold. I'll tell them to stop at the next posting house."

"No." She did not want to stop at anymore posting houses. But more than that, she did not want Rowden Payne to let her go. "Just hold me. I feel better when you hold me."

And so he held her, his hand running lazily up and down her back as her shakes slowly became trembles and then faded away. Wordlessly, she moved to one side of the bed, making room for him. He began to protest, but she pulled him down beside her and turned to face him, snuggling into his arms.

He held her, his arms lightly wrapped about her, but she was close enough to hear the rapid beating of his heart and the way his breath hitched. He was as aware of her as she him. She looked up at him then, his face so close to hers, and his gaze met hers. She put a hand on one of his cheeks and tilted his head down then kissed him. He kissed her back, his lips tender against hers. She could feel the tension in him, knew he was restraining himself. She moved to kiss his cheek, his jaw, his temple.

"You said earlier," she said, brushing her lips over his ear and hearing him suck in a breath, "that you wanted me. I want you too."

He moved back, away from her, which had definitely not been her intention. "You don't know what you're saying."

"I do," she said. "I've read Song of Solomon."

He smiled. "What I want is more than pretty poetry."

"You think I don't know what you want?" she asked, looking down at him. "I spent years of my life outside taverns and brothels. I saw what happened in dark nooks and crannies. I wasn't supposed to look, but I saw enough."

"And that's what you want?" he said.

"I want you to touch me. I want you to show me what drove those men and women into those dark nooks. Why I heard them moaning in pleasure."

"You want me to show you pleasure?"

Her cheeks heated, but she was not about to shy away now. "Yes," she said. "And show me how to give it to you."

He reversed their positions, so he was leaning over her. He hadn't pinned her down, but he could do so easily. He was a big man and strong. Still, she wrapped her arms around his neck and tilted her lips up for a kiss.

"What happened to the woman I met dressed all in black? The one who asked if I couldn't find an honest way to make a living but who is now on her way to the biggest mill of the year?"

"She found out everything she believed was a lie."

"Everything?"

"Maybe not everything." She'd known from the beginning he was a good man. She still believed that. "Will you kiss me or no? I suppose there are other men in Hungerford I could ask..." She had been teasing, of course.

But perhaps she'd done it wrong because his face changed, darkening into a fierce scowl.

"No, you won't," he said. She started to tell him she would never do such a thing, and that's when he lowered his lips to hers. The heat of his touch, his lips, his mouth was undeniable. It was a molten, intoxicating heat that, she would be ashamed to admit, she gave into easily. His kiss was like the brandy. It made her lightheaded and dizzy and thirsty for more.

The rocking of the coach brought their bodies into contact, and she clung to him for stability, even as his mouth unmoored her and left her reeling. When he finally broke the kiss, she felt as though she were floating. She would have held onto his neck as an anchor, but he gently removed her arms and lowered his head to kiss her neck. His cheek was stubbled, and the scratch of that stubble contrasted with the softness of his lips made her moan softly.

He looked up at her. "That's a sound I didn't expect to hear from you. Let's see what happens if I kiss you here." His lips moved to the hollow at the base of her throat, and he darted his tongue out to tease her skin. Modesty inhaled quickly, her hands clutching at his shoulders. "Does that grip mean stop or continue?" he asked. He looked up at her with those beautiful green eyes.

"Continue," she said. "Please."

"So polite," he said, trailing his lips down to the edge of her bodice. "But I've seen the way you look when something illicit excites you."

She imagined she looked that way now as the way his tongue dipped into the top of her bodice was illicit. Her body was tense with anticipation and need.

"How do I look?" she asked, her voice breathy as his hands moved under her breasts. His gaze on hers, he slid his hands up to cup her, his thumbs finding her nipples even under all the layers of undergarments.

"Beautiful," he said, his gaze still on her. She wanted him to touch her bare skin, wanted to feel his warm flesh on hers, but the neckline was too high to be pulled down.

"I wish I could feel your skin on mine," she said.

He froze, his body going rigid.

"Did I say the wrong thing?"

"No, but if you keep saying things like that, I will need a few moments to—er, gather my strength."

"I don't understand. What strength—" She broke off as one hand slid down her body, over her hip, and ruched up her skirts. A moment later, she felt his warm palm on the knee of her uninjured leg. She gasped.

"Is this what you want?"

Oh, yes. It was exactly what she wanted. For a moment, she could hear her father's voice preaching about fornication and the fires of hell, but then she thought of the letters, and pushed the voice away. How could it be sinful to feel this good? How could it be sinful when they were both willing?

"Yes," she murmured. "You're so warm."

"So are you." His hand moved upward. "And soft." His hand covered her thigh, gently parting her legs then slipping onto the tender skin of her inner thigh. He moved his fingers higher, causing her breathing to accelerate. But he paused before reaching the juncture of her thighs and looked down at her.

"Should I move higher?"

She hesitated.

"I won't be angry if you say no." His voice was low and sincere. "I'd rather stop now than have you regret anything. I'd rather stop now than have you feel as though you are damned for what we do next."

"No God would damn a person for this," she said. "He created pleasure."

"Are you convincing yourself, Modesty, or me?"

"I don't need any convincing," she said.

"What do you need?"

"You." She kissed him again, and his tongue dipped inside her lips, causing a jolt of heat to course through her. And then his hand moved higher, brushing over her curls and she made a sound of surprise and pleasure.

His touch was light and gentle as it moved over her, exploring and teasing. He kissed her as he touched her, but when he found that place where she gasped and moaned at his touch, he released her mouth and looked down at her.

"Rowden," she said on a strangled breath.

"I'm here. God, you're beautiful right now."

No one had ever told her she was beautiful before him. She'd always been taught physical beauty didn't matter. But he made her feel beautiful, and she loved that about him. She loved what he was doing with his fingers too, and even as she thought it, pleasure like none she had ever felt before began to spiral through her until her entire body was filled with it, making her cry out.

He kissed her again, covering the sound with his mouth, and she wrapped her arms about him and held him tightly.

Sixteen

Trogdon greeted them at Battle's Peak. Though he had only set out an hour or so before them, he informed Rowden he'd been at the country house most of the day.

"I'm glad you made good time."

Rowden did not mention that his delay had been mostly due to Modesty's attack. She seemed to be recovered from that fright. He liked to think he had taken her mind off it for a little while.

Of course, he'd also like to think of himself as a man with a strong will, but though he had promised himself he would not become involved with her, he'd complicated things irrevocably. Now that he'd had a taste of her, he wanted more. The problem was that, regardless of how often she argued that she'd renounced her former morals, she wasn't an experienced woman he could take to bed for one night. He'd already compromised her enough to warrant a marriage proposal.

Even the thought of marriage made Rowden feel as though the world had begun to spin too fast. He did not want to marry again. And yet, he continued to find himself wanting Modesty Brown and in a position to take advantage of those less than pure thoughts.

"The public coach is fast, sir," Trogdon said, drawing Rowden's attention. "Unfortunately, I was obliged to sit on top. My hands are quite frozen and incapacitated."

"Really? From sitting atop the public coach?"

"I am obliged to ask another servant to carry in your bags."

Rowden raised his brows. Trogdon looked perfectly dressed and his blond curls neat and tidy, so unless he had someone else arrange his clothing, his hands were working just fine. But Rowden had learned arguing with Trogdon was pointless as any attempt at logic was quite useless, and so he summoned one of Lord Nicholas's footmen and asked him to carry his valise as well as Miss Brown's luggage.

The housekeeper had introduced herself and offered to show them to their rooms after they'd had refreshment. Lady Florentia, Lord Nicholas's sister, was waiting for them in the drawing room. Rowden wondered why Lord Nicholas was not there as well, but he knew better than to ask the house-keeper questions about the family.

He took Miss Brown's arm and led her inside, where she paused in the foyer to gape at the grand marble staircase, the high ceiling and crystal chandelier, and the huge paintings by Renaissance masters on the walls.

Trogdon followed the footmen inside, keeping an eye on Rowden's valise, and commenting that the man was carrying it incorrectly. Rowden hadn't been aware there was a correct way to carry a valise, but who knew what other body parts of Trogdon's might be incapacitated if Rowden made the wrong remark. The housekeeper led them upstairs to the drawing room, and Miss Brown leaned in close. "I have never been anywhere as grand as this except Westminster Abbey and St. Paul's Cathedral."

"Lord Nicholas's brother is the Marquess of Averstow. The family is one of the oldest in England and quite wealthy." She smelled a bit of brandy and him. His scent was on her. Her cheeks were still rosy and her lips a bit swollen from his kisses. Rowden would have liked to carry her to his room and make her moan again, but that was the way to marriage, and he was growing tired of reminding himself not to continue along that path. He would turn back now and keep his hands to himself.

"Is the marquess here?" she asked.

"No. I don't believe this is the family seat. The family is known for breeding horses, and I believe this is where they stable and breed them. Lord Nicholas and his sister reside here and manage the horses."

Though the housekeeper had been pretending not to listen, Rowden had not lowered his voice, and now the servant added, "Actually, Lady Florentia does not reside here. But she has been staying here for the winter to keep her brother company." She opened the doors to the drawing room, and Rowden practically had to drag Modesty inside. She stood gaping. The chamber had been decorated in the Greek style, with columns in white and white plaster and moldings all around. The groupings of chairs were spread throughout the room, the furnishings upholstered in pale cream or gold. A lady with dark brown hair and large brown eyes rose from one of those groupings and smiled at them. She wore a white gown with gold trim.

Rowden couldn't remember ever meeting her from the name alone, but he recalled her face. He and Lord Nicholas had known each other before the war, and their families had spent time together in the country.

"My lady," he said with a bow. "Thank you for opening your home to us."

She waved a hand. "Lord Rowden." She curtseyed. "We have a dozen empty rooms. I am more than happy to fill them. Since my brother won't allow any parties, I was so pleased when Mr. Sterling's letter arrived. And who is this?"

"Might I present Miss Modesty Brown."

Lady Florentia came forward. "Miss Brown, a pleasure." She looked toward the door. "Where is Lady Lorraine and her husband?"

Rowden doubted Ewan would enjoy being relegated to Lady Lorraine's husband, but Florentia and Lorraine were of an age and had probably known each other for years. "She is unwell," he said. "They are staying in London. Miss Brown would have stayed with her, but she has pressing business in Hungerford."

"I see. Come sit by the fire and warm yourselves. Tea will be here in a moment. Was the journey awful?"

"Considering we were offered the use of Mr. Sterling's coach, it was very pleasant," he said.

"I want to see that coach later," Lady Florentia remarked. "I have read about it. He sent a note that he will arrive tomorrow in plenty of time to watch your…how did he say it…in time to watch you have your brains beat in? Something like that."

Rowden recognized the joke, but before he could issue a rejoinder, Modesty broke in. "He won't have his brains beat in. He'll defeat the German this time. He only lost last time because I distracted him."

"Did you?" Lady Florentia said, giving Rowden a knowing look. "I want to hear all about that."

The tea arrived and Rowden took the opportunity to ask what he really wanted to know. "Lord Nicholas won't be joining us?"

Lady Florentia's lips tightened. "Not right now. He is here, but he keeps to himself for the most part or spends time in the stables. He was never terribly social, but I do worry he spends too much time alone."

"Has he started riding again?" Rowden asked.

"No. He works with the horses, but he won't mount one. It's been two years now, my lord. I have begun to fear he will never again ride."

Rowden caught Modesty's curious glance but didn't enlighten her. "I'll speak with him."

"You may try, but I believe he's avoiding you. When your manservant arrived, Nicholas walked off muttering that he wanted to be left alone."

"Well, that's quite a normal reaction to Trogdon, I think."

She laughed. "You always could make all of us smile, my lord."

"Just a mister now, Lady Florentia." He rose. "A working man. If you don't mind, I will take my leave. I want to see the venue for the mill."

Miss Brown placed her teacup on the table. "Shall I come with you?"

He shook his head. "It's not the best place for a lady, and it will be dark soon. I'll take you on your errand tomorrow. In the meantime, my lady, is there a seamstress who can repair Miss Brown's dress? She had a bit of trouble at a posting house."

Lady Florentia pretended to just notice Miss Brown's torn hem and promised to have her own lady's maid repair it. Rowden bowed and left them. He made his way to the stable but did not spot Lord Nicholas. Instead, he asked a groom if there was a horse he could borrow to ride into Hungerford and was given a mare who was fast but good-natured. It was only about three miles to the race course housing the exhibition site, and as the mare was quick, Rowden arrived while it was still light.

He dismounted, tossed the reins to one of the lads who was standing about for that purpose, and entered the tent that had been erected to house the mills. The seating had not yet been put in place, but the fighting square and the ropes stood at the ready. He spotted the famous bareknuckle boxer Tom Cribb at the ropes and stood beside him.

Cribb nodded at him. "I hear you're fighting the German."

"That's right." Rowden hadn't realized Cribb was also fighting. He'd certainly be a bigger draw than Rowden and the German. "What about you?"

"One of the umpires."

Rowden felt some of the tension seep out. If he was still the main draw, his share of the prize money and the stakes would be higher. Cribb looked about. "Where's Okoro? He isn't your manager any longer?"

"He had business in London and will come tomorrow."

Cribb nodded. "If you want me to put you through your paces tomorrow, I'd be happy to oblige." He held up his hands. "I'm not trying to take Okoro's place."

"It's a generous offer," Rowden said. "I'll take you up on it."

Cribb's gaze narrowed and he frowned. Rowden glanced at the far end of the tent and spotted Notley. "What's he doing here?" Cribb asked. "He doesn't have a milling cove entered."

"Poaching off others," Rowden said. "He lost the Black Plague and will want to acquire new talent."

Cribb nodded. "I might have heard something about that. You'd better watch your back. Notley's not the forgiving type."

"I can take care of myself."

Cribb slapped him on the back. "I wouldn't put it past him to go after Okoro or someone else in your circle."

Rowden considered. Notley would be sorry if he went after Chibale. Modesty was safe enough at Battle's Peak, but earlier...

"When did Notley arrive?" Rowden asked Cribb.

Cribb shrugged. "This is the first time I've seen him today."

Across the room Notley smiled at him and lifted his hat. Rowden didn't smile back. Notley was surrounded by his usual cronies, and Rowden could hardly march over there and accuse him of attacking Modesty, especially without any proof. And yet, the way Notley smiled made the hair on the back of Rowden's neck stand up.

***

Thérèse collapsed onto the emerald longue in her parlor and gratefully accepted the cup of tea her servant handed her. Chibale took one as well, though he continued to stand.

"Have some tea," Thérèse told him. "You have worked hard today."

"I'm thinking of returning to the shop. If whoever did this comes again tonight, I'll be waiting."

She rose and put her arms about his waist. "They will not return. They did what they came to do."

Chibale turned his head. "Why do you say that?"

She gave a shrug. "Because they did not take anything. They did not break down the door to my office and steal the money. They did not steal the silks and the dresses off the forms. They could sell thees and have coin in their pockets. They wanted to destroy."

"So we are back to assuming they are vandals."

"What else?"

"I don't know. If they come back tonight—"

She slid around to look him in the eye and put her finger on his lips. "If they return tonight, my bully boys will deal with them. All ees safe and well." She kissed him. "Sit down and have some tea."

"Shall we have dessert?" the parrot asked, and Thérèse blew out a breath. She would have thrown curses at the bird, but she would only hear them repeated in the shop the next day. Instead, she coaxed Bleuette to her shoulder, petted her, and then placed her in her cage, covering it for the night.

"That bird," she muttered, sitting next to Chibale on the longue, "annoys me to no end."

"Why do you keep her?"

She looked at him, wondering how much to tell him, wondering why she did not tell him all. He was not like the other men she had known. He was kind and sweet. He had invited her to a ball and to meet his family. But she doubted he would want her to meet his family if he knew the truth about her. Perhaps now was the time to find out, before her feelings for him became any stronger. She could already tell his feelings for her were serious. Thérèse had suspected this before, but after all he had done today, there was little question.

She looked at Bleuette's cage and then back at Chibale. "I keep her because she ees like me."

Chibale raised a brow. "You are both very beautiful, but I think the resemblance ends there."

"That ees because you do not know her story. I took her from a house in Paris. The master of the house, a rich nobleman, had ordered several dresses for his newest paramour. I brought the dresses and conducted the fitting myself. In those days, I had no reputation and took what work I could get—actresses, courtesans. I specialized in risqué gowns, and thees nobleman wanted that for his new paramour. And so I came to the flat, and I did the fitting. The girl was very silly and the nobleman very vain. I could tell he was a collector of beautiful things, but they were just things to him, not treasures. A priceless painting tossed in a corner. An expensive vase used for rubbish. A beautiful bird, neglected and dying."

Chibale glanced at Bleuette's cage.

"Yes. It was she. I could not forget her. I felt...how do you say...solidarity with her? And so when it came time for payment, I asked for the bird."

"What did the nobleman say?"

"He argued, the idiot. The dresses were worth more than the bird, who was in poor condition, but he argued anyway. Finally, his mistress intervened and gave me the bird. I took her home and nursed her back to health. And you see how she repays me?"

"Surely she doesn't know what she is saying."

"No, and she ees very unusual. Ladies come into the shop to see her and then stay to buy. She ees an asset." She leaned closer to him. "But today it ees you who I needed. You who were the asset." She would have kissed him, but he put a hand on her shoulder.

"You said she was like you. How so?"

Thérèse had known he would not let that point go. Hadn't she wanted him to ask? She sat back. "Because once I too was in a cage—not a literal cage—but a cage nonetheless. And I was neglected and ready to die."

Chibale surged to his feet. "Who did this to you? I will kill him."

She waved a hand. "It was long ago and far away. I was a different person then. Literally, a different person. Thérèse Renauld was not my name. I was given to thees man very young. Not a marriage, no. My mother did the best she could for me. The life she gave me was no different from hers."

Chibale took her hand, his face blank and unreadable.

"She sold me," she said bluntly. "She was a courtesan, and she sold my virginity to the highest bidder, who made me his mistress. Thees man was older and wealthy. He took me to another city in France. He took me away from my family and friends. I knew no one and had no friends. He put me in a house and locked the door. I was not allowed to leave. I was to be always available to him, if you understand." Chibale's hand on hers tightened, to show he did understand. "Sometimes he would be gone for a day. Sometimes a week. Once he was gone for a fortnight, and I had no food. I pounded on the door, called out for help, but no one came. I thought I would die. And while I lay dying, weak and faded as Bleuette in her rich man's cage, I made a plan to escape. That was if I should survive.

"He returned, and I waited until I had my strength back, and then when he was asleep, I hit him over the head with a lamp and ran."

"Thank God." He tried to pull her in, but she shook her head. She wanted to tell him all of it now.

"If God was truly to be thanked, he would have died. But he lived, and he came after me. That was why I hid, why I sewed gowns for actresses and prostitutes, why I fled to England. As difficult as it ees to find someone in Paris who does not want to be found, I knew as my dresses became more popular and more sought after, he would find me. I prayed after all these years, he had given up on me, but I could never be certain. I could never stop looking over my shoulder. And so I came here."

"Do you think he is responsible for the damage done to your shop?"

"I do not know," she said. "It ees possible. But if he has found me, then I am in danger of more than damage to my shop."

Chibale pulled her to him now, and she allowed it. She had never told anyone about her past, and she was trembling from the memories that assaulted her. But Chibale's arms were strong, and his body was solid. He held her closely, and when she put her head on his chest, she could hear his heart beating slowly and steadily. This was a man she could rely on, a man she could trust. She had so few people in her life like that, and to find a man who she could believe in, after all these years when she thought such a thing impossible, was akin to a miracle.

The thought struck her as the sort of thing a child would think. And then she realized it was more the thing a woman in love might think.

She looked up at Chibale, and he looked down at her, and she saw the same love she felt reflected back at her. As though to punctuate it, he said, "I love you, Thérèse."

She stared at him, the image of him in shirtsleeves with a broom sweeping up broken glass foremost in her mind. "You really do, don't you?"

He kissed her forehead. "When did you realize it?"

"That night you sent the Black Death away."

"I did that for Phaedra," he teased.

"And for me," she said. She rose and took his hand. "Shall we have dessert?" she whispered.

"Yes." But instead of following her into the bedchamber, he reached down and swept her up into his arms.

"*Mon Dieu*!" she cried. "What ees this?"

"I will protect you, Thérèse." He carried her to the bedchamber. "I will keep you safe. Tonight, tomorrow, for as long as you want me."

Thérèse wrapped her arms around him and when he lowered her to the bed, she closed her eyes and sank into the tender press of his lips, the stroke of his hands, the weight of his body on top of hers. She had watched Chibale all afternoon, and he was a man who took his work seriously. He paid attention to detail. He did a thorough job.

He undressed her slowly, took his time arousing her, watching until she was breathing quickly and clutching him desperately. She was a woman of thirty and…well, one need not delve into specifics. She was an experienced woman, but with Chibale, she felt like this was all new again. She felt as though she'd never wanted a man so much.

And when he finally, *finally,* slid inside her, joining their bodies as well as their hands and their lips, she was happier than she'd ever been. She opened her eyes and looked up at him, telling him silently that she loved him too.

***

"I am not leaving you," Chibale said, setting his fork on the plate and giving Thérèse her own formidable stare right back at her. "Rowden can handle himself."

Thérèse, looking lovely with her hair in waves over her shoulder and the morning sunlight filtering through the curtain behind her, shook her head.

"So can I, *mon chéri*." She lifted a pastry and took a bite, not a dainty bite but a real bite. He liked that about her. She was not ashamed of her appetites.

"After what happened the night before last, I'd like to stay close by."

She shook her head. "Your fighter needs you, and I won't have you mees thees exhibition. I will ask my maid to stay, and the bully boys will watch the shop. Don't shake your head. You will regret it if you do not go."

"There will be another fight."

"Perhaps." She shrugged. "But not another like thees one. You will go, and when you return, it will be time for the ball. I have almost finished the dress. I think you will like it." She winked.

Chibale raised a brow. "Can I see it?"

"Oh, no! I want to enjoy the surprise on your face when I show it to you that night. So you see that I will be fine. Go to Hungerford and win the fight."

"I don't actually fight," he said, folding his napkin and setting it aside. He rather liked watching her eat.

"That does not mean the victory ees not also yours."

Chibale didn't like it. He didn't like leaving her alone after the vandalism at her shop, didn't like being so far away if she needed him. At one time he would have said that this fight was the most important thing in his life. It was still important, but not nearly as important as Thérèse.

"Win the fight," the parrot said.

"There you are," Thérèse said, gesturing with her fork. "Even Bleuette agrees."

"How can I argue with Bleuette?"

"Pretty bird," Bleuette added. "Fine lace!"

"That's enough," Thérèse said. She rose. "You should go now, or you will not arrive until late."

"I hadn't actually made up my mind to leave yet," he said.

"I have. Come to me as soon as you return, *oui*?" She reached for the door handle, but he pulled her into his arms and kissed her. When he finally ended the kiss, she looked at him with a dreamy look. "As soon as you return," she said. She fumbled with the door but finally managed to open it. He saw himself out and went directly to the modiste shop.

Chibale knew Thérèse would be right behind him and did not want her to chastise him for not leaving yet. But he wanted to see how the night had gone. He rapped on the front door, scowling at the boards covering the broken window. One of the bully boys opened it and nodded at him. "Was hoping ye'd come by. Have something for ye."

Chibale refrained from asking what that might be and followed the man into the back room. There he found another man with dark skin, though lighter than his own, who was tied up and gagged. Chibale gave one of the men—the bully boys—a look.

"Found him skulking about last night, we did."

"I spotted 'im," Twig said, stepping into the room, chest puffed out and hands on hips. "I saw 'is shadow pass the door, I did."

"Good job," Chibale said, tousling the boy's hair. He crouched down and lowered the gag. "Who sent you?" he asked.

"I didn't do nothing!" the man said, the words coming out in a rush. "I were just walking by, minding my own business."

"No. 'E was skulking, 'e was," the bully boy said.

Chibale looked back at the bound man. "What business takes you near a dress shop in the middle of the night?"

The man looked from the bully boy to Chibale, obviously frantic to think of a lie. "I...I...me ma lives nearby."

Chibale leaned back on his heels. "Really? Where? I'll take you to her." He stood the man up and gestured for Twig to open the back door. Twig gave him a pained expression.

"Ye don't believe 'im, do ye?"

"Open the door," Chibale said. The lad obeyed, and Chibale ushered the man outside. Then he leaned close. "Now that there aren't any witnesses, you'd better tell me the truth. Because if you don't, even your ma won't recognize your face."

"Ye'd better not touch me."

"Then start talking."

The man stared at him, lips compressed.

Chibale released him and stepped back. "If that's how you want it." He raised an arm.

"Fine! It were Notley."

Chibale's arm dropped as though it had been weighed down with lead. He hadn't expected the man to say Notley. He hadn't expected the damage done to the shop would have anything to do with him. He gestured to the shop. "So this is because of me?"

"I don't know why. I'm not paid to ask questions."

"What did he pay you to do?"

The man glanced at Chibale's fist, now balled. Slowly, Chibale opened it.

"He paid me to break the window and toss it. Overturn tables and shred the fabrics and the like."

"Just you?"

The man compressed his lips again, obviously unwilling to give the name of the men who'd done this with him.

"I'll try a different question. Was Notley here?"

The man shook his head. "He had some fight to go to. Said he had business there."

Chibale hissed in a breath. Notley had no business at the fight as his only fighter was on a ship right now. And who was responsible for that? Chibale and Rowden. Rowden, who was in Hungerford right now.

"Why'd you come back last night?"

"I don't know. Guess I wanted to see what I'd done. Should have stayed away."

Chibale grabbed his coat and pushed him against a wall. "I'll give you some advice, friend. When I untie those binds, run home and don't ever come near here again. Next time I see you anywhere nearby, I'll do to you what you did to those dresses inside." He drew out a knife he carried and made a slashing motion and the man's eyes widened. Finally, he nodded his head. Chibale spun him around and used the knife to cut the ropes.

"Get out of here."

The man ran.

Chibale took a breath and went back into the shop. "Say nothing of this to Madame Renauld. But I want one of you"—he pointed to the bully boys—"here at all times. If anything happens to her—"

"It won't," one of them said. "We care about her too."

"Good. I'll be back in a couple of days."

"Where are you going?" Twig asked.

"To settle some scores."

Seventeen

"Oh, good, I've caught you," Modesty said as Rowden strolled into the breakfast room the next morning. His brows rose when he saw her, and she definitely noticed the way his eyes warmed.

"You are up early."

"I missed you last night. I wanted to wait up, but the day tired me more than I thought."

"I was out late." He gestured to the sideboard. "Would you like something with your tea?"

She shook her head. "I'm not hungry."

He piled food on his plate as he would need energy for Cribb's coaching and then for the fight later this evening. "I'm sorry I left you with Lady Florentia."

"I don't mind at all. She was very kind, and look." She stood and showed him her dress.

"It looks as though it was never torn," he said.

"Her maid was wonderful."

He glanced at her hair as she sat again, and she felt her cheeks warm.

"Did she do your hair?"

Modesty nodded.

"I like it."

Modesty did too. It had been pulled back in a loose bun with a generous portion falling down her back in auburn curls. The maid had commented how lovely the color was, and Modesty had almost believed her. For so long she had thought of her hair as a curse. But perhaps it was pretty. Rowden seemed to think so.

The dining room door was open, and she spotted Rowden's manservant pass by, peer in, then keep walking. Rowden saw him too but ignored him. "Did Lord Nicholas ever join you?" he asked.

"No. Lady Florentia said he doesn't care for company."

Outside the doors, the manservant passed again.

"Only the company of horses. But I thought he had better manners." He slammed his fork down, and Modesty jumped. "Stop pacing in front of the door, Trogdon, and come in."

The manservant slid inside and bowed. "So sorry to bother you, sir."

"I thought you'd be gone by now," Rowden said.

"Yes, about that. What was I to do again, sir? My hands, you know—"

"Shut up about your hands. I asked you to go into town and buy oranges, Trogdon. For the fight this evening."

"Ah." Trogdon nodded confidently then shook his head.

"Why are you shaking your head?" Rowden asked.

"It's the middle of winter, sir. There aren't any oranges."

Rowden sighed and muttered, "This is why I need Chibale."

Modesty decided to help. "Mr. Trogdon, is it?"

"Yes, miss." He bowed to her. "Good morning to you."

"Good morning. You make a good point about it being winter."

He smiled at her. "Citrus fruits don't grow in the winter. I learned that in school." He gave Rowden a sideways glance as though to imply his employer had *not* learned much in school.

"I learned that as well, but there is an exhibition this evening, and there are perhaps a dozen"—she looked at Rowden—"what do you call them? Milling coves?"

"Yes." He was watching her with a curious expression.

"There are a dozen or so milling coves in town. They will all want oranges for the fight tonight, yes?"

Trogdon tapped his chin with his hand, which he had wrapped with linen strips. "They will, miss."

"Is it not reasonable that some enterprising shopkeeper has thought of this and purchased oranges to sell in town?"

Trogdon's eyes lit up. "I wish I had thought of that, miss. I'd make a bundle."

"Next time, Trogdon," Rowden said. "Right now I'd like you to go buy several oranges."

"Very well, sir. I'll do my best." He bowed again and departed.

"I'd like to strangle him with those so-called bandages," Rowden said. "There's nothing wrong with his hands. I caught him tying his neckcloth this morning."

Modesty sipped her tea. "I think you will get further with your servant if you play along and give him sympathy." Rowden stared at her as though she had lost her mind. She couldn't help but smile at his expression. "Hear me out. I have known people like him before, often older widows who complain incessantly and drive everyone away. But they just want attention. They want someone to acknowledge them and hear them. Often their lives have been difficult, and they want sympathy. I imagine a bit of sympathy will go a long way with Trogdon as well."

Rowden stared at her. "You want me to coddle my manservant?"

"It couldn't hurt. Give him some salve for his hands and ask how they are. I imagine they will heal much faster if he is given attention for them."

"There's nothing wrong with them," Rowden muttered.

Modesty put her hand on top of Rowden's and squeezed. He looked up at her, and she thought he might say something about what had happened in the coach yesterday. She thought he might give some indication as to whether it had meant anything to him. But he pulled his hand back and lifted his fork again.

Modesty tried not to feel hurt. He'd told her he wanted her against his better judgement. Perhaps he was regretting what they'd done in the coach already. She wondered if she should tell him she wouldn't demand he marry her. Certainly, her missing father wouldn't demand it either. But it might be better to leave things alone.

"I know you must have much to do in order to prepare for this evening," she said. "I was wondering if you could have the coach take me to…" She wasn't certain what to call the woman in the letters. "To the woman my father wrote to."

"I'll take you," Rowden said.

"You will?" Modesty set her teacup down. "But I thought you would be busy. I don't want to be a distraction.

"I can't believe I ever thought of you as a distraction. I want to take you." He straightened. "But I'll wait in the coach. I'm sure you'll want privacy."

Modesty hadn't thought that far ahead. All of her planning had to do with finding a way to reach Hungerford, not what she would say once she faced her father's mistress.

"I saw Tom Cribb at the exhibition last night," Rowden said.

"The famous pugilist?"

"You've heard of him?"

"We used to preach repentance to the crowds who came to see him."

"Since Chibale isn't here yet, he offered to put me through my paces this morning. Come with me, and when we're through I'll take you to—I'll take you where you need to go."

Modesty cocked her head. "You want me to come to the exhibition with you?" Why was she asking him? He didn't *want* her to come. It was simply more convenient for her to be there so they could leave afterward for her business. "Never mind," she said. "You already explained that it's easier to leave from there."

"That's true," he said, cutting his food. "But I do want you there." He looked up. "I could use the support. The bookmakers put odds-on the German."

Modesty stood in surprise and what felt like outrage. "That's ridiculous. Of course, you will beat him."

Rowden raised his brows at her. "I will?"

"How can they not see that?"

He sat back. "Modesty Brown, you never stop surprising me." She thought he might reach for her then, drag her onto his lap, and kiss her...or something more. But the door opened, and a footman entered. And so Modesty sat back in her seat and Rowden continued to eat, and she wished they could be alone again.

***

The exhibition was unlike anything Modesty had ever seen. In what looked to be a large race course, a huge tent had been erected. Subsequently, smaller tents and booths had sprung up around it with vendors selling everything from food—including, she noted, oranges—to artistic representations of the well-known pugilists like Gentleman Jackson, Mendoza, and Tom Cribb.

"None of you?" she said as they passed a stall on the way to the main tent.

Rowden gave her a quelling look. "Thank God."

"You don't want the fame?"

"I've already turned my father's hair white. I don't want to make him apoplectic."

The day was sunny but still cold. She was dressed warmly, and still she felt a shiver run up her back. Rowden had tucked her arm into his, drawing her close to him, keeping her safe. He led her into the exhibition tent, which had several braziers in the various corners, and she was happy for the warmth. A man in nothing but breeches danced about the arena while another man called directions to him. Modesty knew she shouldn't be looking at a man who was half undressed but she glanced at him under her lashes. He was thick and broad, but she'd seen Rowden without his shirt, and there was little to compare to him.

Rowden led her to a seat and sat beside her, his gaze on the arena.

"Do you know him?" she asked.

"I know his name." He glanced at her quickly. "Tom Pease. Fought him once. Beat him." He nodded at the pugilist. "We call him Pretty Pease because he has a pretty face."

Modesty hadn't looked at the man's face, but she did so now. It was not as handsome as Rowden's, but she was probably biased.

"He's fond of that pretty face and protects it. Not now that he's throwing practice jabs and darts, but when he has an opponent, he ducks his head or raises an arm to cover it. Then you can hit him in the ribs or the breadbasket."

"I never realized there was so much strategy in pugilism."

"You were busy telling all of us we were going to hell."

She nodded. "I still don't like it. It's dangerous, unnecessary violence. Men are hurt and people pay to see it."

"It's a barbaric world," Rowden agreed. "But after the war, I'm not really capable of being shocked by violence or inhumanity. Nothing anyone does to anyone else surprises me anymore."

She took his hand. "I've heard other soldiers say the same thing. I'm sorry you were sent to war. That there is such a thing as war."

He squeezed her hand. "So am I."

"You spoke of your father earlier." His grip tightened on her hand. "Lady Lorraine said everyone thought your father would forgive you when you came home a war hero. He didn't, I take it."

"No, he didn't. Killing some of the enemy and saving a few of our own men pales in comparison to the sin of marrying without his permission. Marrying a Catholic, nonetheless. I don't suppose Lady Lorraine mentioned my late wife was a Papist."

He was hurting her hand with his grip, but Modesty didn't think he realized it. "She did, actually. I've always thought the Protestants and the Catholics had more in common than they did differences."

His grip loosened and he gave her a dubious look. "Don't let your father hear you say that."

Modesty looked down.

"I'm sorry," he said. "I didn't think before I spoke."

She smiled at him. "I understand the sentiment. Most people are intolerant."

He smiled back at her. Now was her chance to ask him. She wouldn't have another opportunity so perfect, and she'd been wanting to know. Summoning all her courage, she asked, "Is that why you wish to never marry again? Because your first marriage caused the break with your father?"

The shouting from the arena quieted and it seemed silence hung in the air. Rowden released her hand, and though she wore gloves, her hand felt cold. "That's not why," he said, standing. "It's because when she died, she and my unborn child, she took half of my heart to the grave with her. I'd rather keep the other half," he said. "Though I can't imagine anyone would want such a paltry thing at any rate."

He walked away, raising a hand to a man she recognized from the drawings as Tom Cribb. Modesty watched as he stripped off his coat, waistcoat, and shirt. She saw what no one else saw, though. He still wore his armor. He hadn't spoken those words to her to hurt her, but they'd stung nonetheless. She understood him perfectly. He had nothing left to offer her. He'd loved and lost that love and wouldn't risk his injured heart again.

But as much as Modesty wanted to accept that, to walk away—figuratively, if not literally—it was becoming more difficult every day. Because her heart, which had never thought it would feel love, was falling more and more in love with Rowden Payne. She deserved more than what he could give her, and yet she wanted him all the same.

Watching him step into the ring in nothing but breeches made her face heat. His chest was muscled, his arms powerful, his back broad. He'd put his hands on her in the coach, and she wanted to take those same liberties. She wanted to touch him, kiss him, hold him. And all of his warnings and cautions hadn't lessened that desire even one ounce.

***

The coach was stuck. Chibale and the other passengers stood on the side of the road as the coachman and the outrider tried to dig one of the wheels out of the mud. Chibale had his suspicions the coachman had been drinking. His face was quite red—though that might have been from the wind—and he'd also driven straight into a muddy section of road when a drier path was an easy option. Some of the other men moved to help push the coach, and together they freed the wheel from the mire. Unfortunately, the coach still didn't sit right, and a cursory look underneath revealed a broken axle.

Chibale put his head in his hands. At this rate, he would never make it to Hungerford. He wanted to be there for the mill, but that wasn't his main concern any longer. His main concern was protecting Rowden and Miss Brown. If Notley was in Hungerford, and Chibale had no doubt he was, he would go after both of them. Miss Brown would be the easier target and by hurting her Notley could—as the saying went—kill two birds with one stone. Hurting her would hurt Rowden. And that was the point. Notley wanted to hurt the people he blamed for his own situation.

Chibale had to make it to Hungerford and warn Rowden. And yet here he was, standing on the side of the road, in the freezing cold, watching the coachman and outrider discuss the situation. If the distance hadn't still been so great, Chibale would have walked and risked freezing. But he wouldn't make it before the mill started even if he ran.

He eyed the horses the coachman was unhitching from the coach. He could steal one of them, but he was no horseman, and he would probably be thrown off or pulled off by the coachman before he got very far. Filled with frustration, he began to pace. The movement had the added effect of keeping him warm. At first when he heard the sound of wheels approaching, he didn't believe it. And then he glimpsed a coach in the distance. Chibale paused and blew out a relieved breath. The coach could travel to the next town and send help back.

And then as the coach drew even closer, Chibale's smile grew. He knew that coach. It stopped abreast of the broken public coach and Aidan Sterling lowered the passenger window. "What seems to be the problem?" he asked.

The coachman told him about the broken axle, and Sterling listened, his gaze landing on Chibale then back to the coachman. "We will send help back at the next posting house."

The coachman thanked him.

"Mr. Okoro," Sterling said. "Why are you standing on the side of the road? I thought you'd be in Hungerford by now."

Chibale approached the coach. "I had personal business and couldn't leave yesterday."

Sterling pulled out his pocket watch. "Well, if you stand about here all day, you'll miss the mill." He opened the door. "Get in."

Chibale climbed in and settled back on the seat as the coach drove away.

Sterling offered him a brandy, and Chibale took it.

"I heard your coaches were the most luxurious ever built. I see that wasn't exaggeration." Chibale admired the fine curtains and upholstery as well as the custom wood cabinets and the painting on the ceiling.

Sterling waved a hand. "Have to do something with all of this blunt. I don't like traveling, so this is my way of making it more bearable. You should have written to let me know you were departing today."

"I didn't know if I was." Chibale told him about the vandalism at Madame Renauld's and what he'd discovered about Notley.

"Little weasel," Sterling said. "I've always hated his sort." He rapped on the roof of the coach. "Change of plans," he told the coachman. "Take us straight to the exhibition. And hurry."

***

Something about having Modesty watching him gave Rowden more energy. Even Cribb commented on how light of foot he was and how sharp his jabs looked. Of course, it didn't hurt to have Tom Cribb coaching him, but it was Modesty that made the difference. He could spot her out of the corner of his eye. She sat on the edge of her chair, leaning forward, eyes large and focused completely on him. Those eyes. He had a weak spot for them—especially now when he recognized the look in them.

He'd seen it in Aidan's coach when he'd kissed her and touched her. It was desire. She wanted him.

Plenty of women had looked at him like that. Plenty had done more than look, but he hadn't ever felt toward any of them like he did toward Modesty. He wanted her too and badly. He channeled that raw frustration into his training and punched harder, moved faster.

When he was finished, he went to the corner, accepted a towel and water from Cribb and wiped his face. It was no surprise Trogdon was nowhere to be seen with the oranges. Cribb leaned his elbows on the ropes. "You fight like that tonight, the German doesn't stand a chance."

"I'll fight like that tonight," Rowden said, aware of the men standing around, listening. He could see them putting their heads together, probably already placing bets. If he did win, he and Chibale would take home a bulging purse. He hadn't thought much about retiring before, but if he won tonight, he would leave when he was at his best. Rowden preferred that to spending several more years being pummeled in the arena.

He glanced at Modesty, who was trying not to look at him. But what would he do when he retired? He could always buy out Colonel Draven and work with Mostyn in the studio. He liked coaching. He could do that all day and come home to…Trogdon.

His manservant had just entered the tent carrying a basket. As soon as he saw Rowden, he shifted it from his hands to his arm. Rowden rolled his eyes, wondering how long Trogdon would drag this on. He grabbed his shirt from the ropes and pulled it over his head. "Did you buy the oranges?" he asked.

Trogdon paused midstep. "About that, sir."

Rowden saw Modesty walking their way and held his temper. "Go on."

"They were out of oranges."

Rowden refrained from pointing out that was because Trogdon had wasted time, not going when Rowden had told him. "What did you find?"

Trogdon offered the basket, and Rowden removed the covering since Trogdon was still pretending his hands were injured. Inside were half a dozen lemons and limes. Rowden started to open his mouth to chastise Trogdon but then he glanced at Modesty. She had a worried look on her face and glanced at Trogdon sympathetically.

"Good work," Rowden said.

Trogdon's head snapped up. "Sir?"

"You know I don't like oranges. Much rather have lemons or limes, and they're all citrus. Good work."

Trogdon stared at him. "I did well, sir?"

Rowden glanced at Modesty, who was beaming.

"You did." Rowden took a lemon from the basket, peeled it and took a bite. He winced at the tartness but preferred it to the taste of oranges any day. "Let me take that," he said. "Why don't you go back to Battle's Peak and apply salve to your hands? I told the housekeeper to leave a bottle in your room. Maybe they'll be feeling better tonight."

Trogdon stared at him. "Mr. Payne?"

"Yes, Trogdon?"

Trogdon shook his head. "Just checking, sir. I'll do that, sir." He left, and Rowden set the basket down and pulled the rest of his clothing on. He'd expected Modesty to turn her back, but she watched him quite hungrily. She'd probably forgotten she wasn't supposed to ogle men. Rowden shook Cribb's hand again and ducked under the ropes. One glance at his rumpled shirt and the coat hanging over his arm told him he should go back to his rooms and prepare before going anywhere, but he didn't want Modesty to wait any longer.

"I know I look a bit of a wreck, but I'll stay in the coach," he said.

She froze and he inadvertently tugged her forward before he realized she'd stopped. "What's wrong? You don't want to go?"

"I do," she said. "It's just now that the moment is here, I'm…scared?"

"It's your father's mistress who should be scared," he said. "Give her that disapproving look you gave me the first night we met. She'll burst into tears."

Modesty laughed and started walking again. He liked hearing her laugh, liked knowing he could make her smile, make her happy, make her…well, best not to think of that.

Rowden left her with the basket at the edge of the field and went to find Aidan's coachman. Most of the coachmen were playing dice or cards, but Aidan's was standing by his horses, ready. Rowden waved to him and walked back to Modesty. She looked so pretty standing with the basket in both hands, the green of her dress peeking out from under a blue pelisse, and her hair blowing gently in the breeze. But he caught a movement a little behind her and frowned when he spotted Notley. The man was leaning against the edge of a stall, hands in his pockets, looking deliberately innocent. But Rowden didn't like it. Notley had obviously followed them. The man was making it clear he was watching them.

Modesty turned to see what had caught Rowden's attention, but he moved beside her and put his arm about her, effectively blocking Notley's view of her. He pulled her close and when the coach pulled up, he opened the door and lifted her inside. He gave the coachman directions then took his seat opposite her just as the coach started away. He set his coat down and reached for the buttons of his shirt. "I'll just fasten these and tie my cravat," he said.

"Don't bother," she said. His gaze met hers just as she moved across the coach and slid onto his lap.

Eighteen

Modesty didn't allow herself to think. She just acted. She probably couldn't have stopped herself even if she'd wanted to. She'd never wanted anything as much as she wanted to touch Rowden Payne in that moment. Watching him half naked in the arena, his muscles flexing and rippling as he punched and shuffled, she'd felt uncomfortably warm.

And then she'd felt uncomfortably aroused. The place between her legs where he'd touched the day before throbbed and ached, and she had to squeeze her legs together to keep from shifting uncomfortably. Even her breasts felt tender and heavy. He looked like those statues of the Greek god Apollo she had seen at the British Museum, before her father had made her leave, saying the art was indecent. And now she understood why her father hadn't wanted her to see those statues because the things she was thinking when she looked at Rowden were indecent.

She slid onto his lap, and his arms wrapped around her as though she had done this a dozen times and he always reacted thus. He pulled her close, sliding her against his chest and gripping the back of her neck to pull her mouth down in a kiss. His lips and his tongue tasted of lemon, and his body was warm from his earlier exertions. She was warm being pressed against him, and she untied her pelisse and let it drop down. His hands were on her back, while her hands were in his hair, her lips on his mouth, his neck, his ear.

"Modesty," he groaned, and she liked the way his voice sounded. It was low and husky. Her lips met his again, and then she realized what his hands had been about. He'd unfastened the back of her dress, and now the shoulders slid down. Rowden's mouth was hot and tantalizing on the bare skin of her collar and shoulder. His hands came up, cupping her breasts, and she moaned because they were so heavy with need and his touch felt so good. She had never imagined anything could feel so good. She pushed her own bodice down and out of the way, and Rowden's mouth kissed the tops of her breasts, visible above the chemise and stays she wore.

He tugged down the chemise and stays until her nipples were visible, puckering with the sudden exposure to the air. Rowden lifted his mouth and looked at her. Modesty should have felt embarrassed, but her nipples hardened, and she found she liked his gaze on her.

"You're even more beautiful than I imagined," he murmured, his breath warm on her skin. One hand came up and cupped her breast, and his thumb slid over her distended nipple. She gasped in a breath, the sound somewhere between pleasure and pain. His thumb moved back and forth over her nipple while the other hand reached under her skirts.

She shook her head, trying to hold onto her thoughts, even as her mind reeled from his touch. "I wanted to kiss you, touch you," she said.

"Then touch me."

It was all the permission she needed. Her fingers moved tentatively to touch the skin of his throat. He stilled as she touched him, brushing her hands down into the V at the neck of his open shirt. "More?" he asked.

She nodded, and he adjusted her on his lap and lifted the hem of his shirt then tugged it over his head. He tossed it aside. Modesty looked down at his bare chest and licked her lips. He was so beautiful. She had been itching to touch him, and now that he was in reach, she didn't know where to start. She decided to begin with his shoulders, which were broad and well-defined. She put her hands on them and skated down over his muscled biceps and to his corded forearms. His hand slid under her skirts again and rested on her knee, stroking it lightly and playing with the ribbon holding her garters.

Her hands went to his shoulders again, but this time she allowed her fingers to creep down over his chest. She placed a hand over the center of his chest and felt his heart beating fast and hard. In surprise, she caught his gaze.

"You think I'm unaffected?" he asked. "A beautiful woman is touching me. *You*, Modesty, are touching me. Of course, my heart is racing."

She licked her lips again, and her hands moved lower, down to his taut abdomen and the tight row of muscles there. He flinched a bit as she ran her fingers over his belly, and she smiled at him. "Ticklish?"

"Apparently."

"Should I stop?"

"Never." But he seemed to be at the end of his patience because he pulled her close and kissed her. Modesty's bare breasts pressed against the skin of his chest, and she felt heat flare between her legs, even as his hand slid higher onto her thigh. Her legs were on either side of him, giving him easy access to her rapidly heating core. As he moved to touch her inner thigh, he kissed her neck then her breasts. "I want to touch you where I touched you before. I want to give you pleasure again."

"Yes," she said on a breath as his fingers brushed over her.

"You're so warm." His mouth took her nipple as his finger slid inside her. She clenched around him without even thinking of what she was doing. He sucked her nipple as he withdrew his finger and slid the wetness over that part of her that felt the most pleasure. Slowly, he stroked and tapped until she was squirming with need. The road grew bumpy, and she braced her hands on Mr. Sterling's beautiful painted ceiling. The pleasure and need in her grew until she looked down at Rowden. The expression on his face was so similar to those she'd seen at church when people were worshipping. That's what he was doing now—worshipping her. With a gasp, her body came apart, and she bit her lip to keep from crying out. Then she collapsed upon him, pressing her lips onto the skin of his shoulder and tasting salt, sweat, and Rowden.

***

Either the coachman had taken a detour or Fanny Smithson's farm was further from Hungerford than she had thought, but it was another twenty minutes or so before they arrived. The delay gave Modesty time to rearrange her clothing, and with help from Rowden, refasten her bodice. Although Rowden was not all that helpful as he insisted on kissing her back and shoulders and making her wish they could start all over again before he finally finished fastening all the tapes and pins.

"You seem to know quite a bit about how to dress a woman," she remarked, settling across from him.

"I was married," he said with a smile.

She smiled back. She couldn't help it. She probably should have been mortified at what they had just done and the way he had just made her feel, but she wasn't at all embarrassed. She liked when he touched her. She liked kissing him and being with him. She wished she didn't like it quite so much because they would return to London tomorrow, after the fight, and that would be the end of everything. Rowden had made it clear he never wanted to marry again. Even though she knew he was as attracted to her as she to him, that didn't mean he would ever want to risk his heart again.

Perhaps that was for the best. She did not know what her future held, but what kind of life would she have married to a prizefighter? She might have strayed from her strict upbringing, but that didn't mean she wanted to spend the majority of her time in taverns and at illegal bare-knuckle brawls.

The carriage finally slowed, and Modesty parted the curtains and looked out at the brown, barren fields. In the summer and fall, these fields would be full of wheat and barley. But now the fields lay dormant and waiting.

"There it is," Rowden said, pointing. Modesty looked in that direction and spotted a small house with a thatched roof and smoke curling out of a chimney. It was built of stone and was surrounded by a dirt yard and a small shed where a cow chewed and watched their approach with interest. As the coach pulled closer, the wooden door opened and two children—a boy and a girl—stepped outside. Modesty judged the boy's height and long limbs and put him at about fourteen. The girl was closer to twelve. Neither wore shoes, but both were dressed in sober black. And both had wide, hazel eyes. Eyes Modesty knew she had inherited from her father's side of the family.

"You look white as a sheet," Rowden said, taking her hand. "And your hands are like ice."

"Did you see their eyes?" she asked.

He looked at her. "It's an unusual color," he said. "Quite striking."

She nodded. "I didn't want to believe the letters." The coach slowed and stopped. She could hear the children's voices now. They were high and excited, calling out that a grand carriage had arrived.

He squeezed her hand. "I hope you find answers."

She could hear the coachman jump down. He would open the door any moment. She tugged at Rowden. "Come with me."

He raised his brows. "I don't want to intrude."

"I don't want to go alone. Please."

"Of course."

When the door opened, he went first and then handed her down. She tried to focus on his face, and it was a relief to see the strength and calm in his expression. He had always been there for her. She only need to ask.

The girl took one look at her and curtseyed, and the boy gave a stunned bow. Modesty realized she must look like a fine lady in her Renauld. "Good afternoon," she said, her voice sounding strong and far more confident than she felt. "Is Mrs. Smithson at home?"

A woman appeared behind the children. She was only slightly taller than her son and plump with a pink face and curly blond hair under her cap. She too was dressed in black, but she had a white apron tied about her waist and her sleeves rolled up. "I am Mrs…Smithson."

Modesty stared at the woman who had written those love letters to her father. She was not at all the villainess Modesty had imagined. She looked kind and jolly. She was nothing like Modesty's mother, who had been tall and slim and regal—at least in Modesty's memory—but she seemed to be the kind of person one might want as a mother. She was the kind of woman who would hug a child hard and wipe her tears away.

The woman's expression changed, and she stepped forward. "Go inside," she told the children.

"But—" the girl began.

"Go inside now."

Heads hanging low, the children stepped back into the dark of the small house.

"You're Modesty, aren't you?" Mrs. Smithson said.

Modesty nodded. "And you are Fanny Smithson."

She was untying her apron now and rolling down her sleeves, obviously attempting to look more presentable. "Then you received my letter."

"Letter?" Modesty asked.

"I sent it a few days ago. I didn't know what else to do."

Modesty shook her head. "I never received it."

"Then how did you—" She waved the thought away. "No matter. Come inside. Your father will want to see you."

At the mention of her father, Modesty felt as though she might collapse, but Rowden was right behind her. He took her arm and held it firmly. She wanted to speak, but no words seemed to come from her mouth. Finally, Rowden spoke.

"Allow me to introduce myself, Mrs. Smithson. I'm Rowden Payne, a friend of Miss Brown's."

She bobbed a curtsy. "Mr. Payne. You're one of the brawlers at the exhibition?" She glanced in the direction of the race course and the town.

"I am. Did you say that Mr. Brown is here?"

"I did, Mr. Payne. He's inside."

"Then perhaps he could come outside to speak with his daughter."

Modesty looked at him, feeling a rush of gratitude. She did not want to enter the house. She couldn't bear to see the life her father had created with this other woman.

"I would ask him," Mrs. Smithson said, her gaze moving to Modesty as though she understood. "But his leg is broken, and the doctor says he can't put any weight on it. It's a bad break."

"I see," Modesty said, her voice sounding faint. Her father was alive. He was inside the house with a broken leg. Rowden leaned down, speaking in her ear.

"Do you want me to go in and speak with him?"

Yes, she did. She wanted to go hide in the carriage and pretend none of this ever happened. Instead, she squared her shoulders. "I think you'd better wait outside. It looks small for so many people."

"I'll be right here if you need me."

She nodded and gathered her skirts, following Mrs. Smithson into the house. The interior was dark, and it took a moment for her eyes to adjust. When they did, she saw the house was quite simple but comfortable. It looked far more comfortable than her house in London. She supposed the small touches Mrs. Smithson had added made it seem that way. Woven rugs lay on the floor and a knitted blanket had been thrown over one chair. That chair was beside another close to the hearth. And on the mantel above the hearth were pretty things like a glass vase and a watercolor painting of a house—this one, she realized—in the spring.

"He's here," Mrs. Smithson said, gesturing to an area in the back of the house that had been separated from the front with a blanket draped over a clothesline.

"Who is it?" the familiar voice of her father asked.

Modesty immediately wanted to cover her exposed neck and dip her head, hiding her red hair under an imaginary black hat. Instead, she cleared her throat. "It's Modesty, Father."

Mrs. Smithson pulled the blanket aside, and Modesty stared at her father, one leg supported by wood splints and wrapped in linen. The leg was propped on a pillow to elevate it. More pillows were behind his back on the bed, keeping him upright. Modesty stared at him, at the growth of his beard, at how informally he was dressed—in shirtsleeves. And then her gaze drifted to the empty pillow beside him. There was just enough space on the bed for another person. And Modesty had no doubt who that other person might be.

***

Rowden wasn't cold, even though the breeze had picked up. The sun was still warm and his exertions in the carriage had certainly warmed his blood. He rather welcomed the cool air to dampen his ardor. As much as he liked giving Modesty pleasure, it was never easy to deny oneself.

It might not be easy, but it was necessary. Her husband should take her virginity. Not he.

He shouldn't even be kissing or touching her. He'd known this would happen if they traveled alone together. This was why he'd wanted to end their association. The more he was with her, the closer they became and the more he wanted from her. The more he wanted *her*.

That was an easy fix. He'd met women he liked in the past, women he wanted a longer relationship with. He need only close his eyes and bring to mind the image of Mary, deathly pale, belly distended, a sheen of sweat over her sweet face. "Save the baby," she had whispered to him before her hand went limp.

They'd tried, but in the end, his son had died as well.

The pain of that day and the months and years following it, was enough to dampen his ardor. It was enough to remind him that he wanted to be alone. He could never allow himself to feel pain like that again. He wouldn't survive it the next time.

He tried to bring that pain back into focus now, to remind himself. It flickered to life and began to smolder, the pain still raw like a new burn. But his mind also conjured the image of Modesty. She straddled him, her glorious breasts upthrust as she threw her head back from pleasure. Her sex was warm and wet as his fingers probed it, and her body welcomed his touch. Her eyes met his, wanting more. She might not know precisely what she wanted, but he did.

Rowden paced away from the coach, swearing softly. It had been this way from the start. He couldn't keep the pain centered with her. The pain of his loss faded, the pleasure of being with her blotting it out.

Rowden supposed that would last until he got her with child. An act of love might very well kill her. Even now Rowden imagined Ewan was home wondering if his own child would survive or if he might lose both his wife and child in pain and blood.

No, Lorrie was strong, and she was not as far along as Mary had been. She would survive, and if she and Ewan lost this child, they would try again. Rowden had lost everything, though, and he couldn't face that pain a second time.

The sound of footsteps shook him from his memories, and he turned to see a young man approaching. He was of medium height and build, his hair light brown under his hat, a sack with tools slung over his back. He was dressed warmly with a scarf about his neck and the lower half of his face, but he pulled it down now as he approached the carriage and spotted Rowden.

Rowden recognized the pointed jaw, which could set so stubbornly on Modesty, and the shape of the man's lips. They reminded him of Modesty as well. He didn't have the hazel eyes his siblings—all three of them—shared, but the resemblance was clear enough.

"Good afternoon," the man said cautiously.

Rowden reached for his hat then realized he'd left it in the coach. "Good afternoon." He held out his hand as the man approached. "Rowden Payne."

The man removed his work glove and shook Rowden's hand, his own hand callused and weathered. "Samuel Brown. What brings you here?"

So her father had given his by-blows his surname. That, at least, was honorable. "I'm escorting a friend." No point in keeping it a secret. "A Miss Modesty Brown, who was hoping to find her father."

Samuel's brown eyes widened then softened with understanding. He knew of his half-sister and had probably expected she would come one day. "She is inside with him?"

"She is. I would say she is relieved to see him as when he disappeared, she thought him dead. Of course, now she finds a very different reality."

The man nodded. He was perhaps twenty, certainly no older. And yet he carried the weight of an older man on his shoulders. Perhaps because his father had been so often absent, and this Samuel Brown must have taken on the role of protector and provider at a young age.

"Have you seen him?"

"No."

"His leg is badly broken. It was injured when he fell off the roof."

Rowden glanced at the thatched roof speculatively.

"He shouldn't have been up there, I know," Samuel said. "But he's a stubborn man, and he was angry that we'd kept the state of the cottage from him. We're tenants of Lord Chesterton. He owns most of the land in this area. He's not a bad landlord, and his land steward was only doing his job. The roof leaked and was in danger of caving in. I'd gone to Reading to find some work that would pay in coins so my mother could buy material to make my brother and sister new clothing. They'd grown out of almost everything, and the fall harvest barely paid the cost of buying seed for the spring planting. When I returned, the situation was dire. So I went to Town to ask for some coin and my father ended up coming himself. I was out in the fields that day, but when I came home for dinner, the doctor was leaving. He said my father couldn't be moved for at least six weeks. He fitted him with a splint and medicine for the pain and took half my coin for the trouble. It wasn't until a few days ago that he was lucid enough to ask about Miss Modesty and my mother wrote to her."

Rowden shook his head. "She never received the letter."

Samuel frowned. "Then how did she find him?"

"She discovered old love letters between your parents in your father's room at—er, his London home."

Samuel's face went white. "I see."

Rowden wasn't quite sure he did see. Modesty's life had obviously been very different from his. He was almost certainly a God-fearing man, but he didn't quote scripture as Modesty had when Rowden had first met her. It appeared to

Rowden that in the country, Mr. Brown had been a farmer, and in the city, a preacher, and now those two worlds were about to collide.

***

"Modesty." Her father reached out a hand to her. Part of her wanted to take it. Part of her wanted to rush into his arms and hug him because he was alive, and she hadn't lost him. But part of her did not know the man lying in the bed. The bed he shared with a woman who was not his wife and not her mother.

"You received my letter?" he asked.

She shook her head and pulled the packet of letters from the pocket where she'd stuffed them just before stepping out of the coach. Mrs. Smithson—or was it Brown?—made a soft sound from behind her, and Modesty knew she recognized them immediately. Her father held his hand out imperiously, took the letters, and frowned down at them. "I wish you hadn't found these."

"I wish you hadn't disappeared without saying a word. I thought you were dead."

"I thought I would only be gone for a day. I knew if I sent you on an errand, you would take hours. You always dawdle."

Modesty straightened. She wanted to argue that she hadn't dawdled that day, but she had.

"I left in a hurry and hoped to return as soon as the repairs here were finished. The roof was about to fall in on Mrs. Brown and the children."

Modesty inhaled sharply at the name he'd given his mistress.

"I couldn't allow that to happen," he said, seeming not to notice. "I should have left you word."

"Yes, you should have. You should have told me about"—she gestured at the room—"all of this." She looked at her father's mistress—wife. "About her."

"Excuse me." Mrs. Brown ducked around the blanket that hung as a barrier, leaving them alone. Although they weren't really alone. A blanket would not even mute the sound of their voices. How strange to speak to her father like this now, when for so many years it had only been the two of them. And yet, they had never spoken freely. She understood that now. She had never even known him.

"I don't even know who you are," she said now, echoing her thoughts. "All my life you have been the man standing on the corner, admonishing men and women to repent of their sins. You chastised people doing nothing more than entering a tavern or watching a fight, and all along, you were... *fornicating* here with your *mistress*."

"I'll thank you not to refer to her in those terms."

"How should I refer to her then?"

"She is my wife."

Modesty reared back as though slapped. She'd known already, but hearing it from his mouth was still a shock.

Her father nodded. "I married her a few years ago. I didn't tell you because I couldn't tell the church. I didn't want to lose my position."

"*That's* what you cared about? Your *position*?" She turned to go. She had to go before the tears started streaming down her cheeks.

"Modesty," her father said, and she stopped because she couldn't *not* obey him. "I wanted to tell you as well, but I knew how you would react. I know how much you loved your mother."

"More than you, as it turns out," she said.

The silence that followed let her know her words had hit their mark.

"Your mother knew I was a flawed man. She forgave me."

Modesty rounded on him. "And how did you repay her? By reforming? No, by continuing to do just as you had before. As I said, you are not the man I thought you were."

"And what about you?" He pointed to her. "Where did that dress come from? And your hair is down in the style of a harlot. How did you manage to come here? I wonder if you are the young woman I thought you were."

Modesty looked at him, lying on the bed with his immobilized leg. She felt sorry for his injury. She felt sorry for his wife and the children who had always lived in the shadow of his other life, in her shadow. The truth was revealed now, and she had always been taught that the truth would set them all free.

"I'm not the woman you thought I was," she said finally. "And I'll never be that woman again." She reached for the blanket, which felt much heavier now when she pulled it back. Her father called her name again, but this time she didn't obey. This time she walked through the house, dimly aware of the children that stared at her, and out the door.

Nineteen

Rowden stopped midsentence, forgetting his train of thought as soon as Modesty walked through the door. He could see by her stricken expression that the meeting with her father had not gone well. She walked briskly across the yard and when she reached him, she said, "I want to go."

Her gaze flicked to Samuel Brown and then back to Rowden and then to Samuel. Rowden gestured to the young man. "This is Mr. Samuel Brown."

He saw her flinch when he said the surname.

Her brother gave a quick bow. "Miss Brown." She said nothing for a long moment, and Rowden thought she would demand to leave again, but cruelty wasn't part of her being. And he could see her softening, even as she wanted to cut the man.

"Mr. Brown," she said, and held out her hand. "Or rather, I suppose you are Samuel Brown, Junior.

Rowden could see her try to push the hurt away.

"These are difficult circumstances under which to meet," she said.

"Yes, they are. I'm given to understand you didn't know about me—about us."

She looked at Rowden, and he felt immediately guilty that he had revealed something about her.

"I did not know until recently."

Samuel nodded. "I'm sorry you found out this way."

"Yes." She paused, seemed to consider. "Mr. Brown? Might I ask how old you are?"

"I'm twenty, Miss Brown. Is it presumptuous for me to ask your age?"

"Three and twenty, Mr. Brown." Her words were stilted. Of course, she'd known she would be older. Rowden thought she had a different reason for asking. Her brother must have realized it as well.

"When did your mother die, Miss Brown?" Samuel asked.

"Seventeen years ago," she said. "Almost eighteen now." She looked at Rowden. "I'd like to go, Mr. Payne."

Rowden wanted to tell her to stay, to talk to her brother. She'd been looking for her aunt, for family, and now she had found it. Instead, he opened the door to the coach and helped her inside. He shook Mr. Brown's hand and wished he knew what to say to ease the pain he saw in the young man's eyes. That same pain was reflected in Modesty's eyes when she looked back at him as the coach pulled away.

He would have liked to jump from the coach. He knew what was coming, and he hated when women cried. But this was Modesty, and he couldn't leave her alone in her pain.

He opened his arms, and she only hesitated a moment before she rushed into them. Almost immediately, she began to sob, and Rowden could do nothing but hold her. He couldn't even offer her reassuring words. Though her father was alive, the circumstances in which she'd found him were not comforting.

"He broke his leg," she said, looking up at him through wet, clumped lashes. "That was why he did not return to London."

"I know," Rowden said. "He was repairing the roof. Did you truly never suspect? Did he never have any other unexplained absences?"

"I see it now," she said. "Of course, I see it now. The times when he needed solitude to write his sermon and was away for several days. I always thought he was at the church. The times he sent me to spend a couple nights with the Plineys so he could spend time in meditation and prayer. I thought he was so pious, so holy. But he was lying."

"He should have told you."

"Yes!" She nodded. "I would have understood. I think I might even come to like Mrs. Smithson—er, Brown. But not like this—not like this!"

He pulled her close again, held her. "What will I do?" she asked.

And though he thought the question was rhetorical, he answered, "Whatever you want to do. You're free now. You could seek out your aunt or come live here with your siblings."

"No!"

"Why not?" He pulled back and looked down at her. "The children did not ask to be born. They did nothing wrong. You've lived all of your life thinking you had no family, and yet you have a sister and two brothers. You still have your father."

He was well aware that his voice broke on that last phrase.

Modesty looked at him and then swiped her tears away. "You're right. How selfish I must seem, crying over this when I have a family."

"You are upset, and you have every right to be."

"So do you!" she insisted. "Your father treated you most unfairly. And your sisters and brothers all fell in line. It's not right."

"In their minds, I did the unforgivable. Just as in your mind, your father has done the unforgivable."

She slumped back onto the seat beside him. "I don't want to forgive him."

"Then don't."

"I have to. Seventy times seven." She was quoting the Bible again.

"Well, you don't have to forgive him today. Tomorrow or next week or the next week will be soon enough. Or is there a Scripture as to how soon?"

"There is not." She smiled at him, and he was glad to see her tears seemed to have passed. "I do not want to think of him tonight. Tonight I want to see you beat the German's brains in."

He gaped at her.

"Isn't that what you say?"

"I didn't think *you'd* say it."

Her smile faded. "I suppose what my father said is true then."

"What's that?"

"He said I was not the woman he thought I was."

"I don't think he ever knew you any more than you knew him."

"That's just it," she said. "He never knew me. *I* never knew me. All I wanted was to be the daughter he wanted me to be. One he would love. One my mother would have been proud of. I thought I had to be perfect. I had to follow all of his rules. But he didn't even follow them!" She shook her head. "So many years wasted, trying to be what he wanted, and I never thought once about what *I* wanted."

"And what do you want?" he asked.

She looked at him, and the answer was plain. She wanted him. Rowden would have moved heaven and earth to give her anything she wanted—anything but himself. That he couldn't do. She looked down, obviously seeing his answer on his face. "I don't really want you to beat anyone's brains in," she said quietly. "Just knock him down long enough to win."

"I will. You can count on it."

***

Aidan and Chibale were waiting for them as soon as they returned to Battle's Peak. Lady Florentia was entertaining them in her drawing room, but she was intelligent enough to know when the men wished to speak privately. She drew Modesty away, saying she looked weary and should rest before the evening's events. Modesty must have been weary because she did not argue and allowed herself to be led away.

When the door closed and the footsteps faded, Rowden looked expectantly at his two friends.

"Bad news," Chibale said. He was never one to mince words. "Notley is in Hungerford."

"I know," Rowden said, sipping the tea Lady Florentia had poured him and wishing it was something stronger. But now that Chibale was here, Rowden should be relieved he didn't have orange juice poured down his throat. "I saw him at the exhibition grounds."

"Did he approach you?" Aidan asked. He withdrew a silver flask from his coat pocket and added a splash of brandy to his tea. Rowden glanced at Chibale, who shook his head slowly.

"Not really, but he was lurking about. I suppose he's looking for a new fighter."

"He's looking for revenge," Chibale said. "For what we did to the Black Plague."

"If he is, he's a fool."

"No question of that," Aidan said. "And no question he wants revenge. He sent men to vandalize Madame Renauld's shop."

Rowden shot up, his gaze darting to Chibale. "Was anyone hurt?"

Chibale shook his head. "No. The shop was empty. The damage was monetary."

"I'm sorry to hear that," Rowden sat back again. "How do you know it was Notley?"

Chibale explained how he knew, and then added the last point. "If he's come after Madame Renauld because of my association with her then he may very well come after Miss Brown."

"I *knew* it was him!" Rowden said, standing again, fists clenched. "I should have killed him before. He deserves to die for touching her!"

If Aidan wasn't so quick, Rowden might have made it out the door, but Aidan caught him, and with Chibale's help, they pushed him back to his seat. It took some time for Rowden to calm down and finally be able to explain what had happened to Modesty at the posting house.

"It probably was him," Aidan said. "Or one of his toadies."

"But you go for him now, they'll disqualify you from the mill tonight."

"I don't care."

"*I* do," Chibale said.

"You'll be more effective if you make a plan," Aidan said. "I'm not as good at strategy as Fortescue is—"

"Fortescue?" Chibale asked.

"One of our troop in the war," Rowden said. "Stratford Fortescue."

"—but I always liked a good ambush," Aidan said. "I say we ambush him after the fight. There will be a few magistrates at the mill. We have one lie in wait with us and force Notley to confess."

"Too much planning," Rowden said. "Let's just beat him until he begs for mercy."

Aidan winced. "Let me worry about the plan. You save that anger for the German."

"Yes!" Chibale said, brightening. "Channel it. And speaking of anger, what is this I hear about Tom Cribb taking over your training?"

"He's not taking over my training," Rowden said.

"Good." Chibale pulled an orange from his pocket. "Because only I think to bring you gifts like this."

Rowden sighed, took the orange, and peeled it.

***

The tent was full to bursting with men wanting to watch the mill. Modesty even spotted quite a few ladies—true ladies, who were dressed well and richly. She felt she could almost be one of them as she wore a burnished gold dress embellished with velvet ribbons in a deep russet color. Apparently, Madame Renauld had sent it with Mr. Okoro so Modesty would look her best for the event.

Lady Florentia had declined to attend, but she had her maid style Modesty's hair, and it was a profusion of curls, elegantly arranged about her head with pieces down about her face and shoulders. She could not wait until Rowden saw her. She knew she looked well, and she wanted to see his expression when he spotted her. "Do you see him?" Modesty asked Mr. Sterling.

He was escorting her this evening, keeping her close to his side but not so close that she couldn't look about.

"Not yet." He pointed to a section of the tent that seemed to contain another tent. "He's most likely in there," he said. "The organizers like to increase the suspense by keeping the milling coves out of sight until they fight."

"Do you think he's nervous?"

Mr. Sterling pushed past a man and offered her a seat with a perfect view of the roped off area in the center. It was just high enough that her view would not be blocked and not so close that she would be splattered with blood or sweat. Modesty took the seat and looked around at the other spectators doing likewise.

"I doubt he's nervous. But he's probably pacing back there with all the pent-up energy."

She nodded. "He did say it was difficult to sleep after a fight."

Mr. Sterling pointed to the arena. "There are the first fighters."

"They look so small," she said, observing the men. They were both bigger than she but looked quite young and would have been outweighed by Rowden.

"They're young and new," Aidan said, "but don't discount them. They're light and fast. They'll put on a good show."

But Modesty couldn't watch more than a moment of the fight before she turned her attention back to the crowd. She didn't like to see anyone being hurt and found no pleasure when a man was knocked down. Except for the German. She would rather he be knocked down than Rowden.

She thought she recognized a few people from London—men she had seen at the Cock and Bull. Mr. Okoro sat with a group of them. They huddled close, speaking in low voices, their eyes on the fight. Mr. Sterling had said when Mr. Okoro went back into the inner tent it wouldn't be long before Rowden's match. The manager would go inside to make sure Rowden was ready.

"Is Mr. Trogdon with Rowden?" she asked.

"Who?" Mr. Sterling looked at her then back at the arena. "That worthless manservant? He didn't even remember the citrus fruit." He pointed to a bag at his feet. "I had to bring it."

"Oh, dear. Poor Trogdon."

"Poor Trogdon! Poor Rowden. Lord Nicholas sent them both off in my other coach an hour before we left."

Modesty glanced at him. "Lord Nicholas?" She had yet to meet their elusive host.

"He spends all his time in the stables," Mr. Sterling said. "He's horse mad, always has been, from what I hear. A horse fell on him during the war, though, and crushed his leg. He hasn't ridden since and doesn't like to be seen in company because of the injury."

"Oh, how awful. Did he lose his leg?" she asked.

"No, but he walks with some difficulty. And don't let him hear you pity him. He dislikes it."

Modesty surmised she would not be meeting Lord Nicholas. She would have liked to thank him for opening his home to them. She looked down at the sack of fruit again. "Should you bring that to Rowden before the fight?"

He glanced down at the sack then at her. "I was thinking you might like to do that."

Modesty shook her head. "I don't think that's appropriate."

"Look around." He gestured to the men yelling and waving their fists, the money exchanging hands, the pickpockets and prostitutes moving through the crowd. "There's nothing appropriate about you being here." He leaned closer to her and smiled. "And who cares? I think Rowden might like a kiss for luck before the fight."

Modesty felt her cheeks flame. "Mr. Sterling!"

He shrugged. "On the cheek, of course." He lifted the sack of lemons and limes and offered them to her.

"Fine." She stood and took them then allowed him to lead her through the crowd and to the tent where the milling coves waited for their turn in the arena. A large man guarded the entrance, and he shook his head as Modesty approached. She started to turn around, but Mr. Sterling motioned her forward.

"Igor, my good man," Sterling said to the large man as though they were old friends.

"No one is allowed. Them's orders," Igor said, crossing his thick arms over his broad chest.

"Igor, I thought we were friends. Friends do favors for each other."

Igor frowned at him and Modesty almost ran back to her seat again. But Sterling motioned for her to wait.

"Name is not Igor," the large man said.

"I know your name is Tom, but Igor fits you so much better." Mr. Sterling reached up and awkwardly wrapped an arm about Igor-also-known-as-Tom's shoulders. "Listen," he said, pulling the man down slightly. "I wanted to talk to you about a business proposition."

It took Modesty a moment to realize while he was speaking, he was motioning with his free hand for her to duck into the tent. Modesty did so, stepping into a smaller area lit by a few candles rather than the elaborate torches and lanterns in the bigger tent. When her eyes adjusted, she searched for Rowden, but didn't see him. The place was crowded with half-dressed men, most of them looking at her.

"I think you'd have more luck if you came to see us after the mill," one of them said to her. Modesty swallowed. He obviously thought she was a prostitute. Most likely a highly paid one as she was well-dressed.

She cleared her throat. "I'm looking for The Royal Payne."

The man who'd addressed her nodded. "He has all the luck. He's in the back."

She followed his finger and made her way through the men, most of whom stepped aside to let her pass. Rowden sat on a chair in the back, deep in conversation with another fighter, but as she neared, he looked up then jumped up. "What are you doing here?"

Modesty had a difficult time comprehending what he had said. He wore only breeches, and they were snug on his legs, ending just below the knee to show off his calves, which were bare like his feet. His chest was also bare and somewhat shiny in the candlelight. He was either sweating or had rubbed something on it. She had the intense urge to run her fingers along his skin and see if it was as slick as it looked.

"Modesty," Rowden said. "Where is Aidan?"

She gestured vaguely toward the front. "With Igor."

"What?"

She held out the sack of citrus, still unable to take her eyes from him. "I brought these. Mr. Trogdon forgot them."

Trogdon suddenly popped up from behind one of the other fighters. "Ah, good. I was just looking for those." He took the sack.

"Your hands feel better?" she asked, noting briefly that he had taken the sack with his hands and that the hands were no longer bandaged. Then she looked back at Rowden.

"The salve worked wonders," Trogdon said, opening the sack. "Lemon?" he offered Rowden.

"In a moment." Rowden took Modesty's arm and pulled her deeper into the tent. She thought he was looking for a dark corner to kiss her and have his way with her—at least that was what she hoped—but he pushed out of the tent and into the evening just outside. Modesty took a deep breath, glad of the fresh air and space. No one else was outside and Rowden backed her up against the tent.

"What are you doing?"

"Taking a look at you in that dress," he said. "Madame Renauld has outdone herself." Modesty felt her cheeks heat and looked down. His finger lifted her chin. "Now you look down? Your eyes were practically eating me up inside."

She couldn't stop her gaze from drifting back to his chest, and her tongue wet her lips.

Rowden groaned. "You'll be the death of me if you keep looking at me like that. You don't understand how badly I want you." He moved closer, one hand reaching out to finger a curl. He was careful not to touch his body to hers as he did have something rubbed on his skin.

"I think I understand," she said. "I want you too."

He leaned down and whispered in her ear. "If I wasn't covered in this, I'd take you right here and right now."

"What is it?" Modesty asked.

"You don't want to know, but it's saving your virtue."

Modesty shivered with the anticipation of pleasure. "Come to me tonight." She hadn't known she would say it, but she didn't regret the words. She meant them. She wanted him in her bed tonight.

He groaned. "You know I can't."

"Why?" She looked at him, put a hand on his cheek, which was rough with stubble. "I want you, Rowden. I love you."

He closed his eyes as though the words hurt him. "Don't love me." But he tilted his head so his cheek was pressed closely against her hand.

"It's too late. I already love you. I think I've loved you for days. I know you don't want to marry, but don't you think you could love me—"

He stepped back. "No. I can't marry, and I can't love you. I told you—"

"Because of your wife, yes, You mourn her still."

He didn't speak, and she straightened. "I understand. I can wait."

"No." He moved close to her again, so close that this time she did lift a hand and press it to the center of his chest.

"I don't mind waiting."

"You think I'd ask you to wait? You deserve better than that and better than me, Modesty."

Her hand trailed down his chest to his flat belly. She felt his muscles tighten. "There is no one better than you," she said.

He caught her hand and held it. "It's not that I mourn her. I was barely one and twenty when I married her, and she's been gone ten years."

"There isn't a time limit on grief," she said. "Clearly you are still in pain."

He let out a breath and released her hand. "No. I'm far more of a coward than you think. That's the real problem."

"You're not a coward." She wanted to touch him again. She felt as though she always needed to be touching him, but she knew he didn't want that at the moment.

"I am. I did mourn Mary, and—" His jaw worked as though he wasn't sure how to say the next words.

"And the baby," he said. His voice was so low, she barely heard him. For a moment, she said nothing and then she grasped his hand, hard.

"She died in childbirth?"

He nodded, and she could see the sheen of tears in his eyes. "The baby was…" His voice broke, and he swallowed and took a shaky breath. "Stillborn."

"Rowden." She tried to hug him, but he held her at a distance.

"I'm covered in this," he said, but even if he hadn't been, the divide between them would still have been there.

He swiped at his eyes, seeming annoyed by the wetness. "I can't go through that again," he said, his voice stronger now. "I can't risk it. The pain. I'd rather die."

Modesty didn't speak. She didn't have the words. There were no words. She knew the pain of loss, and she couldn't provide any reassurance that her fate would be any different than Mary's. Life was uncertain. Childbearing was dangerous. She'd wondered why he hadn't taken any pleasure those two times they'd been alone in the carriage. It seemed to her, watching the men in the alleys of London, that they always took their pleasure.

But she'd thought Rowden did not want to take her virginity or risk getting her with child and being forced to marry her. The idea of another pregnant wife probably terrified him. And how could she ask him to ignore his fears? She couldn't discount them. She couldn't promise him things would be different with her.

"So you see, I am a coward," he said.

She looked up at him. "You're not a coward. You're afraid. Only a fool would risk pain like that again. I don't blame you for protecting yourself." She gave him a smile she hoped would make her look braver than she felt. It must have failed because he frowned with concern. "I still love you," she said. "Even if you can't love me back."

He closed his eyes, and she knew she was hurting him. She didn't want to hurt him. Especially not now. "You have a fight to prepare for," she said. "And I expect to see you win this time."

"Modesty, I don't want to leave it like this."

"We'll talk after you beat the German's brains in," she said, making her voice lighter than she felt. "Right now you have lemons and limes to eat."

"Don't remind me." He gave her a ghost of a smile, but it was better than nothing.

"We'll talk later," she said, leading him back into the tent. She knew they would not, but she didn't want to end it this way either. And he still had a formidable opponent to face in the arena.

Once inside the tent, she found Mr. Okoro, whose worried expression immediately fell away. "Your fight is next," he said.

"Lime?" Trogdon offered.

"I'll just go back to my seat." Modesty nodded at Rowden. "You'd better win this time."

"Count on it."

She did. That was all she could count on anymore.

***

Mr. Sterling looked relieved to step away from Igor and escort her back to their seats. "I thought you'd eloped," he told her.

She shook her head. "I don't think Mr. Payne is the marrying sort."

"You'd be surprised," he said as they sat again. "I've seen men less likely than he marry. It seems to be an illness spreading through the countryside."

She glanced at him. "You seem immune."

"Because the only thing I love is money," he said. She thought he was joking, but he didn't smile.

"You know what Christ said, that it's easier for a camel to pass through the eye of a needle than for a rich man to enter the Kingdom of Heaven."

"I have heard that said." He watched the roped off arena as the fighters inside pummeled each other. "You know my solution?"

"What's that?"

"Build a really big needle."

She laughed. "I don't think that's the point of the saying."

"No? Damn."

"I wouldn't consider you damned yet—"

"Damn because I didn't want to leave you, but I had to ply Igor with drinks to keep him busy and drank too much myself."

"I see. I will be fine for a few minutes. I'm sure I am safe in this crowd."

"Don't move," he told her. "I'll be right back."

She watched him maneuver through the seats and the crowd and then disappear out the tent entrance. The crowd quieted slightly, and she craned her neck to see the German and Rowden walking out of the back tent. Modesty clutched her hands together tightly. The German looked so much bigger than Rowden when they stood side by side. That was hard to believe as Rowden always seemed so large and strong and powerful. For the first time, she began to worry about Rowden's safety. Of course, he made his living fighting large men, but she hadn't considered what that actually meant. Now she realized it meant he would be dodging punches from the veritable blond giant.

The master of ceremonies led both men into the arena, calling out their names and accomplishments. Rowden looked about the crowd, and though he seemed to be surveying them as a king might his subjects, she knew the moment he found her.

His eyes softened, and his face broke into a smile. He'd been looking for her. He'd wanted to see her, perhaps needed to see her. Modesty smiled back at him, trying to look brave and as though she felt far more confident than she truly did. He needed her to believe in him. She could see it in the way his gaze locked on hers and held.

And she saw something else too. He loved her. He might not want to love her. He might not acknowledge it or accept it, but she saw the love in his eyes.

It was undeniable.

Her own heart clenched in response as she stared back at him, showing him she loved him too. Then the moment was broken when the men were directed to go to their corners. Mr. Okoro and Trogdon were waiting at Rowden's corner. Trogdon offered water, which Rowden waved away, and Mr. Okoro seemed to offer last minute advice.

Then the umpires called for the fight to begin and the German lumbered into the center of the roped off area and

Rowden swaggered toward him. There was no other way to describe the way he moved. He gave every appearance of being cocky and sure he would win the day. Modesty wished she felt the same.

The German threw the first punch, and she pushed her fist against her mouth to keep from gasping. Rowden ducked and danced around the German, forcing the lumbering man to turn and plod after Rowden. Rowden threw a few test jabs, and the German easily deflected all but one. That hit, and though she heard it land, the German seemed unaffected. She could see the German's strategy already. He was not fast, but he did not need to be. He was big and could take a beating. One punch from him was enough to knock out an opponent.

Rowden moved about the arena now, forcing the German to come after him. Rowden bobbed and weaved as the German threw hard punches, but even though Modesty screamed inside at every punch, Rowden was fast enough to evade them all. She saw his strategy now as well. He would tire the German out then pummel him until he was down. Modesty just hoped Rowden's strength would not falter first.

The German threw another punch and then another. Rowden actually ducked under one of the fighter's arms, came up behind him, and booted him lightly in the arse. The crowd roared with laughter, and Rowden gave them a winning smile. Modesty tried to smile too, but she just wanted the fight over.

She shifted forward as something pricked her in the back. But the feeling didn't dissipate. Before she could turn to see what the bothersome object might be, a voice whispered in her ear. "Don't say a word. Stand up and walk out of here. Slowly. Draw attention to yourself, and I'll gut you."

Modesty froze, all of her muscles tensing. She looked toward the tent's entrance, but Mr. Sterling was not back yet. She looked toward the arena, but Rowden was fighting for his life. No one would notice her leave. No one would notice if this man stabbed her. Everyone's attention was on the fight.

The knife in her back pricked harder. "Stand up," the man said.

Modesty stood and pushed through the crowd. She prayed someone would look at her, notice her. She wanted to meet just one person's eyes and mouth the words, "help." But no one paid her any attention. As soon as she was outside, the man grabbed the back of her neck and pushed her toward a group of other men who were waiting.

Twenty

Rowden was actually enjoying himself. It had been a long time since he'd enjoyed a fight. Maybe it was because the German was a worthy opponent. He wouldn't be easy to beat. Maybe it was because of the roar of the crowd or the purse waiting for him if he won.

But mostly it was because Modesty Brown was in the crowd watching him. He'd looked for her as soon as he'd stepped into the exhibition area. He glanced about for that beautiful red hair and that gold gown. It hadn't taken long to find her. She was watching him, her stunning eyes fixed on his face. Her lips curved in a smile, but he saw the way they trembled. She was worried for him, and he gave her a cocky smile to let her know there was nothing to worry about. He intended to beat the German heartily. It wouldn't be a quick fight. He'd have to wear his opponent down, but he could do it.

And then he'd be through with this business, and he'd... he'd what? He wanted to go to her, to kiss her, hold her, tell her what it meant to him to have her there for him. But he couldn't do that. He'd told her good-bye before the match tonight, and that was the right decision.

In that moment, when she was smiling at him with hope and love in her face, it didn't feel like the right decision. He needed her there. He needed her always.

Rowden had gone to his corner, and Chibale had told him to focus. Rowden had taken thoughts of Modesty and put them in another room in his mind, closing the door. He'd open it later. He'd figure out what to do with his churning emotions later. It wasn't hard to concentrate on the fight. When a man like the German threw punches at him, it got Rowden's attention. But he was aware he was putting on a show of sorts too. The more the crowd enjoyed themselves, the more money they would wager. So he dodged the German and ducked behind him, giving him a playful kick in the arse. It wasn't illegal—not much was in these fights—but it did little except anger the German.

Anger worked in Rowden's favor, though. The German threw harder punches and more of them, and Rowden had to work harder to avoid them. Still, if he had to guess, he'd say the German was breathing harder than he at the end of the first round when the two men went to their corners and Chibale handed Rowden the flask of water.

"Where's Trogdon?" he asked, wiping his mouth. He could have used a knee to sit on for a moment. He would happily forego citrus fruit for the next five years.

Chibale looked uncomfortable, which was strange.

"What's wrong?" Rowden asked.

"Nothing. Trogdon had to use the privy."

"In the middle of my fight?" This was it. This really was the last straw. Trogdon had fluff for brains, but Rowden could forgive that because he was always there when Rowden needed him. But if he couldn't even count on the manservant at a time like this, the man's employment was at an end. "You can tell him, if he returns, he'd better look for another position," Rowden said.

Chibale waved a hand. "Let's not worry about that now. You have a fight to win."

"Right." Rowden squared his shoulders and moved his neck about to loosen it.

"Go out there and hit him hard," Chibale said. "Nothing to worry about. Sterling must be with Miss Brown."

The umpires shouted and Rowden moved back into the center of the arena. He ducked and swung, making contact with the German and for the first time, hearing him grunt. But something niggled at his brain. Chibale had said *Nothing to worry about.* Rowden had taken it to mean that he needn't worry he would win the fight. But then why had Chibale added, *Sterling must be with Miss Brown*?

Why did it seem like Chibale was reassuring him that Aidan was with Modesty? Rowden hit again, punching the German in the face. That was the time he should have struck again, slamming the man in the chest when his head was thrown back and he was unprotected, but Rowden froze instead.

Aidan Sterling had promised to stay with Modesty and never let her out of his sight. It was the only reason Rowden had agreed to let her come to the mill because he'd known Notley would be there looking for a way to strike back at Rowden.

Rowden's first impulse was to look for Modesty in the crowd, find her, and reassure himself she was safe. But that impulse would get him knocked out, and he'd be no good to anyone. The German was angry now and fighting back. He'd recovered and was advancing on Rowden, his face bloody and snarling. Rowden hadn't given himself as much room as he would have liked to maneuver so he had little choice but to fight, rather than duck or feint. And so he fought. He took a glancing punch that left his ear ringing and delivered a hard dart to the German's jaw. The German stumbled back and went to his knees. Instead of following up, as Chibale and the crowd urged, Rowden stepped back and looked up into the crowd.

Modesty was not in her seat.

Aidan was not in his seat.

The umpires called for corners, and Rowden marched to his. "What the devil is happening?" he demanded, pushing the offered water away. "Where is Modesty?"

"Trogdon went to find her," Chibale said.

"Trogdon? *Trogdon*? The man can't even find an orange. I'm going."

Chibale grabbed him around the shoulders and made it seem as though he were imparting some important information. "Half of the men in this tent have money on you. You think they'll let you leave? You have to finish this fight or be torn apart."

"Modesty—"

"Trogdon is looking for her and Sterling. It's the best I can do at the moment. I'm sure she's with Sterling."

The umpires called for the fight to begin, but Rowden didn't move. "When did you notice her missing?"

"I didn't. Trogdon did. He said she was leaving, and he was going after her." Chibale took a step back. "Bloody hell. He's coming."

Rowden looked just in time to duck and avoid the punch. It was strong enough that he felt the breeze whip over his head. Since his head was down anyway, he plowed into the German's solid chest, pushing him back and thrusting him against the ropes on the other side of the arena.

The crowd screamed for blood. Rowden was ready to give it. This fight was over, and he just needed to land the death blow.

***

Modesty's mind raced. She needed to get back to the tent, back to the mill. The one thing she had learned in all her years preaching in the rookeries of London was never to allow anyone to separate her from the crowd. The man with the knife had just done that, and now he pushed her into a group of three other men. The men laughed as she stumbled.

"Is this Payne's woman?" one of them asked.

"That's right. Get her to the wagon," the man with the knife said.

Modesty backed up. "I'm returning to the tent. I won't go with you."

"Oh, yes you will." He brandished the knife. "One way or another."

Without warning, she turned and ran, but she only made it a few feet before she was caught and yanked back by the arm. The men were rougher now as they pushed her further away from the tent. One of them closed his hand over her mouth to keep her from calling out—not that anyone would have heard her. The crowd watching the fight was screaming and chanting. She hoped Rowden was winning.

She could imagine his smile when he won. He'd look for her, and she wouldn't be there. She struggled, trying to slow down the men dragging her. "Where are you taking me?" she asked when her mouth slipped free of the man's hold. She could see they were heading for the area of the field where conveyances had been left. Perhaps she'd be able to cry out to a coachman for help.

"Somewhere The Royal Payne in me arse will never find you."

"Why?"

"Because he took something of mine."

Modesty didn't have a chance to ask what that might be before the hand clamped over her mouth again. She tried to struggle, but one of the men punched her lightly in the belly and she doubled over. It might not have been hard, but it was enough to startle the breath from her lungs. She was bending over to protect her body from further harm when she heard a familiar voice.

"Stop right there, gentlemen."

Modesty looked up, thinking it must be Mr. Sterling. But it wasn't Sterling standing in front of the men, blocking their way. It was...Trogdon?

"Move aside," the man with the knife said. "This doesn't concern you."

"It concerns Mr. Payne," Trogdon said, "and so it concerns me. Release the lady, Mr. Green. Put that knife away, Mr. Notley."

No one moved. Modesty glanced from the man called Green to the leader, Notley. They seemed uncertain what to do, and uncertainty worked in her favor. With a mighty tug, she broke free of Green and plunged toward Trogdon. One of the other men caught her, and she fought as though her life depended on it.

Her life probably did depend on it.

She kicked and scratched and bit, and the man released her. Trogdon swooped in, caught her arm and pushed her ahead of him. "Run!" he instructed.

She tried, but her legs were tangled in her skirts, and she tripped and fell. She scrambled to her knees, her eyes closed as she waited for the rough hands to grasp her again, but instead she heard a loud *thump*.

"Ow! Hey!" one of the men called.

Trogdon moved beside her and pulled her to her feet. And then he handed her an orange. She stared at it and then him. He was holding a sack of them, and as she watched, he pulled one out and lobbed it at one of the men. He had excellent aim as he hit the fellow on the center of the forehead, sending him reeling back.

"Throw it!" Trogdon ordered, still backing up. Modesty threw. Her aim was not as good, and she missed.

"Good try, miss," Trogdon said. "Could you scream for help, do you think?"

That she could do. She screamed as loudly as she could, while Trogdon threw another orange, hitting Notley in the center of the chest. The orange exploded, and Notley reeled back, dropping the knife. But he wasn't incapacitated. It would take more than citrus fruit to accomplish that. He looked angry now as he lunged for them.

***

Rowden was aware he was acting against all his training. He punched and pummeled and wore himself out in an all-out offensive against the German. The crowd was so loud he couldn't even think. Out of the corner of his eye, he could see Chibale yelling, probably telling him to focus and remember his training.

But Rowden didn't have time to wear the German out. He needed to knock him out and find Modesty. But the German, who'd seemed initially taken off guard at Rowden's attack, recovered and punched back. Rowden grunted as one punch landed on his shoulder. Pain exploded, and he gritted his teeth and fought to stay on his feet. The German punched again, but Rowden ducked and launched his own offensive into the other man's breadbox. He was out of breath and dizzy by the time he shuffled away, and the German was still on his feet, and still lumbering toward him.

For the second time that night, Rowden wanted to run. He wanted away from this fight, away from these people. He needed to find Modesty. But he knew Chibale was right. The crowd wouldn't let him leave until one of the men in the arena lay unconscious.

Rowden threw another punch, and it landed in-effectually off the German's temple. And still the blond man came for him. Rowden moved around so he was facing the side where Modesty and Aidan had been sitting. Where the devil was Aidan? Rowden's only consolation was that Aidan was with Modesty. Aidan had been a thief who'd lived some of his life on the streets. He could take care of himself and Modesty.

He ducked another punch then jolted out of shock. He ducked under the German's arm and ran to the other side of the ropes. Aidan had just stumbled into the tent, his temple bleeding. "Where is she?" he yelled. But Aidan couldn't hear him over the dozens of men already shouting.

Too late, Rowden realized they shouted a warning at him. The German landed a punch in his side, and Rowden crumpled but stayed on his feet. Holding onto the ropes for support, he managed to right himself just as the German struck again. Rowden managed to avoid the worst of it, but the blow glanced off his jaw and the pain was like a hot iron placed on his skin. He tasted blood, spat, and looked up to see the German coming for him again.

"Fuck," he said through blood and spittle. He was about to lose.

***

Notley was still coming for them, even as Trogdon threw another orange. This one hit Notley's shoulder and barely slowed him down. He looked angry. Very angry.

"Uh oh," Trogdon said.

Modesty glanced at him. "What's uh oh?"

"No more oranges." He grasped her wrist. "Now we run."

He started away, and Modesty tried to keep up. For a lazy man, he was remarkably fast. He pulled her with him as they finally reached the carriages and wagons the Fancy had taken to the mill. Trogdon darted between them and pulled her along, slowing now to listen for pursuit.

"They're coming," Modesty whispered.

"Here." Trogdon pulled her close to a large carriage wheel and scrambled underneath. "Come on!" he hissed.

Modesty silently apologized to Madame Renauld as she followed. Under the carriage, her elbows sinking in mud, she glanced at Trogdon. He had a smear of mud on his face, but he didn't look frightened. "There you are. Safe as the Bank of England," he said.

Modesty would have liked a bit more security. "Where are the coachmen and the grooms?"

He jerked his head toward the glow of fires, just now lighting up the darkening evening sky. "Playing dice or cards," he whispered. "Too far away to hear us."

"Where are they?" one of Notley's men asked, and Modesty tensed. Trogdon put a finger to his lips, as though she needed to be reminded.

"They're here somewhere," Notley said. "You take that side, and I'll take this one. Look under the vehicles too."

Modesty pressed her lips together and held her breath as a pair of boots came into view.

***

Rowden ducked just in time to avoid the dart. He was aware he was retreating and ducking and basically using nothing Mostyn or Chibale or even his own experience had taught him.

He'd planned to wear the German down and then knock him out. No time for that now. Modesty needed him. He ducked again and ran to the far corner of the area, even as the boos and jeers of the crowd followed him.

The German lurched toward him, and Rowden used those extra seconds to channel all of his anger and fear and panic into a tight, black ball. He could imagine it swirling together as he compressed it and pushed it out and into his hands, his arms, his muscles.

His pain was in that swirling sphere. The pain of losing Mary and now the fear of losing Modesty. He would not lose Modesty. He would *not* lose Modesty.

The sphere seemed to grow as the German came closer, and with a roar, Rowden launched himself. The German paused for just a moment, his brow lowered in confusion, and Rowden struck, landing a hard punch to his face and then another.

He tried to punch again, but he was drained of strength. This was it then. He'd lost.

Except that the German didn't come for him. The German very slowly fell back and down, making the floor bounce as he fell unconscious.

Rowden didn't even wait for the count. He staggered to the ropes and climbed out. Chibale was at his side, yelling for the crowd to move, to part. The men did so, looking from Rowden to the downed German in confusion.

Aidan met him at the tent's exit. "It was Notley," he said, blood covering half his face. "He ambushed me. I think he has Miss Brown."

***

The boots moved on, but just as Modesty started to breathe again, they paused. Then a hand came into view and then knees and finally the face of Notley. "Found you," he said.

Trogdon threw a clump of mud at Notley and scrambled out the back. Modesty followed, but her skirts were heavy now, and Notley caught her arm.

"I have them!" he called. Modesty heard the sound of footsteps coming. Trogdon ran at Notley and tried to free Modesty, but Notley only held on tighter. The tug-of-war on her arm left her crying out in pain. Green and another man ran around a wagon and tackled Trogdon, sending him back down into the mud. Modesty tried to wrest free of Notley's hold, and even though her sleeve ripped, Notley held on to her.

"Let me go!" she yelled. "Help!"

"Modesty!" The voice was far away, but she knew it.

"Rowden!"

Notley cursed and released her so suddenly she fell to her knees beside Trogdon. The men beating him looked up at Notley's expletive and all three of them tried to place Rowden's voice.

"Rowden! I'm here!" she called.

"This way," Notley yelled.

"No, this way!" Green said. In the end, it didn't matter because Rowden came around one corner of a coach and Mr. Okoro and Mr. Sterling came around the other. Rowden grabbed Notley, shoved him to his knees as though he were a doll, and looked about.

"I have her, sir," Trogdon said, waving from the mud. "She is safe."

Rowden's green gaze found hers, and she gave him a little wave. He stared at her then Trogdon. Finally, he looked away. "Chibale, fetch a magistrate. I must have seen at least three watching the mill."

"I'll be right back." Mr. Okoro took off, while Mr. Sterling shook his head at Notley's two accomplices.

"Stay right there," he said, "Or I'll want to know which one of you did this to me and repay you twofold."

Modesty stood and tried to swipe mud off her dress. She reached down to help Trogdon up, and they both went to stand beside Rowden, who was still holding Notley in a painful grip between his neck and shoulder.

"What the devil happened?" Rowden asked.

Modesty could feel the urge to laugh, and she knew it was shock and hysteria. She pushed it down and looked at the manservant. "Trogdon saved me."

"Tell me the truth," Rowden said.

"He saved me!" she said, laughing. She had to press a hand to her mouth to keep the laugh from turning into tears. The dirt on her skin brought her back to reality. "He threw oranges at them and stopped them from taking me."

Rowden looked at Mr. Sterling. "We'd better fetch a doctor."

"I'm fine," she said. "He really did throw oranges. See?" She pointed to the orange stain on Notley's shirt. It was difficult to see as night was falling. Then she looked at Trogdon. "Where did you get oranges? I thought you couldn't find any."

Trogdon gave her a sheepish look then glanced at Rowden, who looked back at him expectantly. "Mr. Payne doesn't care for oranges. I purchased them in case I couldn't find lemons and limes."

"What?" Rowden asked, sounding dumbstruck. In the distance Modesty could hear voices heading toward them. Thank God the magistrate was almost there. She didn't think her wobbly legs would hold her much longer.

"I grabbed the bag when I saw Miss Brown leave the tent with that one." He pointed to Notley. "I had a feeling I might need them."

"That you might need oranges?" Rowden demanded.

Trogdon gave a small shrug. "You do seem to always need them, sir. They must be good for something."

The magistrate and a group of men converged on the party, and Modesty was pushed out of the way. Vaguely, she heard Notley yelling and Mr. Sterling arguing, and she thought she might just sit down on the ground for a moment and catch her breath.

Rowden caught her, picking her up as though she were a child and cradling her in his arms. "Looks like you've spent enough time in the mud. Let's go back to Battle's Peak."

She gave him a weak smile. He was still bare to the waist, and she liked being pressed against his chest, though she was probably smearing mud all over him. "Did you win?" she asked.

He looked down at her, clearly confused. And then his features cleared. "Ah. The mill. Yes, I won."

"Oh, good. I didn't want to be the reason he beat you a second time."

Rowden pulled her closer. "I'll lose a hundred mills if it means I can hold you," he said, and he carried her to Sterling's coach. And then, after what seemed like hours and a thousand questions, the five of them—Rowden, Modesty, Mr. Okoro, Mr. Sterling, and even Trogdon—left the exhibition grounds behind.

Twenty-One

Rowden waited until the house was quiet before stepping out of his room and into the long shadows of the corridor. He knew where Modesty's room was. He'd loitered in that wing of the house on the pretense of making certain she was well and watched a pair of footmen deliver a tub to her chamber earlier tonight. Lady Florentia had shooed him away to take his own bath. That was hours ago, and now he carried a lamp and walked across the gallery to the opposite wing. He chanced to look down the wide staircase as he passed and stopped.

"How long have you been sitting there?" he asked Lord Nicholas, who was sitting with one leg extended about halfway up the grand staircase.

Lord Nicholas looked up at him from under a mop of golden hair that had fallen over his forehead. "Not long."

"I'd ask if you want my help, but I assume you're attempting the stairs in the middle of the night precisely because you don't want help."

Lord Nicholas rubbed his outstretched leg absently. "I used to run up and down these stairs a dozen times a day. Now it takes me a half hour just to haul myself up."

"Why do it then?" Rowden asked. "You have more rooms than you need in this place. Make one of the rooms downstairs your chamber."

Nicholas shook his head. "Then my legs win."

"They were crushed under a horse, Nick. That doesn't make them the enemy."

Nicholas waved a hand. "Don't try that with me. All that damn logic and reason might work with Nash—"

"Actually—"

"But it's nothing I haven't told myself."

Rowden sighed. "You might have noticed I'm attempting a midnight rendezvous. As stimulating as this conversation might be, I had other ideas in mind."

"Your destination isn't my sister's chamber, is it?"

"Absolutely not."

"Fine. Before you defile my house guest, help me up these stairs. It will be recompense for all the horses I stole for you."

Rowden set the lamp on the wide banister and started down the steps. "I never asked you to steal a horse. That was Neil."

Nicholas had risen to his feet, and he draped an arm over Rowden's shoulders, which were sore from the mill earlier that night, but he didn't complain.

"You never complained about riding instead of walking," Nicholas said, his voice breathless as he used one hand to steady himself and Rowden hauled him up the stairs.

"Florentia says you don't ride anymore."

"She talks too much."

They reached the top of the stairs, and Nicholas unhooked a cane he'd draped over one arm. He leaned on it, breathing heavily. "I have it from here."

"I can take you to your room," Rowden offered.

"You have debauchery to attend to." He waved a hand. "I can make it. Good night."

"I hope so," Rowden said, picking up the lamp. He left his friend to shuffle along the gallery and tried to ignore the way his heart beat harder and faster the closer he came to Modesty's room. What if she was asleep? What if she told him to go back to bed? What if she made him wait until they were formally wed? What if she didn't want to wed?

Shut up, man, he told himself and stopped in front of her door. He looked left and right to make sure no one else was up and about, then tapped quietly on her door. He held his breath for what seemed ten minutes before the door opened and Modesty, dressed in a white nightgown with her damp hair about her shoulders, stood before him.

He looked down at her. She seemed smaller than he remembered and younger. And, with her hair down and the white material around her, she looked softer and more inviting.

"What's wrong?" she asked, probably because he was standing there staring at her. "Did the magistrate—"

"No." He did not want her thinking about Notley or the magistrate or the awful events of the evening. Notley was in custody, as were his men, and she was safe. "Nothing is wrong. I was just thinking how beautiful you look."

Color rose to her cheeks. "And you look battered and bruised. Your poor chin." She reached out and ran a finger over the darkening bruise the German had given him. Rowden felt lucky he hadn't lost any teeth. He turned his head and kissed her fingers.

"May I come in?"

Her gaze flew to his, and he could see the question in her eyes. She'd asked him to come to her earlier that night, right before he'd told her he could never love her. She was wondering if that had changed. But she didn't ask, merely stepped back so he could enter. He closed the door behind him and turned the key. When he turned back to her, she wrapped her arms about him, reaching up to kiss him.

He kissed her back, trying to keep his balance and set the lamp down safely. Her mouth was warm and eager and when he was able to draw a breath, he said, "Modesty, I need to tell you something."

"I know you don't love me," she said. "I know lying with you is a bad idea, but I want you anyway." She reached for the ribbon at the neck of her nightgown, and he realized she was about to tug it. The garment would slide right to her feet if she did that.

"No!" he said, more loudly than he wanted. "I mean, I want you to take that off. God, I want you to take that off."

"No need for blasphemy," she said.

He almost laughed. "Just wait until I say what I came to say. If I don't say it while you're dressed, it'll be hours before I have enough sense left in my brain to say it."

"If you make me wait too long," she said, "I will lose my nerve."

"Give me three minutes touching you, and you won't be thinking about your nerves," he promised.

"When does that three minutes start?" she asked breathlessly.

"As soon as I do this." He sank to one knee, his legs protesting since they were sore and tight from the fight earlier. But he'd forget about his stiff muscles soon enough. It had been a long time since he'd played the gentleman, but he still knew how to do it. "Miss Brown, forgive the suddenness of this proposal, but it cannot have escaped your notice that my feelings for you have deepened and ripened into a feeling that I can only describe as love. Would you do me the honor of becoming my wife?"

She stared at him, and he went over the words in his mind again. He'd said them correctly, hadn't he? That was the way to propose.

"You love me?" she asked.

"That's what I said."

"You said something about ripening, and I wasn't certain if you meant me or fruit."

He'd done this all wrong because he was a coward, as she'd claimed earlier. He'd thought by relying on formality he could avoid the emotion of the moment.

But Modesty was obviously having none of that, and bully for her. He took her hand. "I love you," he said simply. "Is that clear enough?"

"But you said earlier—"

"Earlier I was a fool. I knew I was being a fool even then. I knew I didn't mean it because even though I didn't want to fall in love with you, I already had. I already *have*."

"But you said you couldn't bear to feel that pain if you loved and lost again."

His hand on hers tightened. "I had a taste of that pain tonight when you were missing and when I found you with Notley. And you know what I realized?"

"You should give Mr. Trogdon a raise?"

He grinned. "Besides that."

"What?" She stepped closer, and he caught the scent of lemons that must have scented the soap she'd used.

"That I don't want to live without you. That not having you is as bad as having you and losing you."

"You won't lose me."

"There are no guarantees of that."

"Agreed. But I am here now, and so are you. We have right now." She reached for that ribbon again, and it pained him to put his hand over hers, stopping her.

"You didn't answer my question, and I don't want to take you to bed until you do."

She put her hands on either side of his face and looked at him with so much love it made his heart ache. "I will have you for a husband, Rowden Payne." She stepped back, just out of reach, and grasped that flimsy white ribbon. "I." She tugged one side loose. "Will." She tugged the other side loose. "Marry." She let the garment slip off her shoulders. "You." The nightgown slid down her body, leaving her naked and golden in the lamplight.

Rowden didn't breathe for several heartbeats. She was beautiful with her curves and her angles and those lovely breasts with the rosy tips. A triangle of auburn hair invited him at the juncture of her thighs, and he went to her and sank to his knees. He pressed a kiss to her belly, and she inhaled sharply. His hands skated up the backs of her thighs, pressing into her round bottom then over her hips and up her ribs to cup those heavy breasts.

He wanted to sink into that soft body, to explore every inch of it. And he knew just where to start. "Lie on the bed," he said, standing and removing his coat.

She gave him a nervous look, and he wanted to kick himself for forgetting this was her first time. He took her hand and led her to the bed, then sat on the edge and removed his boots. "Have you ever seen a naked man?" he asked.

"In a museum. And well, you are almost naked when you fight.

He yanked his shirt over his head. "Then this much nudity doesn't bother you."

"On the contrary." She reached over and ran a hand across his shoulders and down his chest. "I have been wanting to do that all night."

"Usually, I would let you have your way—ladies first and all that—but I don't trust myself to do this right if I let you have your way."

"There's a right way to do this?" she asked, looking a bit worried.

He lifted her onto the bed, resting her head on the pillow then looking down at her. His chest was pressed against her side, and her skin was soft and warm. "Not a right way," he murmured, dropping kisses over her face. "But I want you to have as much pleasure as I do."

She wriggled against him, obviously anticipating the pleasure she already knew he could give her. But instead of sliding his fingers between her legs, he rolled over on top of her and kissed her, slowly making his way down her body.

He pressed teasing kisses behind her ear; long, luxurious kisses on her lips; and delicate kisses on her neck. He worked his way down, tracing the curve of her breast with his tongue and then sucking lightly on her distended nipples. She arched her back, and he sucked harder, using the distraction to wedge a knee between her legs and open them. She stiffened slightly, but then he slid his tongue between her breasts and down to her navel, and she was gasping for air and trembling. He pressed his knee upward slightly, into the warm heat of her sex.

She moaned and moved against him, even as he slid down further to press kisses on her hip bone and then that soft hair between her legs. He opened her legs further, sliding his mouth down to lick between her legs. She gasped in shock and sat, staring at him as though he were mad.

"Not in Song of Solomon?" he asked.

"No!"

His fingers trailed lazily up and down the skin of her inner thigh. "Solomon had how many wives? Ten? Twenty?"

"Seven hundred," she said, her voice breaking as his fingers moved upward.

"Then he surely knew something about cunnilingus," he said. "What are the verses?" He'd never thought he'd be quoting scripture in bed, but all those years of being forced to read the Bible were finally proving useful. "I remember. *Let my beloved come into his garden, and eat his pleasant fruits.*" Her eyes were shining now, her breasts rising and falling with heat. "Let me taste you. One word from you, and

I'll stop." He lowered his head again, kissing her outer lips then parting them to sweep his tongue along her until he reached the small pink bud hidden in her folds.

She fell back, her legs trembling, her breaths coming in fast pants now. He spread her legs wider, and she didn't protest, opening for him, as he teased her with his tongue. Her hands fisted on the bedclothes and she began to moan faster. His tongue moved faster as her hips began to writhe. "Please," she begged. "Yes, oh yes."

He could have slowed down, taken his time. It had been a long time since he'd done this, and he'd forgotten how much he liked it. But there would be time to tease and torment her later, time to draw out her pleasure until she was wild with need. For now, he pressed his tongue to her until he felt the way her body tensed and lifted, and she cried out with release.

***

Modesty had thought she knew pleasure. Rowden had touched her in the coach, bringing her to climax twice before. But that was nothing to the pleasure he gave her now, nothing to looking down and seeing his dark head buried between her legs as his tongue flicked wickedly over her...fruit.

This time when she climaxed, she felt like her entire body would break into a thousand pieces. Every single ounce of her was thrumming with glorious release. But she didn't shatter, she held together, and came back down and into his arms. His large, solid body was on top of hers, and he was kissing her belly and her breasts, then her neck and her lips. Modesty dug her hands into his hair, tempering her own kisses because she knew his face was bruised.

"Should we wait?" he asked, his voice low and breathless.

"Wait?" She could barely understand him, her mind was fuzzy with pleasure.

"Wait to consummate the marriage until we actually say the vows. I'll wait if you want."

She pulled back and looked him full in the face. "I don't want to wait. I love you."

His face softened, and despite the cuts and mottled bruises, he looked almost sweet. "I love you. I don't know why I fought it."

She gingerly touched the bruise by his eye. "You're a fighter. It's what you do."

"Not anymore."

Before she could ask what he meant, he was kissing her again, his body pressing against hers with a delicious heaviness. She ran her hands up and down his muscled back, and then found a measure of bravery and cupped his buttocks. "Shouldn't you remove the breeches?" she asked.

"Definitely." In a few movements, he was as naked as she, his body warm and hard as he pressed against her. Now when she ran her hands down the length of him, all she felt was sinew and muscle and skin.

He was touching her as well, his hand moving between her legs to stroke her. She didn't think she could feel pleasure again, but her body responded and her breath caught in her throat.

"I don't want to hurt you," he said. "But you have to relax and trust me. Do you trust me?"

"I've always trusted you." It was true. When her father had disappeared, Rowden was the one she'd gone to for help. Somehow she'd always known she could count on him.

The pressure between her legs grew more insistent as he entered her, but her pleasure grew as well as he continued to kiss and stroke her. She pulled him close, wanting this joining, wanting to be one with him now and forever. As her pleasure mounted so did the insistent pressure. It was not unwelcome, just novel. And when he finally brought her to climax, there was pain with the pleasure, but the pain was not so great that she couldn't watch his face as he found his own pleasure. He would have thought her daft, but she thought him beautiful in that moment.

Afterward, he pulled her close, kissing her, whispering how much he loved her, how he did not want to wait to marry her. She was almost asleep when he said, "I'll go see your father tomorrow."

Modesty's eyes opened and she sat. "What?"

"To ask his permission to marry you."

She shook her head. "He won't give it, and I'm of age. I don't need his permission."

He lifted himself onto his elbow and looked up at her. "You don't want his blessing?"

"I don't want anything from him."

He laid back and looked up at the canopy of her bed. It was a grand bed, and she'd felt very small sleeping in it alone last night. Now she looked down at him, and he looked as though he belonged. Of course, he belonged. He was the son of a duke.

Modesty realized her mistake. "Rowden, I didn't mean to upset you."

He waved a hand. "I used to think that way. I didn't need or want anything from my father, or my mother, for that matter. The pain of your father's lies is still raw, but think of how you'll feel years from now." He looked at her, his green eyes dark. "The absence of family leaves a hole."

Modesty hugged him, holding him close. "I'll be your family now."

He stroked her hair. "And I'll be yours, but reconsider cutting your father out completely. If you don't want me to go to him, I'll respect your wishes. Just be sure that is what you want."

She looked up at him. "Did you ever try to make amends with the duke? After your wife died or after the war?"

He nodded. "I've tried several times over the years, but I'm dead to him now. He's a hard man and a stubborn one. But I'm lucky."

She frowned. "I fail to see how."

"I lost my family, but in the war, I gained a new one." He gestured to the room. "Lord Nicholas, Mostyn, Sterling. They're all part of my family now. They're my brothers."

"Then they're my brothers as well." He pulled her down for a kiss. After a long while, she said, "How long until we can marry? Three weeks to call the banns seems a lifetime."

He gave her a roguish grin. "I may be the disinherited son of a duke, but I still have a few connections."

***

The evening after the much-discussed exhibition in Hungerford, Thérèse stood in her parlor and wondered if she was as much an idiot as she feared. She'd dressed in her finest gown, a ruby silk with a beaded bodice she set off with a ruby necklace and earrings—not real rubies, of course, but good copies. She'd had her maid style her hair, piling it high on her head and adding hundreds of rubies to the dark, glossy locks so that she would glitter under the candlelight at the winter ball.

That was if she attended the ball. She'd had no word from Chibale, and it might be too much to expect him to be able to travel back from Hungerford to London in time to escort her to the ball.

She'd probably wasted her time dressing. She checked the clock on the mantel, sighed, and thought about calling her maid back to undress her again.

"Bleuette ees pretty," her parrot said, watching her from atop her cage.

"I'm the pretty one tonight," she told the bird.

"Fine lace!"

Thérèse wasn't wearing lace, but she took it as a compliment anyway.

"Shall we have dessert," Bleuette squawked.

"I hope we can have dessert," Thérèse said. It had only been two days, but she'd missed having Chibale in her bed. She'd missed having him nearby, missed seeing his smile across the breakfast table. He was probably tired from celebrating his fighter's victory the night before. She'd sent her maid out to gather all the news first thing this morning. Thérèse was so proud of Chibale. She wished she could have been there to tell him so and to celebrate with him.

It seemed the more time she spent with Chibale, the more difficult it became to remember their time together was fleeting. He was in love with her, but she couldn't allow herself to fall in love with him. She could never allow herself to be vulnerable to a man again.

But Chibale had made it very hard *not* to fall in love with him. She remembered him sweeping up broken glass in her shop, his sleeves rolled to his elbows as though he were a common laborer. She remembered the way he touched her in the dark, as though she were someone special to be protected and cherished.

Thérèse bit her lip. She was an imbecile. She had fallen in love with him and not even realized.

A knock sounded on the door, and Bleuette called out, "Merde!"

Thérèse shook her head. If she did not watch her tongue, she'd not be able to bring Bleuette to the shop any longer. Thérèse's heart was racing as the knock sounded on the door again, and she took a deep breath and smoothed her skirts before walking calmly to the door and opening it.

Her mouth dropped open when she saw him. Chibale stood in the doorway in a blue coat of superfine, a ruby waistcoat, and fawn breeches. His beaver hat sat at a jaunty angle, and he had a walking stick draped across one arm.

In his other arm he held flowers. "For you," he said.

She took the mixture of tropical flowers that were so exotic she could not even identify them. "Where did you buy flowers thees time of year?"

But his gaze was traveling down her and then back up again. "You look...I don't have the words."

Thérèse felt her cheeks heat as they hadn't since she'd been a young girl. "I see you wore red, as instructed."

"Red is my new favorite color," he said, looking as though he might eat her up. She almost wished they could forego the ball and skip to the eating up part of the evening, but instead she reached for her wrapper and took his arm.

A grand carriage waited on the street below, and she gave him another look as she climbed into what could only be described as opulence. "Exactly how much money did you win in Hungerford?"

He laughed, sitting beside her, rather than across from her. "Not this much. Mr. Sterling offered the coach, and the flowers came from the conservatory of Lord Nicholas."

"You have generous friends."

"Yes, I do." He gazed at her for a long time. "I'm a lucky man."

She smiled. "Where ees your sister, Bethanie? I thought you were to escort her to the ball?"

"She will arrive with my parents."

Thérèse understood then that he had made these arrangements for her. She'd told him she didn't want to marry him and didn't see the point in coming to know his family. Now she felt selfish. That young girl deserved to ride in this carriage to her first ball. "Ees it too late to fetch her—all of them?" she asked.

Chibale stared at her. "No. I don't think so. Are you certain?"

Thérèse looked back at him and nodded. "Very certain."

***

His parents were warm and kind. Charlotte and Gamba Okoro were almost as starry-eyed as their daughter when they climbed into the lavish coach. The family seemed to genuinely love each other, and she watched as they teased one another and exchanged warm smiles.

"But the best part about tonight," Charlotte said, "is meeting the amazing woman who designed this dress." She indicated the gown Bethanie wore. Thérèse had to admit it looked lovely on the girl. "You have a rare talent, madam."

"*Merci*, but it ees easy to dress one so lovely as your daughter."

"Chibale tells us you dress all of London," Gamba said. And before she knew it, they had her talking about some of her famous and not-so-famous clients. And then the talk drifted to their work and Chibale's brothers, and Thérèse was surprised when they arrived at the assembly hall. The time had passed so quickly, and she'd felt completely comfortable.

Once inside, the Okoros introduced her to the president of the Negro Merchant's Guild and his wife. She quickly fell into conversation with him and other members of the guild, who were eager to have her join their ranks. Finally, she realized Chibale was standing at her elbow. He gave her a deep bow. "May I have this dance?" he asked.

"You should dance the first dance with your sister," she told him, stepping away from the guild and talk of business.

"I have danced with her twice, and now she dances with that man there. My father is keeping an eye on them, so I might dance with you."

Thérèse laughed. "Her partner looks harmless enough." She gave him her hand and allowed herself to be led to the dance floor. She danced with him twice more as well as several members of the guild, and at the end of the night her feet hurt, and she was happily exhausted.

Bethanie recounted every moment of the ball on the ride home in the carriage, and before they stopped at the Okoro house, Charlotte put a hand on Thérèse's arm. "I do hope you will join us for dinner soon. Chibale says I make the best currant buns in London."

"I would love to try them," she said. "I adore currant buns."

"Tomorrow evening then?" Charlotte asked.

"*Oui. Merci beaucoup.*"

When they were alone again, Chibale leaned forward. "That was kind of you, but I'll make your excuses."

She tapped his arm with the tip of her fan. "You'll do no such thing. You just want the currant buns all to yourself."

He tilted his head. "I thought you didn't want to go to dinner with my family."

She flicked her fan open and waved it in front of her face. "That was before."

"Before?" he asked as the carriage sped across London toward her flat.

"Before I realized I'm in love with you," she said. Her fan was snatched out of her hand as Chibale grasped her wrists and pulled her to him. He looked her directly in the eyes, his own eager and hopeful.

"Did you just say you love me?"

"You should see a doctor about your hearing."

"Say it again, Thérèse."

"I love you, Chibale."

He kissed her, the kind of kiss that melted all of her reservations away and made her want to do all sorts of wicked things to him. She barely noticed when the carriage stopped, but he opened the door, gathered her in his arms, and carried her up the stairs and to her door. She was laughing by the time he set her down so she could retrieve the key from her reticule. "You should save some energy for dessert, *mon chéri*."

"I have stamina to spare," he said.

"I'm counting on that." She opened the door, and they tumbled inside.

A long time later, he looked down at her and spread her hair out on the silk pillow. She smiled lazily up at him. "You know what I want to ask now," he said.

"Another marriage proposal." She pretended to yawn, but inside her heart was pounding.

"Should I ask again?"

"Definitely. And one of these days I promise to say yes."

Twenty-Two

Earlier that day near Hungerford, Modesty had been reading in the library at Battle's Peak when the butler entered and cleared his throat. She looked about and realized she was the only one in the room. "Are you looking for me?"

"You have a visitor, miss."

She sat straighter. "*I* have a visitor?"

"Shall I show him in, miss?"

Modesty didn't know how to answer, but the butler was already retreating. He returned a moment later with Samuel Brown. Samuel held his hat in his hands, his windswept brown hair falling over his forehead.

Modesty stood. "Mr. Brown. This is…unexpected."

"I'm so sorry to intrude." He glanced back at the butler, clearly uncomfortable.

"You're not intruding. Please, sit down."

The butler closed the door, and Mr. Brown sat on the edge of one of the straight-backed library chairs. He didn't speak right away, and Modesty had to curb her own desire to fill the silence. Her father had always told her listening was more important than speaking. On that point, she agreed.

Finally, her half-brother spoke. "I heard Mr. Payne won his fight."

"He did." She smiled. "Did you wish to speak to him? He's not here, I'm afraid." He had ridden to see about obtaining a special license so they could marry. He'd left very early this morning, kissing her gently before climbing out of her bed. "I don't expect him to return until tomorrow."

"No, I came to see you, actually. I was surprised you were still in the country. I thought you would return to Town immediately."

"That is the plan upon Mr. Payne's return." Modesty felt the need to do something with her hands, besides clutch the book she held. "Should I ring for tea?"

"No. I wouldn't want to trouble anyone. Miss Brown—"

"We are family. You should call me Modesty. May I call you Samuel?"

"Of course. Modesty, I'm here on behalf of our father."

Modesty gripped the book tighter, her hands beginning to ache. She looked down at her white-knuckles and tried to relax her fingers.

"He regrets the way you parted."

"Is that what he regrets?" she said archly. Immediately, she wished she could take the words back. "I'm sorry. None of this is your fault."

He passed his hat from one hand to another. "I feel as though it is, in part. I knew about you, and there were times I thought of going to London and confronting him and meeting you. I never did so."

Modesty gave him a sad smile. "The threat of his disapproval is a powerful deterrent."

He nodded. "Yes. You understand." He set his hat on his knee. "But I think the threat of your disapproval was also a powerful force in his life. When you left him yesterday, he sank into a melancholy I have never seen before. I heard him speaking with my mother when he thought we were asleep. He fears he has lost you forever. He told my mother that would be the biggest regret of his life. He loves you, Miss Brown."

Modesty pulled the book into her belly, clutching it tightly. "What do you want me to do?"

"I don't feel as though I have the right to ask anything of you, but if you could find it in your heart to forgive him, I know he would like to see you again. I think we would all like to see you again. We'd like to be part of your life."

Modesty shook her head, and Mr. Brown rose, his hands outstretched. "Don't feel as though you need to give me an answer. I came to tell you how we felt. I hope one day to see you again."

Modesty stood. "I hope so too," she said, extending her hand. He took it, squeezed it, and then was gone. Modesty sat again and opened her book, but she couldn't read a word.

***

The next day Mr. Sterling returned to London. Before he set off, he delivered Modesty to a small tenant farm a few miles from Battle's Peak. Modesty wished him safe travels and started up the walk.

Her legs felt wobbly, and her heart was in her throat. She was not at all certain this was the right decision, but she'd thought and prayed about it all last night, and this morning she'd been resolute in her desire to see her father.

The door opened and the same boy and girl who had greeted her last time stood in the doorway again. "Miss Brown!" they cried.

Modesty couldn't help but smile at a greeting like that. "Call me Modesty," she said, pausing at the entrance to the cottage. "And what are your names?"

"Grace," said the girl.

"John," said the boy.

"Grace, John, how lovely to see you again. Is your mother here?"

"I'm here," said Mrs. Smith—Brown, coming into view behind the children. Modesty gave her a formal nod.

"I've come to see my father, if that's agreeable to you."

"Of course. Come in."

Modesty entered, her back stiff and straight in the presence of her father's mistress. She might not blame the children, but she did not know when or if she would ever be comfortable around her father's second wife. Mrs. Brown led her to her father's bed. He was seated much as before, but this time, he sat forward, having heard her arrival and anticipating speaking with her.

As before, Modesty entered the makeshift chamber, and Mrs. Brown pulled the curtain closed. Modesty stood awkwardly before him. "How are you feeling?" she asked.

"Better," he said. "Stronger every day."

"I'm glad to hear it. I will be returning to London soon. I imagine you intend to stay here."

"I think that's best," he said. After a long pause, he added, "Where will you live? I could write the Plineys."

Modesty shook her head. "I'm to be married."

The jolt that went through him at this news was visible. She could see his face tighten, see him resist the urge to argue with her. After all, he hadn't been consulted about a marriage. Finally, he took a deep breath. "And who is the lucky man?"

"He's a pugilist, Mr. Rowden Payne."

Her father's eyes grew wide, and she raised a brow, waiting for him to express an objection. An objection he would make while lying in his mistress's bed.

"I wish you every happiness," he said through gritted teeth. "Is it possible for me to meet him before you wed?"

At his response, his acceptance, a heavy weight seemed lifted off her shoulders. She sank into a chair beside the bed. "He wanted to come and ask for your blessing. He has gone to fetch a special license. I can send him when he returns."

The minister frowned. "He has the influence to obtain a special license?"

"His father is a duke." The rest of the story was Rowden's to tell, if he ever chose to reveal it.

"Modesty," her father began, and she tensed at the way he looked at her. As much as she wanted to hear what he would say next, she dreaded it too. "I am sorry for my actions. I never wanted to lie to you. I knew it was wrong. I knew my relationship with Fanny was wrong, while your mother was alive. Sometimes love makes us do things we wouldn't normally do. It's not an excuse, I know, and I ask for your forgiveness."

Modesty looked at him for a long time. *Sometimes love makes us do things we wouldn't normally do.* That statement resonated with her more than any other her father had ever made. She had certainly done things she had never expected for love. "I forgive you," she said.

Her father's face broke into such a huge smile that she wished she had forgiven him earlier. His joy was undeniable. "If you will allow it," he said, "I'd like to be the one to perform the marriage ceremony."

Modesty nodded, feeling tears prick her eyes. "I will have to speak to Rowden. If he agrees, we would still need to postpone for just a little while."

"Why is that?" her father asked.

"I would like my Aunt Augusta to attend."

Her father blinked. "Your mother's sister?"

"Yes. I'd like to meet her. I'd like to write to her and ask her to come to the wedding."

Her father looked away. "She never approved of me, you know. She said your mother should marry someone of her own class. Someone deserving of her. I suppose I proved her correct." He looked back up at her. "But she will want to see you. I regret that I tried to keep her away from your mother and you. It's past time, you came to know her and your mother's family."

Modesty took his hand. "It's past time I came to know your family too."

He nodded. "I'd like that."

"So would I."

***

The wedding was held a fortnight later in the chapel at Battle's Peak. Lord Nicholas did not attend, but his sister Lady Florentia was thrilled to have a reason to open the house to visitors. The ceremony was small, but the wedding breakfast was crowded and raucous. Mostyn and Lady Lorraine had not come from London, but Lady Lorraine had written to say she was quite recovered and directing all about her from a comfortable chair. Her husband had taken to spending more time with her—she lovingly called him her jailer—and Rowden had told Modesty Mostyn was pleased Rowden had agreed to partner with him at the boxing studio. With the new baby coming, he could use the help.

Mr. Okoro and Madame Renauld attended. They were not yet engaged, but Modesty did not think it would be long. Madame Renauld had sent a wedding dress as a gift, and

Modesty adored the pretty sprigged muslin in pale green and blue.

Mr. Sterling had also attended, bringing some of Rowden's other comrades in arms and their wives. Modesty was trying to learn all of their names, but she feared she'd have to be reminded when she next saw them.

Even Trogdon was there. He was supposed to be helping the other footmen serve champagne and tea, but he had mysteriously injured his elbow this morning and now simply stood by a door looking distinguished.

Most importantly to her, her family was there. Her Aunt Augusta had come, and Modesty had spent a great deal of time with her the night before. Her aunt had told her stories of her mother and promised to spend a great deal of time with Modesty when they both returned to London. Her half-siblings and her father and his wife were also in attendance. Her father had tears in his eyes when he performed the marriage ceremony. Modesty thought she might have seen the sheen of tears in Rowden's eyes as well. But now he was all smiles and laughter as he spoke to his friends and accepted congratulations. While his attention was on the others, Modesty knew his thoughts were always on her. He kept a hand on her back or her arm or her shoulder. He seemed to always be touching her, keeping her close by him. Modesty didn't mind. She wanted to be close to him now and forever.

***

After a light supper with Lady Florentia, Rowden led Modesty to their bedchamber. Lady Florentia had made an early exit easy for them, saying they must be so tired by the events of the day that they would certainly want to retire early.

Rowden hadn't argued. He closed the door behind Modesty, locked it, and took her in his arms. She laid her head on his shoulder and sighed.

"Happy?" he asked.

"Perfectly."

He looked down at her, amazed at the changes in her. Gone was the little figure in black with the pale face and the large, hollow eyes. In her place stood a beautiful woman in a lovely green and blue dress that seemed to shift the color of her hazel eyes every time she looked at him. Her cheeks were rosy, and her auburn hair no longer hid under a cap.

But the biggest change, he thought, was in himself. Before his life had been all about the next mill, the next big purse to be won. Now he didn't care if he ever fought again. That might be in part because his jaw still hurt where the German had punched him weeks ago. But mostly it was because he didn't need the roar of the crowds and the thrill of the fight to block out the loneliness and pain. He would always love Mary. He would always mourn the loss of her and his child.

But there was enough room in his heart for Modesty, and perhaps, one day, children with her. The light and the dark could exist together, and he could allow himself to live in the light.

"I hope you're not too disappointed we must wait for our honeymoon."

She tilted her head. "I told you I didn't mind. The weather is too cold to travel at present anyway. Besides, Mr. Mostyn needs you. You are the co-owner of a boxing studio now. You have an obligation to your business."

"My mother will swoon with shame when she hears."

"Who cares?" Modesty said lightly. "I am proud of you. Your friends are proud of you. And you have a new family now."

"Your family?"

"Yes." She led him to the bed and began to strip off his coat. "My aunt is thrilled we will be in London and able to spend time with her."

He angled his body so she might start on the buttons of his waistcoat. "And your father wants you to visit him every other week."

"Yes, well…" She concentrated on maneuvering the waistcoat from his shoulders. She took his hands to unfasten his cuff links.

"You may have forgiven him, Modesty, but that doesn't mean you have to forget. No one would blame you for taking time to rebuild your relationship."

She looked up at him as she tugged at his neckcloth. "He will blame me."

"Let him." Rowden plucked a pin from her hair and then another until it began to fall from its confines. "You're a married woman now. Your husband needs you."

"You don't need anyone, Rowden Payne," she said unfastening the buttons at his neck.

"Not true, my love. I desperately, desperately need you." He bent to kiss her as she tugged the tails from his shirt out of his breeches and slid her hands underneath to touch his bare skin.

"And I need you," she whispered.

He pulled the shirt over his head and then pulled her hard against his bare chest.

"You have me now, Modesty Payne. Like it or not, I'm yours forever."

She put her hands on his face and looked up at him adoringly. "There's nothing I want more..." She smiled shyly. "Except perhaps for you to remove the rest of your clothing."

He raised a brow, pretending to be scandalized. "Mrs. Payne, what will you do when I strip down?" He reached for the fall of his trousers, but she covered his hand and unfastened it herself, causing him to inhale in sharp surprise.

"Let's find out."

About Shana Galen

Shana Galen is three-time Rita award nominee and the bestselling author of passionate Regency romps. Kirkus said of her books: "The road to happily-ever-after is intense, conflicted, suspenseful and fun." *RT Bookreviews* described her writing as "lighthearted yet poignant, humorous yet touching." She taught English at the middle and high school level for eleven years. Most of those years were spent working in Houston's inner city. Now she writes full time, surrounded by three cats and one spoiled dog. She's happily married and has a daughter who is most definitely a romance heroine in the making.

Would you like exclusive content, book news, and a chance to win early copies of Shana's books? Sign up for monthly emails here for exclusive news and giveaways.

Want more Rowden?

Keep reading for an excerpt from Sweet Rogue of Mine, Nash's story, on sale now!

Someone was in the house. Nash Pope might be half asleep and half drunk, but he knew when someone was in his house. He was a trained sharpshooter, and his body was attuned to even the most subtle changes in atmosphere. Just a few minutes before, the air in Wentmore had been stale and still, the only sounds were of mice scampering in the attic and the creak and groan of the ancient timber beams and floorboards settling.

But now the mice had gone silent and the air stirred. The house seemed to straighten and take notice of someone new, someone far more interesting than its current occupant. In the dining room, the curtains closed against the daylight, the lone candle that burned flickered as though the house exhaled softly in anticipation.

Nash raised his head from the sticky table and heard the shuffle of feet and the squeak of a door hinge.

He reached for his pistol. He didn't need to see it. It was an extension of his arm and his favorite pistol by far. He owned at least half a dozen, including a brace of matching dueling pistols made by Manton, a pepperbox pistol made by Twigg, a more decorative pistol he'd purchased from the London gunsmith Hawkins—who liked to advertise that the former American President George Washington owned one of his creations—and this one, made by the Frenchman Gribeauval. Gribeauval had made Napoleon's personal pistol, and though Nash was no admirer of Napoleon, he did admire the French armory of St. Etienne.

Nash's thumb slid over the polished walnut gunstock, over the pewter filigree, until his finger curled into the trigger guard as though it were a well-worn glove. He lifted the pistol, not feeling its weight, though it was heavier than some, and then waited. It would do him no good to seek out the intruder. The world, what he could see of it, was gray and full of shadows. Better to let the interloper come to him. He could still shoot straight if he was still.

All had gone silent. Perhaps the uninvited guest had paused to listen as Nash did.

If the game was patience, Nash would win. As a sharpshooter, he had waited more than he had ever fired at the enemy. He often stood in one spot, unmoving, for four or five hours. He stood in the heat or the cold or, if he was fortunate, in the cool, scented breeze of a spring day. The weather might change, but his rifle at his side never had.

The rifle had been put away. He couldn't sight in the rifle anymore, and it was basically useless to him now, but hitting his target with his pistol and one poorly working eye was possible.

"Nash!" a voice called out. If he hadn't been trained as well, he might have jumped. But Nash's jaw only ticked at his name shattering the silence.

The floorboard creaked again. The intruder was in the foyer. He was not directly outside the dining room. The voice was still too distant.

"Put your pistol down, Nash. I came to talk to you."

Nash did not lower the pistol, though the voice sounded familiar now. Stratford? No, this voice wasn't refined enough. Stratford had been here a few months before. Apparently, he'd sought out Nash's father, the Earl of Beaufort, in London and told him Nash needed him. Stratford obviously didn't know that the earl didn't give a damn about Nash. He'd sent his solicitor, and Nash had fired the pistol he held now over the bald man's head and sent him running back to Town.

A door opened and the man said, "Nash?"

It was the door to the parlor.

"Nash, if you shoot me, I'll kick your pathetic arse all the way to Spain and back."

Nash felt his lips quirk in an unwelcome half-smile, as he finally recognized the voice. "And if I kill you?" Nash asked.

"Then I'll come back and haunt you." Rowden was just outside the dining room now, standing at the door. Nash and Rowden had met in Spain, both serving in His Majesty's army. They'd become close friends, even if their skill sets were quite different.

"If I open this door, will you shoot me?" Rowden asked.

"It depends," Nash said, still holding his pistol at the ready. "Did my father send you?"

A pause. "Of course, he sent me." Rowden spoke like he fought—directly and plainly. He did not pull punches.

"Then don't open the door."

"Shoot me and the next to arrive will be men from an asylum. Beaufort is ready to send you to an institution right now. Mayne and Fortescue managed to talk him out of it and arranged to have me sent instead."

Nash considered. The Duke of Mayne would have done the talking as he was the negotiator of the group. Stratford

Fortescue would have decided to send Rowden. Fortescue was always the strategist.

"Why you?" Nash asked. Seeing that Mayne was the negotiator, it would have made more sense for him to come.

"I needed the blunt."

Nash winced and set the pistol down. That hurt. His father was paying Nash's friends to intervene. He expected as much from his father, who had given up on Nash a long time ago. But his friends…still, what could he expect when he had shot Duncan Murray this past summer? That misstep was bound to have repercussions.

"I'm coming in," Rowden said, his tone one of warning. The latch lifted and the door opened. In the flickering candlelight, Nash made out a dark form. Of course, he remembered what Rowden looked like. He was broad and stocky with short brown hair and coal-black eyes. He had a pretty face, or he would have if his nose hadn't been broken so many times. Nash remembered what every man he had ever served with looked like. His memory was more of a curse than a blessing, though, as he remembered every woman and, yes, child he had ever shot too.

"You look like hell," Rowden said, still standing in the doorway.

"I wish I could tell you the same, but I can't see worth a damn."

"Still feeling sorry for yourself, I see."

Nash's hand itched to lift the pistol again, but he was not hot-tempered. He would not have lasted a week as a sharpshooter if he had been. "What do you want, Payne? To what do I owe the pleasure of a visit from one of Draven's Dozen?"

Rowden pulled out the chair at the opposite end of the table and sat. Nash saw only a gray, amorphous shape but his other senses filled in the missing information. "Considering you're one of us, I'm not sure why you're surprised. We Survivors take care of our own."

It was a lie, but Nash decided not to point that out. Not yet. The Survivors were a troop of thirty highly skilled military men who had been recruited as something of a suicide band to kill Napoleon or die trying. Eighteen had died trying. Twelve had come home. They had been brothers-in-arms, but Nash did not feel any fraternal affection now. The others were moving on with their lives, while he would be forever alone, locked in a world of darkness.

"You're thin," Rowden observed. To a stocky fighter like Rowden Payne, thinness was a liability. "Don't you eat?"

"You must need my father's money badly if you're playing nursemaid now," Nash said.

Shot fired.

"I want to keep you alive, and no one has to pay me for that."

Missed target.

"I'm alive." But Nash knew that wouldn't be enough. Not after the accident with Murray a few months before. Nash had known some intervention was coming. He supposed he should be glad the Survivors had convinced his father to send Rowden before the men from the asylum. Very little frightened Nash anymore, but the prospect of the next fifty years locked in an asylum drove a spike of fear into his heart. He would put the pistol in his mouth and pull the trigger first. "What do I have to do to keep the asylum at bay?"

"So you haven't completely pickled your brain yet."

"What do I have to do?" Nash repeated. He would do what was required and then, hopefully, the world would leave him alone. After all, he'd given his sight for King and Country. Why couldn't they leave him in peace?

"I don't have a comprehensive list," Rowden said after a pause, during which, Nash assumed, he was looking about the dining room. "Off the top of my head, I would say this old pile needs some repair. It looks like there was a fire at some point."

Nash did not comment.

"And clearly you need to ingest something other than gin."

Nash lifted his empty glass. "This was whiskey." At least he thought it had been whiskey. Maybe it had been brandy.

"You need staff."

"No staff," Nash said.

Rowden let out a quiet grunt. "We'll discuss it. But suffice it to say, I can smell you all the way over here. When was the last time you put on a clean set of clothes or took a bath?"

"Will you scrub my back?" Nash sneered and then was sorry for it. None of this was Rowden's fault. None of this was anyone's fault. Nash had known the risks when he went to war. He just hadn't thought anything would happen to him. He'd been so young. Like most young men, he'd thought he was invincible.

Rowden rose. "I'll make you some coffee. We can start there."

Two hours later, Nash was willing to concede life might be easier if he had a few staff members. Not that he needed them to tend to him personally. He could damn well take care of himself. But he did grow tired of Rowden's muttering as he crashed about in the kitchen making awful-tasting coffee, hauled water up to the tub in Nash's bed chamber, and even laid out Nash's clothing. The muttering had ceased once Mrs. Brown made an appearance. Nash didn't know why she still came every few days. She hadn't been paid for months, and Nash wasn't exactly welcoming toward her. Half the time he didn't even eat the food she set in front of him. But he supposed he owed it to her that he had clean clothes and a bar of soap and something edible in the larder.

Nash wanted to be left alone, and she did her best to leave him alone. That was why he hadn't run her off completely.

Now, dressed in clean, uncomfortable clothing with his too-long hair still damp on his neck and forehead, Nash made his way gingerly across the foyer. His belly rumbled. He'd had a bit of bread with the coffee and now his body seemed to want more. Nash thought he might see if any more food had been left in the dining room, but then he heard voices. Rowden and Mrs. Brown were in there. Nash turned his head to catch their words.

"—so glad you have come, Mr. Payne. I've been so worried."

"You're a good woman to have endured all of this."

"Pshaw. My family has worked for the Earls of Beaufort for generations, and I remember Mr. Pope when he was just a baby. I couldn't leave him. He was always such a good lad. Not a bit of temper in him. Always smiling and laughing. Always with a kind word. It was the war what did this to him."

Nash didn't know if Rowden answered. He couldn't stand the pity he heard in Mrs. Brown's voice, and he knew he would either explode in rage or get away. He chose the latter, and before he knew what had happened, he was outside, squinting in the sudden brightness. He could see even less in the sunlight than in the shadows. The light seemed to wash away what little vision he had left in his right eye, making everything into a white blob. Nash closed his eyes and used his walking stick to feel for any obstacles before him. He remembered walking the streets of London with this same stick. He'd swing it about or twirl it, trying to appear dashing to the young ladies. Now he needed it to keep from falling on his face.

How pathetic.

He moved toward the back of Wentmore, where there had once been an informal garden of tall flowering trees, vines, paths, and foot bridges over babbling brooks. It was certainly overgrown now, but at one time he had known that garden so well, he could have walked it blindfolded. Ironic that now that was, in essence, what he would need to do. The informal garden was one of the reasons his father had given Nash the care of Wentmore. The estate was not his, of course. All of the Beaufort properties would go to Nash's eldest brother when he inherited the title. But no one in the family had wanted Nash at the estate in Richmond. It was too close to London. Too close to Society, where everyone might see the horror of his injury.

So they'd sent him north, to Wentmore, which was buried in the countryside and close to nothing but a tiny village named Milcroft. The family had come here when the children were young as Lady Beaufort thought it was quaint and had wanted to expose the children to "simple people." And indeed, the area surrounding Milcroft was inhabited by dairy maids, blacksmiths, bakers, a country doctor, a vicar, and many crofters—some of them Beaufort's tenants. The people had been kind and welcoming, and Nash had spent a few weeks each year running about barefoot along Wentmore's extensive grounds.

How he had dreaded returning to the formalness of the estate in Richmond and, when he grew older, the schoolroom. Although he had patience and focus, Nash had never been a good student. His mind worked quickly, solving problems and working out rationales. But his professors seemed to drone on and on about the same material until Nash was bored senseless and stopped listening. He had done well enough as most of his studies required rote memorization and he could memorize easily, but he had never truly excelled.

Nash paused now, having lost himself in his thoughts and remembrances and tread deep enough into the garden that the sunlight had been somewhat obscured, and he could make out shapes here and there. He hadn't been outside in weeks, but from the crisp feel of the breeze, he knew it must be autumn, late September or early October. He could imagine the colors--quite a bit of green and patches of yellow and red and brown as well. In the distance, he heard the burble of the brook. He would walk toward it and sit for a while on the footbridge, listening to the water rush by. It seemed no matter how much his life changed or how many years passed, that water was always traveling under that bridge, undeterred.

Using his stick, Nash moved toward the sound of the water. He had a good idea where he was now, could picture the path in his mind. Of course, it was more overgrown than it had been before he'd left for the war and the brambles caught on his trousers, forcing him to pause every few minutes to free himself. He wasn't even sure if he was still on the path—or if there was a path—but the sound of the brook grew clearer.

Nash lifted his walking stick to feel for the wood of the bridge and hit what felt like a tree trunk. He moved around it, to the left, thinking maybe he was too far south of the bridge. But then the ground began to slope downward, and he realized that he had misjudged. The bridge was on higher ground and he was now on the banks of the brook. He swung his stick again and, moving forward a bit, he finally found the gentle rise that led to the bridge. He turned that way, but his foot was mired in the soft earth of the bank. He pulled it free, but he'd had to lean on his stick to do so, and then that had become stuck. Nash had to yank it out, which threw him off balance and his foot sank back into the mud.

So much for his clean clothing. His trouser legs must now be muddy almost to the calf. He vaguely remembered hearing thunder a couple of nights ago and the crash of heavy rain on the roof. If he'd remembered before he would not have headed for the brook. Without his sight, everything was so goddamn difficult. Before he would have walked directly to the bridge, dangled his feet over, and sat for as long as he liked. Now he couldn't even manage that because he couldn't navigate well enough to stay out of the mud and muck.

He pulled his foot free again, and struggled to take a step, but he only sank into more mud. Was he moving toward the brook or away from it? He'd become disoriented and made himself pause to listen. He needed to pinpoint the location of the brook and move away from it.

Nash went still, cocking his head to listen. He heard the rush of the breeze through the tree limbs, the chirp of birds high ahead, the singing of a woman, and the burble of the water.

The water was to his…

Nash frowned. Singing?

"I met a young girl there with her face as a rose
And her skin was as fair as the lily that grows
I says, My fair maid, why ramble you so
Can you tell me where the bonny black hare do go"

Her voice was clear and sweet, but Nash knew this song and it was anything but sweet. He tried again to wrest his foot from the mud, but he all but lost his balance and only righted himself at the last moment from falling backward and landing arse-first in the mud.

"The answer she gave me, O, the answer was no
But under me apron they say it do go
And if you'll not deceive me, I vow and declare
We'll both go together to hunt the bonny black hare"

The voice was closer now, the song sung lustily and without any self-consciousness. She obviously did not realize she was not alone. Nash tried to clear his throat as her voice came closer, but she was singing too loudly to hear.

"I laid this girl down with her face to the sky
I took out me ramrod, me bullets likewise
Saying, Wrap your legs round me, dig in with your heels
For the closer we get, O, the better it feels"

Nash was still now, wanting to hear the rest of the song. He'd heard the bawdy song many times in one tavern or another, but never sung with such abandon or enthusiasm. Indeed, on that last line, she had belted out, "For the closer we get, O, the better it feels."

"The birds, they were singing in the bushes and trees
And the song that they sang was"

"Oh!"

Her singing had ended abruptly, and Nash realized she'd seen him.

"What are you doing here?" she asked. Nay, it was more of a demand. As though she owned this garden, and he were the one encroaching. Nash tried to stand up straight and turn his face toward the sound of her voice. She was on the other side of the brook, as near he could calculate, possibly on the other side of the footbridge.

"I think the better question, miss, is what *you* are doing on my land and how quickly you can leave. Unless you fancy a charge of trespassing, that is."